REDROBES

"MOCKINGLY THE FROG WALKED TO THE FIRES AND TAKING A KETTLE OF
BOILING WATER . . . HE POURED THE STEAMING LIQUID ON THE HEAD OF
ECHON [FATHER BREBEUF].

(PAGE 262)

REDROBES
NEIL BOYTON, S.J.

ST. AIDAN PRESS, LLC
Morning View, Kentucky

Redrobes.

First published in 1936 by Benziger Brothers, of New York, Cincinnati, Chicago, and San Francisco.

Typesetting, layout and cover design copyright 2023 St. Aidan Press, LLC.

Cover art from 1936 edition.

ISBN-13: 978-1-962503-04-4
ISBN-10: 1-962503-04-6

For more information, contact:
www.staidanpress.com
staidanpress@gmail.com

We have made no intentional change from the original text except to correct mistakes in spelling and punctuation.

FOR REV. CARLOS BORJA

CONTENTS

TO THE MEMORY

OF

SAINT JOHN BREBEUF

JESUIT

MISSIONER

MARTYR

AND

GIANT OF GOD

REDROBES

Chapter One

Jacques the Little

ALL THE DAYS of his life, and they were to be many, Father Jacques Bourdon could recall the incidents of an afternoon in June, 1644. But if you knew Jacques intimately he would hasten to explain: "It was a sad day, M'sieur, but a glad one also. For in place of the one I lost, I gained an hundredfold the friendship of one of God's great martyrs. Blessed be the Good God!"

And as Jacques continued his explanation, it would unfold this way. Sister Portress, whose tongue Jacques had known on occasions to be keen-edged, came seeking him at play with small Louis Joliet on Mountain Hill Road. Pity shone in her eyes as she stooped and said: "Come, little one."

Wonderingly, hand in hers, the lad walked with Sister Portress up the narrow steep road till they came to the gray walled Hotel Dieu. Little Jacques had always associated the hospital with pains. Babies' shrill cries had come to his ears. He had seen men of the woods, after a rough fight at the river's edge of the town, carried within. Bearded sailors from the ships and silent Indians also had been taken there. Jacques had held his breath at the groans which even the thick walls could not shut in. Little Jacques knew that stiff still things, that had been these strong men, were borne out of the

1

Hotel Dieu and put in the small God's Acre—there to sleep till that Archangel blew his trumpet.

Sister Portress stopped at the lodge room and there another nun awaited them. Little Jacques knew her name. This was Sister Angela. Once she had given him an Agnus Dei to wear and, better, a cake to eat. She also smiled down tenderly now. Then she did a startling thing. She knelt on the stone floor till her headpiece was on a level with Jacques' wondering upturned face. Her hands rested on his shoulders and her lips brushed against Jacques' brown curls.

It was all so strange, this new kindness, and it made little Jacques silent and fearful. The woman, who casually looked after him in her small wooden cabin on Notre Dame Road, gave blows if he did not obey with a jump. And, when she was sober, her tongue was as keen as the winds of winter that swept across the St. Lawrence.

Sister Angela took the lad's hand in hers and led his steps into the softly lighted chapel. God was there back of that golden door. He was more powerful than King Louis across the ocean. This Jacques knew. God could do terrible things to bad children. If boys repeated the words the sailors from the ships used in their cups He would hear and be angry. God owned the terrifying lightning and He could make the earth open and swallow you up like that, if you made Him angry. You had to be good for God. Once God had sent some hungry black bears right out of the woods and they had eaten up a lot of boys who were bad. Jacques had never forgotten that Biblical story, heard around a winter's fireplace.

But now Sister Angela was saying, "Kneel down, little one, and ask the Good Boy Jesus in there to keep you always His sinless boy."

With silently moving lips Jacques obeyed, wondering if Boy Jesus would speak back to him.

Then Sister Angela whispered: "Now ask Little Jesus to make you brave and watch you always."

"I did, Sister."

"Then come with me. Your father is calling for you."

Jacques started up. His father was working on a farm on Orleans Island, some miles below the settlement, and would not be back in Quebec till next month.

It was with a timid clasp that the lad took Sister's hand. She squeezed his hand affectionately and smiled down on him. When Sister Angela smiled she was good to look upon and little Jacques smiled back. The woman who looked after him never smiled. One of the woodsmen who came to her cabin had told Jacques jokingly that the woman's smile had been cut out by an operation and he believed it.

Into the ward they came. Jacques knew the statued Lady they passed represented God's Mother. Neat and white were the beds down either side. In the further corner in the bed directly beneath the big crucifix of Jesus, Who had died for all people many, many years ago, lay a bearded white-faced man and it was some seconds before little Jacques recognized him.

Very weakly Jacques' father lifted his hand and Jacques dutifully bent down and kissed it. He was afraid of his rough father.

Sister Angela brought a stool and when the lad was placed on this the nun stole away.

Was this his woodsman father's voice, Jacques puzzled. The words came in a hoarse whisper.

"Jacques . . . not long now . . . don't know what will become of you . . . could have been a better parent . . . the Good God forgive. . . ."

The lad was beginning to be frightened and tears started to come unbidden. His father had never spoken in such terms before.

"What's the matter, my father?" There was a catch in Jacques' voice. "I thought. . . ."

Hoarsely came the words, "The great tree fell . . . I saw it too late . . . my poor back . . . they brought me here."

Little Jacques could see that giant timber crashing down and his woodsman father leaping desperately to get out of its path. Suddenly he remembered that Louis Joliet's cousin had been crushed that way and how Louis had described the accident. "And when the men took the tree off, my strong cousin René never walked again."

Jacques' father was looking at the lad with staring eyes and it seemed as if he was trying to force words that would not come.

In his extremity the father turned his head slowly and looked down the long white ward. Something comforting that he saw seemed at once to be reflected in his eyes. He sighed contentedly.

Little Jacques turned his head curiously and he beheld Sister Angela returning. With her was a man whose presence instantly made Little Jacques think of giants. The tall man wore a long blackrobe, belted at the waist and patched in many places. Jacques knew he was a Father, who lived at the Jesuits' House. The tall priest seemed to swell up as he approached. Severe were his bearded features. Wide were his shoulders and although graying hairs were scattered freely among his naturally brown hair and beard, he carried himself with the easy, ever youthful swing of the woodsman. Sister Angela seemed immensely tiny, walking at the tall priest's side.

When the two stopped at the bedside, Jacques' father was whispering, "I knew you would come, my father.... It is almost too late. ... Quickly stoop and listen."

The gigantic priest bent low and Little Jacques' gaze took in the thickness and the bronzed roughness of this strange priest's hands. They were so wide at the knuckles and sunbrowned, like a sea captain's.

"My Father . . . this is my neglected little son. . . . His mother, she went to God when he was an infant. . . . Now I know I. . . ."

Big Jacques stiffened with pain and his words came in gasps. "Before . . . I go . . . please . . . my Father . . . be a . . . father . . . to . . . to my little one."

Then Little Jacques, as the meaning of the words became evident to him, looked up tearfully into this strange priest's countenance. At once, the lad's first impression that this priest's features were stern vanished like morning mists on the Great River. For the blackrobed one was beaming down on him and Jacques heard him saying, "Big Jacques, your family, the Bourdons, and mine were close friends, back in Conde-sur-Vire. Go home in peace. I shall be Little Jacques' father always."

The lad could see the look of contentment like a softly dawning light in a morning lake, spreading over the face of his woodsman father.

While he was gazing down on the bed, Little Jacques felt a rough hand steal gently around his shoulder and draw him close to the patched black robe.

The next event of that afternoon came so immediately that its memory always blurred in the lad's recollections. He remembered his gaze had traveled to the neighboring cot where lay a wizened old Indian. He looked a century of years. His hair was furrowed after the manner of the Hurons and Little Jacques was watching the alert squirrel-like eyes of the old brave, when he felt himself lifted bodily. As he swung in the air he glanced down on his father. A ruddy torrent was pouring over his lips. Then Sister Angela was holding Jacques' face pressed close to her shoulder. The deep voice of the tall priest began to say prayers in a strange tongue and Sister Angela was making the responses. Other nuns came running. One carried a lighted candle. Then Sister Portress gently took Little Jacques, too startled to weep, and carried him out of the ward.

.   .   .   .   .

Jacques' last remembrance of his woodsman father was the silent figure in the rough coffin being carried to the open graveside in God's Acre. Jacques was in the van of the small group of mourners who followed. A thunder storm was coming down the river and the lightning was flashing above the proud promontory of Cape Diamond.

Little Jacques never liked lightning. It always seemed to him louder than the guns in Fort St. Louis that guarded the town from the despised English and dreaded Iroquois. Then as the procession reached God's Acre, a crash came, more terrifying than any that went before and a vivid bolt rent a nearby oak.

The boy's fright overcame his grief. He ducked out of Sister Portress' care. He heard her call in vain. But his legs twinkled and he never stopped running down the hill road till he was cowering, soaked to the skin, safely in the lodge room of the Hotel Dieu.

It had rained with all the fury of a summer storm and the artillery of heaven flashed and boomed.

Once over a year before, when Jacques was on Orleans Island in the broad river below the great cliff of Quebec, he vividly remembered another such thunder storm. That time his woodsman father was with him and Little Jacques had stood it as long as he could. Then he had cowered in Big Jacques' arms, trembling with fright at each thunder clap. His rough father had laughed at his timidity and held him up to the open window, where the boy had screamed and kicked impotently.

Now, seemingly without connection with this cruel recollection of a year ago, his present loss came home to Little Jacques. There were no arms of a father—such as he had been—into which he could creep. The stiff silent form of Big Jacques in that rough coffin would be all dripping wet. The gnarled old grave digger would never have had time to throw back all the loose earth before the grave would be half full of mud. This picture made Little Jacques feel very miserable and he wept, while outside the rain was falling dismally.

Finally in his lonely misery Little Jacques had slumped down from the wooden bench and great sobs shook him. Never had his neglectful woodsman father seemed dearer than that rainy afternoon, when the lad had lost him. He knew Big Jacques was with the Good God up in the skies and he wished the Good God would take him too, that he might be near Big Jacques again. New misery engulfed the boy till his shoulders shook and shook. . . .

It was a quiet step that made Jacques aware that he was not alone in the lodge room. He thought at first Sister Portress had come back and she was going to scold him for running away from her care. Even that would be better than this awful feeling.

But strong arms were lifting Little Jacques and he was nestled to a black-robed breast. A deep voice, softly lowered, was soothing him with words that a mother would utter. Little Jacques looked up into the bearded face of the tall priest.

"My little adopted son, so here you are! Now let me give you a piece of good advice that I myself follow occasionally. Next time you feel lonely, you steal into the room where the red light burns on guard. Kneel down there, little son, and tell the Good Boy Jesus why your heart is burdened. He is the special friend of all orphan boys and He knows how to soothe you better than an old bachelor."

Little Jacques asked timidly, "Please, my Father, what is a bachelor? Is it like a bear or something?"

The tall priest laughed and his teeth were very white. "I suspect it is more like the bear than something. Now a bachelor like I am, is a man who gives up the pleasant thought of having his own little sons that he may—so it seems—have the charge of many other nice little boys. For instance, the Good God has sent me another only recently and I hold him in my arms now."

The tall priest had seated himself on the bench and Little Jacques quite contentedly was resting in his lap.

"Now that I have answered that one, permit me to ask Jacques a question. How old are you now, my child?"

Little Jacques counted carefully on his fingers. Finally he held up the result. "My Father, all the fingers on this left hand and all but the thumb on the right."

"Well, unless my friends, the Iroquois, have hacked off several fingers, then I take it you are nine?"

"My Father is right."

"And when was your birthday?"

"Our Lady's Day, last March 25th."

"Now that's interesting!"

Jacques looked his puzzlement and the priest whispered mysteriously, "Are you good at keeping secrets?"

"I never tell what shouldn't be told. That my father taught me."

"Then, little secret sharer, know that you and I were both born on the Feast of Our Lady's Annunciation. Only I came under her loving care a year over a half a century ago. So we both have the same loving Mother in Heaven. Always invoke her with confidence, for I will testify all the days of my life this Lady All Fair looks after her own better than their sins deserve."

The tall priest had taken out his pocket handkerchief and gently was drying away the big tears that trembled on the lad's eyelashes.

Jacques, now that they shared birthdays and a secret, had lost his shyness of this strange priest and he felt emboldened to ask: "Would my Father be pleased to tell me his name, for I do not know it yet?"

"My name! I have had three names. When I was your age and lived in beautiful Normandy, my people called me Johnnie. Up in the lands, many leagues away, where my dear Hurons dwell, I am known as Echon. That is their word which means 'He who drags the loads.' You see, my little one, the Good God has given me more strength than He has given to most men. May I always use it for His greater service! Now here in the settlements along the St. Lawrence, my countrymen call me Father John Brebeuf. At your service."

"Father John Brebeuf," Little Jacques repeated several times aloud so that the tall priest's name would stick in his memory.

"And very shortly now I will be addressed as Echon again. For I go once more to Huronia. But first I have arranged to place you at Our Lady of the Angels, the school that our good Father Anthony

Daniel started some years ago. Now listen closely. There I want you to play with the Huron boys as much as possible and begin to learn their language."

"Why, my Father?"

"Because, when my Jacques is a few years older, I will send for him. He will be placed in a canoe of the returning Hurons. He will travel up to Huronia——"

Little Jacques' eyes sparkled. This promised adventures. He interrupted: "My Father John Brebeuf will pardon, but where is Huronia?"

"Huronia? Well, listen attentively and I will tell you how to get there. It is three hundred leagues from Quebec's Rock. The Huron flotilla paddles up the St. Lawrence, past Three Rivers. At Ville Marie de Montreal the canoes turn into the Ottawa, where the portages begin around the white waters—Allumette Island—Upper Ottawa—many portages—Lake Nipissing—the River of the French. Then through the ten thousand beautiful islands, right down to our Residence at Fort St. Mary.

"Here I will be waiting for you and you will be placed with the boys, who are learning to be mission interpreters. You see why I tell you to play with the Huron boys now and learn all the Huron words you can at Our Lady of the Angels."

"Yes; my Father John Brebeuf."

Now that something definite lay before him, Little Jacques Bourdon felt better. "But if I am to be a Huron interpreter would it not be better if I went to Huronia with you this summer?"

"I'll risk no little boy's life in the Huron-bound canoes this summer. Too many of our good friends, the Iroquois, lie in wait along the St. Lawrence. As a result up in Huronia our missioners are in dire straits. For the poor Fathers sadly lack supplies. You see the Iroquois have disputed the passage these past two summers and few Huron canoes got down the Ottawa and the St. Lawrence and no supplies for the missions got through.

"Two years ago dear Father Isaac Jogues fell into Iroquois hands and was their captive till the kindly Dutch at New Amsterdam ransomed him. But last June when the French fleet arrived here he came back to seek his palm branch once more."

Jacques looked puzzled. "Why a palm branch, my Father?"

"Has my little Jacques seen pictures of Christ's blessed martyrs?"

"Of a surety."

"Then what do the painters put in their hands to show——"

Jacques interrupted eagerly: "I know, my Father. A palm branch to show they died for the Good God."

"And that is what gentle Father Jogues came back to seek again."

Jacques sat up. "A thousand pardons, my Father, but I have seen him. Is he not the priest with the fingers the savages bit off?"

"That is good Father Isaac Jogues. Then, my little one, you have seen a living martyr of Christ. Next time you meet him in the roads of Quebec, kiss those mangled hands very reverently for they are very dear to Our Good Master."

"I would be afraid, my Father," confessed Little Jacques.

"Afraid of gentle Father Jogues! My foolish little one——"

The tall priest broke off. Then he whispered softly, "Speaking of angels!" And Little Jacques looked up.

Another blackrobed figure stood in the doorway of the lodge room. He was a man of medium height, brown bearded, with a high forehead and modest eyes. His hands were hidden in the folds of his much patched blackrobe.

Now those eyes were smiling as they took in the tall priest and the little lad with tear-stained face, who sat in his lap.

"Father John, Sister Angela told me that I would find you here—er, comforting the sorrowful."

"Come in, Father Isaac, and share my spiritual work of mercy. This is my newly acquired Jacques, our future Huron interpreter."

Father Brebeuf whispered to the lad: "Kneel down now and ask Father Isaac Jogues for his blessing."

Jacques slipped to the ground and kneeling before the other blackrobed priest bowed his head.

He heard Father Jogues giving the blessing in Latin and he could feel the priest's right hand clumsily tracing the Sign of the Cross on his forehead. Then as Father Jogues finished Little Jacques reached and lifted that right hand to his lips.

Where finger tips should have been were cruel scars and red healed stumps. Remembering Father Brebeuf's words, Jacques kissed this mangled hand very reverently. He arose from his knees smiling happily.

Father Brebeuf had been looking through the small panes of glass in the window and now he said: "Come, Jacques, the thunder storm has gone down the river and here, out from behind the clouds, comes what my dear Hurons call 'The Old Man Above.' Father Jogues and I have a call to make at the Ursuline Convent. You are to stay here at the Hotel Dieu tonight and in the morning I will take you to Our Lady of the Angels myself. Good-bye, my interpreter-to-be, go and seek Sister Angela and you will very likely find your supper."

Obediently Little Jacques went in search of his supper. He felt so happy within his breast that he was smiling broadly.

Chapter Two

Pounder of Savages

THAT MONDAY NOON in early May, 1648, Jacques Bourdon had no official business near the south gateway into Fort St. Louis. In fact, at that moment he should not have been near the white flag of France, floating lazily overhead. He should have been with his fellow students at Our Lady of the Angels, a quarter of a league away.

But if you had Jacques' confidence, you would have known that the boy, thirteen past now, and small and sturdy for his age, was daydreaming as he idled along and the gossamer of his dreams was Father John Brebeuf's promise to make him a Huron interpreter. That promise, given four years ago, shortly before the gigantic Blackrobe had departed for Huronia, had been a shining star in the dark of the school grind. All the bitter winter months, when school discipline irked, Jacques had thought of the adventurous land, where his Blackrobe guardian toiled. Now that Jacques spoke Huron as fluently as his Huron fellow students, he felt that school should be over for him.

The rat-a-tat-tat of a drum caught Jacques' attention and he turned his steps hopefully towards the sound. It came from within the gray stone gateway, where a white uniformed sentry with his squatty arquebus across his shoulder was pacing his beat. Jacques nodded familiarly to the sentry and passed the guard house into the fort yard.

More white uniformed soldiers lolled in the sun before their quarters. A rare creature in pioneer Quebec settlement, a gray cat, stretched her furry stomach to the rays where she dozed on top of a warm cannon.

Across from the sentry was the source of the sound. Jacques hastened his steps as he recognized the small drummer, Robert Le Duke. He had been a conspicuous failure as a student at Our Lady of the Angels and the Fathers were rather glad when the boy enlisted in King Louis' soldiery.

Small Robert, looking smaller in his tight fitting white uniform with the blue trimmings, was importantly practicing. Drums had always held a fascination for Jacques. The roll increased as the drummer saw his admiring audience approaching. In a few minutes Jacques was eagerly begging the use of the sticks. Soon his amateur efforts came echoing back from the walls of the fort. The problem of Our Lady of the Angels was happily forgotten in a delirium of sound.

A party of skin-blanketed Hurons, their hair characteristically shaven into ridges of bristle that had given their nation its name from the French word for "wild boar," had been admitted into the enclosure. They were evidently bound for an interview with the Commandant or they would not have gotten past the sentry. The furious roll of the drum roused their curiosity.

The shadow of a brave fell across Jacques' drum and he looked up into the blue and white striped features of a young warrior. Jacques had the usual whiteman's contempt for the neighboring savages, but now that he had an audience, boylike he redoubled his drumming.

The young brave said to his companions in Huron, "The white stripling makes more noise than the thunder."

This innocent remark angered Jacques. He shouted, "Go away, you dirty savage!" And he added a sailor's frank expression not allowed to be used at Our Lady of the Angels. He raised his drum stick and struck out sharply.

The blow did more damage than Jacques had intended. For

it caught the Huron on his high cheek bone and inflicted a flesh wound. At once a crimson streamlet poured across the blue painted streak on the Huron's chin.

Robert shouted: "Jacques, you are a big fool! Look out! He may have a knife under his blanket."

But if the Huron brave had one, he did not draw it.

The rest of the party had seen the blow struck and they started to come across the fort yard. Their angry voices made the drummer boy prudently grab Jacques by the arm and drag him to the neighborhood of the sentry.

Jacques was of a mind to continue past the sentry but that soldier of France promptly held him a wiggling prisoner.

At this moment Father Jerome Lalemant, Superior of the Jesuit Fathers in Quebec, having finished his business with the Commandant, appeared in the doorway.

Jacques welcomed the sight of a friendly face and shouted: "Father, Father Lalemant. This stupid old soldier won't let me go." Jacques struggled to free himself from the sentry's iron grip, but his efforts were futile.

Father Jerome pushed through the crowd of angered Hurons to demand: "Jacques, why are you not with your fellow students?"

The boy hung his head. He had just realized here were further explanations of an embarrassing nature.

An old Huron, with the captain's three eagle feathers in his hair, named the Blackrobe: "Nikanis," he used the Indian word for "Superior," "Nikanis, this small nephew of yours has struck one of my people. See he bleeds."

For the first time Father Jerome noticed the cheek of the young brave.

The old Captain continued: "Nikanis, you know our custom."

The Blackrobe nodded gravely. He well knew the universal Indian custom of demanding a present when a wound, even a death wound, was inflicted on a person.

Quietly he moved closer to the boy. "Jacques," he questioned, "is it true that you struck this brave?"

"Yes; my reverend Father."

"Why did you strike him?"

"I did not like the way the savage looked at my drum playing."

"That is hardly a reason to draw blood. Suppose he had resented your insult with a tomahawk blow? These Hurons are a proud tribe. Do you realize if this had happened outside the fort grounds in all probability you would now lie scalped?"

Jacques had nothing to say.

"Now you will pay the present this chief demands."

Jacques waited in apprehension. He was not long kept in doubt of the Blackrobe's meaning.

"My brother," Father Jerome Lalemant addressed the Huron captain gravely, "I know your custom. You have demanded a present for the wound this senseless one has inflicted on this brave."

The captain interrupted the Superior. "He who bleeds is my son, Nikanis."

"All the more reason that you should receive the present."

Father Jerome beckoned to the small drummer who stood grinning on the outskirts of the rapidly growing crowd of idle soldiers. When the boy Robert pushed his way through, the priest whispered something to him and he grinned more broadly and nodded.

As Robert departed, Father Jerome turned to the silent Huron group and singling out the captain said: "My brother, you are not any of the Hurons whom I know by sight."

The captain answered: "We came with the canoes to your settlement to barter furs. We live in the Praying Village where Echon is. He is my friend and also my son's, whose blood flows."

"From Father Brebeuf's village! Then you are Christians?"

"We are Praying Indians," said the captain, "since Echon poured Saving Waters on our heads two summers ago."

Father Lalemant knew the Indians dislike to mention their names directly, so he turned to the young brave and asked, "What name has your father?"

"He is called Paul."

Paul supplied the further information, "My son is called Bernard."

"Then know you are my brothers," welcomed Father Lalemant. He pointed to the culprit Jacques and he continued in the Huron tongue: "My brothers, let me tell you something. We French have a salutary custom. When any of our number does wrong, we punish him. This boy has wounded one of your people. He gave the wound in your presence and he shall be whipped in your presence."

Jacques had heard entirely too much. He attempted to pull out of the sentry's grasp. The sudden jerk succeeded, but he had not run two yards before grinning soldiers of the guard gripped him a helpless prisoner again.

The drummer boy returned from the guard house and he carried three birch switches.

The Blackrobe turned to the soldiers who held the helpless Jacques and commanded: "Take the shirt off this little pounder of savages."

Jacques struggled in vain. Willing soldier hands stripped him and he stood naked from the waist up.

Stolidly the Huron group had watched the French proceedings. Now when they realized that the Frenchmen were in earnest several broke out in Huron: "He is only a papoose. He has no sense. He did not mean to wound."

The young brave Bernard stepped forward. Blood was drying on his cheek. "The young white lynx has no sense, Nikanis."

But Father Jerome Lalemant, knowing from what slight causes grave collisions had occurred between white and red men, refused to heed the Hurons' pleadings.

"The young white lynx," he concluded, "has years enough to realize that a hasty temper brings its own pains. He has offered an insult to a friend of Echon. He will pay the gift you demanded according to our custom.

"You, soldier," the Blackrobe Superior motioned to a thick set member of the guard, "lay on the switch. Five times will stanch this Huron's blood."

Roughly soldiers pushed Jacques forward and held him helpless. He well knew that however painful paying the gift would be, he would have to go through with it.

He pleaded in an aside to his executioner, "Remember, soldier, my back is tender and let your hand be gentle. You may be sentenced to the chevalet sometimes and will want a drink. I will bring it to you."

The soldier laughed: "My tender one, it is for taking too many drinks that one rides the chevalet."

For the last time the boy looked around the circle of grinning soldiers. Even Robert, his drummer friend, was enjoying the anticipation of the punishment. Then Jacques bent over and clinched his fingers in his fists. He closed his eyes tight and awaited the blows.

But they never fell.

Bernard had stepped forth. Now he lifted his elk skin robe off his shoulder and threw it over Jacques' bare back. Standing there in his breech clout he folded his arms and said in Huron to Father Jerome Lalemant: "Nikanis, tell the white soldier I will pay the present myself. Strike me, but this young white lynx is not to be touched. I have spoken."

Affirmative "Ho Ho Hos" from his tribesmen seconded this statement.

A twinkle came into Father Jerome's eyes.

"Jacques," he addressed the boy, "return Bernard his robe and put on again your shirt. From what I heard recently at Our Lady of the Angels without doubt you richly deserve a taste of the birch. It will come later, fear not. Run back to school now before this tender hearted Huron changes his mind."

Jacques snatched up his shirt and did not stop to don it till he was well out of Fort St. Louis' enclosure.

Standing there, waiting the painful touch of the birch, a thought had come to him. It was an amazing thought. Now he dropped into the brush beside an immense pine tree, where he could keep Fort St. Louis' entrance in sight.

Soon Father Jerome Lalemant, grave-countenanced, came out of the gateway and walked by on his way to the Residence of the Jesuit Fathers. Jacques never moved. Then he could hear the distant roll of Robert's drum being beaten in practice, but it did not interest him any longer.

An hour he waited. Finally, his vigil was rewarded. The group of Christian Hurons, their business with the Commandant finished, filed out the gateway of the fort. They passed close to Jacques' hiding place. When they had gone on, the boy rose and stealthily followed them. He kept a weather eye open for the sight of a black-gown, for a meeting with one of the Fathers would of a certainty lead to embarrassing explanations.

William, who hunted for the Ursulines, came by. He carried over his shoulder five wood pigeons. Unnoticed by William, one of the pigeons slipped down from his back. Jacques waited till William had turned the corner, then he retrieved this bird. It was a plump one. Jacques smiled as he realized what chance had given to him.

Down Mountain Hill road into the Lower Town of Quebec the Huron visitors walked. The wood and stone cabins of Quebec held their eyes. These were wonders of the whitemen and their size and magnificence would be retold back in Huronia.

Curiously they paused when they came to the chevalet. This was the iron horse on whose back was usually strapped a Frenchman, paying the penalty for over indulging in strong drink. At present it was unoccupied. Jacques, in his mind's eye saw a thick set soldier strapped to the chevalet, begging him in vain for a drink of water. The boy muttered, "You would birch me, would you. Now stay thirsty." This imaginary scene was pleasant to contemplate and Jacques almost lost sight of the savages he was stalking. He had to run till the winding road again brought the Hurons into sight ahead.

He followed them down to their encampment near the St. Charles River. Here in the open country three shelters of leafy branches had been erected. The birchbark canoes that had brought this party three hundred leagues and would carry them as many more back to distant Huronia were hauled out. But Jacques' eye sought the smoke of a kettle. When he saw it, he sauntered closer.

The young brave Bernard, whose cheek Jacques had laid open, was the first to notice the boy. Jacques held up his hand in the universal peace sign. The Huron grunted and the boy approached.

Speaking their language, he said: "Uncle, that was a hasty blow I struck this morning and I bring a gift to wipe away the blood and the anger out of your heart."

With this Jacques offered the wood pigeon that the Ursulines' hunter had dropped.

The young Huron accepted the peace offering and, pleased to find the French boy spoke his language, invited him to join the group around the kettle. Bernard opened the wood pigeon deftly with his knife and then dropped it into the steaming kettle.

When Jacques was squatted with the rest, he asked: "My Uncles, one of you said this morning that you know Echon. Is that a true word?"

"It is true, young white lynx," replied the Captain, "we all love Echon."

"Then know that Echon, whom we call Father John Brebeuf, loves me. He it was who took charge of me when my own father died."

Jacques proceeded to relate to the silent Hurons the story of that afternoon in the Hotel Dieu four years before.

"Now, Uncles, listen. Schools are not for me. I plan to go to Echon."

Said the Captain Paul: "The small one has a brave's heart." Then turning to Jacques, he inquired: "Does my nephew know the leagues and the many Iroquois, our blood enemies, who lie in wait between this settlement of the French on the Great River and our lands by the Great Fresh Water Sea?"

"Uncles, I know there are many many leagues of paddling, but were they twice as many as the stars I would prefer to endure their weariness rather than remain longer in Our Lady of the Angels."

Here a brave spoke up: "My son spent two winters at the Black-robes' school. It is a good cabin. Now he speaks the words of the French. It is good."

Jacques did not heed this recommendation but pursued his topic. "You see that I know much of your language. In Huronia I would easily know more and Echon would be better pleased with me."

"What does our nephew plan to do? He knows that we cannot take him in the canoes or the bearded Frenchmen would be angry with us."

"That I well know, Uncle. But if I ran away from Quebec of my own accord and you found me, Onontio, the Governor, would not have anger in his heart against you, neither would he expect you to turn your canoe's bow downstream and deliver me back to the school."

He continued persuasively: "Echon will give you many presents for the trouble you took in transporting me to his village."

The old Captain Paul spoke in low tones with the other Hurons and then he announced: "No; boy of the French, Onontio would not like it, Nikanis would not like it. Echon would not like it when we return to our villages——"

Here one of the older braves said without a twinkle in his eye, "This pounder of savages might cause the blood to flow on the cheeks of our nephews. We are afraid."

Hastily Jacques claimed seriously: "No; no; elder uncle. Never again will I do that. This brave is my friend."

The old Captain announced finally, "Boy of the French, if you come with us to our country, it will be after we have heard the words of permission from Nikanis' lips. Now eat with us and then go back to the school cabin where our nephews learn the French words and you white boys learn to speak our language. I have spoken."

Jacques was silent when Paul finished. He well knew that it would not be possible to change the Hurons' decision.

Gladly, however, Jacques shared their meal. He ate with relish the smoked eel and his portion of the wood pigeon. When there was nothing further to eat, the boy stood up.

"My Uncles, I thank you for your food and your wise words. I see I had no sense. I will return now to Our Lady of the Angels. Come to the school tomorrow and you will be shown all the whitemen's cabins there."

Gravely the Captain accepted this invitation and Jacques walked away. It was towards evening now, with the sun just disappearing behind the opposite high cliffs of the St. Lawrence.

The boy had no intention of returning to the birching that undoubtedly awaited him after his all day truancy.

He decided to seek a particular friend of his own age, Louis Joliet, who lived near the Great River.

It was a quarter of a league walk to Monsieur Joliet's wooden house. As Jacques crossed the little clearing and rounded the side of the house, he came upon Louis' mother seated in the doorway, where she could get the fading light for her knitting.

Jacques looked at Madame Joliet and his courage failed him. He had always stood in awe of her since the luckless day last autumn she had caught him and her son red handed, each with a tart they had extracted from her shelf. She has the sharpest tongue in Quebec, thought Jacques, so he would have kept on, but Madame Joliet noticed him and she demanded: "You, Jacques, what do you want? Why are you so far from your school at this hour?"

"Please, Madame, I—I——"

The woman cut his stammering short. "If it's Louis you are looking for, know he's with his father at St. Joseph's, Sillery. Father Gabriel Lalemant wanted a calf and the two drove it to Sillery. They will not be back for two hours. Now run along and tell the Reverend Fathers they shouldn't let you roam around like a little savage. I wonder what their Reverences are thinking about!"

"Yes; Madame, I'll tell them," Jacques hastened to assure Louis' mother.

"So will I, next time I meet Father Jerome."

"Here, wait a minute, Jacques," Madame Joliet gathered up her knitting and disappeared within the doorway.

Doubtfully the boy waited. He had half a mind to run before the woman returned. But in an incredibly short time she came back and thrust a warm tart, sugar coated, into Jacques' hand.

"Here, all you school boys look half starved. I doubt not the Reverend Fathers make you fast too much. Eat this as you trot along."

Gratefully Jacques thanked Madame Joliet, but his smile faded as she added: "Yes; you thank me now, but if I was out of the cabin I doubt not you'd steal like any savage. Off with you now to Our Lady of the Angels. May she protect us all from thieves, especially youthful ones!"

"Amen," said Jacques before he realized the lady's implication.

He needed no further urging. But the truant now had definitely made up his mind not to return to his school. He had been absent all day; certainly a memorable birching awaited him there, that no tender hearted Huron could avert.

It is doubtful if the boy had ever heard of Julius Caesar, but like that ancient Roman general, when Jacques skipped from stone to stone across the little unnamed stream that flowed into the St. Charles, near Madame Joliet's home, he was also "crossing the Rubicon."

Chapter Three

The Stout Cook

A N HOUR LATER, with night coming on shortly, Jacques Bourdon had wandered down to the waterfront, where he could look up to the proud promontory, now in deepened shadows, that dominated all the background of the rude settlement.

A bell rang in the steeple of the Infant Jesus Church. That would be the Angelus. Instinctively Jacques bowed his head and recited his three Hail Marys.

He was still undecided in his mind what his next move would be, but he was certain there was less chance of one of the school Fathers coming across him down here by the bank of the St. Lawrence.

It had been a sunny May day—too warm for this time of the year—but now with evening near there was a wintry chill in the air.

Then Jacques saw the "Saint Anne," the small scallop that cruised between the trading posts, had come to anchor. The boy knew she had come down from Three Rivers.

Jacques' problem of a lodging for the night was settled. The cook on board the vessel, Claude Mangre, had been a great friend of his dead father. Often had Jacques sat in that galley and listened to the cook's talk, while he sampled the choice food supply.

Jacques sat himself down on a log and finished Madame Joliet's tart. It was delicious. While he ate he heard a boat being rowed ashore. He looked out eagerly at the members of the "St. Anne's"

crew in the boat. Jacques was looking for the grossly fat figure of
the cook, easily discernable in the fading light. The cook was not
among them.

Slowly a solitary sailor returned the boat to the "Saint Anne."
Then it came back with the rest of the crew in it. Jacques heard
them singing a rollicking sea song—all about "small Genevieve
who had the rosiest cheeks in St. Malo."

Softly Jacques hummed the song, while he waited. Again the
cook was not in the boat. The crew drifted along the water front.
Now was Jacques' time. It was quite dark. A light moved on the
scallop. Jacques knew his friend was to be the watchman for the
night. All about was the dark St. Lawrence. The opposite cliff just
a deeper black.

His hope was that the careless crew had left oars in the boat.
But when he reached the rowboat, drawn up beyond high water
line, a short search convinced him that the prudent crew had taken
all oars with them.

An hundred yards out in the river he could see the night light
swaying slightly. That would be the mast. A faint glow came from
below. That would be the cook's galley. The lights looked quite near
and comfortable and Jacques knew his father's friend would give
him a welcome and a meal.

Off from the settlement came the songs of the sailors. Here it
was lonely. Again the boy reconnoitred the black bank in the slim
hope that he might chance on a canoe. But he soon gave up the
search and returned to the shore nearest the anchored vessel.

There was nothing for Jacques to do but to swim out. He remembered that the sailors would return late, so he made a bundle
of his boots and clothing and stowed them under the stern seat. He
knew that there would be a current so he picked his way up stream
fifty yards.

Then he waded out up to his waist. The waters of the St. Lawrence were not warm. It was still May. Hastily he blessed himself

and dived forward. He swam slowly and surely. He recalled that this was his first swim of the year and he tried to remember back to his last swim. Yes; it was that afternoon in early September when he and Louis Joliet were down to Orleans Island. The water was much warmer then.

Steadily he swam down to the ship's light. Then the light was swaying overhead and the boy grasped the anchor chain. He clung to it a moment to recover his breath. But his teeth were chattering and with difficulty he hauled himself out of the cold river and fell on deck.

Along the silent shadowy decks, littered with casks and piles of furs, he walked aft to the galley's light.

Then he was standing in the doorway and he was trying to grin despite his chattering teeth.

The fat cook, who had been tending to a pot on the fire, turned around. He blessed himself hastily, but his words were not exactly a prayer.

Jacques, continuing to grin, waved a hand in greeting.

The cook held out friendly arms as thick round as small cannons and cried: "It is the little Jacques, grown so big! Come to see fat Claude, his friend! Come in. Come in. But where is the shirt of civilization?"

Jacques, assured of his welcome, gladly obeyed. He explained: "There were no oars in the boat, so I left my clothes for the crew to bring out."

"Then, my infant, you will wait sometime for your shirt. But you chatter like five little monkeys. That will never do. Hold, I have it!"

The cook waddled into the shadows and came back with a blanket.

"Here, I will make of you a brave at the council fire." He draped the blanket about the boy's figure. "Sit on this and stop chattering."

Claude had kicked a wooden meat block before the galley stove and Jacques huddled in the delicious warmth.

"So, the little monkey, Jacques, dressed like a savage, swims out to see Claude!" The stout cook poured wine into a mug. "Drink this, my infant, and be warm within too. Then I will give you food.

"I was just wishing I had some one to talk to and behold—the little one—here, polish the inside of this bowl." The stout cook thrust a heaping bowl of stew into Jacques' eager hands.

Claude had seated himself comfortably. "My infant, when I saw you first I thought of the two youths who escaped from the Iroquois hands three springs ago. You hear about them?"

"No; M'sieur Claude." Jacques settled himself more comfortably before the fire.

Claude Mangre needed no further invitation. "They were named after two of the Lord's Apostles—Philip and Bartholomew—but that was as far as the resemblance went. For they were wilder than some of those little Huron devils Father Anthony Daniel brought down to start his school at Our Lady of the Angels. After a year's attempt at schooling the good Father called them, 'wilder than wild asses.' Maybe that was why Father Daniel is now back in that Huronia.

"Well, anyway, my brave Philip and Bartholomew dropped their dish rags. Did I tell you they were working in the scullery of the fort at Three Rivers? No; well, they were, though I can't believe they ever did much honest work.

"One day they took an arquebus—I don't say they stole the gun, for no doubt they intended to restore it to the soldier—and a horn of powder. They took—again with no thieving intentions—a canoe that belonged to the Commandant. Leave it to them to pick the best one in the settlement!

"Thus equipped they paddled across the river and landed on the southern shore of the St. Lawrence. Their plans were to hunt elk. But at this particular time there were wilder beasts than any wolves hunting on that shore. This was a Mohawk Iroquois war party, up for early spring pickings in the enemy's country. They heard the report of the boys' arquebus and they quietly began stalking this prey.

"As I heard the story these would-be elk hunters were walking through the forest, chattering gayly, when Iroquois braves rained on them."

Impressively the stout cook kissed his finger nails. "Some of these, my infant, the Mohawks bit away."

Jacques had been listening attentively. The chill of the May waters had left his body. Now he volunteered:

"That's the usual way the Iroquois start to torture their captives."

"Well, I hope to give my ten finger nails Christian burial some day," said Claude piously, "and I'm going to take care of them till then.

"Anyway, Philip and Bartholomew soon were bleeding captives bound to the bottom of Iroquois canoes. Then the Iroquois started up the St. Lawrence for the river named after them, and they must have told the boys too graphically the attentions that awaited them at the end of their journey. Three days they canoed and the youths watched till the Mohawks' vigilance relaxed.

"A night came and Philip and Bartholomew made their escape. They fled and hid, fled and hid, and a week later they came to the southern bank of the Great River, not so far from the place of their capture.

"What little clothing they had were almost shreds, after that week's flight through the forests. In vain the youths searched for the Commandant's canoe that they had carefully concealed. Some sharp-eyed one had found and taken the canoe. The fear of recapture and all the horrors that awaited them made their search for a canoe—anything—thorough.

"There across the river was safety. Here was death by starvation or, worse, by savage slow fire. Thoughts of this sort spurred on the fugitives. Together they recited a prayer to St. Joseph and he did not fail them. Though, personally, I'd appeal to his mother-in-law, good St. Anne.

"In a little cove, cut off from the sunlight, the youths found a cake of ice that had been left when the gorge went out. The cake was less than ten feet across.

"Philip and Bartholomew jumped into the icy water. They tugged and they pushed, till, I imagine, they were perspiring profusely. But eventually the cake floated free of the shore.

"A sentry on the fort at Three Rivers saw something strange floating down the middle of the river. He called his officer who came with his spy glass.

"At first, he thought there were two animals, trapped on a cake of ice, floating down the river. He wondered why they did not swim ashore. Then he made the discovery that the animals were human beings and he ordered some soldiers to take a canoe and investigate.

"When the soldiers paddled closer they saw two thin boys, bare as your hand, scratched by brier and with wounds blood-coated, who were standing on the ice cake. Stretched between them for a sail, they had the wreck of a shirt.

"And that was how Philip and Bartholomew came back to Three Rivers. So you see, my infant, why I thought of them when I saw you in the doorway."

Jacques asked: "Did they ever get the Commandant's canoe?"

"Some Frenchmen of the woods had returned that, but the Mohawks kept the arquebus and the two youths, when they came out of the fort hospital, got a public birching for stealing the Company's property."

The word "birching" recalled to Jacques an unpleasant episode of the morning. Briefly he told the stout cook of his experience in Fort St. Louis and his attempt to get the Hurons to take him back to their country in their canoes.

Claude Mangre shook his head violently and then he shook a pudgy finger at the small blanketed figure.

"So you would trust yourself to savages. You have the sense of the donkey—almost!

"My monkey, did you ever hear what happened to the Basque boy about your age?"

Jacques settled back contentedly, eating the handful of raisins that Claude had thrust upon him. He knew the cook was windy with words and could not be rushed into answers to direct questions.

"Basque Boy? I never heard about him, M'sieur."

The fat cook put on a grave face and continued: "Yes; my infant, that unfortunate boy—Peter was his name—was your age and build. I crossed the ocean with him in 'The Cardinal' before it happened."

Jacques sought to humor Claude, "Did you ever meet him again?"

"What a question! Eat those raisins that came from France and listen. That Basque boy was not bright enough to be a ship's cook. No; he decided the Good God had intended him to be an interpreter and he begged Captain Charles Daniel to take him to the Commandant at Tadousac——"

Jacques interrupted: "Was that Captain the brother of Father Anthony Daniel, who works for God in Huronia?"

"Own blood brother. They are both fine men. Eat your raisins and don't interrupt, my infant.

"The upshot was my brave Peter was left ashore with some savages who lived along the Gaspé, when 'The Cardinal' sailed for Dieppe."

The cook paused dramatically.

"Next summer when we came back to the St. Lawrence and anchored off this very Quebec, Father Le Jeune came on board—he was a kindly man—and I heard him telling Captain Daniel the fate of that foolish Peter.

"It seems those savages went hunting and the brave Peter went along. The elks and the moose kept out of sight. Rank starvation set in and one cold morning the famished savages tomahawked Peter and their kettles cooked him and their stomachs got him. And that's what happened to the Basque boy who would be an interpreter, if you please."

"I hope Peter gave them all indigestion," wished Jacques seriously. He was feeling normal again and his swim in the St. Lawrence was but a cold memory.

Now he asked: "But, M'sieur Claude, did you see any Iroquois traces when coming from Three Rivers?"

The stout Claude paused in the process of wiping a very greasy pot. Then he came back to Jacques' question.

"See any Iroquois coming from Three Rivers? Yes; we thought we saw three of their canoes in a little cove before we breasted Cape Diamond, but Captain was not sure they were not Montagnais canoes.

"You know, my unsheathed infant, you never see trace of those painted devils from the southlands, unless they wish you to see them. They are clothed with invisibility till they are ready to attack. May the good Saint Anne shoot all of them!"

"Amen," said Jacques laughing.

The boy's eyes twinkled. "M'sieur Claude, they'd have trouble getting you into their kettles."

"They are going to have considerable trouble getting me at all," asserted the stout cook. He had finished wiping the pot and now he settled himself in his chair. He took out a silver box and sniffed up a pinch of snuff.

He was reminded of something. "I heard tell at Three Rivers trading post last trip of the sudden way the Iroquois savages captured that holy Father Jogues some years back. One of the Hurons who was with him, a big fellow with one eye, said the Iroquois were all around the Huron canoes before they were discovered. The big fellow got to the bank and ran and hid in the forest till the Iroquois had tortured and taken their prisoners to further horrors at the stakes in their villages."

Again the cook shook a pudgy finger at the listening boy, while he piously vowed: "No painted savage of these savage lands will ever set his dirty thieving hands on Claude Mangre! That's why I stay on board my ship."

"Don't you ever go ashore?" inquired Jacques.

"Yes; when there's a sun in the heavens I step on the land at Three Rivers and here at Quebec, but you don't catch me returning to the 'Saint Anne' after dark! That's why, when the crew goes carousing ashore, they leave me as watchman."

Jacques laughed. "M'sieur Claude, what would you do if the Iroquois came alongside in their canoes now? Just you and I are on board."

The fat cook looked out the galley doorway apprehensively.

"Don't talk that way, my infant! Now I'll never shut an eye till the crew gets back. That is, those who won't have to ride the chevalet tomorrow."

Claude waddled out on deck. It was black night, save for the stars that twinkled on the broad river. A few lights shone in Quebec settlement. A bell rang in one of the convents. From the houses nearer the water front came sailors' songs. The Iroquois menace seemed leagues distant. The cook finished his tour of inspection and returned to the warm galley to find Jacques dozing on his stool.

The boy straightened up. "Did you find any Iroquois?"

"And if I had, my infant, all Quebec would have heard Claude's voice."

The cook settled himself comfortably. "It's a warm night and soon the spring will green up the bleak cliffs and I'm thinking, my infant, that when the ships come from France, I'll ship on one that needs a cook. The thought of these Iroquois, or for that matter, all the pagan savages of this land, makes me lose weight daily."

Jacques looked critically at his friend. He shook his head and announced: "If you are, it isn't showing yet."

The boy had been yawning prodigiously the last five minutes, while his stout friend talked and now Claude noticed it.

"My infant, take the blanket and curl up in the corner there."

The cook indicated a dark angle of the galley.

Obediently Jacques obeyed.

The next he remembered it was broad daylight. He awoke with a start. The cook was busily engaged over his fire and the aroma drove all sleepiness out of the boy's head. He started to throw off his blanket when he remembered his lack of clothing.

Then Jacques saw his shirt and breeches and boots lying nearby. As he dressed, the disagreeable thought came—what would he have had to do, if the crew had discovered and thrown them out of the rowboat.

While Jacques ate his breakfast, Claude Mangre talked and the substance of it was that the boy should return to Our Lady of the Angels.

"A birching stings and then you cool off, my infant. But if you start for this Huronia, you may not get there and," he added ominously, "there may be no cakes of ice handy when you desperately need them. Remember that well."

Jacques did not commit himself and he was glad to drop into the first rowboat going ashore. He waved gratefully to the stout figure that filled the galley doorway till the boat grated on the beach.

His plans, except that he was not going back to Our Lady of the Angels, and he was going to try and find a way to Father Brebeuf in Huronia, were vague. But then Jacques had never been one to plan ahead. He took what came.

Walking warily through the town, he dodged into a narrow road when he saw a familiar Blackrobe ahead of him. He had recognized Father Jerome Lalemant on his way to say Mass at the Ursuline Convent and Jacques did not care to discover himself at this early hour of the day. He knew that his absence from his school was known now and a search for him would be on.

By the Hotel Dieu he passed and the remembrance of his father's death scene there four years ago came to him. Again he recalled Father Brebeuf's promise to his dying father. Then came up the treasured recollection of the gigantic Blackrobe and the conversation they had had that afternoon of his father's burial.

Father Brebeuf had said: "It is three hundred leagues from Quebec's Rock . . . right down to our Residence at Fort St. Mary. Here I will be waiting for you and you will be placed with the boys, who are learning to be mission interpreters."

Jacques' present problem was to get up those leagues that separated him from Fort St. Mary. As he had never been further from the settlement than the few leagues down stream to Orleans Island, his ideas of the distance were too vague to deter him from the unknown dangers.

Jacques had a mind to stray into the enclosure of Fort St. Louis and seek his friend, Robert Le Duke, the drummer boy, but the remembrance of the unpleasantness he had barely escaped yesterday prevented. He did scout before the fort's gates, keeping himself well hidden, Iroquois fashion, behind the boles of available trees, but Robert was not in sight and the white uniformed sentry, slowly pacing his beat, was.

Jacques' vigil was rewarded by the sight of Governor Montmagny, a gallant scarlet and white figure, with a great floating plume in his hat, riding out of the gateway. Stiffly stood the guard, the drums rolled and the Governor trotted his bay horse away from the fort. Jacques' eyes were more on the beast than on its magnificently dressed master. For the Governor owned the only horse in the settlement. Well did Jacques remember the day last June when the animal was brought ashore from the ship from France. He and Louis Joliet and the other boys of the settlement had followed the horse to the Governor's house and had shouted when His Excellency had mounted and cantered the beast away. How the savages, Algonquin, Montagnais and Huron, had scattered when this strange beast—"Moose without the Horns," as they named him—had snorted his fright at his unaccustomed surroundings.

Now Jacques was used to the sight of the horse and he had even petted the animal's flank that occasion when Monseigneur Montmagny had visited Our Lady of the Angels. His Excellency had graciously offered to let some of the pupils ride, but all, savage and French, had politely declined.

Now Jacques watched and regretfully he wished he knew how to ride. In that event the Governor's horse might have been "borrowed" and Jacques' immediate problem solved.

Finally, Jacques withdrew and skirting around the fort's walls, climbed the slope that led up to Cape Diamond. He knew this path he was on led to Sillery.

It took him an hour's climb to scale the heights and come out on the cape. He had met nobody. He sighted some white partridges and many wood pigeons. The pine forest ended abruptly and Jacques was looking down on a glorious panorama.

Below him lay Quebec settlement. The wooden roofs, the steeple of the Ursulines, the house and church of the Jesuit Fathers not yet completely finished, the gray squared enclosure that the boy knew was Fort St. Louis, and anchored, seemingly a spring from the shore, the tiny "St. Anne" on which he had spent the night.

But Jacques raised his eyes and looked across the great St. Lawrence. He recalled that the priest at Sillery, young Father Gabriel Lalemant, had told him once the meaning of Quebec. It was a word of a nearby tribe and it meant "Where the waters narrow." Now looking down from Cape Diamond, it was easy to see why this place had been so named. Across were the heights, crowned with gloomy pines, but below the settlement the St. Lawrence widened rapidly till it disappeared behind distant Orleans Island.

Jacques' attention now was attracted to some tiny moving spots far below. These his keen eyes knew were Indians, paddling their canoes upstream. Maybe, they were the Huron group he had met yesterday.

A remark that Bernard, the young brave who knew Echon, had made, came back to the lad. It was to the effect that there might be a better chance of getting into a canoe at Three Rivers, where the Huron flotilla stopped. Only a few of the Hurons ventured down to Quebec. The rest did their bartering at the trading post of Three Rivers.

But Jacques' immediate problem was how to get to Three Rivers, 76 miles up the great river.

Then the thought came, almost like an inspiration. Why not try to find some friendly Montagnais Indians at their stockaded village of St. Joseph, Sillery. This settlement, smaller than Quebec, was only four miles upstream. Really, only three miles from where the boy stood.

Jacques cast a last look over the glorious panorama stretching for miles below him. Then he turned his back on the sight and began to make his way along the trail.

Quickly he was in the midst of the pine forests. For half an hour he went along through the silent woods. He was recalling the last time he had been to St. Joseph's, Sillery. It was only last September. He and Louis Joliet had heard the rumor, when they were passing the Church of the Infant Jesus and they had started to run to Sillery. Le Fortune, the blacksmith, told them that the Montagnais had captured an Iroquois warrior, who had two Montagnais scalp locks hanging at his belt.

Jacques remembered Le Fortune's exact words: "That Iroquois will be at the stake this very minute. For the council has decided to burn him."

Jacques had looked at Louis and when they were beyond the blacksmith's ken, he had hurriedly explained his signal.

"Let us run to Sillery and, maybe, we will be in time to see some of the torture."

Louis had made a wry face, saying, "It will mean the birch for both of our backs, but if we are in time it will be worth the sting."

So the two boys had walked sedately till they were beyond possible French eyes and then they had run till exhausted along the Sillery trail.

All their efforts came to naught for when they arrived at St. Joseph's stockade, a Montagnais squaw had told them: "French boys, you are too late. The Iroquois lived but an hour. The young Blackrobe"—they knew she meant Father Gabriel Lalemant—"the young Blackrobe poured Saving Waters on the warrior before he expired."

All Louis Joliet's fears about the birch switchings were verified that evening when the two weary boys returned to Quebec settlement.

Reminiscently Jacques rubbed his shoulders as he trudged along and he muttered to himself, "Nobody will put a birch to me again."

By this time the boy had come out on a plain, still thickly wooded. Naturally, he did not know that in the following century this level stretch, back of Cape Diamond, would be immortalized by a bloody battle between white men and would be known by the name of "The Plains of Abraham."

The trail led nearer to the river again and as Jacques saw the water below, he stopped and silently slipped behind the shelter of a great pine.

There below him was a cove and from his height he could see three canoes, each laden with four Indians.

He thought they were Montagnais or Hurons, a fishing party. Possibly, Montagnais. If so, he hoped to paddle in a canoe the rest of the way to St. Joseph's, Sillery.

And thereby Jacques, the truant, made a dreadful mistake.

Chapter Four

Stripling Tree

JACQUES BOURDON turned off the trail to Sillery village and plunged into the forest. Quickly he was slipping and sliding downward. He dislodged a cone and a startled groundhog dashed away into the brush. Ahead he heard a wood pigeon call. Then it was quiet as he slid downward, ever downward, into the dim light beneath the thickly growing pines.

Somewhat breathless the boy came out at the foot of the promontory. Jacques discovered that he was close to the shore. The still water of the cove and, beyond, the broad river appeared. The only sign of life was an eagle sailing majestically across the sky. He looked for the canoes but they had disappeared from cove and shore.

Some instinct warned Jacques to halt in his tracks. There was an ominous feeling creeping over him that innocent Montagnais fishermen would leave their canoes drawn up on the beach. He had just about decided that prudence called for him to climb back up the side of the promontory and retake the trail to Sillery, when a tattooed warrior, naked but for his loincloth, slid out of the shadows right beside him and stood with raised tomahawk.

It all happened in a wink. One look at the red and blue streaks of war paint on the young warrior's face and Jacques knew that he stood helpless before, not an Algonquin or Montagnais, but a dreaded Mohawk Iroquois. The threat of instant death was held in that bare raised arm.

The warrior silently grasped Jacques' trembling arm. Quickly he searched the boy's body for weapons. Then he took a deer fibre thong from his belt and tied the boy's wrists tightly together behind his back.

Then Jacques cried out in sudden pain as the point of the tomahawk prodded him forward. All the lurid tales he had ever heard of the fate of Iroquois captives rushed through his imagination. Jacques wished heartily that he was back at his hated school tasks in Our Lady of the Angels a league away.

The silent brave halted his captive. Then he called softly like a wood pigeon. Jacques listened and from the hidden forest ahead another wood pigeon seemed to answer. Again was Jacques prodded painfully forward till he saw the hidden canoes.

He stepped around the three upturned canoes and into a circle of pines. There seated were the rest of the Iroquois party. In broken French one of the older warriors asked: "Nephew, why did you come alone to the shore of this cove?"

Jacques decided that the truth was his best defense.

"I was on my way to the Montagnais village of Sillery. Up there one hour's walk."

On the chance that he would be better understood Jacques repeated this information in Huron.

At once one of the warriors replied. "Nephew, where did you learn that tongue?"

"I am a student at Our Lady of the Angels, and the Huron boys there taught it to me."

"Why are you not now in the school cabin?"

"I am running away."

"Why?" The question was hurled.

"I did not like school and I want to go to the lands of the Hurons where my friend, the Blackrobe Echon is."

The Iroquois demanded. "Nephew, you know Echon?"

"He is my guardian since my father died in the big cabin of the

Virgin Squaws four years ago. Echon it was who placed me in the school cabin and ordered me to learn the language of the Hurons."

"Why?"

"Echon promised to take me to Huronia and make me an interpreter at the Fathers' Residence."

"Where is Echon's village in Huronia?"

"It is the fortified village the French call Fort St. Mary's."

"And were you going all the leagues alone to Echon's village?"

"I thought I would find a seat in a Huron canoe when the flotilla leaves Three Rivers."

While Jacques was being questioned the throbbing in his bound wrists made him moan occasionally. One of the older Iroquois, evidently the chief of this war party spoke a low command and the warrior who had captured Jacques came forward with a sharp stone knife in his hand.

Jacques faced him outwardly brave.

The young warrior flourished the knife till it gleamed in the sun. Then he passed it swiftly across the boy's throat, the keen edge just grazing the neck. Instinctively the boy winched. The warrior grinned and, reaching back, cut the thong. Jacques with relief commenced to rub his red swollen wrists. He was still engaged in this massage when the chief spoke to him.

"French boy, who speaks the Huron tongue so well, listen. One will come here soon. When he comes I will know if you have spoken with a split tongue." He paused and, pointing to the blazing sun above, added ominously, "If you have, you have looked on Old Man Above for the last time."

The warrior who had released his wrists, now threw Jacques on the ground. In a few seconds his legs and arms were bound securely. Then he was lifted and carried to the canoes under the pines. There under an upturned birchbark canoe Jacques was left to think his bitter thoughts.

But they were driven from his mind by a shout of delight from nearby. Jacques turned his head and saw Louis Joliet. Like himself, his chum was lying on the ground securely tied.

The two boys wiggled and squirmed closer. Quickly Jacques told of his capture and he listened while Louis explained: "My mistake was just as foolish. I did not return from Sillery with my father last evening. You know, we sold a calf to Father Gabriel and the domestic who was to take charge of it was out hunting. So when I learnt that Father Gabriel was coming to Quebec this morning, to see his uncle, Father Jerome Lalemant, I volunteered to stay overnight and take care of the calf till the man returned. My father went home last night. I served Father Gabriel's Mass this morning. Then we started from Sillery village and when we came along the trail on the cliff above, I was telling Father Gabriel about the trap we lost along here last winter."

Jacques interrupted: "So we did! I had forgotten all about it! It was somewhere in this neighborhood. Remember, Louis, we thought, when we did not find it, some large animal must have sprung it and dragged it away."

"Yes; I told Father Gabriel that and he would have stopped and searched for that missing trap with me, only he would have been late for his appointment with his uncle. So he went on to the settlement and I started down to the shore."

"Did you find any trace of the trap?" asked Jacques.

"No;" Louis Joliet replied disgustedly, "I didn't have time, for I foolishly stepped into another trap."

"It was a blessed thing Father Gabriel did not go searching with you!" exclaimed Jacques, "he'd have followed Father Jogues into captivity."

Louis began to chuckle. "It was funny the way I almost walked into a waiting Iroquois. I actually fell over his leg and he had me bound helpless before I hit the ground.

"Then just when I was recovering from that fright, you come tumbling into the same Hot Ashes——"

"What?" Jacques was puzzled.

"That's the name of the young warrior who captured both of us. The one who just left you here."

Here Louis laughed outright.

"There's nothing to laugh about," complained Jacques. "Do you realize our captors are Iroquois?"

"Isn't there enough! When I think of you trying to dodge the school fathers and escaping from them only to fall into Iroquois hands!"

Even Jacques joined in the laugh at this aspect of his taking.

Louis continued: "Listen, Jacques, I don't think this band of savages is going to hurt us. I overheard that chief speaking to another warrior. One of the party is an apostate Huron, adopted by the Mohawks. He is a spy and I think—I didn't overhear enough to be certain—but I think he is spying in Quebec this very moment. Our French don't believe there are any Iroquois savages nearer than Three Rivers. So that's why this war party is encamped here so close to the settlement.

"But when I think of you, running away from Our Lady of the Angels to escape a birching and then to fall into Iroquois hands!"

"Go on and laugh," urged Jacques, "it's funny, isn't it? But if you ask me, I think it was funnier about you coming down to look for an animal trap lost months ago and then to walk into a savage trap——"

"Well, funny or not," was Louis' final fling, "here we both are trussed up like two hens in the market place in front of the Infant Jesus Church, and, at least, those chickens know what's going to happen to them."

"If you ask me," observed Jacques, "I'll tell you right now what'll happen to us. We'll lie low and escape at the first favorable opportunity."

"Hush! Not so loud," cautioned Louis Joliet, "Someone's coming."

The boys twisted their heads and saw the Mohawk chief was approaching. With him was another warrior. Jacques thought at once that he had seen this latter savage before. Then in a flash recognition came.

Yes; he had been among the savages who had visited Fort St. Louis the day before. He had stood silently by, while the boy was escaping a deserved birching.

The young warrior looked at Jacques and then he said: "Yes; this is the little French cock. He's not afraid of Hurons for he struck a Huron. A Blackrobe chief told a big Frenchman warrior to switch him. Then the Huron interceded and he escaped and now this pounder of braves has come visiting us. We are all afraid," grinned the warrior.

"It was good, nephew," said the chief, "that you did not speak to me with a split tongue. I hope you will enjoy your visit."

Jacques noticed that back of the chief's smile, grimness lurked and he felt better when the Mohawk captain turned and walked off.

The warrior remained. He took out his knife and the two boys looked at each other apprehensively. Once Jacques had heard an interpreter at the Fort tell that when an Iroquois warrior grinned at a captive he very likely was about to inflict some peculiarly fiendish torture on him.

But this time that interpreter's observation was wrong.

The warrior cut the thong that bound Jacques' arms and legs. The boy attempted to stand and take a step, but he fell helpless on his face. As he lay there the savage tied his feet together with a thong. This time it was not so tightly bound. Jacques felt that this warrior was friendly to him and he was emboldened to request: "Please, Mohawk brave, do the same for this boy." But the warrior shook his head and silently withdrew.

Both boys saw that some member of the party always kept them in sight and so the day dragged towards evening.

Then Hot Ashes and the friendly warrior came with some smoked eels and while the boys ate ravenously, Jacques' curiosity got the better of him and he asked: "I want to know something. How is it you are a member of this Iroquois war party and yesterday you were with Hurons in the Fort?"

The warrior smiled: "I am the eyes of this party. I am a Huron by birth, but I am an Iroquois in here." He touched his heart. "It is convenient sometimes. Now eat, for we do not feed captives often."

When it was early evening the two warriors returned. They removed the leg thongs and tightened the hide bands about the wrists of each boy.

Then with a cuff the captives were herded down to the shore of the cove.

Jacques lost sight of Louis, but he knew he was somewhere nearby. The three canoes were carried to the water and Jacques was kicked into one.

The chief, Hot Ashes, and a strange brave, who had one ear missing, got into this canoe and Jacques could see the rest of the raiding party in the other canoes. With hardly a splash all paddled away from the cove. Soon they were out on the St. Lawrence. It was almost dark now, yet the boy could see, looking aft over the gunwale, the black looming heights of Cape Diamond and he knew beyond its bulk lay Quebec and all the world of his young life.

The lapping of the waters was soothing and Jacques began to repeat the prayer that he was accustomed to recite with the other boys at Our Lady of the Angels.

It was one that Father Anthony Daniel had composed, back in 1636, when he had brought the first Huron boys down from their villages and begun the school.

"Little Master," prayed Jacques, "I thank You for keeping me from morning till now. Keep me the rest of the way. Forget my faults and help me to overcome them. I give You my acts. Give me Your grace to perform them well. Amen."

Then he finished with a prayer to the Queen of the Angels. Somehow the dread of the unknown horrors of Iroquois captivity ahead, seemed to soften and he had the feeling that this captivity would bring him, eventually to that distant Huronia, where his beloved Father Brebeuf toiled.

With this pleasant last thought, the tired boy slept, while silently the birchbark canoe was paddled up the great river.

While it was still dark the grounding of the canoe on a black shore awoke the lad. Many figures were moving about. With a cry of delight he saw Louis Joliet, sleepily rubbing his eyes. Before he could speak, Hot Ashes led Jacques into the depths of the thick forests till they came to a camp of Iroquois.

Into the blackness of a shelter he was thrust. It was too black to see, yet Jacques knew he was not alone. A man, lying there bound in the other corner, was moaning continuously.

With the coming of the gray dawn light Jacques awoke again. At first he did not know where he was. Then he heard a moan of pain. He twisted stiffly.

Now he could see that he was in a rudely constructed structure of branches. In the strengthening light he saw that a strange young warrior, his two eagle feathers silhouetted against a patch of eastern sky, was on guard outside the shelter. Beyond the figures of other Mohawk warriors were moving about.

The moanings continued and now Jacques could make out his fellow prisoner. He lay fastened face down. He was a young white man. Roughly the boy guessed that he was a woodsman in his early twenties.

When it was light enough in the shelter, Jacques' eyes were fascinated by the sight of the man's hands and feet. They were bound so tightly that the deerhide thongs were buried in his flesh at wrists and ankles. The hands had bloody tips and the lad saw that according to Iroquois custom most of the nails had been torn off. But the soles of his feet had been burnt off. . . .

Jacques with relief thanked his youthfulness for saving him from a similar fate. He knew that if he had been several years older his fingers would be in the same swollen shape. He remembered gratefully that Hot Ashes had treated him considerately so far.

This not too reassuring thought brought up the image of the Huron who was not a Huron, but a member of this Mohawk band. There was some mystery here.

Jacques lay thinking of this puzzling thought, while his unknown companion moaned with pain.

It was broad daylight now and the Iroquois band outside were active. Food was being cooked over fires and the appetizing aroma floated into the shelter.

But no food was brought to the captives. And hunger began to gnaw at Jacques' stomach. He was feeling very miserable and wishing that he had stayed at Our Lady of the Angels, when he heard his fellow sufferer speaking in French: "Stranger, who are you?"

The boy replied: "I am Jacques, the son of Big Jacques Bourdon, who died four years ago."

"Was your father a woodsman?"

"Yes, sir."

"Then I knew him. A good man was Big Jacques. A tree crushed him, didn't it?"

"Yes, sir. God rest him in God's Acre!"

"And who are you?" asked the boy, delighted to know that his fellow sufferer was French.

"I? I am a dead man, whom these painted devils from the south lands keep alive for a few days longer. These Mohawks ambushed me. Philip, my companion, was helping me tow a boat upstream and we walked into their ambush. I think my companion died at the first arquebus shot. I was less fortunate. They brought me here. Yesterday the band tortured me. You see what they have left.

"Philip and I were captured by Mohawks three years ago when we went out hunting from Three Rivers. After a few days we escaped and crossed the St. Lawrence on a cake of ice. Some of this party recognized me as an escaped captive. They plan to take me to their castles in the south and there I will go to the stake."

The young man was about to speak further, when three warriors came to the shelter. They kicked the man over and for the first time Jacques saw him. His face, with beard plucked out, was livid from blows and clotted blood covered his chest and thighs.

Ignoring the listening boy, one of the Mohawks spoke to the man in broken French: "My nephew, you are rested now. Here is some strengthening sagamite and meat." The warrior pretended to hand the captive food. "Eat, my nephew, for you will travel many leagues today."

"Where do you cursed savages take me?"

"Close to the French trading post, my nephew. You will see your friends and they will be helpless to help you. You will ride in a canoe till we come to our River of the Iroquois, near to where your tribesmen had the Strong House."

Jacques recognized the Indians' designation for Fort Richelieu.

"Then you will sail down our river till you come to our castles."

"And when I get to your accursed country, what then?"

"What then, my nephew? Why our squaws and children will be awaiting to give you the caresses you deprived them of before. They will caress you, but they will not stop your heart beating. When you are rested, you will be led to the platform and the fires will be lighted under the kettles."

The young Frenchman laughed. "My uncles, it's many a league to your country. How do you know that I will not escape again?"

"Our nephew will never walk again," said one of the Mohawks.

The captive attempted to stand on his burnt soles but fell face forward on the ground. Then two of the savages began to carry the Frenchman away. He shouted back to Jacques: "Boy, listen well.

Escape and tell my friends in Three Rivers that Philip died and I, Bartholomew Dablon, go south in the company of these gallant gentlemen. May they all burn forever!"

The captive's voice died away.

It must have been over an hour later, when the Huron Iroquois, who had befriended Jacques the evening before, appeared at the shelter. He carried a birchbark dish of steaming sagamite and some smoked eels.

Jacques' first question was: "Where is Louis, my friend?"

"He is nearby, little nephew. He was eating when I passed him a few moments ago. His example is a good one to follow."

Jacques gratefully wolfed down the half cooked food. When it was finished he thanked this friendly warrior.

"Tell me," he asked, "what is your name and why do you befriend me?"

The warrior did not reply to the lad's first question and at once Jacques remembered the warning a soldier at Fort St. Louis had given to him, "Never ask a savage his name directly. They do not like to be so questioned. Always ask the name of another savage."

"Befriend you? You are a young boy. I liked you, when your countrymen would beat you with switches. That is enough. I have spoken. Come."

He cut the leg bands and led Jacques out of the shelter. At once he was in the midst of the Iroquois camp. It was neatly hidden from all eyes on the nearby river. Jacques looked in vain for the place of Louis' captivity. He counted some thirty braves in camp. Some were bending over the fires, that did not send up betraying smoke. Others were repairing an upturned canoe with patches of birchbark. Two had wounds on face and shoulders that told of recent fighting.

When they approached the upturned canoe that three young warriors were repairing, Jacques noticed one of them was hardly more than a boy of fourteen, slim and immature. He wore but a skin breechclout.

Jacques' captor said something to this boy and he laughed. Then the Iroquois boy came forward and taking Jacques by the arm with a grip that hurt, led him to a small tree and in a trice had lashed his arms to the bole.

The Huron said: "Stripling Tree will watch you. He is Hot Ashes' younger brother. He is anxious to kill his first Frenchman, so don't attempt to loosen your bands, my nephew."

Then the warrior left Jacques and the Mohawks laughed and went on with their mending of the canoe.

Jacques decided to try some of his Huron on this Stripling Tree. "Mohawk boy, I ask a question. What is the name of the warrior who led me here?"

The boy replied: "I thought you spoke only the whiteman's words. It is good. Now we talk some."

The boy squatted before his prisoner. "That one is The Frog. He was born a Huron, but was captured when a boy and was raised in Ossernenon. He is Mohawk by adoption and he has sworn to kill all Hurons. They should be killed, for they are allies of your people, whom we always kill."

"Thanks," said Jacques, "we French kill many of you too. Why don't you kill me now?"

"I wish I could. It may not be done, for you belong to Hot Ashes who captured you. But loosen your bonds and try to run away. See what will happen, nephew."

"What?" asked Jacques, "I could kill you in a fight."

The Iroquois boy smiled wickedly. "Listen, white boaster, three summers ago there were two French youths captured by us near the shore of the Great River. We were taking them to our castles. They got away and returned to their cabins on the Great River. Yesterday the two fell into our ambush, as they were towing a boat upstream. Unfortunately one of them died at the taking. Last night, when the fires were burning brightly, we warriors held the live one over the fires till the soles of his feet touched the live coals' embers. He

49

will crawl on his hands and knees till he gets into the kettles at Ossernenon. That is the punishment of those who try to escape and are recaptured. Now do you know, white boy?"

The name of Stripling Tree's Mohawk village had sounded strangely familiar to Jacques. He was trying to connect it with some incident he had heard.

"Iroquois boy who boasts what the warriors do, say again the name of your long houses?"

"Ossernenon."

"Ossernenon, Ossernenon," repeated Jacques, "now I have it!

"Listen, Iroquois boy, wasn't it at Ossernenon that a Blackrobe and his young companion were put to death more moons ago than there are fingers on your hands?"

Stripling Tree grinned. "A summer and half a summer ago— yes. It was in the nutting time before last."

Jacques hastily figured back and murmured to himself: "That would be about October, 1646." Aloud: "Yes; that was the time. Did you see their deaths?"

Again Stripling Tree grinned cruelly. "The Blackrobe was the one with the mangled hands, whom the Broad Breeches ransomed and who came back?"

"That's the one. His name with us is Father Isaac Jogues."

"He was a bad medicine man. When he came to make the peace treaty he cunningly buried evil spirits in a box under a cabin in Ossernenon. Then he went away to the French villages along the Great River. The evil spirits came out of the box and spread disease through all our castles."

"You speak with a split tongue," cried Jacques angrily. "Father Jogues was gentle. He never killed anybody."

"French boy has a split tongue. He did with his evil spirits in that box. So when he came back again he was tomahawked by a brave of the Bear Clan. I did not see that killing but I saw his wicked head when it was stuck above the gateway of our palisades.

With the other boys and girls I threw stones at it often. A bad medicine man was that Blackrobe. I have spoken."

Jacques was silent as he recalled the blessing of a blessed martyr he had received that long ago afternoon when his own father had been buried.

Stripling Tree was eager to talk and he continued: "But he should not have been tomahawked so swiftly. He should have been roasted three nights over the slow fires."

"You have no sense, Stripling Tree. That Blackrobe never injured any Iroquois. He never carried an arquebus and he certainly never buried—what you call—evil spirits to spread disease through your village. I know what was in that box. We boys at Our Lady of the Angels heard all. In that box were some clothes for the winter months. For Father Jogues planned to spend the white months in your Ossernenon and teach you The Prayer——"

"You speak with a split tongue, white boy," interrupted Stripling Tree in anger, "I hope my brother Hot Ashes takes you bound to Ossernenon and turns you over to the scaffold and the slow fires. I may not touch you now, unless you attempt to escape. Then it would be different."

Stripling Tree went on: "That bad medicine man's companion had not seen many more moons than you. He was staked down in our Long Houses the whole night after the Blackrobe was tomahawked.

"I was one of the boys who caressed him. Do you want to know how?"

"Yes," said Jacques, eager to learn details of the death of John Lalande, Father Jogues' youthful companion in martyrdom.

"It is our custom—you will learn it when we reach Ossernenon, or sooner——" Again Stripling Tree grinned cruelly. "It is our custom to thong down the condemned captive this way."

The Mohawk boy lay on his back on the ground and spread-eagling his arms and legs showed Jacques the helpless position in which the Iroquois victims were bound. "Then when the French boy who was the companion of the Blackrobe was bound that way, we boys of the village and the girls too, were permitted to caress him with live coals. We would laugh when he attempted to shake the burning coal off his chest and stomach."

"How long did this last?" asked Jacques, seeing in imagination the helpless Lalande enduring his martyrdom.

"Till the east brightened. Then a captain cut off his nose. He was tomahawked and his head was stuck on a palisade spike alongside of that of the Blackrobe.

"That is the way to treat all French. They are the allies of our blood enemies."

"I wish I had you alone in an Huron village," thought Jacques, eyeing the Iroquois boy.

Suddenly a crow cawed thrice and instantly all the Mohawks, who had been working in the camp, disappeared behind boles of trees. Jacques found Stripling Tree holding a keen-edge knife before his startled eyes as he hissed: "Cry out a tiny warning and——"

He did not finish the threat, but he poised the knife suggestively above Jacques' heart.

Jacques listened. Out on the nearby St. Lawrence he began to hear catches of a sailor's song. Often he had heard it on the ships that came from France. It was about a maid who waited for her sailor lad in Dieppe. The words came clearer and with rising horror Jacques realized that this French sailor was sailing into a Mohawk ambush. The warriors had crept noiselessly down till they were hidden close to the water's edge. Jacques had a vanishing thought to shout, but the sight of the grim Stripling Tree with raised knife, kneeling before him, silenced any sound in his throat.

Jacques, by twisting his head, could see between pines a small sector of the river and the distant green northern bank. Now into this visible space sailed a scallop, bound downstream. Jacques recognized it as one that belonged at Tadousac, leagues down the river.

The words of the song came from the lips of the bearded sailor at the helm. As the craft cleared the point of the woods, instead of following the shore and sailing into the ambush of crouching Iroquois, the sailor threw over the helm and the sail filled, heading the boat towards the safety of the opposite shore.

Only when the words died away on the river breeze did the silent Mohawks come out of their positions. Stripling Tree reluctantly lowered his knife and Jacques breathed easier, but his heart was still beating fast at that close escape his countrymen had had from capture and lingering death.

Soon the hidden camp resumed its activities.

Before dusk Hot Ashes came. This time Jacques was led to the kettles and he squatted delightedly across from Louis Joliet. But he was forbidden to speak to him. The two boys smiled across the fire. They ate heartily and listened to the snatches of conversation. Jacques gathered that the camp would be broken as soon as night fell. And in this he was correct. For when shadows were indistinct on the water, the party in eight canoes pushed off and began to paddle upstream.

Jacques found himself bound securely to the thwarts in the middle of Hot Ashes' canoe. He slept and he woke to peer over the birchbark side and see night and its deep shadows on the Great River. The Mohawks were paddling upstream, close to a dense pine forest.

Again Jacques had been sleeping soundly. He awoke with a start. For a growl from the dark bank nearby told him that a startled bear had scented the canoes. Then he dropped off to sleep again and sleepily he awoke, when, near dawn, the party went into hiding.

So another day and another night voyage. Occasionally Jacques caught glimpses of his friend, and he saw that Louis fared as well as he did.

The third night the Mohawk party passed Three Rivers trading post, paddling close to the far shore. Jacques looked across the wide river at the lights that told him where sentries were on guard in the fort.

Quickly the canoes were paddling up the St. Lawrence and Three Rivers, like Quebec, was behind him.

Now Jacques realized that he had seen the last of his countrymen, unless he and Louis managed their escape. But try as they might, the boys were never left close enough to carry on a conversation.

Once Jacques asked Stripling Tree directly: "Take me close to that French boy. I want to speak with him."

The Mohawk guard replied bluntly: "It is not Hot Ashes' wish that you two have words together. You talk and, like all captives, you plot how to escape the caresses that await you in our Long Houses. It is not good."

After that Jacques was silent, biding his time. Now the Iroquois party, once Three Rivers' settlement was left astern, reversed their procedure and paddled openly by daylight. One canoe always kept half a league in the lead.

On a sunny afternoon this scouting canoe signalled and at once the other canoes headed into the shore. The whole party lay hidden. Quarter of an hour later, Jacques saw a scallop sailing down the middle of the broad river. He recognized it as one that belonged to the new settlement of Ville Marie de Montreal, leagues up the St. Lawrence.

When the vessel had unsuspectingly rounded a lower point and was lost to view the Mohawk party resumed their monotonous paddling up the lonely stream.

Jacques could see Louis seated in another canoe. Like himself, he was not bound now, except when camp was pitched. But though he tried repeatedly, and he could see Louis tried also, never once was he able to exchange a word in private with his fellow captive.

Jacques, however, kept constantly on the lookout for an opportunity to communicate with Louis, but all schemes were discarded as impractical.

The boys' captors evidently had a rendezvous somewhere up the St. Lawrence, for they waited a whole day in camp till a lone canoe came and then the party followed it to the meeting place, where the largest band of Mohawks Jacques had ever seen were assembled in the pines, close behind the river's bank.

From a remark Stripling Tree let drop Jacques learnt that the combined party was about to start on a raid up the Ottawa into Huronia.

This bit of information changed Jacques' outlook completely. All the dread of unknown horrors that awaited captives in the south lands disappeared and he became cheerful at the prospect of reaching Huronia, even in Mohawk canoes.

Then a ready means of communication with Louis Joliet was almost forced on Jacques' notice.

Mohawks of the new party in camp kept drifting by the spot where Jacques was tied. They looked at the French boy sullenly and it was with relief that Jacques realized that he was Hot Ashes' property and by tribal law none of them could lay murderous hands on him.

Then came a couple of young braves. They stopped before Jacques and one said in Huron: "My nephew, the other boy says you are able to do whiteman's magic and make this piece of bark speak. Has he a split tongue?"

Jacques took the strip of bark that had been recently torn from a tree. He turned it over and saw scratched there some rude letters. Holding the bark at an angle he was able to spell out the words.

"What does the bark say to you, my nephew?"

"This bark says to me this message, 'The wood pigeon coos twice.'"

When Jacques had uttered this cryptic sentence, the smaller Iroquois, who had red and blue stripes on his cheeks, and banded around his arms and legs, looked his amazement.

He took the piece of bark from Jacques and examined it closely. The boy, seeing the Iroquois' evident ignorance of the whiteman's alphabet, laughed heartily when that warrior shook the bark vigorously, and even held it to his ear, listening attentively, as though he was trying to hear it breathe.

"My nephew, what makes this speak like a stupid Frenchman?"

Then it was that the idea came to Jacques. In a flash he realized what might have been obvious to him days ago. If these captors were ignorant of writing and curious to see the "whiteman's magic," why here was a easy way to communicate with his fellow captive.

Jacques looked solemnly at the Iroquois warrior.

"You have never seen speaking bark before?"

"No; my nephew, though in my long house I have heard of it."

"Well, my uncle, bring me a silent strip of bark from that white birch there and I will tell it to say your message to the other boy."

Obediently the Mohawk stripped off a piece about ten inches long.

"Now lend me your knife and I will make this talk to the other French boy."

"No, my nephew, captives may not have knives. It is not allowed by the war captain," said the warrior.

"Then get me a sharp stone. And——" Jacques hastened to add as he saw the brave was about to refuse, "——you can take it away when I am finished."

This evidently was not forbidden. The warrior walked to the fire place and returned with a sharp stone. With him came Stripling Tree. Jacques paid no attention, but he saw the Mohawk boy was watching the proceedings intently.

"Now, uncles, you tell me what to say. I will tell it to this strip of bark. Then take it to the other boy and he will make it speak."

The two warriors gravely consulted and then one said: "Make it say this message. 'Two bears found the honey in the tree.'"

Jacques cut the words in the soft bark and handed the message to the warriors. They also demanded the stone knife and without thanking him walked to where Louis Joliet was held captive.

Jacques smiled to himself as he saw Stripling Tree following the braves curiously.

As he suspected Stripling Tree came running back. Jacques had never seen him so excited.

"The braves brought the speaking bark to the other boy. He looked at it and at once said: 'Two bears found the honey in the tree.' I myself heard him. That is great magic.

"Here," Stripling Tree tore a piece of bark from a nearby birch, "make it say, 'The canoe is on the water.'"

Jacques scratched the message and then he added, "Secret. Don't read out. Hello, Louis. How are these savages treating you? Jacques."

"There it is, ready to speak to the other boy." He handed the illiterate boy the bark strip. "Take it to him and see if the bark does not speak."

Delightedly Stripling Tree ran to the opposite side of the camp, where Louis Joliet was detained. Five minutes later he was back and with him were three interested warriors. He carried another bark message.

Jacques took it and holding it at an angle saw that Louis had scratched this, "Three squirrels are in the oak. Secret. Hello, Jacques. Fairly well. Louis."

The boy turned to the silent Iroquois who were watching his every movement.

"This bark tells me thus: 'Three squirrels are in the oak.'"

"It is great magic," said one of the warriors gravely.

For the rest of that afternoon the two boy captives were kept busy writing and reading various simple statements, as more of the warriors in camp learnt of this exhibition of "whiteman's magic."

But under the very eyes of the Iroquois, Jacques learnt that Louis, like himself, was less securely watched at night, that he did not get enough to eat and was anxious to escape at the first opportunity.

In one of the last messages that Jacques was able to send he informed Louis of the party's intention of raiding into Huronia and he advised Louis to be on the lookout for a sharp stone. It was agreed that the first one who was able to secure and conceal this sharp stone, would, come night, cut his own thongs and then attempt to release the other.

Jacques took huge delight in getting the ever-suspicious Stripling Tree to carry these messages to and from Louis.

At the end he had high hopes that his guardian would forget the stone knife with which he was scratching the words on the bark, but the Mohawk boy held out his hand for it, and, reluctantly, Jacques lost this opportunity.

However, lest he excite the boy's suspicions, he concealed any sign of his disappointment.

At the dawn of the fourth day the large body of warriors broke camp and started canoeing up the St. Lawrence. Before high noon, the Iroquois flotilla came to the mouth of a river. To Jacques' intense disappointment Hot Ashes left the main party and turned his canoe into this river.

Three canoes turned south into this mouth. Jacques did not have to be told that this was the River of the Iroquois and it led directly to the dreaded Long Houses. The main party paddling silently, as was their custom, disappeared up the broad stream.

To his relief Jacques saw that Louis Joliet was in The Frog's canoe, so they were not to be separated in captivity.

Scarcely a quarter of a league's paddling along this much narrower stream the canoes turned into the reeds and the Mohawks went ashore. Jacques and Louis were landed close together. Before they could do more than smile at each other, Hot Ashes had Stripling Tree unbind the arms and legs of the two boys.

"Come," commanded Hot Ashes, "and don't speak."

Louis took Jacques' hand in his and squeezed it warmly. Then obediently the boys with Stripling Tree between them dropped into Indian file and started away from the bank.

Five minutes' silent walking brought them to the evidently

burnt ruins of a French fort. This could only be one place, Jacques thought, the abandoned Fort Richelieu. He remembered hearing in Quebec that after the small French garrison had been withdrawn a few years before, a raiding party of Iroquois had burnt this fort.

Now he was gazing on the blackened rows of what once had been the palisades.

But Hot Ashes did not let the boys delay. He led them beyond the fort's ruins, till nearer the river's bank again, they came to a blackened tree that evidently had been struck by lightning. In its low branches a board had been stuck.

Hot Ashes gave an order and Stripling Tree halted the two captives.

The boys saw rudely scrawled on the wood the outlines of some eighty heads. Most of these were recognizable as Hurons, but Jacques' quick eye saw the pictured heads of two bearded Frenchmen.

Hot Ashes had taken out some red paint and now he was silently sketching two heads.

Stripling Tree in the meantime was explaining: "This is our way of making wood talk. See, those heads tell our brothers who come this way how many captives have been taken back to the fires in our Long Houses. Those two heads much larger than the others represent two great captains of the Hurons. See the feathers. They mean they were very brave."

"Then," interrupted Jacques, "I understand what Hot Ashes is painting now.

"Look, Louis, he is outlining our heads. See they are smaller than the men's. That bearded head before must represent the young Frenchman, Bartholomew Dablon, we saw taken away when we were first captured. I wish I knew whom the other represents.

"Tell me," Jacques asked the Mohawk boy, "why is one of the Huron heads painted in black?"

"He was not taken to our Long Houses but caressed somewhere along the Great River."

"Who did that caressing?" Jacques asked.

"The warriors whom we left this morning. That was the night before we came to their camp."

Louis Joliet looked his horror at Jacques. Both boys knew the grim significance of the black paint.

They learnt by further questioning that a group of thirty heads represented a party of Hurons who had been ambushed a week before. All the bundles of furs and pelts that they had planned to barter at Three Rivers had been taken and the wretched captives, bearing their bundles, were somewhere ahead on the trail, if they had not already been tortured over the slow fires in the Mohawk Long Houses.

Silently Jacques and Louis watched Hot Ashes finish his painting that would tell other Mohawks what success he had had on the warpath.

Then Jacques was back in the canoe, bound, and Hot Ashes was steadily paddling up the River of the Iroquois.

Jacques said fervent Hail Marys to Our Lady of the Angels till the monotonous motion of the birchbark canoe made him drowsy. And as he drifted off to sleep it seemed to him that gigantic Father John Brebeuf, toiling for God in the lands of the Hurons, many leagues to the north, was nearby. Again he was resting, a little boy in his Blackrobe's lap, as he had that rainy afternoon of years ago. His fears gave way. Father Brebeuf—Echon—was his protector and, somehow, all would be well.

Chapter Five

The River of the Iroquois

HE SECOND afternoon after Jacques Bourdon and his fellow captive had seen the last of the broad St. Lawrence, the River of the Iroquois narrowed and the water began to run swifter. This, Jacques now knew, meant his captors were coming to another stretch of white water.

Stripling Tree was paddling in the bow and Hot Ashes in the stern. Small whitecaps began to show nearby. Then Jacques' canoe lurched, stopped, water rushed by, and the next Jacques knew it was turning over. Wildly the boy grasped the thwart and he was spilled into the water and the canoe had crashed on top of him.

When he came gasping to the surface, the force of the current was sweeping him along. Jacques saw the naked shoulder of Hot Ashes alongside him. The current turned the body and the Iroquois' face came into view. Jacques noticed that Hot Ashes' eyes were closed and there was a jagged cut on his forehead. He made no effort to swim and the force of the water drove his face under again.

Jacques struck out after his captor. But the rush of the water was stronger than he had imagined. Some undercurrent had Hot Ashes and it was pushing him unresistingly along.

Slowly Jacques overhauled the unconscious figure. Then he was five feet away. Three. He grasped the slippery arm, lost it, took two vigorous strokes and he had his fingers in Hot Ashes' long black hair. He turned him face up and began to kick towards the swiftly passing bank.

The two were hurried along and as Jacques' strength began to wane, he realized that possibly he was not going to make the bank with his burden. He was tempted to let the unconscious Mohawk go to his death and strike out for the shore. But he downed this thought when he recalled that he owed his escape from torture to this warrior.

It was impossible to reach the shore, thought Jacques. Then he saw that the canoe that had followed his and had not yet come to the beginning of the rapids had noticed him and his burden.

The Frog and another Mohawk, who was named Deer Tracker, turned their canoe and began to paddle out from the eddy. This sight gave new strength to Jacques. He abandoned his efforts to close in to the bank and went with the current. As the canoe swept down on them, he made a last desperate effort and grasped the paddle that Deer Tracker held out.

At once he was sucked into the side of the birchbark. The canoe tipped dangerously, but the expert canoemen balanced it. Then Jacques was holding to the thwart with one hand and supporting the unresisting Hot Ashes with the other. Thus they were towed into shallow water. The Frog leapt out of his canoe and took Hot Ashes.

Jacques collapsed on the shore with half his body still in the water, where he lay, attempting to recover his breath. He found himself wet and sweating at the same time.

Then strong arms had lifted him and he knew he was being carried further up the bank. Great drowsiness and blessed sleep overcame him.

Later, it seemed as though he sensed the warmth of a fire and sunshine had become starlight. More sleep.

Jacques was aroused suddenly by being kicked. He rolled over and then he was on his feet and partly awake. Stripling Tree was the one who had aroused him.

Jacques tried to smile at his tormentor as he was prodded down to the bank, but it was hardly a success. He felt weak and was glad to rest back gingerly in the center of the canoe where he could see the tireless shoulders of Hot Ashes as they swung forward and back, forward and back, over his paddle.

He had thought this Mohawk warrior would at least have thanked him for his rescue in the white waters yesterday. Not much hope of kindness there, the boy concluded hopelessly, as he watched the densely forested shores of the River of the Iroquois slip by, carrying him further and further away from Quebec.

Then the water shoaled and all had to wade and drag the canoe upstream. Jacques stumbled and fell head-first into the deliciously cool water. He floated there, face down. It was such a relief.

Jacques opened his eyes under water. Yellowish pebbles and low growing green aquatic grasses showed before his gaze in the clear water. A startled killie fish darted away.

His eyes lighted on a find! There lay a stone knife, that some Iroquois had evidently lost overboard. Jacques' hand shot down and closed over this treasure. It was the work of a moment to conceal the knife in his ragged breeches' pocket. When he straightened up in the waist deep water he saw with relief that Hot Ashes was bent forward as he towed the canoe and had not noticed. The eagle-eyed Stripling Tree was busy on the other side, steadying the canoe. Further downstream The Frog and Deer Tracker were occupied in pulling their own canoe through the white waters. For once the Mohawks' vigilance had been relaxed.

Jacques stumbled on and concealed the joy that had sprung up in his breast. His pains were momentarily forgotten. He would have liked to shout out his find to Louis, but prudence shut his lips.

To make sure that it was not a pleasant dream with a cruel awakening, he felt the satisfying hardness of the knife in his pocket.

The rest of that day Jacques' captivity was easier to bear.

He saw Louis Joliet sitting dejectedly in The Frog's canoe. But no opportunity came to tell his fellow captive of the find of the morning.

Before dark the canoes were drawn up on a low bank. The Frog and Deer Tracker went at once to a hidden cache. Here was a supply of smoked eels and corn. A fire was lit and the two boys were permitted to share in the abundance of the cache.

Jacques and Louis wolfed down all the food that was given to them. The boys were seated about ten feet apart and Jacques watched for an opportunity of whispering to Louis. But the vigilance of Stripling Tree who sat between them, made this impossible.

The Mohawk boy made one remark that Jacques treasured. He said, as he handed his prisoner a roasted ear of Indian corn, "White boy, two suns and we come to the end of the canoe paddling."

"Are your Long Houses there?" asked Jacques.

"Not yet. We hike through the forests along our trail," explained Stripling Tree, "two suns more and then you will see our Long Houses. They are on a ridge above a beautiful river, high on the opposite bank. There will be caressing," he added with that grin that Jacques noticed these Iroquois always accompanied any mention of torture.

"May I tell this to Louis," Jacques pointed to the small figure, seated silently across the smoke of the fireplace.

"You have no sense," was Stripling Tree's only reply and he turned away.

Later the young Mohawk tied each boy's feet securely. Jacques saw another thong in his hand. "If you bind my hands, I will not sleep. Is it not enough to tie my feet?"

Jacques waited in anxiety for the Mohawk's reply, but Hot Ashes spoke from his place in the circle. "The feet thongs are enough."

Stripling Tree laughed. "Sleep as well as you can. Later you won't feel like sleeping." Grinning he threaded the wrist thong in his loin cloth and walked away.

Jacques watched Louis being tied hands and feet and left on the ground just beyond the light from the camp fire. Hot Ashes did not give any command not to tie Louis' hands and Jacques realized gratefully that he had been shown a kindness by his Mohawk captor.

With nightfall the party rolled up and slept. They were well within the borders of their own territory now and they felt no alarm at any enemy's attack. So no guard was posted.

Jacques said his night prayers and he added three fervent Hail Marys to good Saint Joseph and three more to his Guardian Angel to make this coming attempt at escape successful.

He fought against sleep. It was hard after the day's journey and at last drowsiness conquered and Jacques joined the sleeping camp.

But somewhere in his brain the thought he must keep awake persisted and out of deep sleep he woke.

It was pitch black everywhere, except where the last embers glowed feebly. What he had planned to do this night came to Jacques and he was wide awake. He listened intently. The regular breathing from the surrounding figures told him all slept. He sensed rather than saw that the savage nearest to him was Stripling Tree.

Softly, softly Jacques turned away from the Mohawk boy. He rolled over and over till he was completely beyond the faint light from the embers.

Then he sat up and carefully withdrew his treasure of a knife from his pocket. He reached down between his ankles and began painfully to saw the thong. Sooner than he had expected the deer skin strip parted and he was unbound. The boy could have shouted.

He rubbed his chafed ankles and then, lying stomach down, began to creep around the fireplace to where he knew Louis Joliet slept.

Fortunately the ground was sandy. That would deaden any noise, but Jacques ever felt ahead with his right hand to discover if there were twigs that might crack and so betray him. Once he found one and thankfully lifted it to one side.

He began to say Hail Marys to the Guardian Angels of these Mohawks that they would keep them all in deep sleep.

He had in mind the location of the savages and he made a detour to pass well outside of them. When he was satisfied that he was near Louis' place he began cautiously to creep in again. He made out Louis' slim form. The exhausted boy was sleeping on his face with his bound hands stretched before him. Jacques made out the bulk of a Mohawk not five feet away. It was Deer Tracker.

He realized that if Louis made an outcry when he was awakened, the escape would be frustrated then and there.

Jacques muttered the hasty prayer, "Angel of God of Louis, make him know me at once and keep quiet. Please do not let Deer Tracker hear."

Then he resumed his edging closer. When he came to Louis' hands over his head, Jacques was tempted to squeeze them, but he feared Louis' startled outcry.

He drew himself up till he was lying alongside his chum. Then very softly he laid a hand on Louis' shoulder and breathed in his ear, "Louis, Louis. It's Jacques."

Louis Joliet stirred. His hands came down, brushing the warning fingers away and the boy turned on his side towards Jacques.

Again Jacques cautioned: "Louis, Louis, it's Jacques. Are you awake?"

The whispered reply came, "Yes; how did you—what!"

Jacques pressed his chum's hands and pulling his head down, whispered in his ear: "Quiet. Quiet. We're going to escape tonight. I have a knife. Push your hands towards me and don't speak while I cut your thongs."

Obediently Louis' bound wrists were pushed towards him. Jacques felt and then began to saw the bonds. The sharp stone knife hacked through and Louis was squeezing Jacques' hands in an excess of delight.

Jacques heard sobs and he hastily warned: "Quiet, while I cut the ankle thongs."

Jacques stopped to listen but the regular breathings in the darkness about him continued. He squirmed till he could reach Louis' feet. When these were free, Jacques turned himself till he was lying alongside his fellow captive again and drawing Louis' head down whispered in his ear: "Creep after me. Not a sound till we are beyond the firelight. If a savage moves, lie still. Say your prayers and come on."

Now they were beyond the camp light and Jacques judged it safe to stand up. Through the branches the boys could just make out the faint glow of the embers. Jacques took Louis' arm and said: "Well, we've made a start, but we must be hidden before they discover our escape."

The boys felt rather than knew that it would be dawn soon in an awakening camp. This unpleasant fact made them desperate. Quickly they came to the sloping bank of the River of the Iroquois.

Louis exclaimed: "This is fortunate! Let us walk in the shoal water and cover our tracks."

The first splash of the water sounded startlingly loud. Both listened.

"I have it, Louis. We'll swim across and try to find a hiding place on the other shore. Can you make it?"

"I think so." And he added gratefully, "Thank God that we are free from those Mohawks."

"We are free," Jacques corrected, "but we have a long way to go to freedom."

And in this observation Jacques was correct.

Chapter Six

The Welcome St. Lawrence

HE BOYS struck out. Side by side they swam. It was lighter here on the river and in no time the dark looming other shore appeared.

A startled animal, surprised drinking at the bank, crashed away through the brush. The boys floated till the noise of his wild flight died down. No telltale sound came from the camp bank and the two touched bottom and, rather winded, the swimmers rested, sitting in water a foot deep.

"Listen," said Jacques, "when the Mohawks discover our escape, they will naturally think we have started at once towards the St. Lawrence——"

"In that case," Louis counselled, "it will be safer for us to go up this River of the Iroquois, and hide. I think the nearer to the camp we conceal ourselves, the better chance of escape we will have."

"That sounds reasonable," Jacques agreed, "wait here a moment."

He got up and explored the dark shore. Here was a bank, maybe, five feet high. He returned to Louis.

"Let us swim up the river a bit and look for a marsh. That will be the best place to hide in."

So together they resumed their swim. They were opposite their camp site. Jacques remembered one of the canoes was close to the shore. He told Louis his sudden thought and Louis agreed. So very quietly the two boys crossed to where the canoes were hidden.

More quietly they lifted a canoe and set it afloat. First Jacques took two paddles and put them in the canoe.

Now he whispered, "We will let this drift down stream and as soon as the Mohawks discover a canoe is missing they will conclude that we took it and they will follow. That will give us more time to hide upstream."

The boys watched the canoe drift out of their sight as the current caught it. Then they resumed their swimming upstream. Shortly the river bent to the eastward. When they were exhausted the boys touched bottom and taking care to keep in water waist deep they waded on.

Dawn was coming shortly and the chance of meeting an Iroquois canoe increased. Then Jacques saw what he had been hoping for. The bank sloped away and low marshy grass appeared. Into this welcome retreat the two crawled and quickly they were hidden.

Daylight had broken with low hanging clouds. They saw that they were in a jungle of thickly growing marsh grass. In their sodden clothes they lay, not daring to raise their heads above the marshy barrier.

It started to rain gently from the leaden skies.

Louis said: "That rain is what I have been praying to Saint Joseph for."

"I know," Jacques replied, "it will wipe out any footprints we may have left. Hot Ashes and his party will trace us to the river and find a canoe missing. That's certain, Louis. But beyond that the trail is lost. For never once did we step ashore and even the sharp eagle eyes of Stripling Tree can't detect our footprints under the water."

"They all can read the forest signs and we may have broken a twig or bent a blade of grass and then they will be hot on our trail. It's dreadful to think what they will do to us if they catch us again."

"That they are not going to do," Jacques reassured him, "remember, we are upstream and they will naturally trail us downstream."

He noticed that Louis was shaking with the cold, for the marsh dampness had penetrated to the bone. They could not lie there much longer.

"Listen, Louis, say Hail Marys till I get back."

"Where are you going?"

"I'm going to explore a bit. Don't lift your head above the grass."

"I won't and don't be gone too long."

The rain by this time was coming down steadily.

Jacques snaked his way through the marsh grass. At length he came to a muddy hillock that rose, maybe, a foot above the water and mud. On this stood a gaunt dead tree, blackened by an ancient stroke of lightning.

The boy carefully circled the hillock. There was an opening in the northern side of the tree. He crawled back to where he had left Louis. He found him shivering with the cold and whimpering in his misery.

"Come on. I have found a shelter. It will be better than nothing and it should be drier."

Jacques had to turn and drag Louis through the mud.

Mud coated the boys thickly as they reached the hillock. Prudently they crawled, keeping their heads below the tops of the marsh grass, till both could see the black opening in the tree.

It was gray morning now, raining dismally. When they stood on the hillock the downpour washed some of the mud from their bodies, but left them chilled to the bone.

Jacques had to boost Louis into the hollow tree. Then he scrambled in and dropped to the bottom. It was soft with rotting wood, but fairly dry.

The two boys filled the opening, leaving little room to move. There in the gloom, lighted only by that gray opening just above their heads, they passed the long dismal day.

Once Louis, wakening from a troubled sleep, thought he heard voices. He shook Jacques awake. With hearts beating like triphammers they listened.

Jacques ventured to raise himself and peek out. The swamp, dismal in the persistent rainfall, greeted his gaze. Somewhere nearby a bird, hidden in a leafy tree, chirped and chirped. This lone cry, piercing against the monotonous beating of the rain drops was the only sound.

But as Jacques' eyes travelled over the reedy grass, beaten down by the heavy falling rains, he saw a bird—then another—whirl up with sharp cries. His eyes searched the land below the startled birds. Then his heart almost stopped. There standing at the edge of the swamp were the figures of The Frog and Stripling Tree.

Jacques realized at once that if these keen-eyed savages had picked up any telltale marks and were tracking them, he and his companion were held in this tree as effectively as any animal, caught in a woodsman's trap. This gaunt lightning struck tree, standing out against the low marshy gray would be a landmark that the woods-wise Iroquois would certainly investigate.

He dropped back and explained to Louis: "I've just learnt something. We will have to get out of this hole at once."

"Why?"

"Because The Frog and Stripling Tree are searching this marsh and this will certainly be a spot they will investigate. Come on, we'll be safer lying in the grass."

Louis reluctantly admitted the wisdom of this. The boys left their shelter and dropped into the world of mud and water. They crawled away from the river to where the grass grew thicker and here in the muddy cold water they lay.

Nearby they discovered some sassafras roots and chewed on them ravenously. The aromatic roots, while they did not deaden the boys' hunger pangs, at least lessened them.

Occasionally they could hear the Mohawks. Again Jacques breathed a prayer of gratitude to his Guardian Angel that it was raining heavily and wiping out any marks that would give them away. After a couple of hours, the boys crawled on.

Deep in the reeds they came upon a fallen tree. Then they both heard the sound of a splashing quite near. Jacques ordered Louis to crawl under the fallen tree. Noiselessly the boys moved under the tree. As still as growing things they listened.

Some one was splashing nearer.

"Move up, Louis," Jacques hissed, "I think my feet show." He pushed his companion. Louis started to squeeze further under the tree, when his alarmed whisper came to Jacques' ear: "There is some animal up here."

"Never mind. Say Hail Marys that we are invisible."

Louis squeezed Jacques' hand in acquiescence and the boys waited, their heart beats increasing.

Suddenly Louis let go of the hand and Jacques heard, "Ough!" He did not need to question further. The overpowering odor that poured over him told him the nature of the attacking animal that was nearby.

The splashing came nearer and nearer. It was evidently a lone Mohawk searcher. Jacques would have liked to have twisted around and seen whether it was The Frog or Stripling Tree, but he dared not move. He did grasp the stone knife in his right hand, determine to plunge it into his captor when he was dragged out feet first. It would be better to die now than later.

The Mohawk was coming alongside the open end of the trunk. Then Jacques felt a moccasined foot come down on his ankle and bury it further in the mud.

The Mohawk caught the odor and he retreated hastily.

No longer could the two boys endure that awful suffocating smell that had saved them. They very weakly crawled out from under that hollow tree and lay in the mud and water, while the blessed rain drove down on them.

The morning dragged on. The odor clung to their ragged clothes till finally they buried most of them in the mud and crept into the wet grass.

There had been no further sound of tracking Mohawks—though both Jacques and Louis knew of a certainty that Hot Ashes' party was somewhere in the vicinity, seeking relentlessly for their lost captives.

The endless afternoon faded into gloomy twilight. The rains fell intermittently and Jacques as he recalled the narrow escape from discovery thanked in fervent prayer the kindly Providence that had sent the skunk.

With dusk the rain seemed to have definitely ceased. But a new torment plagued the two fugitives. These were the gnats and mosquitoes that came out in myriads as the skies cleared. Soon the boys' faces and arms and backs were swollen and they were forced to lie almost under water to escape these insects.

Then it was night.

Jacques said: "We're fairly safe till daylight, Louis. I've been thinking of a plan. You remember the river bends sharply north of where we lie. We're on the opposite bank from Hot Ashes' last camp. So if we cut north through these forests in a few miles we will strike the river again. Then we will wade or swim till we come to another swamp and spend the day.

"There was a marsh on the other side, remember, Louis. We passed it shortly before we made camp. That's our next hiding place. Come on."

"No; wait till it's black night," cautioned Louis, looking about apprehensively. He had thought he heard an owl screech and he remembered that was one of the bird cries used by the Iroquois to communicate with each other. All too well Jacques recalled that cry of the wood pigeon heard just before he had been captured in the cove above Quebec settlement.

That was only days ago, but it seemed dreary months since he had left Our Lady of the Angels school to escape the deserved birching.

Soon it was dark enough to proceed. The fugitives kept low till they came to the edge of the marsh. Here on higher land they quickly entered a virgin forest. The skies had cleared after the day of rain and now the stars shone out.

Jacques knew the Dipper and the North Star. He took the latter as a pointer, whenever he could glimpse it in a break in dark foliage overhead.

The ground rose gradually till the two came out on a ridge. In the moonlight they could make out the darker curve of the River of the Iroquois as it swung into a bend below them.

Again getting their bearings from their faithful guide, the Polar Star, Jacques and Louis plunged down the other side of the ridge. They encountered myriad thorns and nettles and what was left of their clothes was soon reduced to strips, while their thighs and legs smarted from the scratchings.

It was slow progress—now around a fallen tree—now caught in an impenetrable jungle of undergrowth—now stumbling down, then up a small ravine.

Once Louis heard the ominous rattle of a snake. It sounded almost under his bare foot. He leapt back, upsetting Jacques. Both boys rolled away and said their "Angel of God, my guardian dear," as they realized their narrow escape from another kind of horrible death.

Jacques still had the keen-edged knife. He stopped to hack off stout branches. These he fashioned into clubs.

But the rest of the night as they plunged ahead, seeking the shelter of the water, the boys avoided as much as possible the thick underbrush.

At length, while still under the shelter of the darkness, they stumbled and slid down a muddy bank and were in the cooling River of the Iroquois again. They lay there, bathing their torn legs in the freshness of the water.

"We can't stay here," urged Jacques. "Let us swim over to the other bank and seek a hiding place."

"I feel it will be dawn soon," Louis said, "and I am so tired, I think I could sleep till night."

"I want to find something to eat first."

"No, Jacques, get to our hiding place before it is light." Louis looked fearsomely at the east where a line of light was showing.

The boys waded out till the water came up to their breasts and then began to swim.

Something loomed darkly ahead.

"It's a log!" cried Jacques delightfully. "We're in luck. Come on, Louis, and let the current carry us along towards the St. Lawrence."

So the boys overtook the log, hooking their tired arms about this welcome tree trunk. Rested, they clambered up and lay hugging the trunk.

Then they drifted off into exhausted sleep and the next they knew the log was bumping over a rock. Water was racing by. The log hit another rock, swung sharply over and spilled the startled boys into white water.

It was broad daylight now, and they found themselves being carried along into the smooth waters below a rapids.

Jacques recognized the locality as the waters in which he had rescued Hot Ashes from drowning.

He and Louis struck out for the shore.

"We must get under cover at once, Louis," he panted. "We might have been captured like sleeping turtles."

As they disappeared into the underbrush, Jacques said: "Listen, Louis, Hot Ashes' party camped nearby. Let us find the site."

"Why? It would be too dangerous." This from Louis.

"We'll creep up cautiously. I have a reason."

Further into the underbrush the boys crept, thankful that no Iroquois eyes had sighted them while they slept on the floating log.

As they went along, Jacques explained: "Just behind this camp site is a cache of food. Remember, Stripling Tree got some from it."

"Yes; now I remember where it is too. While you lay unconscious from the water, I saw Stripling Tree take the food from it. He told me it was a cache known to all the Mohawks from his Long Houses."

"If that's the case, we'll gladly help ourselves."

When they came near the former camp site, they saw the blackened cold ashes of the fire place that they both recalled.

The boys kept a sharp lookout, but the camp site was evidently not occupied.

Louis crawled forward and located the cache, hidden under a pile of stones. Here wrapped in bark were a quantity of smoked eels and a pile of corn.

The two fell on the food and ate like wolves. This unexpected food supply put strength into their exhausted bodies. When finished, they carefully put back the stones. Then they crawled into a clump of thickly growing bushes. Jacques covered Louis with leaves and then with a great effort he concealed himself as well as he could.

That long sleep refreshed the boys. It was rapidly growing dark when they awoke.

Remembrance of that log gave Jacques an idea and he promptly told it to his companion.

"Listen, Louis, after we eat again from that cache, let us get another log. It will float on the current all night and we will be leagues nearer the St. Lawrence before daylight."

Louis added: "I wish we had thought of a log yesterday. It would have saved a square foot of skin for my legs."

So under the cover of darkness the boys again raided the Mohawk cache. This time they took a further supply for future needs.

Back to the bank they crept. Wading downstream, they kept a lookout till they came upon a trunk of a medium sized tree. It was broader than last night's log.

With much tugging and pushing they got it afloat. Securing their scant food supply in the crotch of a branch, they lay along the log and, paddling with their hands, quickly had this improvised raft in the current.

"Stop paddling," Jacques cautioned. "The noise of the splashing might reach the ears of a Mohawk war party encamped on the bank."

So they let the trunk drift along the silences of the River of the Iroquois. When the moon came up over the tree tops it lighted the waters in silvery spots, the boys lay low along the trunk, listening for any warning sounds.

They could see the looming shores and above the tops of the trees on either bank etched sharply against the heavens.

Only by watching a top branch blot out a star did they know that the trunk was carrying them steadily northward away from the horrors of the Mohawk Long Houses towards the welcome sight of the Great River.

Just as dawn was gray streaking in the eastern horizon Jacques and Louis paddled their log-raft into the reeds. They crawled under some branches on high ground. Jacques' last act was to pull some leaves over Louis' exposed legs and then he too was asleep.

When they awakened the sun told them it was late afternoon. They ate the smoked eels and added a supply of blue berries that fortunately grew profusely nearby.

While they were eating Jacques looked up and to his horror saw on the river a birch bark canoe with four strange Mohawks paddling silently along.

He and Louis crouched low and watched while another and another canoe came into view and disappeared up the River of the Iroquois.

Both boys trembled to think what would have happened to them, if their log had met this party.

No more canoes appeared and when it was quite dark the two sought their big trunk in the reeds.

Quietly pushing it ahead of them they waded breast deep into the night-hidden river and then straddled the log.

All night long they took turns keeping a lookout into the shadows ahead.

It was in Jacques' watch, sometime after midnight as he judged by the stars, that he suddenly noticed that the looming shores had disappeared. Excitedly he woke Louis.

"Look around you. What do you see?"

"Nothing but night," replied Louis sleepily. "Why—why—that's strange! We're floating on a river much broader than the River of the Iroquois!"

"That's it exactly. We've drifted out into the St. Lawrence."

The two boys slept no more the rest of that blessed night. Iroquois dangers were forgotten in the delightful thought that soon they would be safe at Three Rivers trading post.

A strong current and a downstream breeze sent them along. Occasionally they could make out the darker mass of the northern shore, so they knew they had crossed the Great River.

Then it was dawning light. Jacques and Louis debated whether to abandon the log, the next time the current brought them within an hundred yards of the bank and swim and hide in the pine forests, or risk discovery from a sharp-eyed Iroquois war party.

Louis settled the debate with the remark, "We'll keep low in the water, clinging to the log for the river current is carrying us all the time nearer the trading post!"

Mists on the early morning river helped to conceal the boys, but with the rising of the sun, it promised to be a clear blue sunny May day, the wide panorama of the St. Lawrence opened out.

The welcome warmth took some of the coldness out of the escaped captives' bodies, but it brought back the pangs of hunger.

The two had crawled out on the log and like browned turtles lay their length in the sun.

Quickly they grew drowsy. Then they slept.

Some premonition of danger awoke Jacques. They had drifted within a hundred yards of a densely green forested point on the northern shore of the St. Lawrence. He glanced at the quiet green-ery of the point and then up at the sun's position.

"It must be about the middle of the afternoon," he thought.

Then he turned to glance up the river.

Jacques gave a great shout. Louis raised his head in alarm.

"It's the 'Saint Anne'!—This is luck!"

There sailing down midstream, taking advantage of a fair wind, came the scallop that plied between the French trading posts.

Both boys were trying with difficulty to stand on the log, shouting and waving their arms wildly, to attract the crew's attention. Louis lost his balance and fell backwards into the river with a great splash.

Jacques reached him a hand, crying: "Claude, the cook, will be on board. This is luck!"

As he pulled Louis back on the log, Jacques happened to glance towards the point that they were about to drift by.

He almost backed into the river in his surprise. Hastily putting out from the underbrush was a birchbark canoe and Jacques' glance took in the terrifying fact that the three redskinned warriors who were paddling the canoe, each wore in his hair the two eagle feathers that betoken Iroquois.

"Louis, we're recaptured!"

Joliet's yell of fright carried across the waters.

Jacques looked upstream and he could see that the scallop had tacked from her downstream course and was sailing directly for the log.

It was a race to see whether the French or the Iroquois would reach the log first. The boys leapt into the water and none too soon for one of the braves had dropped his paddle and sped an arrow. It twanged into the log and stuck there quiveringly not three inches from Jacques' hand.

Both boys ducked under the surface. They heard a boom as they came up on the offshore side of the log and Jacques could see the tiny cloud of smoke floating free from the scallop's deck.

Louis cried out: "That shot has scared the savages' canoe. Look, Jacques, look."

Jacques peered cautiously over the log and he could see with satisfaction that the birchbark canoe had already turned and was heading back for the shelter of the shore.

Another shot sailed overhead and the Iroquois canoe seemed to fly through the water. As it touched the sands, the three warriors leapt out, grabbed the bark sides and like a flash, canoe and savages were hidden in the green underbrush.

As the "Saint Anne" drew near Jacques and Louis abandoned the log and struck out for the vessel's side.

Jacques saw his stout friend, Claude Mangre, waving two enormous arms encouragingly. Then the boys were under the scallop's counter and grasping ropes. Quickly the two were hauled on board and lay panting on the deck.

Jacques could hear Claude begging: "Ah, Little Jacques, my poor infant, drink this."

A hot soupy liquid that warmed Jacques' insides was gratefully gulped down.

M'sieur the Captain and a sailor that Jacques remembered having seen before, but he could not recall his name, were examining Jacques' torn sides and thighs.

He could hear their tongues click in sympathy. A great drowsiness was overcoming him. It was delicious and as he relaxed he knew he was being lifted into the cabin. Voices grew far away and Jacques, like Louis Joliet, slept his first real sleep in days.

Chapter Seven

Captain Charles Daniel

THE "SAINT ANNE" had sailed the rescued boys directly to Quebec settlement, where Madame Joliet insisted on carrying Jacques to her cabin for maternal nursing.

This cabin, typical of Quebec homes in 1648, consisted of two rooms. The walls of the rooms, to the height of a man's shoulder, were worn smooth by the backs that had leaned against them. There were no chairs, but solid looking boxes in which Madame Joliet kept her linens and dresses. Rough hewed benches served for seats.

Filling one corner of the main room was a clumsy loom, at which Madame would spend long winter hours, weaving the coarse homespun. Cocoons of flax and fluffy wool hung from the rafters.

The fireplace took Jacques' eye. It was large enough to hold the smoke blackened arms of a crane. A "bake kettle" stood to one side and there was also a gridiron with legs.

In this cabin Jacques Bourdon spent a lazy luxurious week, eating abundantly Madame's fine cooking and sleeping long hours, while his wounds healed. Schoolmates from Our Lady of the Angels listened open-mouthed to tales that verged on the truth.

One warm afternoon in June, while Jacques was dozing on a bearskin in the sun before the cabin door, he heard footsteps. He opened his eyes sleepily to see the tall figure of Father Jerome Lalemant. Jacques attempted to get up, but the priest restrained him.

"No, no; my restored one, do not rise," the Blackrobes' Superior urged, "I see you still look weak, but that three-quarter starved look has disappeared."

Jacques confessed, "Father Superior, I feel much better. Madame Joliet is the finest cook in New France." A broad smile spread over the boy's wan features.

"I know you are in kind hands, and she is treating you as she is her son Louis, but that is not exactly why I have come to converse with you. Where is Louis?"

"He went five minutes ago to carry a message to his father, who is cutting wood over there." He indicated a stretch of forest nearby. As they listened both heard the regular sound of an axe hitting wood.

Father Jerome Lalemant seated himself on the edge of the bear skin, Indian council style, and began: "Jacques, I am much troubled about your future. Each morning at the Holy Sacrifice, since you were almost miraculously saved from a horrible death, I have been asking the Good Lord what we should do with you. Now I wish you to answer me openly. Jacques, do you wish to return to Our Lady of the Angels?"

The boy did not hesitate with his reply. "No; my Father, I don't."

"Then you are still determined to go to Father Brebeuf in the lands of the Hurons and learn to be an interpreter?"

"My Father, there is nothing I wish more."

"You have prayed over this decision, my little one?"

"Yes; my Father, when I went to Holy Communion at the Infant Jesus Church last Sunday, I asked the Little Jesus to let me go to Huronia to Father Brebeuf."

Father Jerome Lalemant was silent for a few moments and Jacques saw the Superior's lips moving in prayer.

"I have had the feeling, Jacques, that the kindly Providence that brought you safely through so many recent perils, is leading you to some hidden service with good Father Brebeuf. To him you shall go."

"Thanks, my Father, and when?"

"That depends. Word came this morning by the fly boat from Three Rivers that some canoes have arrived from the Huron country and with the party is Father Joseph Bressani."

Jacques repeated the name to himself, then said: "He was the Blackrobe who was tortured like Father Jogues by the Iroquois, was he not?"

"The same valiant soul. In a few days he should be here in Quebec. I intend to send you back to Huronia with his party. My nephew, Father Gabriel, is going to the Huron mission and in his care shall you go."

This was welcome news indeed and after Father Jerome's departure, Jacques lay in the warm sun and dreamed of this new adventure.

When the secret was confided to Louis Joliet that chum promptly declared his views. "No, indeed, if I ever leave the settlement of Quebec again it will be in the company of the soldiers or on a ship. I don't want to fall into Mohawk hands again. You forget, Jacques, that you and I are escaped captives to the Mohawks and if they ever get their dirty hands on us we would be made to pay heavily. Just imagine what Hot Ashes or Stripling Tree would do to our bodies before we died!"

Louis Joliet shook his head decisively.

"You may go along with Father Gabriel Lalemant, but I won't, even if my mother would give her permission and she won't do that. Remember what Father Gabriel was telling us when he called here two days ago. He said it is almost three years since his uncle has been able to get supplies through to the Huron Missions and he is none too sure he will be able to this summer."

"Yes; but some Huron canoes have come to Three Rivers. Father Gabriel is to return in one of those canoes."

Louis shook his curls and announced with finality: "I will not leave Quebec with any Father Gabriel."

Both boys looked up startled when a deep voice exclaimed: "Why is my name being taken in vain?"

Jacques and Louis sprang to their feet when they saw youthful Father Gabriel Lalemant smiling down. He was a man of medium height, who was in his late thirties.

"My Father, not in vain," explained Jacques, blushing furiously. "I was telling Louis here he should come along to learn to be an Huron interpreter with us."

Father Gabriel showed his very white teeth in a smile. "With us? So you know Father Jerome's decision already?"

"Yes, my Father. He was here less than an hour ago."

"And I was planning," said Father Gabriel with a wry smile, "to carry the good news to my youthful interpreter myself."

"Can't you speak Huron?" asked Jacques in amazement.

"Well hardly, my infant. I only reached Quebec in September, '46—less than two years ago—and I have had more contacts with Algonquins than Hurons, so I must depend on your glib tongue till I am able to use my own."

"My Father, I will gladly teach you all I know, for I am able to speak with Hurons, Iroquois and Montagnais. I can talk to any savage," boasted Jacques, "and make him understand."

"You will make a fine interpreter, my Jacques."

And the Blackrobe turned to the silent Louis. "And so you prefer the settlement to the forests?"

"Yes, my Father. I am never going to leave it again unless the soldiers are along."

"Now that is unfortunate, my infant."

"Why, Father?"

"Because Monsieur the Captain of the 'Chasseur' has invited me on board this evening and I had intended taking you and Jacques along."

"Oh, my Father," Louis hastened to amend his declaration, "I am always ready to go on board a ship from France."

Madame Joliet, when she returned to the cabin, readily gave her permission.

From the Joliet cabin to the waterfront was not twenty minutes' walk.

Jacques, trotting alongside the young priest, retold gaily his last trip along this route when he had spent the night on the scallop with the stout cook, Claude Mangre.

"That last time I was running away from Our Lady of the Angels——"

"And this time," put in Father Gabriel, "you are going to a rougher school, for the boys at Fort St. Mary's up in Huronia, never know when the raiding Iroquois will come into their neighborhood."

Louis Joliet shook his curly head and repeated: "Another reason why I wish to grow up and die in Quebec."

They had now come into the well trodden road that led to the St. Lawrence's bank.

Roughly hewed cabins of the French settlers were nearer each other here.

Jacques recalled the cabin in which he had lived in the old days when his woodsman father was yet alive. The woman who had given him casual care was now dead and a new family, the D'Altons, who had come from Old France the summer before, now occupied the one story structure.

Father Gabriel Lalemant paused a moment at the doorway to say good evening to Madame D'Alton. Then he rejoined the two boys and soon they were at the shore.

Anchored a hundred yards out was the great ship with its towering masts and spars. The sails were reefed loosely and the white flag of France waved bravely to the breeze.

Jacques pointed and cried: "See! We are seen. There comes a boat for us."

All watched the boat being rowed towards the shore.

Louis pointed excitedly: "Look! Jacques!—my Father!—at that black man among the crew."

"I believe you are right, Louis," said Father Gabriel, "that's a negro and they come from the African lands. I have only seen a few myself."

When the ship's boat was within hailing distance, a bearded boatswain with rings in his ears called across the water. "My Father, Monsieur the Captain awaits you and the boys."

The three passengers sat in the stern and the boys had no eyes for the ocean going ship, for they were fascinated by this sailor with the dark skin and white teeth, who smiled at them whenever he caught their eye.

Father Gabriel asked the negro: "From what country are you?"

"On the west coast of Africa was I born, but I have sailed with Captain Daniel ever since he bought me as a boy."

"A slave from Africa," whispered Jacques into Louis' ear. "He could tell us about elephants!"

"And monkeys!" added Louis.

But before they could question him on those interesting animals, the boat was drawn under the quarter of the "Chasseur."

While a sailor held the boat off, Father Gabriel tucked his blackrobe up around his waist and nimbly followed the two boys up the rope ladder.

On deck Captain Charles Daniel, a tall loosely built man with the bluest of eyes, received them kindly.

"So here are the children who escaped all by themselves from the savages!"

The boys were silent under the Captain's kindly gaze, but their eyes were taking in the world of rigging and tackle all above them.

Monsieur the Captain led his guests to his cabin aft. This was a large half circular room the width of the stern. Under a swinging lantern was a table strewn with papers and charts.

The open stern ports gave a view of the green banked St. Lawrence below the settlement, standing out vividly in the light of the setting sun.

Lockers and bundles of sea clothing hung or were thrown about and Louis whispered to Jacques: "Monsieur is not orderly. If I threw my clothing around that way, Madame, my mother, would box my ears."

"He's a busy man," excused Jacques, "but look at those arquebuses!"

A pair of those clumsy looking weapons were in a rack between the stern ports. In delighted silence the boys examined the arquebuses. It would have been an effort of strength for them to lift the guns, much less fire them.

Then their eyes were attracted to a glass case.

"What's that?" A deep voice behind the boys startled them.

"O, Monsieur," cried Jacques as he saw the captain had come up unaware behind them. "Please, what is this—it looks like a strange fish' skeleton—in a glass case?"

"I was about to call the attention of you boys to that curio.

"Come here a moment, Father Gabriel, and hear this."

The young priest came across the captain's cabin. He had been gazing at the green beauties of the further cliffed bank of the Great River that was visible through the open port hole.

"This is a curio I picked up. It is called the crucifix fish, and if you will examine it closely, you will be able to pick out the various implements of Our Lord's Passion."

Captain Daniel put the rounded glass case on the table where the strong light would fall on it.

Then the boys pointed out the nails, cross, ladder, spear, and other implements of the Passion, that were clearly visible in the skeleton of this strange fish.

"Where did you get this, Monsieur Captain?" asked Jacques as with increased reverence he beheld this curio.

"Years ago when I was cruising on the Spanish Main, I got two of them at some West Indian island, and I gave one to Father Anthony Daniel."

"Is Father Daniel your brother?" asked Louis.

"Blood brother. Him and his companion Father Ambrose Davost I transported across the Atlantic back in 1632.

"I have not seen Father Anthony since he had charge of the boys' school here in Quebec. I remember he brought some promising Huron boys down from their country and commenced his school in a little cabin on the St. Charles River over there. That was about twelve years ago, in '36."

Father Gabriel had been reverently examining the crucifix fish and now he joined in the conversation.

"It wasn't so successful—that start."

"You mean the early deaths of those two youths my brother brought down from the Huron country?" queried Captain Daniel.

"Yes."

"I made port that summer of '36 shortly after Father Anthony arrived from Huronia. He looked like a skeleton and I decided to feed him good French food. So several times I had him and some of his red skinned pupils in this very cabin.

"I remember how broken up he was because two of his few Huron boys died shortly after he opened his school. I had seen these young Huron lads seated at this table. One of them spoke French quite correctly."

"That would have been little Tsi-Ko," put in Father Gabriel, "he was the nephew of a famous Huron orator. I recall an anecdote about him that Father LeJeune told." The Blackrobe's eyes twinkled in anticipation of the point of his story, "Father Anthony Daniel taught his pupils their prayers in Huron and Latin and they would go about the school singing their Latin prayers, especially the Our Father. This noon Sieur de Caen was dining at Our Lady of the Angels. There was not so much to eat but a special dish, a great favorite of Tsi-Ko, was on the table. Just before dinner he came into the dining-room and spied that dish. He thought nobody was looking, but Father Daniel happened to be standing in the shadows and he saw his little savage come close to the table, his hand went out longingly and then in a clear voice the Huron boy began to sing, 'Et ne nos inducas in tentationem.' Then he backed away."

The captain laughed heartily and turning to Jacques asked: "My lad, are you able to translate that Latin?"

"Of course, Monsieur Captain, I'm an altar boy and I know it means, 'And lead us not into temptation.' It's the ending of the Pater Noster."

The big Captain laughed again and slapped his hands against his blue lace-trimmed coat.

"Such Latin knowledge deserves a reward." He clapped his hands sharply.

The young negro, whom the boys had noticed in the boat, appeared at the doorway. He carried a wide tray on which were a bottle of red wine, glasses, and a heap of cakes covered with strange icings.

"Put them there, Matthew," said the Captain.

"And now, my lads, make yourselves sick."

The invitation did not need to be repeated. The cakes were strange to the boys' palate but delicious and they helped themselves greedily.

Finally Father Gabriel called a halt. "You need not take the Captain's invitation literally. It is evident that you two do not know the fate of two of the first pupils of Father Daniel's school."

"What was that, my Father?" asked Jacques with his mouth crammed with the cake.

"Why these two Hurons at your school found a supply of food and they ate and ate before they were discovered. The nuns at the hospital worked over them, but they died."

"No boy would die of eating these sweets," observed Captain Daniel. "Is that not correct, Louis Joliet?"

The boy nodded, unable at the moment to speak.

"Well, I am not going to take any chances. Now you two, one more apiece and then we go ashore."

Captain Charles Daniel behind the Blackrobe's back, motioned the two to fill their pockets. Silently and unobserved the two boys obeyed.

As they stood on deck, Captain Daniel took Jacques aside and said: "My lad, Father Gabriel tells me that you are to go with him shortly to his dangerous country of the Hurons.

"I wish you were voyaging with me instead. It would be safer. Any time you care to come with me to Old France, this ship is yours. Remember that. But now you are set on Huronia.

"You will meet my brother, Father Anthony, there. Give my respects to my good brother and tell him to keep me always in his prayers. He is a holy man, my little one, and he has great influence with the Good Lord. Many a time at sea in a tight place I have invoked my brother's aid and always the situation cleared up. It is good to have a saint in the family."

"What are you two whispering about?" asked Father Gabriel Lalemant.

"That is a little secret Jacques and I share," explained the Captain, "I was giving him an invitation and a message to carry to Huronia."

All too soon the boys were ashore and the adventure was a pleasant memory, but that night while Jacques lay awake reviewing the events of the afternoon, he thought of what Captain Charles Daniel had said of his brother and the memory was pleasant. He, Jacques, was going soon to meet a saint, rather, several saints, for was not Father John Brebeuf very holy too?

Chapter Eight

Father Joseph Bressani

ITHIN TEN DAYS came a memorable guest to Quebec. Jacques Bourdon never forgot that first meeting with this missionary. The boy had recovered his strength and regretfully left Madame Joliet's cabin and was back at the Residence of the Jesuit Fathers. He had been given light duties and one of the pleasantest was waiting on table.

This evening the new arrival was seated next to Father Superior at table. He was a stoutish Blackrobe, swarthy of complexion. There was that gaunt look in his features that Jacques had come to associate with all the missioners who came down from Huronia.

Jacques had heard this newcomer's name. He was Father Joseph Bressani who had been captured by the Iroquois in the same manner as blessed Father Isaac Jogues, and after torture had escaped to the Dutch settlement of New Amsterdam and had been transported to Europe.

Like the martyred Jogues he had returned to New France for more toils. Now he was down to Quebec to gather the sadly needed supplies for the stricken missions in the lands of the Hurons.

All this Jacques recalled as he moved behind the Father's chair, serving the soup. But it was a shock when the boy attempted to hand the newly arrived missioner the bowl and he saw the healed stumps that eloquently told of Mohawk horrors endured for Christ.

Awkwardly Father Bressani attempted to ladle out his soup, till Father Superior leaned over and said very gently: "Permit me, Father Joseph, the high privilege of assisting you."

Father Bressani's hands rested in full view of Jacques and the boy gazed in awe at them. Suddenly he recalled where he had seen another pair of mangled hands. It was that afternoon of his own father's funeral. He was being comforted by Father Brebeuf and there had appeared in the doorway the slender figure of an unknown Blackrobe. The tall Brebeuf had ordered, "Kneel down now and ask Father Isaac Jogues for his blessing."

The recollection passed as Jacques continued his duties in the Fathers' dining-room. But this newly come Blackrobe had a strange fascination for the youthful server.

Next morning, when Jacques, his light household duties finished, idled in the cloistered walk, he saw this Blackrobe seated on the low bench. His breviary was closed and the father seemed to be busy with his thoughts.

There was something kindly in the Blackrobe's face that made Jacques forget the respect that would ordinarily have kept him at a distance. So the lad approached and stooping low, said: "My Father, I would like to kiss your hands. They are so like Father Jogues'."

Reverently his lips brushed the disfigured hand of the missionary.

Father Bressani looked up, a smile lighting his features. "Would that I were more like Father Isaac in The Master's Eyes!

"I think I know you, my child. It is the young Jacques, who has lately been in Iroquois' hands."

Jacques nodded.

"So you are to accompany us back to Huronia to join our boy interpreters?"

"Yes; my Father."

"We have four rogues there now. Claude and Jean and Guy and Nicholas. You will be the youngest, but not by much."

Then the Blackrobe suddenly switched from French into Huron and asked Jacques the way to Fort St. Louis.

Gravely speaking the Indian language Jacques replied, sketching in outline the way from the Jesuit Fathers' Residence to Fort St. Mary.

"Splendid! Splendid! Bravo, you will make a fine interpreter, my little one!"

"Tell me, my Father," Jacques had seated himself confidently alongside this Blackrobe. "How is my Father Brebeuf?"

"I left him at Fort St. Mary, our fortified village in the land of the Hurons. He was still well but his pounds are less. It is a characteristic of those lands where we labor that the less we have to eat, the better our health is. Look at me, who used to weigh 225 pounds in my native Italy and now—I stepped on the scales that the Commandant has in the fort and I tipped them at 165."

Father Bressani dismissed this topic by asking: "You knew the blessed Father Isaac Jogues? Then let me tell you something that happened last summer.

"There is a little village of Hurons half a day's hike from our Residence of St. Mary's. Father Brebeuf was making his missionary rounds and he came to this St. Peter's Mission, as the Christians call it. Then he was sorrowful for in one of the cabins he found a nine-year-old boy, a great favorite of his, whom he had baptized and prepared for his First Holy Communion only six weeks before.

"Now the little lad lay blinded and in pain. It seems that a week before, when this lad was out on a neighboring ridge with two of his age, the boys discovered an eagle's nest. Boylike they were climbing to get at it and this—did I tell you the boy's name was Philip?—this Philip was almost to the nest when out of the sky came the angry eagle. The great bird landed on the boy's breast. Cruel claws scraped his face. The lad in his fright let go. He would have been killed but his small body struck an outstanding branch and fortunately wedged there. The angry eagle was wheeling in the sky to attack again. Philip's companions on the ground had run to their arrows and they quickly drove off the eagle. Then they climbed up and lowered Philip to the ground. His face was covered with blood and when they had led him back to the village his parents discovered that the eagle's claws and beak had ruined the sight in both eyes.

"Now the little lad lay in fevered pain on a skin in the cabin. It was in this pitiful condition that your gigantic friend discovered his small favorite.

"Father Brebeuf told me that the thought came to invoke Father Isaac Jogues, the news of whose happy death at the hands of the Mohawks had reached Huronia. He remembered that there was a tiny crucifix in his Mass kit that had belonged to Father Jogues when he resided at St. Mary's. Father Brebeuf got this and then kneeling down beside the blinded little lad, raised his face to God's Home and prayed: 'Blessed Father Isaac, you who gaze on Light Everlasting, if it be our Master's Will, ask Him that this little one have his sight once more.'

"With this he took the crucifix and made the Sign of the Cross over both the cruelly torn eyes.

"Now listen, my Jacques. At once little Philip sat up and cried out, 'Oh, Echon, it has been black before my face for days but now I can see the fireplace and the flames and your face!'

"Father Brebeuf, so he told me himself, took the small face most reverently in his hands and there where a moment before there had been cruelly torn flesh, now was the healthy red skin and the healthy eye balls.

"The boy ran screaming his joy to tell his parents, while Father John again knelt and fervently thanked Father Isaac who had spoken to The Master."

"That is a fine story, my Father," said Jacques, "but why shouldn't God give Father Isaac whatever he asks for? Didn't he go back to the Mohawks' Long Houses, knowing that he was to die?"

"The Good God is never outdone in generosity. It is true that Father Isaac went knowingly to his death, knowing that it was a high privilege to die for Christ. Would that my sins had not prevented me from sharing his happy death!

"But I seem to have a charmed life. When we had that fight with the Iroquois, two weeks ago, just before we came to Three Rivers, no bullet, arrow or knife touched me, though I found myself in the middle of the fighting."

Father Bressani began to chuckle.

"What is it that amuses my Father?" Jacques asked politely.

"I was just recalling an humorous incident of that fierce fight in the woods. Robert Le Coq was one of the soldiers coming with our party. You may have heard that the Hurons insisted on stopping in the woods to grease their hair and paint their faces, so that they might appear before the French in orderly array.

"It was while the main party of over two hundred Hurons were at their toilet, so to say, that the advance guard in five canoes were attacked almost in sight of the settlement at Three Rivers. They prudently retreated towards the main party and drew the Iroquois after them.

"The fighting was going on in the forest and Robert Le Coq made the horrifying discovery that he could not tell Huron war paint from Iroquois war paint. He stopped short, not knowing whom to attack. Then it was he came upon a tall warrior. Mistaking him for a friendly Huron he clapped him heartily on his bare shoulder, crying, 'Courage, my brother, let us fight bravely! You show me the Iroquois and we will slay them together.'

"At this a Huron captain, whom Le Coq recognized, rushed up and would have plunged his knife in the warrior, only he saw him make the signal, 'I am the senseless white man's prisoner.' The Iroquois explained that when the Frenchman clapped him on the shoulder, he thought that was the French sign for 'You are my prisoner.' And he had surrendered.

"Robert Le Coq took no more chances of mistaken identity in that battle. Afterwards, his fellow French christened him 'Sergeant Jonah' and I believe that he will be known by that nickname for the rest of his life."

Jacques joined in the hearty laugh of Father Bressani, who seemed to enjoy the telling of this anecdote more than describing his own perils in that same fight in the woods.

"May I join in this joke?"

Both priest and boy turned at the voice and saw youthful Father Gabriel Lalemant standing beside them.

He explained: "I could not help hearing your laughter, Father Joseph."

When he was told the story of Robert le Coq's mistaken identity, Father Gabriel said: "I know Sergeant Jonah. That was just like him. He would blunder out of danger."

Father Gabriel's eyes twinkled. "I know another anecdote of the unlucky, or rather, lucky Sergeant.

"Shortly after he came to the settlement from Old France, he was the one who went to Sillery and on the way came across a large turtle. Brave Robert hit it over the head with the butt of his gun. Then he grasped the unconscious turtle and swinging it over his back, hastened triumphantly to our Algonquin settlement. I happened to be walking before our little church, when I espied Robert. He shouted to me: 'Look, Father, at what I caught without going hunting. This will make rare soup——'

"Our soldier friend got no further, for he leapt in the air, shouting that all the devils in New France had hold of him.

"Quickly most of the Algonquins in the settlement came running up, for Robert has a robust voice.

"Several young braves tried unsuccessfully to pull off the turtle, which had revived and had grasped its captor in a grim grip. Finally one of the braves had to cut the turtle's head off and pry the jaws open before Robert's flow of words ceased.

"Then Robert's worry was to learn if these New World turtles had a poisonous bite. The Brother Infirmarian assured Robert that while he would eat standing up for several days, there were happily no poisonous effects.

"However, turtle soup that evening was excellent. I know," concluded Father Gabriel grinning boyishly, "for I shared the Sergeant's turtle."

Jacques asked eagerly: "Please, my Father, is this Robert Le Coq returning to Huronia with us?"

"He is that," Father Gabriel informed the boy, "despite his blunderings, Robert is a faithful donné and has a stout heart, but I advise you now, keep clear of this soldier, unless you wish to have some unusual adventures en route."

Jacques assured the Father gravely that he would.

Then it was time for Jacques to set the table and he departed grinning broadly.

.   .   .   .   .

The next week found Jacques happily busy helping the Fathers prepare the mission supplies. These articles for Huronia were tied up in bundles, wrapped in sail cloth and roughly sewed. The bundles were made small enough to be stowed in each canoe, and light enough to be carried on the shoulders, when the many portages would be met.

At length came the morning, when Jacques, serving Father Gabriel's Mass, received Holy Communion from his hands.

In his Thanksgiving the boy prayed, "Dear Boy Jesus, before evening I will actually be leaving Quebec for the distant lands where Father Brebeuf and these other Fathers labor. Please let me be of service to You and them."

Jacques felt very light hearted all that morning. He paid a patronizing farewell visit to Our Lady of the Angels, where he was looked on as a lucky boy by the students. Then he had taken the well remembered trail that led to Madame Joliet's cabin.

She mothered him and as he was leaving pressed into his hands a package.

"Don't open this till you are unable to see Quebec settlement."

Jacques thanked her and departed with Louis for the Fathers' Residence. His chum kept repeating his protestations that Jacques was foolish to leave the shelter of the settlement.

"Don't you worry about me, Louis," Jacques assured his friend. "Didn't we slip away from the Iroquois once? If necessary I'll do it again. Anyway, Robert Le Coq is along."

"That unfortunate soldier! I wouldn't go out in the sunshine with him, for fear that I would be struck by lightning. He's another reason why you have no sense, going on a voyage with 'Sergeant Jonah' along."

"I'm going to Huronia this time, Louis, and make no mistake about it. Come along. There is time yet."

But Louis Joliet shook his head decisively. "Write me a letter and I'll pray for you to good Saint Anne," was his final promise.

Father Jerome Lalemant and the other Blackrobes were in a little group. When the Superior noticed Jacques he beckoned him to come aside.

"My child, I am sending you to your Father Brebeuf in care of my nephew, Father Gabriel. Obey Father Gabriel and Father Bressani in all things and the Good God and His Angels will see that no harm comes to you. When you get to our Residence of St. Mary's obey Father Brebeuf as your father. He likes you and, always remember, you fortunate child, you have a saint for a protector in the Huron country.

"Now till we meet, wherever it is God's Will that we meet."

Jacques knelt and received Father Jerome's blessing.

He found to his delight he was sharing a canoe with Father Gabriel and two Hurons. He remembered little of the confusion of the departure of the dozen canoes. He was out on the St. Lawrence, sitting before Father Gabriel. The silent Hurons were at their tireless paddling. Canoes about him and either side of him.

Soon the little cluster of the settlement's cabins, the spires of the churches and the white flag that floated over Fort St. Louis were hidden and the flotilla was passing close under the green towering heights of Quebec's Rock.

The cove of his capture some weeks before came into view and Jacques began to speculate if anybody had ever discovered that long missing animal trap. Then a pine-studded point cut off the sight of the cove.

His heart was light as the birchbark canoe under him. Contentedly he snuggled down into a more comfortable position, and opened Madame Joliet's package. As he suspected it contained a dozen of his favorite sugar coated cakes. In his happiness Jacques began to hum the gay words of the sailors' song, "There's a maid in Brittany."

The actual, long anticipated start for Huronia was really begun! Its joys seemed near. Its dangers very remote.

Chapter Nine

Huronia Bound

THE DAYS SPENT at the trading post of Three Rivers on the northern bank of the Great River had been busy ones for Jacques Bourdon. Here he met the main party of Hurons, some two hundred and fifty, with whom Father Joseph Bressani had come down a month before. They had traded most of their furs and pelts. Jacques saw so many skins that now he was able to recognize at a glance the different kinds of hides. Here were piles of the skins of moose, fox, lynx, otter—some of them black and therefore more valuable—martens, badgers and muskrats. But the Hurons seemed to have gathered chiefly the pelts of beavers as these were the ones for which the French were willing to pay the most.

With the credit the Hurons received from these skins they went to the log cabin in which the Company kept their supplies. Jacques had been bewildered the first time he entered the trading post. It was a long cabin that was larger than any building he had ever seen in Quebec settlement.

Here were seemingly inexhaustible stocks of tobacco, crackers or sea biscuits, peas, Indian corn, raisins, prunes, kettles, knives, picks, that the Hurons prized highly for their ability to break the ice in winter, swords, bodkins, iron arrowheads, hatchets, sheets, shirts, hats, nightcaps, blankets, and French cloaks.

Jacques watched with ever growing wonder these French supplies diminish and then he noticed that the Hurons with their hair cut in ridges that gave them the appearance of wild boars, had

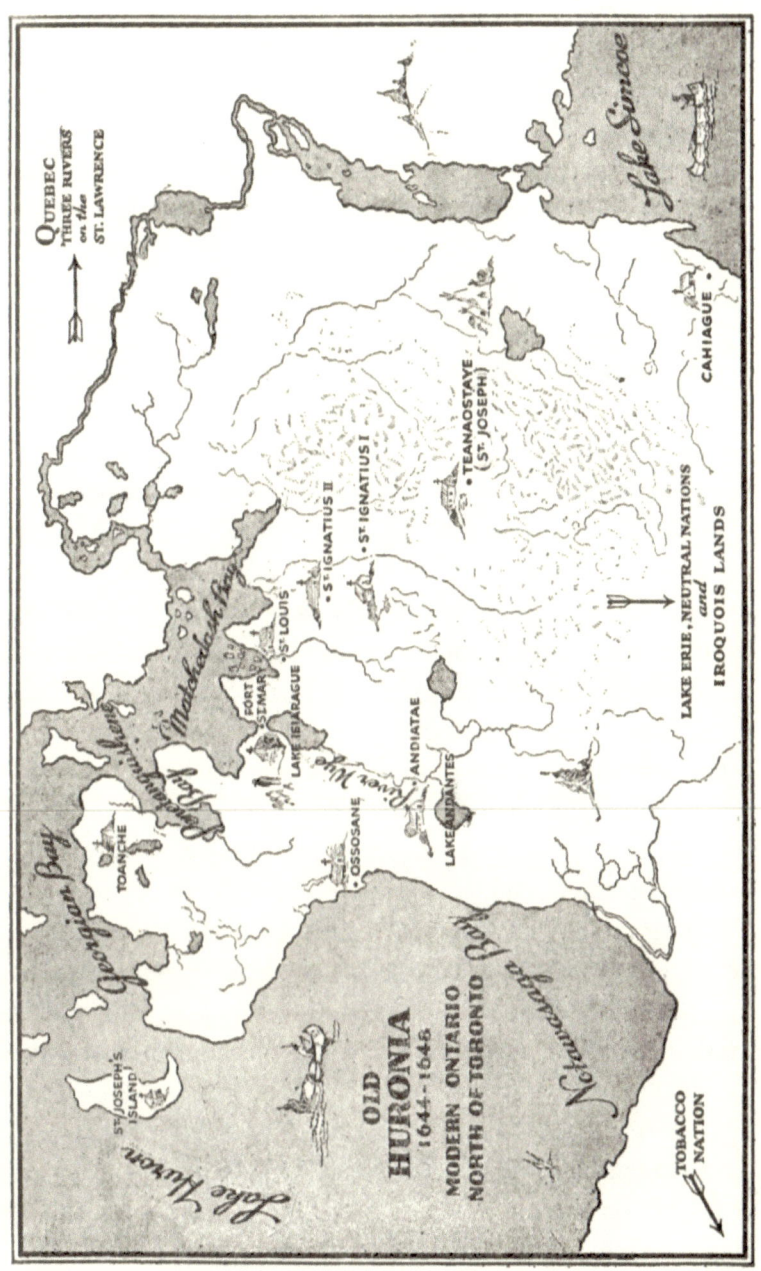

changed their costumes and the French clothing had replaced the rough skins that they had worn down to the trading post.

One day while Jacques was idling in the trading post, Claude Mangre, the stout cook of the scallop, called to him: "Ah, it is the rash little one! Come here, my brave. So I hear that you have not had enough of Iroquois fare. You will not be satisfied till they squeeze your carcass into their kettles and boil you till you are tender."

"No, M'sieur, no Iroquois kettle will ever hold me."

"Why are you so sure?"

Jacques hesitated, but finally he blurted out: "Well, if you must know, I am travelling with saints and where they go, the Guardian Angels go. Father Bressani, who suffered so much in the Mohawk Long Houses, said to me when we were being paddled up here from Quebec, 'My child, serve the Good God faithfully by doing what you are able on the Mission and as He is faithful, you will live to see the rock of Quebec again.' And that's the word of a saint and I believe it. So you see, M'sieur Claude, why I don't fear any Mohawk kettle."

The cook was silent for a moment. Then he observed: "I believe in the Communion of Saints, but it would take more than the whole community to get me into a canoe, headed for that bloody Huronia."

He patted the lad on the shoulder and noticing that the homespun shirt that he was wearing was old, led Jacques to the counter. There he bought the boy shirt and breeches and soft moccasins.

"Wear these, my little one, when you are in those northern wildernesses and sometimes say a prayer for an old friend."

The cook noticed Jacques' eyes were wandering longingly towards a pile of bone-handled knives and he commanded the boy to pick out his favorite.

"Oh, thank you, M'sieur," was Jacques' grateful response.

Claude Mangre suddenly nudged Jacques and pointing to a young Huron brave, who was draping a red blanket over his shoulders, whispered: "He will speak many words, if he sees me. Keep behind this post."

"Why, M'sieur?"

"Because of an incident that happened last evening in Madame Bourgier's cabin. Several Hurons entered and Madame hospitably poured out some wine and offered it to this White Oak—that is his name. This is White Oak's first visit to the Great River and he has heard wild rumors in his villages that the French poisoned their guests, so he was suspicious of all French food and drink.

"He turned to me and insolently said: 'Fat Frenchman, taste this first and if it does not kill you, then I will.'

"With this he handed me the cup. I know the excellent reputation of Madame's red wine, so I took that pagan at his word and uptilted the cup. When I put it down again there were no drops left. The other Hurons present laughed, for they like French wine very much—too much for a lot of them—and they told White Oak what he had lost. When he realized this, our friend White Oak spoke rapidly in Huron. I only wish you were along to translate his words for me—though maybe, the good Fathers would not have approved having you present—but I gathered that he did not like my action.

"Then he had the insolence to demand that Madame Bourgier fill up his cup again. But she had heard of his suspicions and she told him shortly that as he had suspected her good wine the first time, she had no mind to have it fall under further suspicions and if White Oak was thirsty there was a spring nearby and he was welcome to help himself. So White Oak went off in a temper and I don't know yet whether he accepted the invitation to sample Madame's spring water."

Jacques laughed and assured the cook that White Oak had been served right.

When they came out of the trading cabin Claude Mangre pointed out to Jacques a soldier who was passing and he warned, "Keep away from his neighborhood."

"Why?"

"He is Robert Le Coq."

"Oh, so that is Sergeant Jonah!" exclaimed Jacques, grinning delightedly at this first sight of the usually unfortunate soldier.

Jacques thanked his friend again for his kindness, but declined his earnest invitation to dine on the scallop, as he had promised Father Gabriel Lalemant that he would be back at the Residence of the Jesuits before dusk.

When the boy returned to the Residence he found Father Gabriel in conversation with a Huron boy of about his, Jacques' age.

Father Gabriel spying Jacques called out: "You are just in time. Jacques, I want you to meet Peter. He is from Teanaostaye, where Father Anthony Daniel has his mission, and Peter tells me that he serves Father Daniel's Mass often."

Jacques had been shyly appraising this slim red skinned boy, who, except for a loin cloth, was naked. To his black hair was attached an eagle feather and it hung over his right ear. Loosely hung over his left shoulder was a quiver, the tips of four small arrows showing over the top, and a boy's bow.

"Peter is to be in our canoe at the start tomorrow, and he is to help share the bundles that I allotted to you. This arrangement will make the portages easier for both of you."

Jacques had decided that he was going to like this Peter of Teanaostaye, but he had no chance to further his acquaintanceship, for the bell was ringing for dinner and Jacques ran to the kitchen to assist in serving.

Early the next morning Jacques served Father Gabriel Lalemant's Mass and in his Thanksgiving after Holy Communion prayed fervently for all the graces he would need. For he was uncertain when he would have the privilege of hearing Mass and receiving again.

Then Jacques knelt with the little group of voyagers, while the prayer for a safe journey was recited.

From the Residence of the Jesuit Fathers came a little procession. It was made up of the Frenchmen and the Christian Hurons who were about to start for Huronia. Father Joseph Bressani was talking eagerly to the Superior Father Jerome Lalemant, and Father Gabriel Lalemant, walking with downcast eyes, as though he would deprive himself of the innocent pleasure of this last sight of white civilization—rude as it was in this pioneer French outpost—followed behind them.

Jacques found himself walking alongside Peter. Both boys had bundles of mission supplies and Jacques knew that in his canvas package were two small silver chalices and brass candlesticks, gifts from friends of the Huron missioners in Old France. Besides he had the package of precious letters, some of them five years old, that had been waiting for this opportunity to be forwarded to their owners in Huronia.

As he walked along in silence he was recalling what Father Bressani had once said. "It is like hearing from an almost forgotten dead friend to receive a letter from Europe on the Huron Mission."

Now Jacques, like Peter, was all eyes as they came in sight of the canoes lined up on the bank. The hundreds of Hurons, adorned in their newly purchased blankets and trinkets, carrying French hatchets and kettles, and a few warriors, the proud possessors of arquebuses and powder horns, were all converging here. Soldiers in their white uniforms and traders and men of the woods, bearded and sun bronzed, strolled about. There seemed to be utter confusion with the savages running about in all directions.

That July morning of 1648 was a memorable one for the settlement of Three Rivers. For it marked the departure of the Hurons, who had successfully come down the long watery trail from their own lands, despite the constantly growing Iroquois blockade.

To the Jesuit missioners this was more than a successfully concluded commercial venture. It was a Providential opportunity to send sadly needed missioners and mission supplies to the valiant little spiritual outpost in Huronia.

New recruits were going under Huron escort to Fort St. Mary. At their head was the veteran, Father Joseph Bressani, who seemed to savage and even French eyes to lead a charmed life.

With him was the young and eager Father Gabriel Lalemant, who was to wear a martyr's crown within the year. His cheerfully happy countenance seemed to glow with the anticipation of the glory.

Besides these Blackrobes, there were three new lay helpers in the party—young Frenchmen and Canadians, in whose blood the urge for adventure was mingled with the desire of serving God. So these young men had volunteered to serve the mission for board and lodging—such as it would be on the mission—for a limited term of years. These lay helpers were called "donnés."

Such a one was John Lalande, hardly more than a boy, who had volunteered and gone with Father Isaac Jogues into the Iroquois country in '46. The cleft skulls of Blackrobe and donné were now bleaching on the palisades of Ossernenon. Possibly there would be other skulls there.

But thoughts of this kind were far from the mind of Jacques as he walked eagerly to where the canoes were being laden. The wildest confusion prevailed, yet out of it the captain of each Huron village brought order.

Jacques saw Father Gabriel Lalemant and he shouted:

"Oh, my Father, I thought I had lost you in this noisy crowd."

"Well, if you had, my Jacques, I would have sent that sharp-eyed Peter after you. He would have found you in short order. The Fathers in Huronia can't afford to lose you."

"Why?"

"Because you carry their letters from Old France. I know from Father Jerome that some of those letters, addressed to your guardian, Father Brebeuf, will be five years old, when he reads them. That's a long time to wait for news of your family and your friends."

Jacques was silent, thinking this thought over. Then he smiled up into the youthful Blackrobe's face.

"I don't believe my Father Brebeuf has been thinking much of those former friends across the ocean. Do you know, Father Gabriel, I believe Echon has almost forgotten them. His friends today are right in Huronia."

"Not all, Jacques. For I have heard that a very dear friend of his has been living in Quebec, when he wasn't in the hands of the Mohawks."

"I know," Jacques interrupted, "and that friend is now in Three Rivers about to embark for Huronia."

The whole party was afloat. It had come quicker than Jacques ever imagined that a start could be made out of that seemingly endless confusion of departure.

Once out on the wide river and the little settlement of Three Rivers already growing smaller, Jacques strained his eyes to make out Father Jerome Lalemant, the Superior, who kept waving his shovel-shaped hat in farewell. Grouped about him stood many of the Indians, Christian and pagan.

Then Jacques saw the puff of smoke and almost immediately afterwards heard the boom of the first of the saluting guns that the Commandant had ordered to be fired as a Godspeed to the returning Hurons and the missioners. The shots reechoed. Then silence followed.

At last the actual start of the voyage was under way. Jacques and Peter crouched in the center of the birchbark canoe. Soon a green bank hid Three Rivers and Jacques began to point out to his new chum the different places he remembered, connected with his recent Mohawk captivity. While Peter showed Jacques where the battle had taken place with the Iroquois on the trip down and he told again the story of "Sergeant Jonah's" unwitting capture of an unwounded Iroquois brave.

All that day the flotilla paddled steadily up the silent river. The scout canoes ahead signalled no signs of danger and the leagues were made in peace.

Night found them encamped near Cape Massacre, so called from a killing of Iroquois that had occurred near here back in the days of Champlain.

After all had eaten and the party of white men sat around the fire Jacques sought out Robert Le Coq and squatted beside him. Soon the donné asked the boy if he knew this place was holy and when Jacques sensed a story "Sergeant Jonah" obliged.

"Right near here was where I helped discover the body of Father Anne de Noue two years ago last February."

"I knew him in Quebec," interrupted Jacques, "but I did not know that you were in the party that found him. Please tell me about it."

"As we reconstructed the story," said Le Coq, "Father de Noue, who was Chaplain at Fort Richelieu, left Three Rivers with two soldiers and a Huron to return to the fort. All three were on snow-shoes, for this broad river was buried below three or four feet of ice. They made six of the twelve leagues that first day and encamped on the bank in the shelter of some trees for the night. Some time before daylight, while the moon was still shining the Father got up to go on ahead to the fort and, I imagine, let the sleeping soldiers share his blanket, for it was bitter weather.

"He took neither gun nor matches to light a fire and his only food was some bread crusts and a few dried prunes. I remember we found them still uneaten in the Father's pocket. And what a poor cloak! It would hardly keep a summer breeze out, much less that knife-edged winter wind that blew down this broadening of the St. Lawrence which we call Lake St. Peter. We canoed up it today.

"The moon did not last long for snow clouds hid it before dawn. Was it cold that morning! I know for I was on sentry duty in Fort Richelieu that morning and the next. It seems to be my luck always to get the coldest days for sentry duty."

Jacques grinned as he thought of this soldier's nickname.

"During the morning I challenged the Huron of Father de Noue's little band when he came over the snow bank and sought admittance into the fort. He asked us if the Blackrobe had come into the fort yet and that was the first the garrison knew that their Chaplain was somewhere near on the white wastes of the frozen river. All that day we watched in vain for the Chaplain's appearance.

"Next morning a search party was sent out. They discovered the two half dead soldiers and brought them in, but no trace of Father de Noue was found.

"We knew the chances of seeing him alive again were slight. Lieutenant La Touch, who commanded Fort Richelieu, asked for volunteers, who knew the river. I stepped forward. Another soldier—the Iroquois caught and ate him the following summer. Mercy on his soul!—Noel was his name. He also volunteered. We took two Montagnais, who knew this locality and set out.

"It had stopped snowing but was bitter cold. We found the place where Father de Noue had spent the first night. A hole in the snow, lined with pine branches. There the Montagnais were able to pick up Father de Noue's trail. It criss-crossed the river. Evidently the wanderings of a lost man. All that day we followed that pitiful trail. Father had crossed the ice and passed right in front of the fort, only in the snow storm he never saw the white palisades. Maybe, he was snow-blinded by this time and could not see anything.

"He must have staggered on and finally he came to this very Cape Massacre. You see that stream about ten yards up, where that green bank is—that was about the place we came upon the body."

"Where did you say Father Anne de Noue was found?"

Robert Le Coq looked up and saw that Father Bressani had come quietly up behind the soldier and the boy and had been listening intently to the story.

Robert jumped to attention. "Right over there, my Father." The soldier pointed to the spot, now covered with summer's green growth.

"I'll never forget that sight. Father de Noue was on his knees frozen stiff. His shovel hat was lying on his snow shoes. A fall of snow had covered his shoulders like an ermine cape. His body had fallen slightly forward and rested against a snow bank as though he was kneeling at a prie dieu."

"Indeed he was," whispered Father Joseph Bressani reverently.

"We lifted the body back and saw that his arms were composed across his chest and they held in them a little mass of white snow like a white lamb. Father's eyes were wide open and he had died gazing upward."

"You mean on his new and eternal home," said Father Bressani softly.

"Maybe," put in Jacques in an awed tone, "he was looking at the angels coming to take him home."

"That's what we soldiers thought too," said Robert Le Coq unexpectedly.

Father Bressani had risen and he invited, "Come, Jacques, we will make a pilgrimage to a shrine."

"What shrine?" Jacques got to his feet, showing his puzzlement at the Blackrobe's words.

However, he walked in silence through the camp till they came to the bushes and blue wild flowers that grew at the side of a little stream. Here Father Bressani searched a moment and then he exclaimed: "My Jacques, here is the wooden cross, notched on the tree, that Robert and his soldier friend made to mark the place where they found Father de Noue."

Jacques took a step nearer and saw the cross that had been hacked into the bark. He also knelt and said a prayer to Father de Noue.

When the missioner and the boy arose, Father Bressani said: "Jacques, mark well this holy spot. For here the son of the Seigneur of Villers en Prairie began to enjoy his eternal reward. En Prairie is a little market town some six or seven leagues from Rheims in

Champagne. I met Father de Noue's brother there when I was in France.

"Father Anne de Noue was a handsome boy and in his youth was a page at Court. There were strong temptations at Court for a handsome youth. But young Anne, who proudly bore, like so many French boys, the name of the Mother of the Blessed Virgin, had great devotion to Anne's Holy Mary and she kept him pure for thirty years in the world and for thirty-three more in religion."

Father Bressani kept looking at the rude cross cut into the bark. "Do you know, Jacques, I have been thinking that death by immaculate snow was a singularly appropriate death for this good client of Mary Immaculate. That white robe that Robert Le Coq found thrown over Father de Noue's shoulders by the winter's storm was symbolic of the purity of his soul."

Jacques listened in silence and nodded his understanding of the Blackrobe's words.

Suddenly he exclaimed: "My Father, if you had your choice, which kind of death would you like?"

"A death in the state of grace, my child."

"Oh, of course, but I do not mean that way. I mean, by the fire of the Iroquois stake or by freezing alongside a snow bank?"

When Jacques asked this question he happened to glance at Father Bressani's hands. And then he remembered.

Father Joseph Bressani did not answer at once. He lifted up his hands and looked at the places where the finger-nails should have been.

"By cold or by heat! Personally, I seem to have a preference for the flame." Smilingly he spread his tortured finger-tips that had each been burnt. "But the manner of our calling by the Good Master does not matter. It only matters that we serve Him to the best of our abilities. Always remember that, my little Jacques.

"And now as it is growing dark and I still have some of my breviary to read, let us return to the others."

So they did and no sooner had Jacques stretched out by the warmth of the fireplace, than he turned over on his blanket and was asleep.

The next morning after the early start, while Jacques sat in the canoe with Father Gabriel Lalemant, he retold to the young Black-robe what Father Bressani had said the night before.

"And if I had a choice," said Father Gabriel in answer to Jacques' question, "I also would prefer the warmth of the stake to the chill of the snow bank. I am not so old but I have learnt that the Good God always gives us the kind of death that is most suitable to us. The only thing that matters is——"

"I know," broke in Peter, who had attentively been listening to the conversation, "is that we are in the state of grace when death comes."

"Right you are, my child," said Father Gabriel.

He suggested to Jacques that when he got the opportunity at a night's camp, he ask Father Joseph Bressani to tell him about the young lad who had been captured with him four years before and had suffered in the Mohawk villages.

This Jacques resolved to do, but during the next week, when they had left the wide St. Lawrence behind and were struggling up the Ottawa River, he found no opportunity. Now the portages around the rapids had commenced and it was backbreaking work for all.

Jacques and Peter found the bundles they had to carry along the wood's trail left them so weary that when the Huronia-bound party encamped for the night, all they cared to do was to eat and roll over into dreamless sleep.

All too soon it would be before dawn again and the new day's work over rocks, through white water, when they were soaking wet for hours, along mosquito infested portage trails, was upon them.

They came one hot midmorning to a cataract that poured down in silver folds, looking like a curtain. Earlier voyagers had given it this name—Rideau (Curtain) Falls. All through the heat of the midday the Hurons and the missioners portaged the supplies around this obstacle in their path.

Then they were in the canoes once more and only a few leagues gained till it was dusk.

Around that night's camp fire Jacques found his opportunity. He sat silently near Father Bressani till he saw the priest cross himself at the end of his breviary prayers. Then Jacques slipped into position at the Blackrobe's feet. Father Bressani smiled down on him.

"Do you know, Jacques, when you smile you remind me of Jean La Touche. Did I ever tell you about him?"

"No; my Father, but I would like to listen."

Young Peter of Teanaostaye had come silently up and he also sat down.

Seeing the Huron boy, Father Bressani switched his narrative from French into Huron and went on: "Jean was a little lad I had in the canoe with me in April, 1644, when I was attempting to reach Huronia. His brother Guy is a boy interpreter at St. Mary's now. That time I did not get as near as we are tonight, for as you may recall, my party was captured some leagues beyond the spot where blessed Father Jogues fell into the same Mohawk hands. There were six Hurons, Jean and myself in the party who accepted Mohawk hospitality.

"Jean had the same ambition as you, Jacques."

"I don't want to accept any more Mohawk hospitality, if that's what you mean," objected the boy.

"No; no I don't mean being captives. I mean he ambitioned being a boy interpreter at St. Mary's.

"Well, they drove us down their trail to their Long Houses and I needn't describe to you what happened to this lad.

"Let me see your fingers, Jacques."

The boy held out his hands, fingers spread.

"So you still have ten nails left. Little Jean had only one left the last time I saw him."

"How old was this Jean, my father?" asked Peter, speaking for the first time.

"Between twelve and thirteen, but he was brave beyond his years. He was tortured because of his Faith, for I encouraged him to say his prayers and the Mohawks did not like that."

"What prayers, Father Bressani?"

"The same you learnt at Our Lady of the Angels, my Jacques. Especially that beautiful one that begins, 'Little Master, I thank You for keeping me from morning to now. Keep me the rest of the way——'"

Both Jacques and Peter finished the prayer in Huron, "Forget my faults and help me to overcome them. I give You my acts. Give me Your grace to perform them well."

"Amen," said Father Bressani.

Jacques confessed: "I say that prayer every morning and night and sometimes during the day. I like it as well as the prayer to my Guardian Angel."

Father Bressani had been silently thinking and now he spoke: "Do you know, my little ones, sometimes it is given to us to pierce out the workings of Divine Providence. Let me illustrate."

Jacques sensed another story and edged closer to Father Bressani's knees.

"This Jean and I were captured, so it seems to me looking backwards, that we might be the humble instruments of bringing Saving Waters to a poor soul.

"After our privilege to suffer a little for The Master in the same castles of the Mohawks in which Father Jogues had been held captive and before Jean's death and my ransom, we were allowed some liberty.

"We used it to go around the Long Houses. One afternoon I entered the Long House in which most of my pains had been given. There lay an aged Mohawk Captain who was evidently dying. I tried to instruct him through a captive Huron interpreter, for I then spoke Huron quite fluently, but pride hindered the Captain from listening to the interpreter. He answered that a man of his age and standing should teach and not be taught.

"I asked him whether he knew whither he would go after death. He answered me, 'To the Sunset' and here he began to relate the fables and delusions which these wretched people, blinded by the Demon, regard as the most solid truths.

"Sadly I turned away and with little Jean walked back to our Long House. Now see how the Good Master sends us a disappointment just before He fills our hearts with joy. Another captive had been brought into Ossernenon two days before. I had been falsely told he was not of our Hurons and I would not understand his language.

"Little Jean said, 'My Father, do you know the new captive is of the Huron tribe?'

"I told him no. But as soon as the lad said that, I felt an inner urge to go to this poor captive at once. So with Jean leading, we went to the last Long House within the palisades. We passed through the crowd of Mohawks. They formed in line for us and allowed us to approach that man, who was already quite disfigured by the torture. He was lying on the bare ground, without being able to rest his head in any place. Seeing a stone near him, I pushed it with my foot as far as his head, that he might use it for a pillow. Then, looking at me, or by some sign judging that I was a stranger, he said to the person who had him in custody: 'Is not this the white man whom you hold captive?' And the other answered him, 'Yes.' He looked at me the second time with a somewhat pitying glance, 'Sit down, my brother, near me for I desire to speak with you.' I did so not without horror at the sight of that body already half roasted, and asked him what he desired. I rejoiced to understand him a little, because he spoke Huron, and I hoped through this opportunity to be able to instruct him for baptism. But his answer, to my utmost consolation, anticipated me. 'What do I ask?' he says, 'I ask nothing else than Saving Waters. Make haste, the time is short.'

"I undertook to question him, in order not to offer a Sacrament unworthily, and I found him perfectly instructed, having been received among the Catechumens, even in the country of the Hurons.

"While I was conversing, little Jean had quietly gone off and now he returned with a small quantity of water in a gourd. He passed this to me and I baptized the captive then with great satisfaction. The Iroquois present perceived my actions. They informed the Captain. He came and drove Jean and myself out of the Long House with angry threats. At once the Iroquois began to retorture the captive and the following morning they finished roasting him alive.

"Then because I had baptized him, they carried all his limbs, one by one, into the cabin where I abode, and in my presence skinned and ate his feet and hands. My Aunt, as I addressed the squaw of the Captain who had charge of me, put at my feet the dead man's head and left it there a considerable time, reproaching me with what I had done by saying, 'Blackrobe, what indeed have your enchantments helped him? Have they perhaps delivered him from death?'

"What do you think, Jacques?" Father Bressani turned with a smile to the listening boy.

"Yes: indeed, eternal death."

"You are correct," affirmed Father Bressani and he resumed: "All the time the braves and boys would keep threatening me. Their usual conversation was to tell me: 'We will burn you too, Uncle. We will eat you. I will eat one of your feet. And I a hand.'"

The missioner smiled reminiscently. "I just recollect that one evening about this time, while they were burning the ring finger on my right hand for the last time." The Blackrobe held up the mutilated stump. "They commanded me to sing, as the custom was for those under torture. Instead of singing I intoned the Miserere with so awful a voice that I made them afraid. All in the Long House listened to me with deep attention. Even 'my uncle' who

was burning me remitted a little of that severity with which he
had begun. But he did not therefore forbear to continue, for he
feared that they would mock him for cowardice. I thought then I
would die, so cruel was the pain. But the Good Lord preferred that
I suffer and live."

"How did you escape, my Father?" asked Jacques.

"Some weeks later the kindly Broad Breeches, as these savages
called the Dutch of New Amsterdam, came to Ossernenon and
they ransomed me cheaply, on account of the Mohawks' small es-
teem of me, for they believed that I would never get well of my
ailments.

"But here you see me, en route to Huronia once more. Some
people are not worthy of martyrdom."

Father Bressani was silent till Jacques asked:

"What became of little Jean La Touche?"

"They killed him under torture and he is enjoying himself this
very moment in the Playgrounds of Paradise. Jean is my personal
martyr, to whom I appeal often when I need things for my soul.
And he rarely fails me," concluded Father Joseph Bressani with a
smile.

It was getting late and the Blackrobe stood up. Regretfully
Jacques and Peter knew that the story telling time was over.

The next day the flotilla of Huron canoes came to the large
cache of food that the party had hidden on the way down and that
night there was almost feasting around the camp fires.

Jacques learnt that a few leagues above them on the Ottawa
River they would come to the Chaudiere.

Robert Le Coq told him to watch on the morrow and he would
see an interesting ceremony among the pagan members of the
homeward bound flotilla.

With the dawn the party was afloat and, sure enough, they had
paddled only two leagues and the sun was just breaking through
the low-hung clouds, when the portage was reached. Already the

river was white water, and paddling by the silent Huron braves was increasingly difficult.

The landing was made on a sandy beach and the now familiar back-breaking routine recommenced.

Jacques and Peter were struggling along under their heavy loads of mission supplies, and perspiring freely when the roar that they had heard in the forest suddenly grew increasingly louder. They struggled on behind the Hurons and soon the trail came out of the forest and ran close to the edge of a great falls.

Jacques stopped and looked in wonder at the wild scene below him. He saw that he was standing quite close to the edge where the white waves raced up and then poured over in a smooth sheet. It was difficult to speak and be heard and for the first few moments the French boy did not care to utter words.

To Peter of Teanaostaye the scene was not new as he had seen it on the down voyage. But he also looked in silence. Finally he motioned Jacques to come with him. The boys left their bundles by the trailside and walked forward till they stood on the very brink of the falls. A new scene spread out below them. The Ottawa River fell some sixty feet into an immense semicircular basin in which the water boiled up. Jacques imagined that he was looking into the center of a great kettle of boiling water.

He knew that nothing would live long in that maelstrom and instinctively he drew back and bumped into Father Gabriel Lalemant who had come up unnoticed and was also gazing in awe at the wild waters.

The Blackrobe put his hands on the shoulders of both boys and they gazed in fascination at the boiling cauldron below. Then they retraced their steps and each in silence took up his burden.

Quickly the portage trail swung into the dark forests again and the noise of the falling waters lessened. When they reached the end of the portage the Ottawa had resumed its usual appearance and gave no inkling that a league below it took a plunge of sixty feet.

Shortly the camp was made for the night. About the fires Father Gabriel told Jacques why he had detained him at the edge of the falls.

"I wanted that place to be etched on your memory for I am curious to see it with my own eyes."

"Why, my Father?" Jacques stretched himself out comfortably.

"Well, your Father Brebeuf is the cause of my curiosity. The men of the woods named those falls of the Ottawa the Chaudiere and there the pagan Hurons from time immemorial have stopped and offered a sacrifice of tobacco to the demon who dwells, they say, in the caves behind the waters. I have no doubt that good tobacco was offered to this imaginary demon by the pagans of our party today, though I did not see the offering.

"Many canoes have been hurled to destruction over this falls. The unfortunate paddlers did not land at the portage head and then it was too late to land on either bank after the current gripped the canoes.

"Father Brebeuf on his first trip up this river, back in '26, saw that pagan ceremony and it was his account that I had in mind as I stood beside you this morning."

"What was it?" asked Jacques.

"If I recollect aright, the pagan braves stand in a circle, very likely near the spot where we stood, and in their center stands the captain. He holds a bark dish in his outstretched hands. Into this each brave throws some portion of his small supply of tobacco. For these pagans foolishly believe that this demon likes tobacco and nothing but the weed will propitiate him.

"When the bark dish is heaped high with the offerings, it is placed on the ground in the center of the circle. Then the captain in sign language begins one of his long speeches, telling the others the dangers of this falls and afterwards others of the party retell how his offering of tobacco on a former voyage had saved his life.

"After this the dancing began. It must have been a weird sight. The shouting of these leaping figures silenced by the continuous roar of the tumbling waters nearby.

"Then followed foolish and dark incantations——"

"What are incantations, my Father?" The word was new to Jacques.

"Invoking this demon by the falls, my child, which is sinful.

"The ceremony concluded with the Captain walking to the edge of the precipice and throwing that good tobacco into the foaming torrent. So the tobacco ceremony of the Chaudiere would conclude and the braves would take up their canoes and bundles of pelts and resume their journey."

Peter had been an observant listener to Father Gabriel's words and now that he had concluded, he asked Jacques to repeat them in Huron.

Father Gabriel watched wishfully as the fluent Jacques retold the ceremony.

When the Blackrobe and the boy were alone later, the young missioner said: "I wish I had your facility in this native language! For until I am able to speak with these people and without the tongue of an interpreter, I am a useless servant of the Lord."

Jacques remembered this wish next day when he was seated in the canoe with Father Gabriel and he began to instruct the willing Blackrobe in the Huron tongue.

The following week, while the flotilla ever paddled or portaged upstream, was a busy one. But each night's camp fire showed progress.

Jacques began to hear around the fires that they were approaching the country of the Algonquins and there was a fortified village of these people on an island and there were rapids either side of this island and no Huron canoe passed up or down stream without the permission of the old one-eyed Captain of these Algonquins.

Finally late one afternoon the Huron party came to the portage below the Algonquins' island. This island Jacques heard the Blackrobes call Isle des Allumettes.

He listened one evening while Father Bressani retold of Father Anthony Daniel's bitter experiences in this neighborhood.

"When Father Daniel was making this same voyage that we are on, he was travelling with a young Huron. Armand was his name. Father Daniel was ashore at the portage and Armand and an Algonquin were in the canoe about to land. They were doubling a point and the surging of the current suddenly overturned the canoe. Father Daniel saw two Indians and a quantity of precious mission supplies disappear under the waves. He gave not a thought to the invaluable supplies, though his Mass kit and with it all that he needed for saying Mass was overturned with that canoe, but his thoughts were on the drowning boy. Father had high hopes that Armand might some day be of great service to the missions. So Father Daniel, seeing Armand no more on land or water, knelt down by the bank and begged the good Angels to aid.

"The young Algonquin, naked as your hand, had no difficulty in saving himself. But he made no effort to help the French boy. When Father Daniel had almost despaired of Armand, the boy suddenly appeared on the surface. He struggled weakly as the current caught him and hurried him along to his death. Just as he was about to be swept out into the full current, Armand clutched at an overhanging bush and held on.

"Father Daniel jumped up, ran along the bank to grasp the drowning boy.

"When Armand was able to speak he burst out in loud laments: 'O my Father, in that lost chest was your chalice and alb and chasuble! They are all lost through my mishap.'

"But Father Daniel stopped him. 'It is enough, my son, it is enough that you are living. Do not let us speak of our loss, but let us bless God and His Holy Angels for rescuing you from death.'"

Jacques had listened to Father Bressani's account of this near drowning. Now he asked: "Why, my Father, did not Armand learn to swim? Then he would have had more chance of saving himself when the canoe overturned."

"I don't know that, Jacques. But I do know that I have never learnt swimming yet, though I have always wanted to. Maybe some day you will teach me."

Jacques nodded solemnly. He added: "I wonder if I would be making this canoe trip to Huronia unless I knew how to take care of myself if the canoe overturned."

"To know how to swim is excellent, my Jacques, but like Father Daniel, I trust more to my good Guardian Angel and the Guardians of the Huron Mission than my own arms."

"If you know how to swim, you are making the rescue easier for your Guardian Angel, my Father," Jacques assured the Blackrobe gravely.

Father Bressani smiled his assent.

"Mentioning Father Daniel's name, Jacques, reminds me of his own adventures within a day's journey of this Algonquin stronghold island we are near. Do you wish to hear it?"

"Of a certainty, my Father."

"I heard Father Anthony tell it at St. Mary's last winter. He said, as well as I recall his words: 'We departed early in the morning, without eating and drinking. We journeyed with long strides over a very bad road and in extreme heat. I was burdened with my little baggage. The others in the Huron party had gone on ahead. I supposed that my people would stop about noon to eat something, but they left me behind, continuing to advance. My weakness increased with the heat of the day, I stopped there almost fainting, and threw myself upon the ground, unable to do any more. Then having taken a little rest, I found three or four gooseberries, which did not help me much——'"

Here Jacques who had been listening attentively, interrupted: "I do not like gooseberries. They are not sweet enough."

"Anything is sweet when the pangs of hunger gnaw within, my child," Father Bressani observed reminiscently.

"Father Daniels said they did not help him much, for attempting to resume his way, he was compelled to lie down again, as his head ached severely and he felt a great weakness throughout his whole body.

"I well remember—I am quoting the words of good Father Daniel—poor Hagar and the Prophet Elias, whom God had helped in their necessity, but my sins forbade me to hope for this temporal favor; nevertheless, my soul was comforted in seeing itself depart from this world through obedience, in case they should not come to succor me. I remained an hour or two in this condition, when my people, having noticed that I delayed too long, came to look for me. I asked them for a little food, but they answered that they had nothing. They took my little baggage, and urged me to take heart. We found a brook that refreshed me, and gave me strength enough to get to the islands towards evening, where I found our Frenchmen in great anxiety.

"So you see, my Jacques," concluded Father Joseph Bressani, "Father Anthony Daniel threw himself on God's Providence and It never deserted him, or anyone, zealous to labor in His Service. Never forget that and you will be safe and happy. Now that is a wholesome thought to sleep on.

"Good night, Jacques—Peter."

"Good night, my Father," both boys replied.

Chapter Ten

On Alone

URING THE NEXT ten days the party became separated because the captains felt that the Iroquois menace was below the flotilla and those Hurons who were more eager to get back to their country had pushed on ahead.

Jacques and Peter had begged Father Bressani's permission this day to travel with Bernard, the young Huron warrior who had saved Jacques from the birching at Fort St. Louis.

He had promised the boys that a few leagues ahead near a large cache of food was a good hunting place. They had come to the cache and found that the Hurons in advance had taken all the food. They had nothing with them so hunting was imperative if they did not wish to go hungry.

Then fortune smiled on them. Peter heard a rustling in a nearby bush. He froze in his tracks and motioned Jacques to keep silent. Bernard was off to the left, but he had seen the young Huron boy's signal and he crept noiselessly near. In sign language he told the two to let him investigate alone. He approached the underbrush. Without a sound he parted the branches. Then he grunted. Jacques saw him stoop low and when he straightened he held a small black object in his hands.

The boys crowded around the hunter. "Oh," cried Peter, "it's a papoose bear!"

"Yes," added Bernard, "and half famished. This little cub is dying of starvation."

The cub had been weakly struggling, clawing at his captor. Now it raked Bernard's wrist with a needle-like claw. He dropped the tiny animal and it started to scamper clumsily into the underbrush, the two boys in instant pursuit. They stopped when beyond the brush they came upon the carcass of a large black bear. Bernard had followed the boys and he examined the body.

"This is why the papoose bear stays here. See! The squaw bear was killed by an arrow."

He pulled out the shaft and examined it closely.

"It is not the kind we Hurons use——"

Jacques interrupted him. "That's a Mohawk arrow! I remember seeing that kind in Stripling Tree's quiver."

"You speak with sense," Bernard affirmed, "Iroquois arrow means Iroquois braves are near." The Huron was turning over the carcass. "This squaw bear was shot not later than yesterday afternoon. It must have gotten away from the Iroquois hunter and crawled into this place to die. But the meat is good. We stop and eat."

Bernard cut three hunks of flesh from the bear's flank and after making a fire, he and the boys ate ravenously. When they had finished, Bernard hacked off two generous portions of the carcass, and loaded with these, the boys followed the hunter.

Jacques would have liked to have carried the cub, but Bernard reminded him, "It is too dangerous." He set the cub down and before Jacques could protest, the Huron plunged his knife into the animal's heart. There was a sudden stillness in the forest.

"It is better," explained Bernard, "if I left the cub here he would have died of starvation."

The three with their burdens of meat were tracking back to the river's bank. When, wearied and bramble scratched, they broke through the brush late in the afternoon and looked on the wild river, there were no traces of their Huron party.

"This is where they intended to camp tonight," insisted Bernard, when they had journeyed half a league up the bank and came to a clearing. "Something has happened that made the captains change their plans."

Night would fall soon so the three made camp. With his flint Bernard sparked tinder into a glow and quickly a tiny flame blossomed. Over the fire the meat was partially cooked. Then before it grew too dark all trace of the fire was extinguished.

Sitting in the dark Bernard expressed his fears.

"Several signs I have seen today, my nephews, make me believe that all is not well ahead. I think our brothers have discovered Iroquois signs and have taken to cover."

"Then we should do likewise," said Jacques.

"You speak sense," Peter put in. "One never knows when the Iroquois are near. I remember last spring a warrior of that nation lay hidden for a whole week near the northern gate of Teanaostaye till he saw a brave returning alone from the tobacco fields. He cut him down and took his scalp lock and got away. And we in the village only learnt of it next day."

"Sleep now. I watch," ordered Bernard, "and do not dream of Iroquois, my nephews. Much strength will be needed tomorrow and when the sun rises we will know what to do."

It was a warm night and despite the swarming insects sleep finally came. Bernard kept watch and then he decided with the coming of light to wait here on the river bank to see if any Huron canoes would come paddling by.

But though they watched till the sun sank behind the southwestern bank of the Ottawa no canoes appeared. Early the following morning a canoe with a solitary warrior in it darted around the woody point upstream. Jacques was the first to sight it. It was being paddled rapidly along.

Prudently Bernard checked the boys and signalled them to hide in the brush of the river's side. It was well he did so, for as the canoe came closer, all saw the Mohawk war paint, red and blue stripes on face and chest of the paddler.

Silently the boys in the bushes viewed the canoe sweep within thirty feet of where they lay hid. Then there was a twang over Jacques' head. One of Bernard's arrows sped out. The boys saw the paddler half leap up, clutch at the quivering arrow in his side and pitch into the water. The canoe rocked, righted and rode along the current on an even keel.

Bernard had leapt over Jacques and waded out into the stream. The Iroquois corpse appeared. Jacques saw Bernard's knife descend and then the Huron was holding a black scalplock and the corpse was whirling along after the empty canoe.

Said Bernard: "He was a runner carrying messages from a war party to the old captains in the Mohawk Long Houses to the south."

"What does that mean?" asked Jacques, still stunned by this sight of swift tragedy.

"It means we must travel with very wideawake eyes. Where there are runners coming south, there will be a war party north of us. The river is no longer safe travelling."

Peter put in: "It is not many leagues above this spot where the land trail begins. I came down it going to the Big Villages of the French."

The Huron boy explained to Jacques: "We have lost track of our main party and we must go on alone to my village of Teanaostaye. I think I know the way and, of course, Bernard knows it."

So the river was left behind and the three had not gone many leagues till they came on gruesome relics of the passage of a victorious Iroquois war party.

Dead ashes of ten camp fires. The unpleasant remains of a large animal, from which the crows and buzzards flopped up reluctantly. The trampled undergrowth where braves had slept. All these showed mutely that a party of considerable size had spent the night here quite recently.

Peter and Jacques were following Bernard through this

deserted camp site, when the Huron hunter stopped suddenly. The boys came up silently and stood on either side of him.

There lay the body of a middle aged Huron squaw. She had been tomahawked. Said Bernard: "Squaw was too weak to keep up with her captors. They take her lock and leave her here."

Peter stooped and looked closely at the face. "I knew her! She was Arnold's squaw and she comes from Teanaostaye. I was altar boy with Father Daniel when he poured Saving Waters on her head in our chapel last summer."

"Are you sure?" asked Jacques, kneeling by this Christian Huron.

"Certainly," Peter replied. "This is Arnold's squaw. She used to be known as White Humming Bird, but Saving Water made her name Marie. She was Arnold's squaw, I tell you."

"Then," said Bernard, "this Iroquois war party must have raided near your Teanaostaye."

"Maybe," Jacques put in hopefully, "she was in the fields for corn and Iroquois surprised her."

"Maybe," agreed Peter doubtfully, "I hope nothing has happened to my Teanaostaye where my mother is.

"Anyway, we must walk the trail softly, as there may be more Iroquois ahead."

"You speak sense," agreed Bernard, "for the signs show that this party was going south and there may be other enemies ahead of us."

But the rest of that day was monotonous travel and the three spent the night in a clearing.

They travelled warily and as the leagues lay behind them, they came on increasing traces of Iroquois raiders—camp sites and by the trail sides the stark unfortunate captives who were unable from hunger or wounds to keep up with their savage victors.

But in the succeeding week the three never sighted a live Iroquois. Now they were approaching the confines of the lands of the Hurons and Bernard and Peter recognized landmarks.

It was a morning late in July and Jacques had begun to think his long journey was nearing its end, for Peter had said to him as they started that daybreak: "Teanaostaye is only a few leagues over there." He had pointed to the northwest.

Before the sun was high Jacques came close to death. He had been last in the file. He could see the furrowed hair on the back of Bernard's head and Peter's as they silently walked on ahead of him.

Then Peter had turned suddenly as a locust like sound came from the grass beside him. Jacques saw him leap into the air and Jacques quickened his step. The next second he felt something rise out of the grass and strike his leg. He bounded up, crying out with the instant pain and fright. He slipped to his knee. Peter jerked him along the ground. Then he felt suddenly weak and relaxed on the trail.

Bernard came bounding back and his tomahawk flashed into the grass. There was a violent wiggling and Jacques saw a thick-bodied snake writhe in its death agony. All the time the tail was vibrating giving off that locust like sound.

Peter was saying: "Whenever you hear that sound of death, leap as I did. Where did he bite you?"

Jacques looked down at his torn deer skin legging. But before he could examine further, Bernard and Peter were kneeling beside him and the former was removing the legging from his right foot.

There were the tiny punctures with their droplets of blood beginning to ooze out.

Bernard said: "This will hurt, but it is necessary."

He took his keen edged knife and cut into the flesh. Jacques winced, but he saw Peter observing him and he forced a grin to his lips.

"It is good what Bernard does. See the poison flows out."

"I make it flow faster," Bernard put his lips to the wound.

Jacques remembered to say a silent prayer of thanksgiving to his Guardian Angel for this protection that had just been given to him.

They rested by the trailside for an hour. Then Jacques felt able to resume the journey. But he found it difficult following the trail that day and he was glad when, long before evening, he and his two companions came upon a ruined beaver dam across a small stream. The flow of the stream had been checked and the water spread out into a tiny lake with the roots of trees, cut down by keen teeth, showing all over the surface.

Bernard motioned for silence and the two boys drifted behind the boles of nearby trees. The Huron hunter went ahead like a shadow to reconnoiter.

From where he stood in the shelter of the trees Jacques could see the dam and the beaver lake clearly. Right by him were several gnawed stumps and Jacques noticed how sharp the teeth of these busy little animals must be to fell such striplings.

Then a sleek-backed beaver appeared upstream. It saw Bernard and dived.

Peter called softly: "Jacques, Bernard has sighted something suspicious. See he is taking to cover."

The young hunter had dropped into the underbrush and only a slight waving of the bushes suggested his progress to the watching Jacques.

A crow cawed upstream from the upper edge of the beaver lake and Jacques saw it winging its black way straight over the tree tops of the further bank.

Peter grasped Jacques' hand and drew him down. "I do not like this place. Something moves at the upper end of the lake."

The Christian Huron boy's sharp eyes were searching the far shore.

"Bernard has seen it too," said Jacques.

"What's that?" Peter indicated the direction.

"It's a bear possibly."

"You have no sense. A bear makes more noise."

"Look! Look!" It was Jacques' startled exclamation.

The boys saw that Bernard had risen and was running through the marsh grass away from them. Their eyes sought the cause and simultaneously they saw it.

Two Iroquois warriors had straightened out of the underbrush of the upper shore. One was pointing an arquebus at the fleeing Bernard. There was an explosion and Bernard threw up his hands, stumbled and started to drag himself like a wounded bear. The enemy came leaping. Jacques recognized the second one. He was Hot Ashes, his former captor.

In the excitement of this discovery Jacques almost shouted out, but Peter had coolly clamped his hand over his companion's mouth and held him down.

"We can do nothing. If they see us, we are dead men."

Jacques thought he heard the thump of the tomahawk driven home.

Continued Peter: "If they suspect he is not alone we are not safe here. We'll be safer there." The Huron boy had released his breath-destroying hold on Jacques' mouth and he indicated the direction of the beaver dam.

"Come on then before they start the search," said Jacques, "there is no time to lose."

Snaking his way through the sharp-thorned bushes, Jacques followed Peter. When they had come to the open space between the bushes and the marsh grass, Peter wormed his way across the opening, quickly followed by the other boy. The water felt cooling as the two sunk under its concealing surface, only their mouths above the surface.

There they lay an hour and nothing happened. Hot Ashes and his companion had disappeared as noiselessly as they had come upon the scene. Finally Jacques said: "It seems that they believed Bernard was alone and they have gone off.

"I just was thinking of something that William, who is the hunter for the Ursuline Nuns back in Quebec told one afternoon last winter."

"What was that?"

"He told me how two soldiers from the garrison at Three Rivers had saved themselves last summer, when surprised by an Iroquois war party. They dug into a beaver dam and lay there in safety till the danger was past."

Peter turned gently on his side and urged: "That is a sensible idea and it will give us better protection than this grass. Any Iroquois within five feet might see us here. Wait till I scout."

Jacques itched to raise his head and have a look upstream, where in imagination he saw the corpse of Bernard, but he prudently restrained himself and instead began to say Hail Marys for the repose of the Huron hunter's soul.

Peter came crawling through the muddy water sooner than Jacques had expected. "The plan is workable and I know just the place to conceal ourselves in the dam. Follow me and keep low."

There was only one spot of danger and before the two fleeing boys passed it Peter made a headgear of grass and putting it on slowly raised himself to look around. He was satisfied that no Iroquois was near.

Handing the grassy headgear to Jacques, he bade him keep a sharp lookout. Then he wiggled into the marsh grass that grew profusely beside the edge of the dam and began to burrow like a village dog.

Jacques slowly let his eyes sweep the downstream banks of the small stream. He turned and his gaze took in upstream where the beaver lake spread out. There sprawled face down on the sloping edge of the northern bank lay the body of the young Huron warrior who had first befriended him that day in Fort St. Louis.

The gruesome reminder of what awaited Peter and himself if they should be discovered by the enemy caused Jacques to sink beneath the protection of the grass and remember to say his favorite prayer—"Angel of God, my Guardian dear. . . ."

Peter's persistent burrowing brought out a lone beaver who promptly splashed into the water and swam away. Then it was silent along the lake.

At length, Peter backed to where he could motion Jacques to come forward. He found that a tunnel had been neatly excavated between the mass of mud and sticks. When he crawled after Peter into the beavers' home he could sit down and above his head was a roof of dam material.

Through this Peter was busy tearing out peepholes that could command views up and down stream.

"Now, unless we have left too telltale a trail behind us, I think we are safe for the present."

The Huron boy relaxed and wiped the perspiration from his features.

The two boys had been voluntary captives in their beaver home over an hour and they were almost on the point of coming out, for nothing suspicious had occurred, when Peter warned: "Listen, Jacques."

At the time the Huron boy was watching through the peephole that commanded the beaver lake. The two listened, but no unusual sound was heard for a matter of ten minutes.

Then Jacques with his eyes glued to the opening that gave a view downstream gasped. For out of the forest, not fifty feet away, suddenly appeared an Iroquois brave, painted and greased for war. He surveyed the ruined dam and then stepped across the small stream. Before he had disappeared into the southern forest, a line of warriors had come into view.

"Peter, we're lost!" Jacques in his excitement spoke aloud.

The Huron pushed the French boy away from the peephole and silently surveyed the party that now was splashing through the water and disappearing into the forest.

"It is a victorious war party of our enemies. They have many of our people captives, carrying their bundles. We must not move or we are dead men."

Jacques was now beside his companion and with fascinated eyes watched the sad line of Huron captives, who marched along with their backs raw under the weight of the bundles of furs and pelts that were tied on. The Hurons were all young squaws or children. Jacques saw several Huron boys about Peter's height.

Then came a Huron brave. He was a middle aged man and despite his captivity he carried his head high. One bloody arm hung at his side, helpless. His back had been cruelly cut when running some recent gauntlet and the flies were swarming on his wounds. But he bore no bundle.

Peter was whispering. "I know him. That is the Christian captain of the village that is an hour's walk from Teanaostaye. His name is Andrew. He is a brave captain and the enemy are keeping him for the slow fires in their Long Houses."

"I am looking for three Mohawk Iroquois," said Jacques, "they are Hot Ashes, The Frog and a young Mohawk about my age, whom they call Stripling Tree."

"Have you seen them?"

"I am sure it was Hot Ashes who tomahawked Bernard and where he is, The Frog and Stripling Tree should be. For they travel in the same war party."

"We don't want to meet them."

"I don't, I know, Peter, for to them I am an escaped captive and they would burn the soles off my feet before they killed me. That is their punishment for escaping."

"It is a good thing that we thought to hide in this ruined dam, for some of this party would have surely seen us in the forest. Why we might have walked into their scouts! Oh! Oh!"

Peter broke off suddenly and Jacques inquired:

"What is it?"

"There go two squaws from that village of Andrew's. I have seen them in Teanaostaye. I do not like to watch any longer."

But Jacques was fascinated by this sight of the victorious Iroquois returning with captives and he kept his eyes at the peephole till the southern forest edge hid the sight of the last one.

It was almost dusk now. Since the sun had set it had become chilly in this beaver house and Jacques began to feel the pangs of hunger again. Neither of the boys had eaten that day.

When it was black night, they decided to venture forth from their hiding place. Peter crawled out first and, satisfied that it was safe, he gave the signal for Jacques to follow. He did not realize how cramped he was till he attempted to stand erect. With a moan he fell to the ground. But he was determined to get away from this spot, so after vigorously rubbing his legs till the circulation was restored he got up.

In Peter's wake he waded through the marsh grass along the side of the beaver lake. They came to where the body of Bernard still lay.

Jacques recalled the latest kindness of this Christian Huron who had sucked the poison out of his wounded leg only the day before and he knelt and prayed.

"He was good to me, dear Boy Jesus. Please have mercy on him. Please."

The two boys dragged the corpse up the bank and with stones found nearby they covered it as well as they could from the wild beasts.

Then they started to search for something to eat. When they chanced upon a patch of blackberry bushes, they ate ravenously.

Peter finally said: "We must get on to our villages. I think I remember that the stream at the foot of this lake flows into a larger lake. If I am right, we are on the land trail to Huronia. But I am beginning to be afraid for Father Daniel and my people at Teanaostaye."

The two waded back to the beaver dam that had concealed them and then on downstream through the dark night.

"In the water we leave no tracks," warned Peter, when Jacques would go on the bank.

They heard the howls of some wolves on a neighboring ridge and later the snarls and growls of the same hungry animals fighting over a find. These sounds overcame the boys' fatigue and they pushed on all that night.

As the light began to break in the east they noticed that the stream had broadened and now it was some thirty feet from bank to bank. They went ashore and broke through the underbrush, following the general direction of the river.

Before it was broad daylight Peter sighted some pigeons in a tree. He took careful aim and sent an arrow through one. Before it struck the ground Jacques had caught the warm thing and the boys roughly dividing the pigeon, ate it raw.

They had done about half a league further when Peter called a halt.

"I know this place. We stopped here on the way down. I remember that tall white hemlock with the peculiar twist in its trunk. We are in luck!"

More he would not say, but Jacques followed the other boy's assured steps. A short walk through the forest and the two stood on the edge of a blue-watered lake, maybe, a league and a half in width. In length it stretched beyond a green-treed point.

"This is the lake we always cross and my countrymen have canoes hidden and what is better, a cache of food. I know the place. It is near that point."

It took Jacques and Peter two hours to reach the point. Here Peter went to the shore and studied it carefully. Then he retraced his steps into the bushes.

There, skillfully hidden under leaves and branches, were two birchbark canoes.

"How will we paddle the canoe?" Jacques wanted to know.

"Our custom is to hide the paddles in the trees. Look about you and tell me if you see any paddles."

Jacques' keen eyes searched all the neighboring trees. Then he shook his head.

Peter was grinning. "Even our enemies, the Iroquois, can't see our paddles."

Proudly he went to an oak that towered over the rest. He shinned up about ten feet and bent down a limb. Then Jacques saw the paddle, neatly hidden under the branch and tied with thongs and covered with leaves.

Peter cut it away and passed it down to Jacques.

"The cache of food is about a hundred yards down the shore from where the canoe paddles are hidden. It is about fifty steps in from that large rock that juts out down there." Peter pointed.

The two hungry boys followed the shore line till they were abreast of the rock. Then they pushed inland. In a dense brush, concealed and protected by a pile of stones was a most welcome supply of smoked eels and corn. They feasted on this find and then, despite the sting of the mosquitoes, fell into deep sleep.

It was almost night when Jacques awoke. Peter was still curled up alongside him. He awakened the Huron boy. Again they ate and taking a supply of eels and corn from the cache, they carefully covered up the rest of the food and sought the canoe.

When it was quite dark they silently pushed off and as silently paddled out into the middle of the lake. By starlight they set a course for the distant dark point. It took them three hours to reach it. Here the lake narrowed till it was nothing but a wide river.

"We follow this river as far as the canoe will push through," said Peter.

So they canoed until the high dark banks grew noticeably nearer. Several times drinking moose and deer were startled by the noiseless approach of the boys' canoe. There would be a quick lifting of the antlered head and then a wild crashing of branches that died away into the usual silences.

Again before daybreak the canoe was drawn in and concealed in the undergrowth.

Jacques invited: "Before we eat and sleep, let us swim."

So he and Peter cooled off in the delicious water. Then they ate heartily and soon were sound asleep.

It was broad daylight when they awoke, refreshed and heartened by the knowledge that the end of their journey was almost in sight.

As they lay on the bank, prudently hidden from the chance sight of a hostile canoe, Peter was saying: "I will be glad to be back where I can serve Father Daniel; he says I am the best altar boy he has in the village. He said that last spring when I saved the church from burning down."

"You never told me about that."

"You never asked me," Peter replied, "listen and I will tell you all.

"It was Easter Sunday morning and almost the whole village was crowded in and around the church. Father Daniel had been telling my people that Easter was to remind us of the happy times to come for all Hurons if we were faithful to the Good God's laws. He said when we die we begin to live. I thought that a funny way to put it. When you die you begin to live."

"He meant the soul part of us that can't die anytime," Jacques explained, "the Fathers at Our Lady of the Angels told us the same thing. It is true too."

"Of course, it is true. The Blackrobes do not speak with a split tongue."

"Of course."

"Look!" Jacques exclaimed suddenly. He pointed to a tiny bird that was poised on vibrating wings over a blue flower. "I know what that is. It is a humming bird. I never saw one before."

"I have seen many. Father Daniel told me once that the humming bird is just like angel's wings in color, only the angels' wings are brighter colored."

"The humming bird is beautiful." Jacques was lost in admiration at the tiny bird. He approached on his knees and made an ineffectual attempt to grab it, but it darted away out of sight.

"I was telling you," Peter continued, "Father was just about to finish his sermon when I noticed that the candlestick had tipped over and was setting fire to the bark side of the altar. A few minutes more and the dry bark would have caught and then the church would have been in danger.

"I grabbed up the candlestick and the burning bark and rushing to the door, threw them out. My right hand was burnt, but I did not mind when Father Anthony said I had saved the church from burning down. He said so from the altar before my people. He put some cooling stuff on my burns and then he gave me three prunes and some French snow."

"You mean sugar," put in Jacques.

"Yes; it is very sweet and I like it very much."

Jacques got up and stretched himself.

"There is something I like better just now."

"What is that, my brother?"

"Another swim in the river." Jacques started for the bank.

"Wait, I scout first." Peter climbed into a leafy oak. Soon he had disappeared from Jacques' gaze. Then he saw the bare legs of Peter coming down. When the Huron boy leapt lightly to the ground, he approved: "It is safe. From the top of this tree I could see up and down a league. There is nobody near. I go with you."

The late afternoon sun had warmed the waters and the two boys luxuriated in the cooling depths. They seemed to lose some of the weariness out of their limbs and when at length they waded ashore and lay in the yielding sand, they felt refreshed for the night's fatigues.

139

Another night's canoeing brought them to the place where the river ended in a swamp. Here Peter recognized the spot where his countrymen hid their canoes. Carefully concealing the light birchbark canoe and tying the paddle out of sight under an oak's limb, the boys headed across the land.

Peter said: "We are not many leagues from the first village of my people."

"Is that the one where Father Brebeuf is?" asked Jacques.

"No; the first village is Cohaigue, or, as the Blackrobes call it, St. John the Baptist. Echon is leagues away from there. We will go direct to my Teanaostaye. I know the trail from here."

Peter showed that he did for he led the way through the darkness with sure foot. Towards dawn the two, now quite tired came out on a ridge. Peter could see a dark valley lay below them.

"This is the ridge that looks across at the ridge on which is my Teanaostaye. Here we rest. It is not safe to come near a village in the dark. Some brave might put arrows into us."

So Jacques gladly lay down and as his limbs relaxed he thought how his long journey was almost over and of the welcome that awaited him from his beloved Blackrobe, Father John Brebeuf.

As if reading his thought, Peter sleepily exclaimed: "My white brother, it is nice to think that with daylight I will see my Father Daniel and after tomorrow I will serve his Mass again. For I am the best altar boy in Teanaostaye. Father Daniel says so."

The two boys sunk into dreamless sleep.

It was into a hot sun that they blinked when they opened their eyes once more.

Chapter Eleven
Where Daniel Died

LOOKING FROM the fringe of fir trees the two boys gazed in horror. There on the opposite ridge where Teanaostaye had stood, surrounded by its palisades and green outlying fields of corn and tobacco, were now blackened ruins. Too many buzzards sailed lazily in the blue sky or swooped down on sure wing to disappear into the ruins.

"Teanaostaye has been taken and sacked by the Iroquois! My village is gone! What of my squaw mother!" Peter kept repeating this as Jacques stood at his side and looked on the holocaust across the valley.

Along a familiar path Peter led Jacques into the valley. Before they reached the bottom and crossed the little stream they disturbed many buzzards. The ugly birds reluctantly flew up as the boys came close.

Then the two stopped. There by the streamside lay five bodies. Or, rather, what had been left of the bodies by fire and bird and prowling beast.

A little further along as the boys warily advanced into the still valley were other signs of defeat and sudden raid. Dropped blankets, some blackened by fire. Knives and broken arrows.

Peter stooped to pick up something. Jacques looked. "Why, it is a human hand!" he cried in disgust.

"No; it was," explained Peter, "that was dropped by some Iroquois. See. It has been cured and it was his tobacco pouch."

Jacques took the hand and saw where the wrist had been sewed into a pouch. As he tipped it some grains of tobacco fell out. He threw the pouch away in disgust.

Now the two boys were crossing the narrow stream.

Peter explained: "You know, Jacques, Teanaostaye means 'The Guardian of the Beautiful Little River.'" He sniffed. "Ough! This used to be sweet water. Smell it now. It is poisoned water."

Jacques looked at the noisome stream.

"Down there was where the squaws got the water and carried it to the cabins," explained Peter.

Grass had already begun to grow in that once much travelled trail up to Teanaostaye. The two walked along, keeping a sharp lookout for any sign of human life, hostile or friendly. But there was none.

They were walking on blackened remains of fields.

"Here was where Teanaostaye grew its maize and over there the tobacco." Peter pointed to other desolate fields.

The boys stepped into the ashes and a choking cloud of dust arose. They coughed and were forced to detour around the burnt stumps.

The boys had come out on the level plain on top of the ridge now and Jacques paused to look back across the still valley to the other ridge on which they had spent the night. It showed freshly green against the blue sky.

Then at an exclamation from Peter he turned back. The Huron boy was pointing. "Look! Everything is burnt down!" He indicated a low line of blackened stumps. "Over there was where the palisades stood. The main gate into my village was right there." His hand swept to the left.

Peter led Jacques in silence to the wrecked defenses. That there had been resistance here the eyes of the boys readily saw. They passed into the sacked Huron stronghold. Everywhere was grim testimony of fight and flight. But it was the awful stillness of this Huron shambles that struck Jacques with fear.

"Don't you almost hear the silence, Peter?" he wanted to know.

The Huron boy was not listening. He was leading the way to the center of the village. Here he paused before a blackened oblong of stumps.

"Anwennen's," he used the Huron name for Father Anthony Daniel, "Anwennen's Prayer House was right here. Now look at it!"

There outlined in the ashes were the burnt foundations. It was clear that fierce heat had consumed this chapel.

Peter noticed something and he stepped into the site of the chapel. He stooped and picked up what looked like a lump of brass.

"See! I know what this was! Do you remember that I told you the other night about saving the chapel from fire last Easter? See, this is all that remains of one of the altar candlesticks.

"I remember how Anwennen had prized them, for they had come many leagues across the Great Water. Some Virgin Squaws in the chief village of the French had sent them for Father's chapel here."

Jacques knew that the Huron boy was speaking about nuns in Paris. He took the almost shapeless piece and looked closely. There was the outline of a cross still distinct in the middle of the melted brass.

Peter had turned away and now he led Jacques' steps to the northern end of the burnt village of Teanaostaye. He stopped before more gray ashes.

"Here is where my cabin stood." He examined the charred remains. "There are no bones here and I am hoping that my squaw mother may have escaped at the first alarm."

"Where would she have gone?" Jacques asked.

"When the alarm of an Iroquois attack is given by blowing on the conch shell, squaws and children flee to those forests." The Huron boy pointed to the dense woods that hid the northwestern horizon.

"There is the trail that leads to the fortified village of the Black-robes."

"You mean Fort St. Mary?"

"Yes; it is not many leagues away."

"Then we should be on our way. I am anxious to learn if Father Bressani and Father Gabriel Lalemant have arrived safely."

"And I am anxious to know if my squaw mother and Anwennen are safe at St. Mary's. It is good that we start now and leave these dead to the birds of the air."

The boys walked across the ashes that rose in clouds about their feet and when they reached the shade of the forest they paused to look back on the desolate "Guardian of the Beautiful Little River."

Blackened it lay in the sunlight, telling its mute story of surprise attack and massacre, but hiding the fate of those fortunate enough to escape Mohawk capture and death.

Peter, as they trudged along the well remembered trail, pointed out to Jacques the favorite hunting grounds of the village boys and the small stream where he had often fished with Father Daniel.

They were travelling down a trail when suddenly he grabbed Jacques' arm and drew him into the shelter of the trees.

"Some one comes along the trail," he whispered.

At first Jacques could hear nothing suspicious, but then he heard the snapping of a twig.

"Maybe it is a bear," he suggested.

"You have no sense. Bears make more noise." Wood-wise Peter corrected him.

The boys waited in concealment till they saw the approaching one was an old squaw.

Peter sprang out and the woman's eyes lighted with delight as the Huron boy ran to her.

They talked rapidly together and Peter led her to where Jacques still stood.

"This is my mother's squaw, Theresa, and she says my mother is safe in the strong village."

Peter's grandmother looked her surprise when Jacques addressed her in Huron.

"You are the French boy that the Blackrobes at the fortified village think was killed on the way back from the French villages on the Great River."

"I was not killed."

"Then the Squaw in Blue has had you in her care."

Jacques knew that this old Huron woman was referring to the Blessed Virgin.

"She does that always, my aunt," he rejoined.

"What happened to our village?" It was Peter who put the question.

His grandmother sat by the trail side and the two boys did likewise.

"It all happened so suddenly and unexpectedly that I hardly know where to begin."

"Did not the captains know the Iroquois were in our lands?"

"There were few captains in the village. Most of them were down with the canoes to the Great River and many braves were on a hunting expedition. A false rumor had come that bears were seen. It was an apostate Huron runner who brought the false report. This we learnt too late."

"Where was the Blackrobe?"

"Anwennen had come back from the fortified village of the French the afternoon before. He had had the chapel bell rung and he preached beautifully to us. Then he heard the confessions. For he had been away for two weeks at St. Mary's."

"We were crowded into the chapel at dawn, hearing Mass——"

"Did he have an altar boy?" Peter asked and Jacques thought he noticed a trace of jealousy in his tone.

"Of a surety. Charles, your cousin, was serving him."

"Charles has no sense. He does not know all the prayer answers. I should have been there."

"I am glad you were not," said his grandmother, "for Mass was not quite over when a boy came shouting, 'The enemy are at the palisades. The enemy are at the palisades!'

"All the braves in the chapel ran to their cabins for weapons and then ran to the palisades.

"Before Anwennen had finished his Mass prayers the chapel was overcrowded with catechumens, crying loudly for Saving Waters. Still in his vestments, Anwennen turned around and began to pour Saving Waters on their foreheads.

"I saw Charles holding the holy water in the gourd and still the crowd clamored for Saving Waters. Anwennen kept pouring it as fast as he could.

"Then he raised his voice and ordered us squaws to take our children and flee into the forests. I remember he said, 'It is five leagues to the fortified village of the Blackrobes. Go there in haste, aunts. The Blackrobes will take you in and the Iroquois will not attack the fortified village for they know there are French soldiers there and cannon. You will be safe.'

"A squaw cried, 'We will go, but you, Anwennen, come with us.'

"'Go, my good aunt,' he said, 'my place is here. Go now all of you,' and he shooed us out of the chapel as a squaw chases the village dogs from her kettle.

"I ran to our cabin. There was no one there and I could hear the Iroquois cries close to the southern palisades. There were many hundreds of our enemies. A boy came running by. His head was all bloody. 'The enemy have hurt me with a death stick,' he cried, and fell dead."

"Death sticks?" asked Jacques.

"He meant weapons like the French have," explained Peter.

"Oh, arquebuses."

"What could our few braves do with their bows and arrows

against these death sticks. I knew then that Teanaostaye was doomed. So when I came out of the cabin the death sticks of the Iroquois were to be heard on the southern side of the palisades.

"With other squaws I ran towards the center of the village where the chapel was. There was a greater crowd of squaws and children and I could see Anwennen still in his Mass vestments. They were white that day. He was still pouring Saving Waters on the heads of catechumens. Then again he would hear a confession and I could see his hand rise and fall as he said the Forgiving Sin prayers. He was always busy and he did not seem excited.

"He saw me and he said: 'Theresa, my good aunt, you belong on the woods' trail that leads to St. Mary's. Hurry your old legs along.'

"But I was looking for Charles, my daughter's child. He was nowhere to be seen. I knew that at my age the Iroquois would not take me captive. And with so many of my friends dead or soon to be dead, I was not of a mind to run and hide in the forests.

"Some one said that the enemy had made an opening in the southern palisades and they were starting to burn the cabins. I could smell that for the choking smoke was beginning to drift over the whole of the village.

"Now a wailing rose up. Word had come that the Iroquois were killing those in the forests and it was too late to leave Teanaostaye.

"A squaw came from the southern gate screaming, 'We are dead. We are dead. The enemy are swarming over the palisades. Fly. Fly.'

"Many let panic come into their hearts and they sought the northern gate in the palisades.

"Then I saw Charles. He had pushed his way till he stood beside Anwennen. The crowd around the Blackrobe was dense. Blackrobe stopped pouring Saving Waters on each head. There were too many. He dipped his handkerchief into the Holy Water and he scattered the drops over the heads of the pagan squaws and their papooses. Thus he poured Saving Waters on them.

"Suddenly a squaw screamed: 'The enemy are here.'

"I looked and there out of the smoke I saw coming a party of ten or more Iroquois. They were killing as they came. Two had death sticks and the others their tomahawks.

"The squaws grabbed their children and ran towards the northern gate. I was knocked down and many trampled on me. That was what saved my life, for as I lay there, the Iroquois took me for an old squaw already dead. I did not undeceive them. But out of the corner of my eye I saw Anwennen was standing alone before his chapel. He still had on his white chasuble and the vestment on his left arm. I do not know its name."

"Maniple," put in Jacques.

Peter's grandmother nodded and went on. "But I forgot the Blackrobe's vestments when I looked at his face. I had never seen a countenance like it. Anwennen's face seemed to shine like the sun coming over a ridge at early morning. He strode boldly towards the advancing Iroquois. They saw that he did not carry a weapon in his hands and they stopped. I saw a young brave raise his death stick till it pointed at the Blackrobe. But he did not make the death noise.

"When Anwennen had gone about fifteen feet from the entrance to his chapel and it seemed that he would walk right up to the enemy, the young Iroquois made his death stick speak. At once a crimson stain appeared on the left breast of the Blackrobe and it grew larger.

"Anwennen fell on one knee. He swayed for a few seconds. I distinctly heard him say, 'Jesus taitenr. Jesus taitenr.' (Jacques knew this meant, 'Jesus have mercy.') Then he toppled over.

"As if this was a signal, arrows and tomahawks sought him. He quivered once. Again I heard, 'Jesus taitenr.'

"Then Anwennen did not move and his vestments were not white any more, but all crimson."

"That was the proper color for a martyr of Jesus Christ," put in Jacques reverently.

The old squaw nodded her head in agreement and continued: "Now the enemy fell on this body like hungry wolves. They stripped off all the vestments and they chewed his finger tips and they cut and cut.

"I closed my eyes and said, 'Jesus taitenr' too, for I did not know when some brave would see that I was not dead and then I would quickly be dead.

"When I peeped again, I saw that the enemy were throwing bundles of lighted straw and flaming faggots into the chapel. It smoked and burst into flames so quickly. The heat came to me even where I lay so that I sweated mightily. But the smoke that hung over everything was my protection.

"I saw two of the Iroquois braves take up the body of Anwennen and they cast it into the fires of his church. The crackling flames welcomed it and the heat made the Iroquois draw back.

"The merciful smoke hid my old body and it was not seen. When the smoke was almost stifling me I crawled away from the great heat of the chapel and I kept saying, 'Anwennen, you are now with God. Help your good aunt to get away from Teanaostaye.' And he did, for under the cover of the smoke that hung everywhere and choked me mightily I managed to crawl unseen out of the village, through the small opening in the palisades that the boys used when the gates were shut."

"I know it," said Peter, "it is in the northern palisades about one hundred paces from the chapel."

"Once in the forest I fell asleep and it was a pain in my left arm that awoke me. Then I discovered that an arrow had passed through the flesh and I had never noticed it before. I put healing herbs on it and then I started for St. Mary's. Next day I got there.

"Your father's squaw was there, Peter, but many of Teanaostaye never got there. I heard a captain of our people say that 700 escaped from Teanaostaye and 700 more were killed or captured there. That is all that I, Theresa, know."

"What became of the Iroquois raiding party?" Jacques inquired.

"Who knows! They come when nobody expects them and they depart like the night at dawn."

"It must have been some of that raiding party that we saw returning to their Long Houses, when we hid in the ruined beaver house," said Peter, "if I had looked closer I would have recognized many of the captive squaws and children."

The Huron boy returned to the thought of his cousin, Charles. "Charles could never learn the words for serving Mass. I tried to teach him. He wanted to go down to the French villages with the flotilla of canoes. But his father said he was to stay and learn the Mass words."

Theresa put in. "Whether he learnt them or not, he has not been seen since the Iroquois came. The searchers never found his body."

"Then very likely he was taken captive and is now on his way to the Iroquois lands," suggested Peter.

Theresa got up and said to the boys, "I will go on my way to what is left of our Teanaostaye, but you two keep on the trail and go to the Strong Village. They will be glad to see you for they think you have been killed on the trail. So I heard in the Blackrobes' village."

Peter tried to persuade his grandmother to return with him.

"No; boy. Do as I say. I have some trinkets hidden in the forest near Teanaostaye and I will get them. You go on the trail. I have spoken."

So the two boys left the old squaw and resumed their journey.

Two hours later, when the sun was scorching overhead, both boys slid into the underbrush at the trail side. Peter's keen ears had heard a suspicious noise. As they lay hidden they saw a young brave coming openly down the trail ahead.

"If I was an Iroquois and had an arquebus, I would have a scalplock in a few moments," observed Jacques in a whisper, pointing his imaginary arquebus at the approaching figure.

"No; I know this brave. He is a Moose Hunter, a pagan of Teanaostaye. He was in the canoes to the French villages with us."

Peter stepped out into the middle of the trail and held up his right hand in the peace gesture.

The pagan Huron noticed the boy instantly and almost in one motion his hand had grasped an arrow from the quiver, slung over his shoulder, and had fitted it into his bow.

Peter shouted: "A friend. I come unarmed, O Moose Hunter. It is I, Peter of Teanaostaye."

Moose Hunter lowered his bow and arrow and motioned Peter to advance. Before he took a step, Peter told Jacques to follow him. As soon as the French boy came out of the brush, the bow was raised menacingly.

"He is also a friend," shouted Peter.

Moose Hunter cried as they came nearer: "The boys who were in the canoes and disappeared with Bernard!"

Briefly Peter told the Huron brave of their adventures.

"We heard you had been killed beyond the Algonquins' island." Here Moose Hunter added: "I wish I had!"

"Why, Moose Hunter?"

"I came back to Teanaostaye and what do I find. All my family are killed by the enemy. That is what happens to the Praying Indians."

"Had they all received Saving Waters?" asked Jacques.

"All but me. Now I live and they die. It is so with the French. I saw it all in their village on the high bluff of the Great River."

"What do you mean by these words that make no sense?" Jacques asked.

"My words do make sense, French boy. Your people have come to kill all us Indians."

"You speak with a split tongue."

"No; I do not. Listen, my nephews, and I will tell you all."

They were glad to rest by the trailside, while they listened to Moose Hunter pour out his dislike for the Christians.

"My people listen to discourses of the Blackrobes that charm them at first. But you are doubtlessly ignorant, my nephews, of how false these promises are. I have been to the French village on the rock above the Great River. I know everything about the Prayer of the Blackrobes. I do not speak without having had experience of it. Some years ago, you saw the Algonquins in such numbers that they were the terrors of the enemies. Now they are reduced to nothing; disease and wars and famine pursues them wherever they go. It is the Prayer that the Blackrobes teach that brought those misfortunes on them. That you may not doubt that what I say is true, I tell you that I went down to the French village on the rock this summer to see for myself what had been the result of the Prayer on Montagnais and the Algonquins who had received Saving Waters. I was shown a house full of one-eyed, lame, crippled and blind people. They were all fleshless skeletons and people who all carried death on their countenances. Such misfortunes are what happen to those who accept the Prayer. To be a Prayer Indian is to resign oneself to all those miseries. Besides that, one must expect to be no longer lucky either in fishing or hunting."

Jacques had heard more than enough of Moose Hunter's grievances. Now he broke in. "I know the cabin in Quebec that you saw. It is the hospital of the good Ursulines. I have been there. Of course, all those who come there are lame and blind and crippled and diseased. It is a Sick Cabin and the Indians who are well do not go to Sick Cabins. The Virgin Squaws spend their days nursing those sick. They are not obliged to do so. They come across the Great Water to do so. It is The Prayer, or their Faith, as we say, that makes them do so."

"You surely are the blind one," obstinately persisted Moose Hunter, "I saw the diseased Indians with my own eyes. I for one will never listen to the Blackrobes. Then I come back to my own lands and find all my people who follow The Prayer dead at the hands of our enemies."

Without another word he went along the trail.

When he was hidden by a bend in the trail, Peter said: "He is bitter because his family received Saving Waters and were all killed in Teanaostaye."

The two boys resumed their travels in silence.

Night was on them before they came in sight of Fort St. Mary, but they knew it was less than two leagues away and morning would bring them to the Fathers' village.

That last night on the trail Jacques fell asleep happy in the knowledge that on the morrow he would see again his beloved Father John Brebeuf.

Chapter Twelve

Fort St. Mary

ITH THE COMING of daylight Jacques and Peter saw that they were resting near the bank of a lake whose shore line was hardly less than a league around. As Jacques watched a canoe was paddled swiftly around the woody western point. He saw at once that the paddlers were two boys. Jacques warned Peter and both softly disappeared from sight as the canoe came nearer.

Then the watchers saw the two boys stop paddling and for the first time Jacques noticed that they were dressed in rough spun shirts and trousers and that they were not Hurons at all, but French boys. One of them he thought he recognized as Claude St. Leger, who had been at Our Lady of the Angels with him and had gone up to Huronia to be an interpreter.

Jacques was just about to reveal himself, when St. Leger called to his companion: "This is about the place Sleeping Bear said the best fishing was. Let us try, Jean."

The boy Jean already had his line out and a shout followed by a jerk and the triumphant landing of a flopping fish inside the canoe, confirmed Claude's estimation.

Jacques had been so eagerly watching the landing of the fish that he had neglected to stay concealed.

Jean it was who saw him.

"Look at that Indian, Claude," he said in French.

Jacques realized that his bronzed skin and breechclout had

deceived the boy. Now he showed himself, walking down to the shore, with his hand raised.

"That's no savage," said St. Leger, "that's—that's—well, I forget his name—no; I know him. That's Bourdon from Our Lady of the Angels whom Father Brebeuf expected."

Jacques was smiling and now he called in French, "You are right, Claude."

The two in the canoe had forgotten their fishing excursion in the excitement of meeting a fellow French boy and they paddled the canoe towards the shore.

Prudently stopping several lengths from the beach, Jean asked: "Are you alone?"

Jacques looked behind him, but Peter was not visible. "No; there is a Teanaostaye boy with me. We got lost from the flotilla and came on alone."

"O, Peter."

The young Huron now rose out of the bush.

Fishing was forgotten. St. Leger told the two ragged boys to get into the canoe. He explained: "Jean Bonin and I will paddle you to the Residence. Won't you be welcome!"

Jacques and Peter squatted in the bottom of the birchbark canoe and while Jacques answered a rapid fire of questions about the journey up and the news of Quebec friends, they were being paddled up the lake.

In answer to his questions, Jacques learnt that this body of water was Lake Isaragui—meaning "where the sunbeams dance on the waters." Soon they were at the mouth where it emptied into a small stream. Grass grew plentifully here but the two young interpreters knew where to look for the channel. Boldly they parted the tall green grasses and after a hundred yards of paddling in the maze of water weeds a channel appeared that soon widened into a small stream. Jacques was told that this was the River Wye which flowed before the Residence of St. Mary.

Now Hurons in canoes were met, who greeted the boys gravely and paddled by. After less than a league of progress the River Wye straightened out and ran almost north.

When the canoe was well within this stretch Jacques had his first view of Fort St. Mary. His destination in the northern wilderness stood on the eastern bank of the stream. A strong frame palisade stretched away to a far corner where a stone bastion stood out. Atop of this was a block house surmounted by a wooden cross. Many canoes of Hurons were now visible, most of them coming down the river from its mouth that flowed into a larger body of water.

"It's big!" exclaimed Jacques, "no Iroquois war party would dare to attack this fort."

"They have come near," said Claude St. Leger, "on several occasions. They sent their scouts, who were seen from the palisades at the time Teanaostaye was destroyed last July, but they did not attempt to attack."

"The wily Iroquois knew better." Jean Bonin grinned, "We have three cannons in the fort and the soldiers were itching to send a hot present to them."

"Maybe they will attack the next time," gloomily predicted St. Leger, "the Iroquois menace is getting worse and worse. The Hurons have very few villages still unburnt and more and more of the Hurons are living near the Residence."

Jacques now had a better view, as the canoe neared its landing place and he could make out the massive timbers in the palisades that surrounded the whole of the Blackrobes' village.

"This southern end is where the Huron Christians camp. There are many there now for last evening a party of over two hundred came in. See the smoke of their fires over there."

Jacques could see the thin blue columns that rose above the walls.

"Is that moat all around the front of the palisades?"

OLD FORT ST. MARY, 1639–1649

"Around the Fathers' part, yes; and two sides of the Huron section."

The canoe of the boys now was abreast of the southern end of the palisades. Beyond the fields of cultivated corn Jacques had a glimpse of a small cemetery with its many white crosses, row and row.

Now the canoe had come abreast of a wide ditch and he saw that it separated the Hurons' from the Fathers' parts of Fort St. Mary.

Up this in the midst of a number of laden canoes the boys paddled. They passed a side ditch that led under the water gate into the Huron village. Jacques could see several hundred Hurons moving about.

Then they were turning into another ditch on the opposite bank that led to a canoe landing beach.

St. Leger and Bonin leapt out and drew the canoe up. Jacques stepped out and stood close to the rough hewed timbers of the palisades. A sentry on the top watched the boys idly.

"That is the Fathers' Residence and the church is there." Jacques followed the direction of Jean's hand and could see beyond the spiked tops of the palisades a long wooden building with a tall stone chimney at one end, the slanting roof, pierced with five dormer windows and at the nearer end was the cross-surmounted roof of the church.

"Why I never expected to see such a building in the wild Huron lands! It's big enough to be in Quebec!"

"That's the Blackrobes' Long House, as the Indians call it," explained Claude, "it is always a cause of wonder to the Hurons, Christian and pagan, who come from leagues around to see it and the wonders within. Wait till you see them."

Peter had been silent for some time but his eyes had been scanning the features of all Hurons in sight. Now he shouted: "I see my father's squaw!" and he was plunging into the ditch and swimming across. On the other bank he started to run and Jacques saw him headed for a squaw who was bending over a fireplace on the plain.

"You come with us," ordered Claude St. Leger, "and we will find one of the Fathers."

"I want to find Father Brebeuf first."

"Then you will very likely find him in the Residence this time of the morning.

"Come," said Claude, "I will show you the way. You rack the canoe, Jean."

The sun-browned French boy, his only clothes his ragged breech clout, might easily have been taken for an Huron as he passed along.

Some French workmen were engaged in replacing a timber in the palisades that faced the ditch between the two parts of the fortified village and there, inspecting the work stood a tall blackrobed figure. Even at a distance Jacques' heart beat quickened as he recognized that figure. Like Peter at the sight of his mother, Jacques started to run forward. He shouted: "Father John Brebeuf! Oh, Father John!"

The missioner turned at the boyish voice, speaking excited French. Then Jacques had fallen at the priest's feet and was eagerly kissing his hand.

The tall Blackrobe looked down at the slim figure, blackened and scarred by innumerable encounters with the thorns of three hundred leagues of travel. A puzzled expression came into his face. That this strange boy was French, not savage, was evident in his upturned features.

"Don't you know me, my Father?" Father Brebeuf studied the sun-baked countenance. Then his face broke out into a smile of glad recognition.

"Of a surety I do now! You are Little Jacques. But—but where have you come from? Purgatory—Paradise?"

"Not yet, my Father."

"Then for once Father Bressani was misinformed. He and Father Gabriel told me sorrowfully on their arrival a fortnight ago that you had disappeared at a portage on the way up and they suspected that you had fallen at Iroquois hands, as at that time they came upon traces of the large war party that had taken Teanaostaye."

"We lost our main party at a portage," explained Jacques, "for Peter of Teanaostaye and I went hunting with Bernard. He got killed and we tried to find our party but could not.

"Peter thought he knew the trail across country and we—we dodged Iroquois and came that way. Did the package of letters for the Fathers, that I left in the canoe, come?" Jacques concluded anxiously.

Father Brebeuf nodded and he and Jacques passed within the enclosure. The boy felt he had stepped out of the wilderness and was back once more within Fort St. Louis at Quebec. He remembered that morning ages ago. It was with a start he realized it was only about three months ago; only last May, when he had fled Our Lady of the Angels and its dull school monotony to reach this destination.

Now he was actually within the enclosure of Fort St. Mary. Directly ahead of him was the long log and stone Residence of the Fathers. As he gazed in awe at its size he realized why he had heard that the Hurons and neighboring tribes came many leagues to look on its wonders.

Jacques had only a glimpse at the fort entrance. He saw some soldiers and workmen, all in buckskin, and then Father Brebeuf was saying: "Come, my little one, and pay your respects first of firsts, to our Good Master. Verily he hath given His angels charge over thee and they have guided and guarded your footsteps through many dangers to His little chapel in these wildernesses."

Jacques saw that Father Brebeuf was leading him directly to the chapel end of the Residence. Then the two stood at the threshold and Jacques recognized with delight in his eyes the familiar altar and the sentinel light on guard that told him the True Lord of these lands was present in His tiny tabernacled home.

He hesitated to enter the chapel, suddenly remembering his scant clothing. But his tall friend, sensing the boy's embarrassment, stooped to whisper reassuringly: "He understands all, my little one. Go and kneel before Him and tell Him you love Him and you thank Him. Now I am about to recite the Te Deum in thanksgiving."

Jacques dropped to his knees and buried his face in his hands. This sudden renewal of that homely chapel feeling, so different from all other places, had come over him and he prayed easily and fervently. He was at home again.

When he looked up he saw the tall figure of Father John Brebeuf, kneeling erect and rigid. Jacques thought his Blackrobe looked austere, till he caught a glimpse of the priest's face. It was aglow with love, as though the veil of earthly things was very thin and he was actually gazing on the features of a well beloved Friend.

Jacques felt a thrill of awe steal over him and he bowed his head again and prayed: "Dear Boy Jesus, make me good like Father Brebeuf."

When the two stood at the doorway, the Blackrobe whispered: "How does Little Jacques like this Home of our Lord in the wilderness?"

"It's—it's very comfortable," said Jacques fervently. His eye was caught by a painting that hung on the wall. "That's a beautiful picture of Our Lady. Where did they get it?"

"A good friend of the Huron Mission had these painted in Paris." Father Brebeuf pointed to two others, "The Last Judgement" and "The Boy Christ Among the Doctors." "Captain Daniel brought them in his ship to Quebec four summers ago. Then they were transported the long, long way to this Residence. The angels seemed to take a special interest in these paintings for the canoe that brought them to us never sighted an Iroquois nor encountered a real danger en route."

The mention of Captain Daniel's name reminded Jacques of that sailor and he told Father Brebeuf what Captain Daniel had said to him that afternoon on board his vessel.

"I'll remember the good captain's intentions in my Masses, but he has a better patron right now in his own family in his martyr brother."

The tall Blackrobe returned to the paintings. "Our Christians never tire of coming here to this church and gazing and gazing on the likeness of 'The Squaw in Blue,' as they designate Our Blessed Mother. Even the pagans have heard of this picture and only last week three captains and their families traveled a week coming to St. Mary's just to see this painting."

"Is this Our Lady's church?" Jacques asked.

"No; good St. Joseph is patron of the Huron Mission and so this church is dedicated to him and Our Lord's Foster Father takes us all under his powerful patronage.

"You might, my little one, whisper a wee prayer of thanksgiving to good St. Joseph. For when Father Bressani and Father Lalemant arrived and told me that you were thought dead, I decided to make a novena in honor of St. Joseph. It might interest you to know that that novena was finished only this morning."

Jacques promptly dropped to his knees and said three Hail Marys in thanksgiving to the Patron of this church.

When he stood up, he confided: "Now I know why I got here safely. No wonder the Iroquois could not see me."

Father John Brebeuf put his hand affectionately on the lad's shoulder.

"Little Jacques, it is evident that The Master has some special work for you on His Missions. But now that we have paid our respects to the Master of St. Mary's, let me take you to the Fathers."

That was a glad reunion when Father Gabriel Lalemant and Father Joseph Bressani sighted the boy with his gigantic Blackrobe guardian.

Jacques had to sit down there and then and retell his adventures.

After half an hour Father Brebeuf carried Jacques off to the store room in the residence. Here he met Brother Martin—'Little Martin', as the boy quickly understood everybody called him. And he was fitted out with buckskin breeches, leggings, a homespun shirt that felt rough on his shoulders, accustomed to all weather. Soft moccasins completed his civilized outfit.

When he came forth from the store room, Claude St. Leger and Jean Bonin with two strange boys were waiting for him.

Father Brebeuf introduced these two other boy interpreters as Guy La Touche and Nicholas Colivet.

Then he ordered: "Jacques is to have a bed in your quarters. You, Jean, see what he needs and get it from Little Martin."

As the boys trooped off, Father Brebeuf halted them.

"A minute, please. Here comes Father Superior from the Hurons' village. He will wish to meet our newest recruit."

Jacques looked up as a missioner of middle age, with his hair and beard beginning to turn gray, approached. He looked austere, but a kindly light lit his eyes as he paused.

"Father Ragueneau," said Father Brebeuf, "this is Jacques, our prodigal lamb who was lost and has been found."

"Rather, came home all by himself," said Father Paul Ragueneau, as Jacques dropped on one knee and kissed the Superior's hand.

Father Ragueneau patted the boy's head.

"Father Bressani has been telling me all about you. And I noticed that your friend, Father John, has anticipated my thought and has had you outfitted. But," Father Ragueneau laid his hand on his stomach, "has any one thought to outfit you within here? Our new arrivals always are hungry."

Father Brebeuf cried: "A thousand pardons, Jacques!

"You are right, Father Paul. I forgot that this ward of mine has been living on roots and——"

"Not roots alone, my Father," put in Jacques, "for Peter—the boy from Teanaostaye, who came with me, found a cache of food and we helped ourselves."

"I still claim that this new recruit looks half starved.

"Father John, have the boys take Jacques at once to our cook. He will know the correct thing to do."

When Father Superior had departed, Father Brebeuf said: "Boys, do as Father Paul has directed and you might wear a half starved expression on your own faces. Our cook is notoriously soft-hearted."

"Come on, Jacques," chorused the interpreters.

Father Brebeuf detained Jacques. "When you have eaten your fill, come back to me. You will find me in the Residence. I need an interpreter this morning in the Huron village."

Delightedly Jacques went off with the other boys.

Chapter Thirteen

Kettle Hound

N HOUR LATER, Jacques, his hunger appeased, was standing at the doorway of the Residence of St. Mary's. A nondescript brownish yellow dog came around the corner and dropped down in a sunny spot. His tail thumped a friendly greeting to the boy.

Jacques walked over and stooping, petted the dog's head. As he did so, a shadow fell on him and he heard Father Brebeuf saying: "So you have already made friends with my honest hound, Kettle Hound."

"Is that his name?"

"Yes; and he has quite an evil reputation among the Huron squaws for being the cleverest dog thief in St. Mary's. He has been known to snatch a piece of meat from under the hands of a squaw tending her fire.

"Come here, Kettle Hound."

At the command the dog stretched luxuriously and yawned in the Blackrobe's face. Then he attended to an impertinent flea and finally he came slowly to his master.

"See here," Father Brebeuf showed Jacques a long scar, recently healed, that extended along the dog's right flank.

"I almost lost my Kettle Hound. He made a sad mistake last month. He attempted to steal meat from the kettle of a strange Huron visitor to the Residence and the brave scarred him with his knife.

"Kettle Hound, Kettle Hound, when will you stop your thieving. You know well enough that the cook will always give you meat, if you were not so lazy about coming around to the kitchen door."

Father Brebeuf felt the long scar.

"Kettle Hound is clever enough. Do you know what he did when he got this almost fatal wound?"

"No; my Father."

"He dragged himself to the hospital and good Christian, our surgeon there, attended to it. Then every morning Kettle Hound presented himself for attention. He would come into the hospital room and lie quietly in the corner till Christian was free to treat him. That kept up for a whole week. After that Master Convalescent here decided that he was strong enough to resume his evil ways."

Father Brebeuf gave Kettle Hound a pat and said: "Jacques, I could tell you many a tale of 'Echon's dog', as the Hurons call him, but you will hear them soon enough. Now as we walk to the hill over there, let me find out what kind of an interpreter I have acquired this morning."

Immediately Father Brebeuf switched from French into Huron and put Jacques through a stiff language examination.

While they talked they had walked out of the northern gate of the fort and were ascending a rather steep hill. Coming to the summit, Father Brebeuf commended Jacques: "My little one, some of the boys come to us and we have to wait a whole year till they are of use as interpreters. But you come so fluent in our natives' language that you can be of use at once."

Jacques blushed at the praise and stammered out, "My Father, do you not remember that afternoon four—five years ago, when I was a little chap and you ordered me to learn the Huron language?"

"I will never forget that afternoon, my little one, for we became friends then."

166

"Well, I began then."

"Indeed you did and now you are capable of working in this section of the Lord's Vineyard."

The Blackrobe and the boy had come through the trees and now stood on the top of the hill. A cooling breeze and a glorious view met them. Sweeping down from their feet were the green tops of the trees and beyond Jacques looked north and westward over a large expanse of blue water. He could see where the little river that flowed past St. Mary's emptied into this lake through a narrow blue ribbon laid across the green marsh grass.

Half a dozen canoes were being paddled into the mouth of the Wye. Father Brebeuf noticed them and said: "Here come some more pilgrims. Last year over three thousand Indians came to the Residence. This year with our Iroquois cousins getting bolder and bolder, I think we shall entertain more."

"Where do they come from, Father John?"

"Mostly from our neighboring Christian Huron villages, but pagan parties from the surrounding tribes occasionally visit St. Mary's.

"Most of them come to see the wonders of the Strong Village of the Blackrobes, as they call the Residence, but many remain to beg the Sacrament of Baptism.

"So you see, little one, good St. Joseph and Our Lady use these poor creatures' curiosity to give them the great grace of Faith. After they have seen the wonders of the Church and our Christian Hurons at the services, grace works in their souls and we have other converts. You will see. But now," Father Brebeuf had turned till he was facing the northwest, "let me make you acquainted with the geography of this New World into which your Guardian Angel has led you so safely.

"First, this country of the Hurons lies between 44 and 45 degrees of latitude. You understand?"

"We had that at Our Lady of Angels, my Father."

"Good. And the longitude is about an hour more to the west than Quebec's. That is, when it is about eleven o'clock here, as it is now, back in Quebec it is almost noon.

"This lake that you see is really a bay that pours into the Fresh Water Sea (Lake Huron), which is nearly 400 leagues in circumference. To the west of us lies the Tobacco Nation. These peoples are about twelve leagues distant. Our Father Charles Garnier is laboring there now.

"To the south and a little towards the west are the Neutral Nation. Their nearest villages are about thirty leagues distant. I spent one winter there eight years ago with Father Chaumonet. In the lands of these people is a wild river that flows through a great gorge. I followed it up and I saw the most majestic sight I shall ever witness this side of heaven. There, the waters of some mighty lakes pour over a vast circular cliff. The Neutrals call this falls Niagara.

"It was winter time when I stood there with my companion. The snow and ice glistened with billions of diamonds. I thought of all this beauty of the power of God lost in the wilderness. If the people in France and Europe knew there was such a magnificent sight in the world they would come in droves and brave dangers just for one view."

"Maybe some day many white people will see it," said Jacques.

"Maybe, but it will be years after you and I have gone to our heavenly home.

"But I was telling you some local geography. South of these Neutrals——"

"Pardon, my Father, but why do you call them Neutrals?" interrupted Jacques.

"Because they refuse to take part in the warfare between our Hurons and the Iroquois Nations.

"South of these Neutrals is another Fresh Water Sea, called Erie. It is the waters of this inland sea that hurl themselves over that mightiest of waterfalls, pour through the gorgelike river and empty into the third Fresh Water Sea—Ontario. And its waters make up the volume of our familiar St. Lawrence River which empties eventually into the Atlantic Ocean. Did you ever see the Atlantic, Jacques?"

"No, my Father. The largest body of water I ever saw was Lake St. Peter in the St. Lawrence. When it is clear weather you can see both shores."

Father John Brebeuf was now facing north. "There are left the tribes in this direction. These are Algonquin stock. They do not till the soil, but live solely by hunting and fishing. They roam as far as the Northern Sea, which they tell us is more than 300 leagues distant. None of our Fathers have been among these more northern tribes yet. But we hope to go soon.

"Now to come nearer home, our Hurons have most of their villages within a radius of fifteen leagues from the Residence. Over there to the northwest, near the shores of Penetanguishene Bay stood Ihonatiria, the first Huron village where I was over twenty years ago, when I first laid eyes on this blessed land. Good Father Anne de Noue, was my companion——"

Jacques interrupted: "Coming up we stopped for a night's camp on the site where he froze to death."

"So Father Gabriel was telling me. Happy Father de Noue. May he pray us all safely Home!"

Father Brebeuf resumed:

"Now to the south on the shores of Nottawasaga Bay is the village of Ossossane. Swinging around more to the south and east of us stood Teanaostaye or St. Joseph's. That is, it stood till a few weeks ago when the Iroquois surprised the palisades. Our blessed Father Daniel died gloriously there. But I am forgetting that you have been there and know that."

Father Brebeuf had turned till he was facing east.

"Over there, on that green pined ridge you see, are my missions of St. Louis and a league to the northeast, St. Ignatius. Soon I will take you there. This is at present my portion of the Lord's Vineyard. The time is so short and I do wish to cultivate it while I may."

Jacques looked up, for Father John Brebeuf had become silent. He saw at once that the tall Blackrobe had completely forgotten his presence. His eyes were fixed on the hidden villages of St. Ignatius and St. Louis. Father Brebeuf stretched his arms out in a gesture of offering and his face glowed as one who saw sights of delight hidden to mortal eye.

It was Kettle Hound, returned from an exploratory visit to some neighboring grass who interrupted. Unceremoniously he jumped against his master's knee and demanded attention.

Father Brebeuf regretfully dropped his gaze and his hand rested on the yellowish brown head of his dog.

"So, my Kettle Hound, you come back to tell me that the rabbit was too fast for you again. Dogs that would chase and catch fleet-footed rabbits must mortify their appetites and not steal so much from the dining pots. Is that not so, my honest friend?"

A wag of the tail seemed to affirm the master's words.

"So, my Jacques, I have taken you up on a high hill and shown you the kingdoms of this Huron world."

Jacques put in dryly. "My Father is forgetting who did that to the Lord. You were not comparing yourself to that tempter were you?"

Laughed Father Brebeuf, "No, I am afraid my comparison was not apt after all.

"Now it is about time that we descend to the Residence and let you get better acquainted with our good people."

Jacques had let his eyes drop to take in the Indian village that was adjacent to the fortified village of the Blackrobes. He saw that it was filled with Hurons.

"There are many more Hurons here than I thought. Why is that, my Father?"

"Besides our regular pilgrims who come and go, we have at present several hundred refugees from Teanaostaye. The long house you see near the eastern palisade of the village is our hospital. It is crowded to the door with the sick and wounded.

"And there to the north where the tiny white crosses are is our God's Acre. There is a whole new row planted since the Iroquois took Teanaostaye."

Father Brebeuf pointed. "Jacques, do you see that small cross apart from the first row—there in the northeastern corner of the cemetery? It is the grave of a little boy. His parents were pagans and he would have died a pagan only Father Anthony Daniel found him very ill and persuaded the parents to bring him to the hospital here. The little boy did not get any better. I saw him in the hospital and he called to me. When I stopped over him, he asked me to make him a Praying Indian. I instructed him and in baptizing him gave him my own name. Little John lived two days more. Then he flew up to our Home. We buried him in consecrated ground. His pagan parents came to me and begged permission to bury alongside Little John his favorite dog, who had died of grief the day after the boy.

"The Fathers consulted together and permission was granted. So there is a little dog laid at Little John's feet.

"And I think," Father Brebeuf concluded as he looked down at the impatient Kettle Hound, "that another thieving dog will die of starvation and have to be buried soon if we do not return to dine. Is that not so, my Kettle Hound?"

An affirmative wagging of the tail was Kettle Hound's response.

As Father Brebeuf and Jacques walked back to the Residence the Blackrobe was saying: "Your friend Peter of Teanaostaye tried to teach my dog to say his Grace last summer, when I was with Father Daniel at Teanaostaye."

"How was that?"

"Well, we always say the Benedicite before meals."

"That is the Latin Prayer we boys said at Our Lady of the Angels, my Father."

"Excellent. Well, this time some of blessed Father Anthony's altar boys saw Kettle Hound begging me for food and when I gave it to him, one reminded me that Kettle Hound did not say his Benedicite.

"Promptly Peter said: 'Nama irinisionakhi attimoukhi,' which you might translate freely, 'The dog has no mind. He does not say his Benedicite. It is only for men to say that.'"

"That was the correct answer," observed Jacques, "and that reminds me, my Father, that I have not seen Peter since we reached the Residence this morning."

"Do not worry about that elderly papoose. He is with his mother and family in the Hurons' section of the fort. We will meet him this afternoon.

"But to conclude, after that I taught my smart dog to say his Grace after his own fashion. Look."

Father Brebeuf stopped and commanded: "Kettle Hound, if you wish to eat, say your Grace now."

Immediately the dog sat back on his haunches and bent his head reverently over his paws, one bright eye, however, was fixed on the pocket of his master's cassock.

Father Brebeuf withdrew his hand and gave the dog a bone.

"I brought this along in case Kettle Hound did not find any Huron kettle handy to steal from."

Kettle Hound wagged his tail and let this observation on his virtue pass.

"All right, Kettle Hound, but some day you may be too smart and a squaw may hurl an angry weapon at you and catch you. If that day comes, remember I warned you."

But Kettle Hound bounded away unalarmed at his master's warning.

When the two, priest and boy, had entered the fort gate, Father Brebeuf said: "Take a good look at the Residence. It is the largest building you will see this side of Quebec."

Jacques gazed at the wooden structure and then he asked: "Who built that?"

"A blessed martyr of God, Father Isaac Jogues. He was in charge of the workmen here in '39 and I remember him telling me that the Residence was 175 feet long and about 90 in width.

"It was started in '39 and when Father Isaac went down to Quebec the summer of '42 one of his commissions was to procure some simple furnishings for this Residence. As you will recall he was captured on his return voyage and never saw St. Mary's again. Though I do believe his blessed spirit is with us, for sometimes I feel Father Isaac so near that it is a comfort and a strength.

"You will sleep tonight in a room that he built, see if he comes to tuck you in. Do you remember him, Jacques?"

"Yes, indeed. I have never forgotten that time he came when I was with you after my own father's funeral, and you told me to kneel down and ask his blessing. I always remember the sweet feeling I had when I kissed his mangled hands."

"You fortunate boy! You had the high privilege of receiving the actual blessing of one of God's white-robed martyrs."

Jacques looked up into Father John Brebeuf's face and said simply, "And, maybe, of another martyr too."

It seemed almost in a reverent whisper that the tall Blackrobe at his side replied: "Yes; He may yet overlook my many failures to respond to all the graces He has given me. His Holy Will be ever done!"

When they reached the Residence, Jacques had his first opportunity of examining the interior. He found that, as he entered the main door, there were two large rooms, where the new Christians received religious instructions. In the room to the right he heard Father Ragueneau teaching the Hail Mary in Huron to a group of squaws and their singsong responses.

Beyond these instruction rooms were the quarters of the workmen and soldiers. In a room off this was the room where the boy interpreters had their cots and Jacques was delighted to see that his cot had been placed there.

Then came the refectory and kitchen. Across from these rooms was the chapel and at the other end were the Fathers' own quarters, divided into little cells by skin partitions.

When Jacques noticed this arrangement he inquired and learnt from Jean that only four Fathers were at the Residence at present. All the other Blackrobes were at their various mission stations.

At certain times of the year, especially after the labors of the winter and summer, the Blackrobes would all meet here and have their Spiritual Exercises in common.

Jean continued: "Last month most of the Fathers were here and Father Anthony Daniel went back to Teanaostaye only two days before he was martyred."

"Where did he stay?" asked Jacques.

Jean pointed to the last cell and when he was alone Jacques went to this cell and kneeling down made this secret prayer. "Dear Father Anthony, I never met you personally, but from your place in Heaven please help me to be a good boy always and aid me to help these Fathers."

Then Jacques heard a bell ringing and he suspected it was dinner time. He felt sure of this when Kettle Hound dashed in at the doorway and placed himself expectantly in the corner of the refectory.

Jacques saw that St. Leger and Jean were to wait on table. He hesitated at the doorway, not knowing what duties were expected of him, but Father Ragueneau, the grave Superior, coming in, noticed his hesitancy and whispered: "Jacques, you are to sit there today, below Brother Martin with Guy and Nicholas."

The Brother, short of stature, smiled a welcome when Jacques approached. The Grace was said in Latin and Jacques felt proud to be able to give the correct responses with the others.

The community ate in silence, while Eustache Lambert, one of the donnés, read from a Life of St. Francis Xavier.

That morning a haunch of venison had been given to the Black-robes by some newly arrived Hurons and when it was served with roast corn, Jacques ate heartily of this, the first really cooked meal he had eaten in almost two months.

His eyes wandered up to the Fathers' end of the table. There sat Fathers Ragueneau and Brebeuf, Bressani and youthful Gabriel Lalemant. St. Leger was serving them.

Then Jacques noticed that Kettle Hound had stationed himself, sitting on his haunches, close to Father Brebeuf's chair. As Jacques watched, the dog poked his nose impatiently into Father Brebeuf's knee. He smiled as he saw his Blackrobe quietly reach down and press a piece of meat into Kettle Hound's waiting mouth.

Later in the meal he was pleased to find Kettle Hound by his chair. The dog accepted the bone that Jacques contributed and retired to a corner to finish it.

When the dinner was over Jacques followed the community across to the little chapel. The Fathers and a few of the donnés got within the room. Jacques knelt with the rest on the floor of the corridor to make his after-dinner visit.

Little Martin pressed Jacques' arm when the community rose from their knees.

"Jacques, come with me. Father Brebeuf has asked me to make you familiar with our farm."

"Gladly, Brother Martin," the boy acquiesced.

In the northern section of the palisade enclosure were a few sheds and some planted fields.

"Did you like that milk you had to drink at dinner, Jacques?"

"Indeed yes, Brother. I had almost forgotten how milk tasted."

"Then meet Evangeline and Elizabeth who gave it to you."

Near the shed stood two brown and white spotted cows. They mooed at sight of the Brother.

"This is our milk and butter and cheese supply. If Evangeline and Elizabeth could talk they would have a tale to tell you, Jacques, of their adventures, when I brought them up from Three Rivers four years ago."

Jacques looked at the heavy set animals and then he exclaimed in amazement. "But, Brother, how in the world did you ever get Evangeline and Elizabeth from Three Rivers to these Huron missions? Either one would swamp a canoe!"

"Oh, they were small calves with large voices then. I could carry them one under each arm. They were tied down in the canoe like captives of the Iroquois and they expressed their dislike of the indignity practically every league of the voyage. At evening I led them up and down the encampment for exercise. But they did not like our camp sites either and it is a wonder that some prowling war parties did not hear their protests and attack us.

"Of course, at the portages they walked and stumbled and when they fell exhausted, I carried these babies like sheep on my shoulders. Ah, but I couldn't do that now, old ladies!"

Little Martin gave Evangeline and Elizabeth resounding smacks on their flanks.

Jacques showed his interest in the hogs in their pen and the chickens that were so tame that they got under foot all the time. The Brother had a name for each of the fowl and swine and Jacques learnt that their ancestors, like the cows, had been transported up from the settlements on the distant St. Lawrence.

Jacques heard his name called and there at the doorway of the Residence stood the tall blackrobed figure of his guardian. When he came running up, Father Brebeuf said: "I suppose Little Martin has introduced you to all our animal brothers and sisters. He hates to have any of them killed for the table.

"I am going to the hospital now and was thinking——"

"You know I would certainly care to go with you anywhere, my Father."

"I suspected that. My orderly should get acquainted with our catechumens and excellent Christians as soon as possible."

As the two crossed the small bridge that had been flung over the canal between the Fathers' and the Hurons' sections of Fort St. Mary, Father Brebeuf continued: "While we are here and any future time we are away from the French, speak only in Huron. Remember, not many French words while in the presence of the Hurons."

Jacques had not realized there were so many Indians in their village till he entered the gateway. Before him was a large plain enclosed by palisades that formed a rough triangle. One blunt side paralleled the River Wye. There were three wooden buildings within the palisades. The building to the east, with its front facing west was obviously the church. Along the southern side was a slanting roofed structure, resembling the Residence, but not quite as long. This Jacques rightly judged was the hospital, to which Father Brebeuf had alluded. Another small building was in the southwestern part of the enclosure.

"What is that building for, my Father?"

"That is the place where the Fathers instruct the Hurons or others who come inquiring about the Prayer—as they call our Holy Faith. As these are yet pagans, they cannot attend the services in the church, so we answer their questions in that building."

The open plain in front of Jacques was literally dotted with the small Huron cabins of the Teanaostaye refugees. These cabins were constructed of poles covered with birchbark strips. Before many of these wigwams were open fireplaces with the thin spirals of smoke ascending into the clear sky.

Squaws chattered to squaws; children and dogs ran at will in and out of everybody's way. Only a few braves were in evidence. The rest were beyond the palisades, hunting or fishing in the abundant waters of the River Wye or the bay beyond.

As soon as Father Brebeuf was sighted, the cry of Echon! Echon! arose and Jacques could almost see the name leap from lips to lips. The boy walked silently at the tall Blackrobe's side observing everything. Especially he noticed the healing burns on the refugees that told of recent Iroquois torture and escape.

He listened while squaw after squaw came up and engaged the Blackrobe in earnest conversation. Echon always had a word of counsel for each supplicant.

It must have been twenty minutes before the Blackrobe and his escort reached the hospital building.

There stood a Petun brave and two squaws were laughing at him. The Blackrobe asked one of the squaws: "What is wrong with this brave, Anne?"

"This brave has no sense, Echon."

"Possibly he takes after you, Anne," observed the Blackrobe dryly, "but why do you say that?"

"This brave without sense comes from over there," she indicated the general direction of the distant Blue Mountains, "and he sees for the first time the cabins that the French build. We found him walking around and around this cabin of the Sick. He could not find a way to get in and when we showed him the door, he was afraid to go through it."

"Is it true that you have never seen a Frenchman's cabin before, Petun man?" asked Father Brebeuf.

"It is true, Echon."

"Well, this door—see, I open it with my hand." Father Brebeuf turned the knob. "Now come in with me."

"It is no trap, Echon?"

"It is no trap, Petun man."

"I will trust Echon. All the squaws have split tongues. I wish to see my brother."

Father Brebeuf waved the grinning squaws aside, saying "Do not make fun of this stranger, my aunts."

Trustingly the Petun followed Echon through the traplike doorway. Jacques brought up the rear and he found himself in a long oblong room. On the floor in no particular order lay the sick and wounded.

Father Brebeuf had inquired of a tall young donné, whom he recognized as Christian, where this Petun's brother lay.

Christian pointed to the northeastern corner and Jacques saw the Petun squat alongside a younger brave, who lay on a skin.

Jacques had never heard such a babel of sounds as arose from the patients and their visitors.

Finally he asked Christian why there was so much noise allowed.

"Try to stop it! I asked that same question," replied the young donné with an engaging grin, "when I came to St. Mary's four years ago.

"I said to a bull throated brave, 'My friend, I pray you speak a little lower.' Do you know, Jacques, what reply I received?"

"No."

"The brave said, 'You have no sense, Frenchman. There is a bird.' He pointed to one of our roosters who was crowing lustily, 'that talks louder than I do and you say nothing to him.'"

Jacques laughed heartily at the Indian's comparison.

While he was conversing with Jacques Christian had been bleeding a fever patient. He was about to move away, when a young Huron boy stopped him and made a request.

"What is that?" Jacques heard the donné ask.

Jacques saw Christian go to a small table and open a box. He handed the boy two dried prunes and then he beckoned Jacques to come over.

"Why did you give him the prunes, Christian?"

"That small Huron wanted two prunes to cure his brother's sore foot."

"What!"

"You see these pagans have noticed the care that the Fathers take of the sick and many of them believe all they have to do to cure any of their ills is to obtain something from us."

"Well," said Jacques roguishly, "that pagan boy picked out a nice cure for his brother's sore foot. I believe, Christian, that I have two sore feet."

The donné shook his head. "Consult Father Brebeuf for your ills. You get none of the patients' prunes from me."

The mention of his guardian's name reminded Jacques to look around for that Blackrobe.

There was Echon, standing shoulders above the crowd of Hurons near the doorway. Catching Jacques' eye Father Brebeuf beckoned him to come.

"I have finished my morning's business here," said the Blackrobe as the two walked towards the eastern side of the Indian village where the church stood.

As they approached, Jacques noted the rows of tiny white crosses either side of the building.

"Many good friends of mine lie here," said Father Brebeuf as they came into the "God's Acre." "Or, rather, their bodies do. Their souls, I trust, are happy in their Father's Mansions.

"These, Jacques, are the only ones I am so sure of."

"I do not understand, my Father."

"I mean, my little one, these who lie here are safely out of this world's temptations. Peace and reward and joy are their portion for ever and ever."

Father John Brebeuf seemed momentarily to have forgotten the youthfulness of his listener as he went on: "Sometimes when I feel weak I come here and somehow the proximity of these, safe in God's Acre, acts as a tonic and I am strengthened for the rest of the way.

"Now let me tell you about some of these here who await Gabriel's horn."

Father Brebeuf had led Jacques among the rows and now he paused before a small white cross.

"My little one, I want to tell you the story of the two who rest in this grave. Back in '42 a Christian squaw of the village of the

Immaculate Conception went to visit some pagan relatives at a distance of twelve leagues from her home. She felt herself attacked by an illness, that did not seem dangerous. I know not whence the presentiment of her approaching death came to her, but at all events, she set out on her return journey.

"'I leave you,' she told her relatives, 'because I wish to die among the Praying Hurons and my brothers who bring the Prayer to us. They will assist me at my death and I desire that they attend to my burial. I shall rise again with them and I do not wish my bones to be mingled with those who will be nothing to me in eternity.' She was referring to the Hurons' Feast of the Dead—a horrible sight. I know for I witnessed it some years ago. It is held every ten years when the bones of all the pagan Hurons who have died within the past decade are reinterred in one pit. So this squaw got into her canoe and paddled back to the Residence. God alone guides the steps of His elect and holds their hearts in His Hands. This good Christian from her Baptism had been one of the pearls of this infant Church, but the nearer death approached, the more precious she became.

"'If I feared death, Echon,' she said to me once, 'I would not think of believing in a Paradise that awaits me. There is nothing on earth that keeps back my heart.' Her patience was heroic throughout her long and painful illness and she displayed a courage worthy of a Christian.

"She could hardly move when I brought her Viaticum, but her faith gave her strength. She struggled up to her knees and in a dying voice exclaimed, 'Here, my Captain, I firmly believe that it is You Who come to visit me. I die in the Prayer and in sorrow for having lived so many moons without knowing You.'

"On the following day she fell into a coma, and had neither eyes nor ears, except when some Christian squaws who were attending her, spoke of God. Then she would revive and even in her death agony, took pleasure in adoring Him whom she now enjoys.

"She had been expecting a baby for five months and that was her sole regret that death would deprive her child of the happiness she prayed for it. We made a vow in honor of that good mother, St. Anne, that she would obtain from her Grandson Baptism for this little unborn one. God was pleased to grant our prayers at the very moment when we had lost all hope. The little mite came into the world and lived only a few minutes, but still long enough to make him live for ever in Heaven. I named him Ignatius. The mother soon followed her little angel.

"It was then we saw ourselves compelled to consecrate this cemetery near the church, which was to receive as its first seed so blessed a deposit. So we buried the two; one in the arms of the other, in this first grave. And that is my story. Or, rather, I have finished, as my Hurons say."

They had turned away when Jacques asked: "My Father, where is that little John and his dog buried?"

"At the end of that first row over there." The tall Blackrobe's hand pointed. Then his hand swept in a wide half circle around the cemetery.

"You see, Jacques, we have laid at rest many others since. I like to walk here among these quiet rows and think of these Citizens of Heaven. If you are troubled with the trifles of today, do as I have fallen into the habit of doing, walk apart and say your rosary here and you will feel strength for the rest of the way.

"This is a little secret that I am sharing with my interpreter. But of all the graves here, those of the tiny 'Thieves of Paradise'; those who stayed in this world only long enough to have Saving Waters fall on their brows, these are my favorites, the Holy Innocents of Huronia. To them I go when I want special favors and they are prompt to lend their intercession."

Jacques' eye had been roving about for something. Father Brebeuf caught his look and said: "Is it for some friend you are seeking?"

"Yes, my Father, in a way. I was looking for the grave of good Father Anthony Daniel."

Father Brebeuf's eyes sparkled and there was a ring in his voice as he said: "Then you will be disappointed in your search, my little one. For that ardent flame was consumed entirely for God. His blessed body, on which the pagans tried to inflict their cruelest mutilations, was finally thrown into his burning chapel at Teanaostaye and though Brother Martin and the donnés and soldiers and many of the Hurons went over the ruins with the eyes of hawks, not one tiny part of his precious bones were they able to recover. The Master desired a holocaust and Father Anthony gave it. So, much as we would desire them, we have no relics of that Good Shepherd who gave his life for his flock last July.

"Tonight you will sleep in the room that one martyr built, Father Isaac Jogues, and that another martyr, Father Anthony Daniel, occupied while he was making his Spiritual Exercises at the Residence last June just before he went to his flaming reward. You are a fortunate boy."

Father Brebeuf said no more. His gaze was far away and the boy at his side felt a hesitancy to speak. Instead he pondered over Father Brebeuf's last words as they walked silently back to the Residence.

With the coming of darkness Jacques felt drowsiness taking possession of him and he made no objections when Father Ragueneau beckoned to him after supper.

"I saw you yawning prodigiously over your meal. That means only one thing. Father John showed you where you sleep?"

Jacques nodded, suppressing another incipient yawn.

"Go to bed now and see how it feels to sleep on a cot again. After a good night's rest, we will see if you are able to serve Mass in the morning. Do you think you have forgotten?"

"No; no, Father Superior."

"Excellent. Drop into the chapel and say short night prayers and good night to Our Blessed Lord."

Jacques gladly availed himself of this permission to retire early. In the dimly lit chapel he said his favorite prayer, "Little Master, I thank You for keeping me from morning till now. Keep me the rest of the way. Forget my faults and help me to overcome them. I give You my actions. Give me Your Grace to perform them well. And good night. Amen."

Once lying on the rough cot with a real blanket over his shoulder, Jacques felt a delicious sensation stealing over him—he was in Huronia at last—work to be done with his beloved Blackrobe—fishing—hunting—adventures ahead—vague Iroquois dangers too—but they would never attack strong St. Mary's. The boy's thoughts returned to Father Brebeuf's words of the afternoon, "the martyr Isaac Jogues built this room; the martyr, Anthony Daniel, slept in this room. It is good to be where Martyrs of Captain Christ had been—it is safe to know they would aid—it is delightful to sleep here near the holy men of God. And God Himself is right across the corridor.

"Good night, good Guardian Angel," Jacques muttered sleepily, "Good night, Little Master, I thank You for keeping me from morning to now. . . ."

Then he was in deep slumber.

Chapter Fourteen
After Fish

ACQUES BOURDON'S first weeks at St. Mary's were filled with delightful new experiences. Father Ragueneau, the Superior, had said: "My child, Father Brebeuf informs me that you have no need to study the Huron language. This is excellent. We will find plenty of use for your tongue, but these next few weeks rest up and gain back your strength for the work to come. Eat plenty. Sleep plenty and then we will find you plenty of work for the Good God."

The kindly Father Superior had evidently given directions to the boy interpreters, for Claude St. Leger, Nicholas Colivet, Jean Bonin and Guy La Touche sought out Jacques on a sunny morning and Claude said: "You know that other day when Jean and I were fishing, we caught only you and that Peter. Today we have off to fish again. Do you wish to come along?"

"If Father Brebeuf does not need me," objected Jacques. The prospect of a day's fishing delighted him.

Just then the tall Blackrobe with the inevitable Kettle Hound at his heels came up. When he heard of the proposed fishing excursion he gave his hearty approval.

"By all means go, Jacques. It will give you an opportunity of getting acquainted with your fellow noise-makers. I wish I could send Kettle Hound along," added Father Brebeuf, smiling down at his dog.

"We don't want him," chorused the boys.

"A lot of fish we would catch with that thief along," said Claude and Nicholas.

"You see, my honest hound," Father Brebeuf pretended to address his dog, "what it is to bear a black reputation."

But Kettle Hound's wagging tail seemed to be saying "I don't care much for fish, my master."

The five boys descended on Little Martin and that Brother gladly put up a lunch for them. His parting shot was, "There will be peace in the Residence today."

The boys sought the landing beach between the Residence and the Hurons' village. Here Jacques learnt that the young interpreters had their own birchbark canoe. It was the same one in which St. Leger and Bonin had picked him up the first day. But this morning a larger canoe was selected and they pushed off.

Claude suggested: "Let us try the fishing in the bay today. A Huron brave was telling me yesterday about a new fishing ground."

This suggestion was acceptable and when they floated on the River Wye the canoe's bow was turned away from Lake Isaragui and paddled towards the mouth of the river.

"There's Father Brebeuf waving," shouted Jean.

They saw the tall figure standing by the entrance to the village. All the boys waved their hands.

Kettle Hound's barking carried across the waters.

Ordered Claude: "Sing our hymn now for Our Lady's protection on the outing."

The boys' voices broke out into the familiar "Ave Maris Stella," as they paddled along the palisaded side of the Residence. Father Brebeuf kept waving good bye. Then he was hidden by a bastion of the palisades.

Two soldiers on the northern bastion waved down.

When the hymn was finished, Jean Bonin suddenly observed: "It is a good thing that Kettle Hound thief is not along. I think that dog knows he belongs to Echon and so nobody will hurt him. He's too clever for his own good."

"Well," put in Guy, "I would prefer him to a strange Huron."

"Why, Guy?"

"Because, Jacques, you do not know what stealing is, till one of them is around the camp."

"That's right," affirmed Claude and added: "I do not believe there is a people on earth more given to stealing than these Hurons."

"Yes," agreed Nicholas Colivet, "it is necessary to have your eyes on both their feet and their hands, when they enter a place. For they steal with their feet as well as their hands.

"I remember there was a strange brave came into the Residence two—three weeks ago. Christopher Regnaut, the donné who has charge of the carpenter chest, had it open. I noticed this Huron casting his eye on one of the hammers. This one came from Three Rivers and it was too valuable to lose. I thought the Huron wanted it so I watched it and him all the time. But he was more skillful in stealing than I was in spying. He concealed the tool so cleverly that I did not see him make any movement. But the hammer was missing from the chest.

"Father Brebeuf came by and I whispered to him my suspicions. 'It's a Three River hammer too,' I told him. Echon is not afraid of any Huron alive. He's not afraid of Iroquois either. So he said to the brave, 'My brother, we have not many hammers here at the Residence.'

"The Huron said, 'Echon, I have not the Blackrobe's hammer. I am not a thieving Petun.'

"It would have been a deadly insult to search the brave and find nothing, but Echon was clever. He whistled and Kettle Hound came bounding up. Echon stooped down and pretended to speak to his dog, saying, 'My honest hound——' "

"Honest!" Guy La Touche exclaimed and blessed himself piously.

"Well, that's what Echon said. 'My honest hound, what do you think?' Kettle Hound whined and wagged his tail vigorously.

"'What does your dog say, Echon?' asked the Huron suspiciously.

"Father Brebeuf looked at me and I nodded my head that this Huron had the hammer on him and pointed under the Huron's blanket.

"Again Echon stooped down and said something in Latin to his 'honest hound.' Kettle Hound whined again.

"Said Father Brebeuf, 'Uncle, are you sure you have not our hammer under your blanket? For my dog says——'

"'Echon, your dog is too wise to live long.' The brave looked wickedly at the dog. Then he laughed and taking the missing hammer from under his blanket gave it to Father Brebeuf.

"But," concluded Nicholas, "I never saw that Huron steal the hammer and I was watching him all the time."

"I wonder," inquired Jacques, "what was the Latin that Father John said to Kettle Hound?"

"I know," said Nicholas, "for I asked him after the Huron brave had walked away. He said to his dog, 'Omnis homo mendax est,' and that means, 'All men are liars.'"

"Echon is clever, all right," Guy declared, "if the Hurons, pagan or Christian, did not think so, Kettle Hound would have been in their kettles long ago."

The canoe was paddled between the green banks for a few minutes. Then Jean Bonin spoke.

"Robert Le Coq, the soldier, is another one who did not think the Hurons were such clever thieves. Sergeant Jonah knows better now."

Jacques' companions laughed heartily.

"Why the laughter?" inquired Jacques.

Explained Jean: "The others know the story. When Sergeant Jonah was stationed here last summer, he was sent with Father Charles Garnier to his mission village. I went along. That night in a strange cabin Sergeant Jonah sneered at the savages and boasted, 'You think you are clever thieves! I will give you anything you are able to steal from me.'"

"What a thing to say to Hurons!" exclaimed Claude.

"I was seated on the ground beside the Sergeant and I promptly moved away. Some of them might have thought I was making the same offer. The braves present said nothing. But ten minutes later Sergeant Jonah broke out in a great oath which I shall not repeat. He was turning out all his pockets and searching for his tobacco pouch. I had seen it in his hand when he was rashly boasting that no Huron could steal anything from him."

"Did he get it back?" asked Jacques.

"He did not and I do not know to this day who took it but I am sure it was one of those silent Indians seated nearby.

"Great thieves!" concluded Jean, "I would sooner trust Kettle Hound alone in the kitchen with some fresh meat."

The boys had been chatting and paddling steadily along and now were at the mouth of the River Wye. Coming towards them was a line of five canoes.

"Who are these?" asked Jacques.

Nicholas and Claude had been watching the approaching Indians. Finally Claude St. Leger said: "These are strangers to the Residence."

"Look," said Jean, "they wear their hair different from most of our Hurons."

The foremost canoe was passing close by and Jacques noticed the hair of the three braves. Each had a large strip closely shaven, from the crown to the forehead that divided the hair into two hemispheres.

"Where do they come from?" It was Jacques put the question.

Jean Bonin had been observing the Indians. Now he spoke: "I would not be surprised to hear that they come from a village of the Neutral Nation."

"I do not think so," this from Jean.

"Why?" asked Jacques.

"Because travellers from the Neutral Nation usually come on foot."

Here a paddler in the second last canoe suddenly called out: "My nephews, is Echon in the French village?"

"Yes, my uncle," replied Jean, "he was there this morning."

"Good fishing," said the Indian.

"Now I know them," Jean spoke in a low tone to the others, "listen."

He raised his voice. "There is also in the French village that large white brave who was in your village last year with the Blackrobe. The one who boasted that none could take anything from him and he lost his tobacco pouch. He has another smoking pouch. It is better than the lost one. He got it in the villages of the French on the Great River."

The Indian and his companions smiled and paddled on.

Jean explained, "When that one spoke I recognized him as a brave who sat in the cabin near Sergeant Jonah that time I was telling you about. When we return today we must see if the Sergeant is missing anything."

The boys' canoe was skirting the shore of the bay that Jacques placed as the large body of water he had seen with Father Brebeuf from the top of the hill that first morning at St. Mary's.

Half an hour later they came to the fishing grounds. They had caught three fish when water began to seep into the canoe's bottom.

Claude ordered: "Into the shore at once."

As the canoe came closer to the green woods they saw a little beach and there two Indians, a man and a boy, working over a canoe.

"Pagans," Jean whispered to Jacques as their canoe grounded on the sands, "but we know them. They live two leagues from the Residence."

Jacques saw the Indians were repairing with pitch a leak in their own canoe.

At Claude's request the older Indian offered to stop the leak in the boys' canoe and they lifted it high and walked it to a place alongside the Indians' craft.

When Jacques put down his side of the canoe he looked sharply at the older Indian. He thought he had seen him somewhere before. Then it came in a flash. This was the pagan Indian he had met with Peter that morning after the two had left the ruins of Teanaostaye. Moose Hunter was his name, Jacques remembered. He recalled also that this brave had spoken so bitterly against the Christian religion.

Moose Hunter had left his own canoe and with deft fingers was repairing the leak in the other canoe. When he wanted some more pitch he spoke in sign language to the boy and now Jacques noticed for the first time that the boy was dumb.

Guy confirmed this, saying, "The boy cannot speak with his tongue. He is pagan too."

The older Indian stopped work and looked at Jacques. He said: "Nephew, you are Echon's boy who came to the fortified village with Peter?"

"Yes; my uncle."

"It is a wonder that you did not travel to the Village of Souls when you got lost from the main party."

"'Village of Souls?'" questioned Jacques, "I do not understand."

Claude said in French, "He is pagan. That is his way of saying died and gone to Heaven."

"You boys who speak our language are whitemen who follow the Prayer. I like Echon as a powerful medicine man, but I do not believe what Echon and the other Blackrobes say."

"You'll know better when you die," observed Nicholas.

Jean waved him to keep quiet and sensing a story asked: "Uncle, where do you think you will go when you come to die?"

"I go to the Village of Souls. You praying white boys listen and I will tell you about the man who went to seek his dead sister."

"Please do, uncle," begged the boys and squatted expectantly around the working Indian.

"You who follow The Prayer do not believe about the Village of Souls," he began, "but I tell you it is towards the Tobacco Nation eight leagues from us."

"I did not know Heaven was so near," said Jean, but Claude and Guy whispered, "Shut up."

"The road is broad and well beaten and when the soul goes out of the body, it starts to walk this road. On the way the soul passes near a rock called Ecaregniondi. It is marked with the paint that the souls used to smear on their faces. On this same road before the soul gets to the village it comes to a cabin where lives Oscotarach, or the Pierce Head. He draws the brains out of the head and keeps them. Then the soul comes to a river. The only bridge is the trunk of a tree laid across the river. This is very slightly supported on either bank. The trunk is guarded by a dog which jumps and makes many fall, who are carried away in the stream and drowned."

"But they are already dead," objected Jacques.

Jean and Claude nudged Jacques to keep silence.

Nicholas Colivet had been smiling and now he said to Moose Hunter:

"My uncle, how did you learn all this geography of the other world?"

Said the Indian: "Persons brought back to life have reported it. Let me tell you boys what my mother's father, who was very old, told me when I had your years. An Algonquin brave lost one of his sisters whom he loved above all the rest. He wept many days after her death. Then he resolved to go and seek her. He travelled twelve days towards the setting sun. For he had learnt where the Village of the Souls was. He did not eat nor drink all the time. At the end of the twelfth day his sister appeared to him with a dish of meat cooked in water. She gave this food to him and disappeared. The brother tried to stop her but she disappeared. He travelled on for three days more. Each night his sister appeared with a dish of meat. Each night he tried to stop her, but never could. The next day he came to the river. The water was very rapid. He searched but could not find a ford. On the other side of the river he could see cultivated fields, which made him think the souls lived there. Nowhere could he find a place to cross. Then he comes on a little cabin. He calls several times. A man appears and shuts himself up immediately in the cabin. Now the man who is seeking his sister sees the fallen tree thrown across the river. It looks very shaky. But he is resolved to cross and finally does. He goes straight to the cabin. He beats on the closed door. He is told to wait and to thrust in his arm. When he does, the man in the cabin opens the door and is greatly astonished to see a living body. He tells the brother this land is only for souls.

"'I know that well and that is why I come here to seek the soul of my sister,' said the brother.

"'Take courage,' said the man, 'and you will soon be in the Village of Souls, where you will find her whom you seek.'

"The man continued: 'All the souls are now in a cabin where they are dancing to heal Aataentsic who is sick. Do not be afraid to enter.'

"The man went into his cabin and returned with a pumpkin. 'Take this and put into it the soul of your sister.'

"The brother thanked the man and asked him his name.

"'Be satisfied. I am the man who keeps the brains of the dead.'

"So the brother goes on and he enters the cabin of Aataentsic. Here he sees many souls dancing but he cannot see the soul of his sister. For the souls are so startled at seeing a living man that they vanish. The brother remains all day in the cabin. In the evening when he is sitting by the fire they return, but they show themselves faintly and at a distance. The brother does not move. Now he sees the soul of his sister. When he tried to seize her she flew from him.

At length when she danced near, he was able to seize her. She struggled for a long time, all the time growing smaller and smaller, till at last he was able to put her into the pumpkin. He corked her in well and then goes back to the cabin by the river. Here the man gave him his sister's brains in another pumpkin saying: 'When you reach your home go to the cemetery and take up the body of your sister. Bear it into your own cabin and make a feast.

"'When all the guests are assembled, walk through the cabin, holding the two pumpkins in your hands. You will no sooner have resumed your place when your sister will come to life. That is,' warned the man, 'provided all the guests keep their eyes lowered and do not attempt to look at what you are doing.'

"The brother was overjoyed and speedily returned to his village. He did all the things that had been directed and he was already beginning to feel motion in the corpse. He was just about two or three paces from his place in the cabin, when a too curious squaw raised her eyes."

"I knew one of them would," observed Jean.

Moose Hunter went on: "At that very moment the soul of the sister escaped and there remained to the brother only the corpse in his arms. This he had to take sorrowfully back to the cemetery. I have spoken," concluded Moose Hunter abruptly.

The boys had been listening to the tale attentively and had not noticed that all the while he was telling it, Moose Hunter had been finishing the repairs on their canoe.

Speaking for the rest Claude St. Leger thanked him both for the story and the repairs.

Only when they were afloat beyond earshot did Jean express the sentiments of the others.

"My nephews, that Moose Hunter has a fire in his head," he said, using the Huron expression for a fever.

Guy La Touche who had said little for the last hour, now put in. "Jacques, did you ever hear how Moose Hunter got his squaw?"

"No; but I did hear that his wife and all his people were killed at the taking of Teanaostaye."

"This was before that. I heard an old brave at St. Mary's telling it about the fire."

Guy launched into the anecdote. "When Moose Hunter was young, he and another brave were paying attention to an Indian maiden——"

"A beautiful Indian maid," corrected Nicholas.

"All right, beautiful then, but I have not seen many of that kind. Anyway, the old captain who was father of the beautiful maiden, settled the matter in his own way. He declared he would throw a stick and the first of the two who brought it back to him, could have the maiden.

"The two young braves agreed to this and so the father went to the fire and took a brand that was all aflame. He hurled it as far as possible away from him. The two raced after it and Moose Hunter reached the flaming stick first. He raced back and laid it at the father's feet. But he has a burn on his right arm that he will carry with him to that Village of Souls."

"No woman is worth getting burnt for," observed Claude solemnly. The rest nodded. And he wondered why all the rest laughed at him.

"Speaking of sticks," said Jean Bonin, "I heard Father Ragueneau tell a better one."

"What was it?" asked Jacques.

"He was talking about a journey that Father Brebeuf took some years ago. Echon came to a village near the Tobacco Nation. There he found many so well disposed that he stayed several weeks with them, instructing them all the time in The Prayer. Then he baptized the best of them before he had to leave. He called the captain and gave him five books, or rather, five chapters of a book. These books were nothing else than five sticks, each painted a different color, in which they were to read the truths he had taught them.

"The first was a black stick. This was to remind them to keep from their former superstitions. The second was a white stick to remind them of the common prayers they were to say faithfully each day. Red was the color of the third stick and it was to remind them of the Sundays and other feasts, when they were to assemble together and say their prayers and listen attentively to the captain, who would explain the meanings of these sticks to them. The fourth stick was yellow colored and wound with little strings. This was the book of punishments for those who neglected to keep faithful to what they had learnt from Echon. He had instructed the captain what little punishments to assign those who failed. And the last stick was blue and notched. This fifth stick was to remind them to have recourse to the Good God at all times, when there was plenty and when there was little to eat and to thank Him equally and never to forget eternity that would come shortly.

"Echon left the village and months later when the captain and his party came to St. Mary's they reported to Echon that they had been faithful to the teachings of his five sticks. I have finished," Jean Bonin concluded, Huron style.

"That is not a bad idea, Jean," said Jacques. "We might keep such little sticks ourselves. When I get back to the Residence I am going to notch and paint blue a little stick for myself. I like that one the best."

Claude St. Leger broke in. "Stick or no stick, you have just reminded me that it is getting late and if we do not start we will not be back at St. Mary's in time for supper."

"Then," said Guy, "take up our sticks—I mean, our paddles, and get to work. It is always this way, when we go fishing. We return with little fish and big appetites."

"Paddle," ordered Claude, "and let no one talk of eating or I'll faint."

They just made supper.

Chapter Fifteen

With Echon

NOVEMBER HAD come in with a raw wind blowing out of
the northeast. Snow was banked high down to the hori-
zons and the palisades of Fort St. Mary were almost buried. Biting cold penetrated to the very bone and Jacques Bourdon,
resembling a bear cub in his furs, was huddled close to the warm
glow of the kitchen fire in the Residence.

He had just finished serving Father John Brebeuf's Mass and
this morning he was to wait and go with Father Noel Chabanel to
the mission villages of St. Louis that Father Chabanel and Father
Brebeuf were now serving.

Jacques would have preferred making the excursion in company
with his tall Blackrobe, but Father Noel needed him more. Jacques
had taken a liking to this Father Noel. He, of all the Blackrobes,
Jacques had quickly noticed, found the missionary life in Huronia
the hardest. He was not like the gigantic Father Brebeuf, who took
cold and heat, hunger and pain with the same cheerful exterior. But
Father Noel Chabanel, to Jacques' sharp eyes, found the climate hard
to bear. Much as he tried to disguise it, he disliked the Hurons, the
filth and their ways. He spoke a halting Huron that made the pagans
openly ridicule his speech and even the Christians smiled indul-
gently at Father Noel's clumsy efforts to make himself understood.

So it was Father Noel that Jacques had been told to accompany
this cold November morning to the missionary village of St. Louis,
which was distant about three leagues from the Residence.

Shortly after ten the Blackrobe and the boy started out on their snowshoes. The biting wind cast stinging steely particles in their faces and made each step painful as they crossed the frozen plain towards the first fringe of gaunt trees.

Quickly the snow-buried buildings of Fort St. Mary were lost to view. The two were struggling along the crusty trail, the constant crunch of their snowshoes the only sound.

Jacques had been to St. Louis village several times that Fall with Father Brebeuf and he knew the trail, but he had difficulty in recognizing some of the white laden landmarks. Then they sighted the immense pine that stood sentinel to the northern turn on the trail and Jacques felt relieved. From here he knew he was approaching the ridge on which stood the mission.

An hour out of the Residence they saw a furclad figure approaching on his snowshoes; his arquebus in his hand. Jacques recognized the figure and shouted to Father Chabanel: "Here comes Christian."

The donné had seen them and he waved a greeting. When they met, Jacques' eyes were taken by the three snow rabbits that hung from Christian's belt. The donné noticed the boy's approving look.

"See, Father Noel—Jacques—what I was fortunate enough to bag. These foolish little creatures crossed my trail just outside of St. Louis. They will fit snugly into the cook's pot."

The donné saw the hungry look on the boy's face and remarked: "It is too bad that you will not be home to enjoy them, hey, my boy?"

Jacques shook his head. "No matter, Christian. At St. Louis we will have better fare."

Father Chabanel asked: "Where did you leave Father John?"

"He was leaving St. Louis for St. Ignatius as I left. He left a letter for you on the altar. God be with you both."

"God be with you too," repeated Jacques and Father Noel.

Another half hour's silent tramping through the biting cold brought the two in sight of St. Louis village. Mounting snow banks almost hid this collection of Huron cabins, built on a small plain on the back of the ridge. The tops of the palisades alone showed above the universal whiteness.

Some Huron women were gathering wood in the forest before the village.

One stout squaw, who wore a medal of the Blessed Virgin hung around her neck by a strip of eel skin, dyed red, spoke and Father Noel turned puzzled eyes to his interpreter.

"What is she saying, Jacques? I make out that some braves are——"

"Squaw says a runner came with news of moose and most of the men of the village are on a moose hunt."

"Tell our aunt that I shall pray the braves will be successful."

They went on and soon came to a well tramped down trail that led into the village. Towards the center of St. Louis stood the small log cabin chapel. Its bell hung from the gaunt branch of a nearby tree. Snow lay deep around the chapel, but within it was relatively warm. A log lay burning in the fireplace.

Jacques stretched grateful hands to the blaze. Father Chabanel had gone directly to the altar and knelt in prayer. The boy watched the Blackrobe cautiously. He had noticed that this missioner who, like St. Joseph, spoke so seldom, seemed very talkative whenever he knelt before the tabernacle.

Then Father Noel got up and saw Father Brebeuf's message that stuck out from behind the picture of The Holy Family. When he had read it he called Jacques.

"My boy, Father John directs you to go at once to St. Ignatius village. Do you know that trail?"

"I have been over it once before with Father John, but there was no snow on the trail then."

"You should have a guide. A summer trail is not the same trail when snow lies on the ground."

Father Noel Chabanel went to the chapel door and in his halting Huron called to an old man, who was skinning a recently slain deer.

"David, my uncle, who is there in the village who could take Echon's boy to him?"

"At once, Blackrobe?"

"Yes; that is Echon's order."

"My daughter's child, Rabbit Catcher, knows the trail. I will send him with Echon's boy."

Quickly a ten year old youngster, whose sole clothing consisted of a dilapidated brown bear skin and moccasins, came running to the chapel door.

"My mother's father says to take Echon's boy to him at St. Ignatius. We go now."

The small Huron looked his amazement when Jacques answered him fluently in his own tongue and told him he was ready to go.

It was about a league between the two mission stations. The trail led east along the back of the ridge and it was frequently exposed to the cruel wind that was blowing in from the bay.

Despite the wind Jacques kept a sharp lookout for any animals and his vigilance was rewarded. There was a plump snow white rabbit crouched under the lee of an exposed rock.

Rabbit Chaser had seen the animal at almost the same time, but Jacques' arrow sped to its mark a second sooner. A red spot suddenly sprang up on the rabbit's side. The two boys ran to the wounded animal. Jacques struck it over the head with his stick and the quivering ceased.

Two arrow heads stuck into the side of the animal.

Rabbit Chaser said: "Echon's boy, your arrow has pierced its heart. The rabbit is yours."

"I will put it into Echon's pot and you share our meal."

"French boy has a good heart."

Soon the two were within sight of the village of St Ignatius II. Jacques noted that the site itself was a natural fortification, for on three sides deep ravines gave it protection. A start had been made to erect the palisades on the exposed northern side, but as yet only about one-third had been finished.

As they came closer Jacques saw Father Brebeuf. As usual he was towering over the Huron group that surrounded him.

Rabbit Chaser saw Echon and said: "I go back to my mother's father."

"How about the rabbit?" inquired Jacques.

"I will get another and put it into my mother's father's pot."

"Well, come into the cabin and get warm."

"No; Echon's boy."

Jacques saw Rabbit Chaser was reluctant to come closer to Father Brebeuf. A little coaxing and Jacques had the reason.

Confessed Rabbit Chaser: "It is Echon's dog that I do not like."

"Why?"

"Because four days ago Echon's dog told Echon that it was I who took the French snow from Echon's prayer cabin."

Jacques knew Rabbit Chaser was speaking about sugar which Father Brebeuf kept in his chapel to reward the children when they knew their Catechism questions and answers. And he rightly surmised that again Echon had pretended to speak to Kettle Hound and thereby learn the culprit with the sweet tooth.

He did not urge Rabbit Chaser to enter the village and the little Huron boy started back.

When the Blackrobe noticed Jacques' approach he smiled his welcome.

"I was awaiting your arrival before starting, my little one."

"Where to, my Father?"

"I will explain as we tramp along. But first go into this cabin and get warm at the fire."

Ten minutes later Father Brebeuf said: "Take this bundle and I'll shoulder these two."

They had struck out towards the northeast. The tall Blackrobe insisted on going first on his snowshoes and breaking a path for the boy.

Jacques followed him in silence. Then came the explanation he awaited.

"There are several Algonquin families, my Jacques, whom I visited last July before you came. These are now living near the shore of Georgian Bay, maybe, three leagues north of the Residence.

"Word was brought to me this morning by a runner that two of the children are very sick and their squaw wants Saving Waters for them. So we start. I would have had to go on alone if you had not come when you did."

The wind had slackened and the sun had broken through the leaden clouds, but the cold continued. Father Brebeuf seemed, to Jacques, to have the Huron's tireless stride on his snowshoes. So different from Father Noel Chabanel's awkward efforts. For Echon pushed on ahead continuously. Where the going was rough in the snow, he made tracks for the boy.

The trail had gradually swung down from the ridge and now they were crossing a small frozen stream. No Huron had been met since leaving St. Ignatius.

In the middle of the stream, the gigantic Blackrobe was a stride ahead of Jacques when he heard the crack of the ice. He leapt nimbly to the further shore. Jacques, tired from the rapid pace they had been travelling, was not quick enough. He too leapt as the ice started to give under him. But his weariness leaded his legs and he pitched forward, striking his head heavily on a shore rock.

Father Brebeuf turned back from the bank and seeing the boy lying there was at his side in an instant. He picked up the slim burden and carried it to the upper bank.

When Jacques came back to consciousness, he felt the warmth of a fire. It was very comfortable. At first he thought he was near the kitchen fireplace at the Residence.

He opened his eyes. He was lying on Echon's bearskin cloak before a crackling fire. An outcropping of slanting stone behind him acted as a heat reflector. Overhead from the laden branches of a fir tree snow was beginning to melt and drop hissingly into the leaping flames.

Father Brebeuf in his worn blackrobe was coming back to the fire. In his arms were several fair sized logs.

"So, my little one is awake. You have had a fine sleep."

"What—what happened? Where am I?" asked Jacques in amazement.

"You insisted on bumping your head too hard, so we stopped for a while."

Then the boy remembered. He stretched his wearied limbs to the warmth and laid his hand gingerly on the sizeable bump on his forehead.

"It is larger," said the Blackrobe, "soon it will be so big that you will be top heavy and then what will we do?"

"If you ask me, my Father, we will stay right here."

"For an hour," said Father Brebeuf, "we will cook your rabbit and after we have eaten, we will be on our way, for Our Lord is calling us, remember, to those little pagan children."

Jacques was sitting up now and noticed how snugly the camp site was protected from wind and cold. Behind him some rocks rose out of the frozen earth and he could see the white surface of the stream, maybe, a hundred yards away.

But what interested him more was the rabbit which Father Brebeuf had skinned and was expertly cooking on the further side of the fire.

When both had eaten they heard a yelp and up the trail dashed Kettle Hound. He bounded into Father Brebeuf's lap and seemed to be trying to tell his master what he thought of him going off on a journey and not telling him a thing about it.

"So, my honest hound, you trailed us and came into camp just in time to have some bones."

Kettle Hound ceased his protestations of affection and got right down to business on the remains of the rabbit.

The Blackrobe fed the fire skillfully. Then he sat beside the boy and taking his head gently in his lap, said: "My little one, rest now and we'll talk. That will refresh both of us.

"See how the Good God's Providence provides all we need here in His wilderness. For we are as comfortable as though we were in the palace of King Louis across the ocean. His Providence feeds us and brings us our honest hound to finish up the bones." He turned amused eyes on the dog, who had curled up on an edge of the bearskin and was enjoying the warmth of the fire. "I wonder what thieving job you have done this morning that you fled down the trail to my protection. I will hear soon enough."

Father Brebeuf went on: "If need arose you and I, my little one, could spend the night in this sheltered nook under The Sign of the Stars, as Father Isaac Jogues loved to call sleeping out."

"You might even say, my Father," put in Jacques, "that I got this bump on my head when I did so that Kettle Hound might have a chance to catch up with us."

"Why not! The Master Shepherd looks after His beasts as well as His more precious creatures.

"You know, Jacques," Father Brebeuf pursued his train of thoughts, "I learnt years ago that the long hand of His love is ever near in these Huron lands; nearer, I firmly believe, than it was in Old France; that distant land that seems a dream of my remote childhood.

"You never were there, my little one?"

"No, Echon—I mean, my Father, I was born in Quebec. This is the farthest away I have been. And as you have just said, even Quebec seems a dream of my childhood to me. It seems more than mere months since I came here to Huronia."

"Do you like it here in Huronia?"

Jacques looked up affectionately into the gray bearded features of his guardian and said simply: "My Father, I have never—never felt happier in my whole life than I have these three months near you."

The Blackrobe's hand patted the boy's hair.

"It is a big part of my 100% here below to be given the companionship of a good boy—and a useful interpreter too."

"But I never interpret for you, my Father. Why, you speak like a Huron captain!"

"It is but a gift, this fluency in a strange tongue, that the Good God has bestowed on me to use on His service."

"But you have interpreted for Father Gabriel."

"Oh, he is new to the country. He will learn the Huron's language."

Father Brebeuf was silent and when he spoke it was as though he worded his secret thoughts.

"I had a vision——" he checked himself and substituted, "a dream a month ago and I saw many of my companions. They were redrobed. There was Father Charles Garnier, who labors in the Blue Mountains and Father Noel Chabanel and youthful Father Gabriel Lalemant. Their familiar well-worn blackrobes had become royal red. I looked down on my own blackrobe—and I awoke and there were tears of happiness on my cheeks. In my heart was such joy—O my God, how good You are to me!"

Jacques said nothing, but he reached up his hand and rested it in the larger hand that lay on his forehead. At once he had a memory of that fleeting moment back in half forgotten Hotel Dieu, when as a little child, that martyr-elect, Father Isaac Jogues, had once rested his mangled hand on his head.

The same feeling now possessed him and he drew down this warm hand of another martyr-elect and covered it with reverent kisses. Tears of pure joy welled out of his eyes and, boy that he was, he knew that he now shared with his beloved Blackrobe the secret of his strength.

The fire crackled and threw out a spark. It fell on the sleeping Kettle Hound's flank. The dog leapt up with a yelp and then he growled.

"Do not swear, my honest hound," cautioned Father Brebeuf.

The dog came closer and whined as though he was telling his master all about the shock to his nerves.

Said Father Brebeuf, stroking the dog's head: "I saw it all. Next time, don't sleep so close to the logs."

He turned to Jacques. "It is no wonder that some of our Huron friends say this dog talks to me and tells tales on them."

Jacques gave Kettle Hound a friendly pat and then he said: "My Father, I have noticed something about Father Noel Chabanel. I wish to question you?"

"Question what you will, little one."

"He seems to find everything hard in this land."

"Out of the mouth of sucklings," quoted Father John Brebeuf, "your keen young sight has picked out the heroism in that Friend of Christ Crucified."

"I do not quite understand."

"Let me tell you something of Father Noel's history. Then, my child, you will appreciate this Hero of Christ as I do."

The gigantic Blackrobe fed a crackling log towards the center of the fire.

"Father Noel, when he came among us here back in '44 was thirty-one years old. He was the most helpless missioner ever to arrive in Huronia. Don't think I mean he was not a brilliant man, but some men have the—what shall I call it—special gift of the Holy Ghost—the gift of Indian tongues. Poor Father Chabanel, who speaks three or four civilized languages fluently and had taught rhetoric successfully in France, is still struggling with his Huron ABCs and he will be the rest of life's journey.

"Then he never was able to harden himself to the daily filth of the average savage's cabin and customs. Everything nauseated Father Noel. Living as we often have to in the cabins of our Christians has always been a bitter Purgatory to this Father. I long ago became accustomed to their gross ways and customs. It's all in my lifework.

"I don't mind telling you, Jacques, that once when I was a young Jesuit, not yet ordained, I was assigned to teach a classroom of small French boys in our college at Rouen——"

"Where is that, my Father?" Jacques asked.

"Rouen—Rouen, where is it? I have almost forgotten myself. But it is a city in Old France. And, who knows, you may see it some day," added Echon smilingly.

"Has it many cabins?"

"Far more than Quebec settlement. But I was telling you, this class almost ruined my health and my Superiors had to take me out of that classroom as a failure. I could not handle those little savages."

Jacques thought of the manner in which he had seen Echon handle some murderous Hurons, and he smiled at this confession of failure.

"My lifework was to be with these children of the American forests. I'd be out of place back in Old France, and the thought of having to live at our King's Court would drive me so far into the uttermost wildernesses to the west of us that I could very likely come out among the Chinese. Now before you ask. Let me tell you, my little one, the Chinese are people who live on the other side of this earth. Our good Saint Francis Xavier died among them.

"Father Noel though was born to live among the niceties of Court life. He would have made an excellent King's confessor. Imagine this heroic Father sticking it out for years here in Huronia!

"More than this—and I am speaking confidentially to my best orderly—Father Noel Chabanel was strongly tempted to quit last year, when his life seemed so fruitless here. The temptation persisted to ask Superiors to send him back to his native land. His whole nature cried out for France, clean France.

"I do not believe I could have resisted that temptation, if the Good God had permitted me to be tempted that way.

"Oh, but Father Noel deliberately nailed himself to Christ's Cross last year and when he leaves Huronia it will be—I firmly believe—to carry his palm in triumph into Heaven. For—and this, my Jacques, is a secret I am sharing with you, for I think its memory will strengthen you some day—this Hero of Christ took a vow of stability to these wretched missions. It was on the Feast of Corpus Christi last year.

"This vow so impressed me, when I chanced upon it among the papers at the Residence, that I memorized it and several times when the sky of my soul was overcast, just the repetition of Father Noel Chabanel's vow of remaining in Huronia till death, or Superiors recall him, has been a tower of strength to me."

It puzzled Jacques to hear Echon admitting he ever needed strength. He was the symbol of strength to all in Huronia.

"Listen, my little one, and I will repeat the words of that vow——

"'Jesus Christ, my Saviour, Who by a wonderful dispensation of Thy paternal Providence, hast willed that I, Noel Chabanel, though altogether unworthy, should be a fellow-helper of Thy holy apostles in this vineyard of the Hurons; impelled by the desire to obey the will of the Holy Spirit regarding me, that I should help forward the conversion to the Faith of the barbarians of this Huron country; I, Noel Chabanel, being in the presence of the Most Blessed Sacrament of Thy Body and Thy Precious Blood, which is the tabernacle of God among men, make a vow of perpetual stability in this mission of the Hurons; understanding all things as the Superiors of the Society of Jesus shall explain them and as they choose to dispose of me. I conjure Thee, therefore, O my Saviour, to be pleased to receive me as a perpetual servant of this mission and to make me worthy of so lofty a ministry.'"

"Amen," said Jacques reverently as Father Brebeuf stopped, and it was a half minute before the boy realized that he had uttered the word aloud.

"Now, my little one, does not Father Noel shine in a new splendid light?"

"He does and I feel stronger just to have heard his vow, my Father. He is indeed a Hero of Christ!"

"There are two kinds of heroism, my Jacques. It takes courage of body to face, say, our gray wolves whom we have heard howling hungrily in that woods over there. But it takes a higher heroism of soul to face the living Hell of life in Huronia, as Father Noel does daily, without even an exclamation of disgust ever escaping his lips. Remember that always."

The Blackrobe got up from his position before the fire.

"But, my child, we must be on our missionary way, if that head of yours is rested enough. Shake it and see, if that sizeable bump will fall off."

Jacques got gingerly to his feet and found his footing secure. But his head still ached from the blow.

He helped Father Brebeuf put out the fire with handfuls of snow.

Soon they were on their snowshoes, trudging ahead. Kettle Hound when he heard a wolf's howl in the woods to the east, prudently dropped in behind Jacques. The boy on several occasions almost stepped on him as he followed along in Indian file.

Jacques was speechless, strangely thrilled, sharing the new knowledge of Father Noel's high courage.

The lad's reverie was interrupted. For the endless forest of trees ended abruptly. They had come out on a white slope of landscape and there before his eyes stretched the white wastes of a vast body of water. Shore ice extended out a quarter of a mile to where the bluest of waters, cold and clear, stretched to the horizon.

"The ocean must look this way!" exclaimed Jacques.

"The ocean is many times the width of Georgian Bay," replied Father Brebeuf, "there is a great lake to the westward, beyond this lake—the Lake of the Hurons.

"But I think I see the wigwams of our Algonquins."

The Blackrobe pointed to some tiny black dots nearly a league north of where they stood on the edge of the forest.

"Let us be on our way."

It was harder going here in the open as the wind had greater sweep. Jacques bent double and was chilled through, though he was sweating from the exertion of trying to keep his footing on the slippery ground.

Soon the boy could make out the six wigwams of the Algonquin party.

The Blackrobe was sighted and a squaw in a dirty fur skin greeted him. "Echon, you come in time," she said.

"Who are you, my aunt?"

"I am the squaw who came to the Blackrobe's Strong Village last blueberry time. You instructed me about the Saving Waters. I told my people and when they came near I sent for you. My sister's papoose is very sick. Help him, Echon."

The gigantic Blackrobe nodded and stooped low to enter the wretched collection of branches and skins that made up the wigwam.

There on a deer skin lay the sick papoose. Father Brebeuf gave the child a quick look. Then he said to Jacques.

"Get me water."

The mother who had overheard, handed the boy a gourd containing some drinking water.

Father Brebeuf took the gourd and while Jacques watched the Blackrobe poured the Saving Waters on the dying child's forehead. At the same time Jacques heard the missioner repeating the Latin words of Baptism. "I baptize you in the name of the Father and of the Son and of the Holy Ghost."

Father Brebeuf turned to the watching mother and said, "I have given your little one the name of a Heavenly patron who will watch him faithfully. For I have given him the name of the Apostle Andrew."

When Father Brebeuf and Jacques came out of the wigwam, they found about twenty Algonquins had assembled. Among them Echon recognized some children he had instructed a month ago at the Residence. He singled out a twelve year old boy and girl and bade them to come closer. Then he spoke to the older people through these children.

"My uncles and aunts, listen well to what these children say, for their words are the words of wisdom.

"Boy, what is the name of Him Who made all?"

"God, Echon."

"Good. Now, girl, you answer and if your answer is not correct, boy, you correct her."

Eagerly the small boy waited intently for the girl's reply. The Blackrobe continued: "How many Gods are there?"

"There is only one God, Echon."

"How many persons are there in God?"

"Three and they are only one God."

"Which of these three, made Himself man?"

The girl replied promptly: "The Son, Who was born of a virgin squaw named Mary."

"Why did He make Himself man?"

"To die for us and make our sins go away."

"Why was it necessary for Him to do this?"

The little girl hesitated and when she remained silent, at a loss for an answer, Echon turned to the boy. He answered: "I know that. Our first father, the head captain of all tribes, disobeyed God. He was to be thrown into the fire and his children, that is, all tribes, might not enter Heaven, but the Son said to His Father: 'My Father, have pity on men. I will make myself a man and will die for them.'"

"That is correct, boy. Now, did He not rise from the dead after His death?"

"Yes, the third day and He instructed twelve captains, who are called Apostles. He told them that they should teach all tribes the Prayer. Those who believed would go to Heaven and those who did not believe would be sent to the fires that do not go out."

"Now, girl, what is the name of the Son of God?"

"His name is Jesus."

"That is correct. Now, how many things are necessary to go to Heaven?"

"Three, to believe the Prayer, to receive Saving Waters, and to obey."

"That is well known, my little sister," complimented Echon.

He turned again to the boy. "Little one, what must we believe?"

"What we sing in these words, 'Nitapouetaouau outanimau dieu' and what follows."

Jacques knew the boy was referring to the Apostles' Creed.

"Boy, why do I pour Saving Waters on persons?"

"To remove the head captain's sin and to make their souls white like snow."

"Very well said. Now tell me this. Whom must we obey in order to go to Heaven?"

"God Who commands us to love Him, and forbids us to kill our enemies, to rob, to get drunk, and to do bad things."

"Very good indeed." Father Brebeuf reached into the pocket of his blackrobe and taking out four dried prunes, gave each child two. "I see that you have not forgotten anything that I taught you at the Residence."

Father Brebeuf turned suddenly to Jacques and announced:

"Now I will hear this French boy."

Jacques had not expected to be catechized in public and he blushed.

Father Brebeuf began: "Echon's boy, where is God?"

Jacques started to mumble his reply, when he was ordered: "Speak out clearly and loud as these children did. Where is He?"

"He is here. He is in Heaven. He is everywhere."

"Does He really see us all the time?"

"Yes, my Father. He sees everything that goes on in Heaven, on earth, and in the flames."

"Now I have a question that was asked me by a brave in the chapel at the Residence only three days ago. The Virgin Squaw, is she God?"

Jacques studied his answer before he replied: "No; the Virgin Squaw is not God, for the Blackrobes teach there is only one God."

"Right you are, my little one. But always remember the Virgin Squaw—the one you often call the Squaw in Blue, is a creature like us, but she is most powerful with her Son and so ask her often and confidently for all you need."

Jacques said simply: "I always do, my Father."

The older Algonquins had been listening attentively to the series of questions and answers between Echon and the children.

Now a wrinkled old brave spoke up. "Echon, we have listened to the words of our children and your white boy. It is clear they do not speak with a split tongue. What should an older one do who wished to follow The Prayer?"

"Come to the fortified village of St. Mary's, my uncle, there you will learn the Prayer words you should know and believe."

The group broke up. Echon and his boy visited each of the wigwams and finding no more sick babies, they set out on the return journey. The weather had moderated with the sun still high in the blue skies and it was much easier sliding along on their snowshoes.

Coming to a rise in the trail that gave view to a white panorama of some leagues' distance the Blackrobe stopped and pointed to a ridge showing on the horizon.

"Over there, Jacques, lives an old brave named James."

As they went on Father Brebeuf explained: "Last summer James had some ulcers on his feet and one of the donnés treated him at the Residence. James was not getting better and it seemed as though the Good Shepherd had sent the ulcers to give this poor old man the opportunity for Baptism.

"One afternoon I asked; 'James, will you be glad to go to Heaven?'

"'Alas!' said he, 'it is very far away and I have very bad legs. How shall I be able to go there?'

"I laughed and told him when the time came the Good God would provide transportation. He was satisfied with my answer and next morning I baptized him and my happy James received all the transportation he needed three days later."

Observed Jacques: "I suppose James was much surprized when he exchanged his old sick legs for new wings. I wonder, my Father, how it feels to fly with your wings for the first time?"

"We'll all know soon enough, for in a little while eternity will open and that will be the least of the questions we will receive adequate answers to."

The priest and the boy slid along on their snowshoes in silence for a quarter of a mile. The going was rough and slippery and Jacques was perspiring and breathing audibly when they came to the scene of his accident on the trip out.

Father Brebeuf ordered a welcome halt. There were still some unburnt logs lying by the blackened fire place. Quickly the Blackrobe had a log crackling and he and Jacques rested. The warmth was grateful. Jacques sat looking into the flames, making up fire pictures.

"What are you seeing, my child?" asked Father Brebeuf.

"I thought I was looking at Purgatory. Doesn't that look like a Suffering Soul there between the big log and the two branches?"

"With the aid of a healthy imagination, it does. But, my picture-seeing child, you don't have to go as far as Purgatory."

"What do you mean, my Father?"

Father Brebeuf was looking off into the distance as he replied: "I have seen captives of the Hurons at the torture; your pictures might faintly illustrate the actuality of their sufferings. With the screams of the squaws and the shoutings of the braves turned demons, one might easily imagine he was witnessing a scene in God's Eternal Coals."

Father Brebeuf held out his hands, blue from the cold to the flames. Then he smiled reminiscently.

"What are you thinking about, my Father?"

"I was just recalling an incident that happened some twelve—thirteen years ago in this country. Blessed Father Anthony Daniel, Father Ambrose Davost and myself were reestablishing these missions in '35. The friendly Hurons had built us a cabin. But many of the tribe were openly hostile to us.

"When we first preached about the eternal fire and the burning decreed as a punishment for sins unrepented, many were impressed, till a medicine man stood up at the council fire and challenged: 'You Blackrobes have split tongues. There could be no fire forever, where there could be no wood. For what forests of spruce and pine and fir could sustain so many fires through such a long space of time?'

"This objection to the eternity of Hell's fire had a great influence on the minds of the savages and even some of the Catechumens began to waver. But Father Davost was equal to the situation. He solemnly rose and addressed the circle, telling them the lower world possessed no wood, as we understand it, but burnt of itself. Wholesale laughter greeted this statement.

"Then Father Davost announced: 'My brothers, tomorrow I will exhibit to you a piece of this land of Avernus, in order that since you do not believe the word of God that we preach to you, you may trust the evidence of your own eyes—and noses.'

"The novelty of this promise aroused the savages' curiosity for this promise to give them an opportunity of improving their technique in their favorite method of treating captives, that is, torture by fire. Next morning braves assembled from all the neighboring villages and sat down in an immense plain surrounded by hillocks, like an amphitheater. Twelve old captains were chosen to watch Father Davost to see that he practiced no hidden sorcery.

"The Father, who liked to play practical jokes, had told us privately what he was about to do. He had taken a lump of sulphur that we had in our baggage. This he solemnly gave to the captains. Some of these old braves hesitated to handle it, but before the assembly they could not show their fears, so they passed the sulphur silently from hand to hand. They looked at it and they smelt it and then two, bolder than the rest, tasted it.

"'Is it wood?' asked Father Davost.

"'No,' thundered the chorus.

"'Is it coal?'

"'No.'

"In the meantime Father Davost had prepared a kettle containing live coals. He solemnly took back the much inspected lump of sulphur. The captains and the people were watching his every movement. Father ordered the twelve captains to come closer to the kettle and when they had put their noses almost over it, he shook some grains from the lump of sulphur upon the coals. These immediately took fire and filled the captains' curious noses with a stifling odor. The twelve retreated hastily to fresher air.

"More and more grains of sulphur were thrown on the coals and the odor of sulphur which is not the odor of roses penetrated many nostrils. The medicine man who had challenged the question of Hell's fire was one of the twelve. Father Davost had seen that he got more than enough of his share of the sulphur fumes. Now this one rose and placed his hand flat over his mouth. That is, as you know, my Jacques, our Hurons' gesture to express great surprise. At once practically all the assembly made the same gesture. And from that day we had little difficulty in convincing these simple souls that God's word about an eternal fire for unrepentant sinners was true."

Father Brebeuf got up from the fire's warmth and stooping to readjust the thongs of his snow shoes, directed: "We must be on our way or we'll be caught on the trail after nightfall. There are too many wolves around for that. Put out the fire, my Jacques."

The Blackrobe whistled and Kettle Hound came bounding into sight.

Soon they were trudging along the trail they had broken in the morning. At the approach to the ridge on which St. Ignatius and St. Louis village stood, the Blackrobe turned off the morning's trail and started to walk through the shadowed snows.

"This way we will go directly to the Residence and save more than a league."

They came out of the pine forest cut off and onto a trail that was well marked.

Father Brebeuf was the first to sight a party of Indians. They were trudging along, single file.

The Blackrobe said: "Here are some of our Christians, coming to St. Mary's. We'll wait for them."

The Indians had recognized the gigantic figure of Echon, for at a signal from an old brave, evidently the captain, the whole line quickened their steps.

Jacques saw the party consisted of ten people, six squaws and four men. All greeted Echon as a friend. Jacques did not recognize any of them as Hurons he had seen before. They fell into line behind Echon and the boy.

An hour's walk in silence brought the welcome sight of the nearly snow buried northern palisade of the Residence of St. Mary. There was no gate on the northern side of the fort, so the party snowshoed around the eastern palisades of the Hurons' section till they came to the gate.

A crowd of Christian Hurons were within the enclosure. All greeted Echon most reverently.

Christian, the donné, came through the crowd. He spoke to Father Brebeuf and the tall Blackrobe beckoned Jacques aside.

"My little one, it seems that blessed Father Anthony Daniel has need of his small altar boy."

"I do not understand, my Father?"

"Christian has just told me that little Peter of Teanaostaye died this morning of smallpox. He was very happy to go. Another one safely Home."

Father Brebeuf looked down affectionately on his interpreter. He saw the tears in Jacques' eyes.

"Drop into the Presence of our Good Master and say a little prayer for Peter's soul and then I think you need to seek your cot."

Jacques was glad to slip away from the crowd. His mind was full of thoughts of the Huron lad who had been his companion on the hard trip up to Huronia.

After the visit to the chapel Jacques lay down. He was weary from the day's journey. He closed his eyes. . . . "Eternal rest grant Peter, O Lord . . . Another one safely Home."

Later came Nicholas Colivet and Claude St. Leger to call Jacques to supper. Drowsily he told them to go away and eat it themselves. They left him to his dreams.

Chapter Sixteen

Jacques' Letter

Residence of St. Mary
Among the Hurons,
28th. December, 1648.

To Louis Joliet:

It is the feast of the Holy Innocents and we have been snowed in here at the Residence for a week. Christmas Day I never left the Residence. It is still snowing, but a little while ago I was out on my snowshoes with Jean Bonin, Claude St. Leger, Nicholas Colivet and Guy La Touche, who are the other French boys here. Father Brebeuf's dog, Kettle Hound, insisted on coming along. But he had not gone fifty feet before he sank to his nozzle. He would have disappeared entirely—and that would not have been a great misfortune—only he howled so much that Father Brebeuf came out and carried him back to the doorway. He had enough.

We boys had planned to go to the top of the lookout hill that is northwest of the Residence. The wind and the cold proved too much as soon as we got over the palisades and, like "the honest hound," as Father Brebeuf calls his dog, who is a great thief, we also had to come back. Kettle Hound was curled up by the kitchen fire and he thumped his tail on the warm earth floor at the sight of us, as if he was saying, "So you had to give up too!"

That Kettle Hound is a very wise dog and some of the Hurons say—of course, it is not so,—that he scouts about and then comes back and reports to Echon whatever he finds amiss. You know

Echon is Father Brebeuf's Huron name and it means "He Who Carries the Burdens."

Anyway, some time ago Rabbit Chaser, a small Huron boy, sneaked into the kitchen of the Residence, when no one was in sight, except Kettle Hound in his favorite corner by the fire. The boy stole a handful of "French snow," their name for sugar, and he was just sneaking away to eat it, when Father Brebeuf came up. Kettle Hound got up and, as his custom is at the sight of his master, went whining to him. Father Brebeuf looked at Rabbit Chaser and demanded: "Little one, did you have permission to take that French snow?"

The Huron boy was so surprised that he confessed his theft then and there. And Father Brebeuf was so surprised at a Huron admitting a theft that he gave the boy permission to eat the sugar. Rabbit Chaser looked down at Kettle Hound and said warningly: "Dogs who tell their masters all they see, don't live long."

Father Brebeuf smiled and said nothing. He knows the Hurons would permit no one to lay violent hands on his favorite dog.

When I heard this Huron boy, repeating his story of seeing Kettle Hound informing his master, I retold it to Father Brebeuf. He laughed heartily and said: "Kettle Hound is discreet. He always keeps guilty information to himself. That young Huron scamp did not know that I could see into the kitchen from the other room where I was writing. I saw everything. I am afraid that Kettle Hound would never tell on another thief. His own record is too black."

As if in complete confirmation of this observation, the dog on hearing his name spoken, wagged his tail vigorously.

As I told you, we are snowed in today and like the Fathers, I am writing letters. This one to you will be put in with theirs to be taken down to Quebec in the spring, when the Huron flotilla sets out with the furs and pelts.

I know a lot about these Huron people now. They built their cabins different from the Montagnais who dwell near Sillery. The

Huron cabin is constructed of branches, covered with large pieces of ash, elm, fir or spruce bark. The better ones are roofed with cedar bark. The cabins are shaped like the garden arbor back of your cabin. They make them 60 to 80 feet in length and about 30 feet in width. Within, from one end to the other down the middle, is a passage, ten or twelve feet wide. On each side of this passage is a raised platform, 4 feet above the ground. In summer they sleep on this platform to get away from the fleas. Now in wintertime, the Hurons sleep below on rush mats, close to the fires. This way it is much warmer than on the platforms. At one end of these cabins is a space where the corn is stored in large casks, made of bark. Down the middle passage, over head, are suspended pieces of wood, on which they hang their garments, provisions, furs. This is to keep them beyond the teeth of the numerous mice or dogs, or the one or two bear cubs that are in each cabin.

In a large village cabin there will be twelve fires, which means, twenty-four families live together there. The smoke of all these fires, which has hardly any way to get out, makes the inside of the cabin reek and your eyes smart all the time you are within. I have seen Father Brebeuf and other missioners trying to say their Breviary and you would think they were crying all the while.

These bark covered cabins are highly inflammable and last summer, shortly after I reached these lands, I saw a whole village burn up in half an hour. A spark from a fireplace got on one roof and that was enough. The villagers did not get one sick papoose out quick enough and he burnt up. When the Iroquois come they like to burn the whole village down and they throw all the captives they do not wish to be burdened with into the burning cabins.

There is plenty of nice fruit in this Huron country. I have eaten strawberries, mulberries and blueberries. The bears like the berries very much and once I helped some Huron boys catch a bear cub that had eaten so many berries that he was not able to run away. His little belly almost dragged on the ground and he just waddled into a bush and let us grab him. He is now a pet of the soldiers here. They call him Berries. He is not allowed into the Residence, for, as Father Brebeuf says, Berries believes the commandment reads, "Thou shalt steal." Berries likes honey so much that he will even let the wild bees sting him to get at a honey tree.

Berries and Kettle Hound are great friends, but that is natural, Father Gabriel Lalemant says, because they have so many vices in common.

Do you remember Brother Martin, who was at Quebec some years ago? They called him Little Martin. He is the Brother in charge of the farm here now. When Father Brebeuf came up here some years ago your parents gave him a pair of calves. I was milking them this morning in the stables and you would never know them. They are that healthy and big looking. I asked Brother Martin how they ever got Evangeline and Elizabeth to these distant missions. He told me he had charge of them and they were trussed up like fowls for sale in the market place before the Infant Jesus church, and laid side by side in his canoe. One time on the Ottawa River the canoe upset in a rapids. Little Martin dived in and brought first one and then the other helpless calf ashore. They furnish us with good milk. Brother Martin has other live stock—the pigs and the chickens. So sometimes we have pork and eggs.

But you must not get the idea, Louis, that we boys here just eat as the Hurons do at their Eat All Feasts, where it is bad manners to get up from the feast while any meat or corn remains. I have never attended any of these Eat All Feasts, but some times when I was hungry I have wished I had an invitation.

Lately, Father Ragueneau, the Superior here, was telling us of one he attended a year ago. And Father Brebeuf and Father Bressani have been at many. This I know.

You should hear me speaking Huron now. Father Brebeuf says if my hair were black instead of brown and I was better at taking things that didn't belong to me, he would take me for a born Huron boy. I am puzzled to know if this is a compliment or not. Sometimes I am not certain that Father is not having his fun. He is always so jolly, yet he can be serious. And everybody knows he is a saint, who wishes and prays to be a martyr.

Speaking of the Huron language, there is a Father here, Father Noel Chabanel, who has never been able to speak it fluently. He comes to me sometimes and asks me the Huron word for the commonest things. I am always glad to tell him, but he does not seem able to make himself very well understood. I have been with him on several trips to the mission villages and I have had to act as interpreter between him and the Hurons we meet, even the catechumens and Christians.

I teach Father Gabriel Lalemant too. His Huron name is Atironta. He is making progress and though he has been here in Huronia only since last September, he is now able to help instruct the Huron catechumens who come here to the Residence. Every week some come. Not so many now as most of the tribe are away hunting. The summer is the time when they come in droves to the Strong Village of the Blackrobes, their expression for St. Mary's.

Two weeks ago I went to St. Louis Mission with Father Brebeuf. On the way I saw a long narrow animal. Its fur was snow white. I did not recognize it. When I asked Father, he said: "Now that is a weasel in his winter coat. Some of our Hurons will capture him shortly and take his snowy coat away from him. It will be cured and hung up in the cabin till the flotilla goes down to Three Rivers next spring. There it will be bartered for, say, an iron kettle. A French vessel, possibly, captained by Father Anthony Daniel's brother, will carry it across the wide ocean to my distant land, where some day a lady of the Court will wear our little friend's winter coat in company with other similar coats. She will call her beautiful white cloak ermine and King Louis' eyes may admire this particular white coat.

"Thus," said Echon, addressing the little animal that stood not so far from us with its black tip of a tail twitching, "if you are a sensible beast, you will keep far from a Huron's arrow and save yourself a trip to the Court of His Majesty."

As if he had an inkling of the advice the big Blackrobe was giving him, the weasel dropped down and slunk out of sight behind a snow bank. . . .

Father Brebeuf just called me over to the table where he is writing his report for Father Jerome Lalemant and he asked me if I had enough material to write you. I confessed that I had put down about all I could recall. Then Father Brebeuf suggested that I close my letter with a copy of this letter that a fifteen year old Petun boy sent him.

The boy was a catechumen but Father hesitated to baptize him, because he had to return to his pagan village among the Petuns and Father Brebeuf feared the boy might be persuaded to abandon the Prayer, as all his relatives were pagans.

The young Petun went to Father Bressani and said, "Take talking bark and send it to Echon. This is what you are to ask it to say."

Here is an exact copy of the Petun's letter:

"Echon, Grey Squirrel's heart is sad because you will not pour Saving Waters on his head. Grey Squirrel writes to speak to you that your heart may be softened and he may receive Saving Waters. Listen to him. This is what he says, I have left my own country and my parents to come to the Strong Village of the Blackrobes for Saving Waters. For what else would I come to seek here, where I have no relatives or friends? I know all the prayers and the whole of the Prayer Questions.

"If I once receive Saving Waters I do not wish to go back up there where the wicked are. I will remain here and hunt and fish with the Prayer people. I am young but still I know what I am doing. I will keep close to the Prayer all my life. I do not speak with a split tongue. If you will not give me Saving Waters I shall be sad. I shall return to my own country, where I shall perhaps die without Saving Waters. And if I must go to the Village of the Souls, I will tell all that I do not wish to be there. I will tell all that Echon is the cause of my not going to God. You, Echon, will be the cause of it. This is what Grey Squirrel says to you by this talking bark."

Grey Squirrel after he had Father Bressani write the letter himself delivered it to Father Brebeuf. Echon read the letter and next morning he baptized this Petun. He gave him the name Joseph. That's Father Bressani's patron. I was godfather. This boy has gone back to the Petun country and he carried a piece of "talking bark," addressed to Father Charles Garnier, who is stationed at a mission village there. So Father Garnier will look after this Joseph. I hope to visit him in his country to the west of the Residence next summer....

(Two days later.) I resume. You should see some of the cunningly made tobacco pouches our Hurons have. I have seen one made of a muskrat. The animal was skinned and cured in such a way that there is only a little opening in the back of the head.

Another one which a pagan brave carries is not so nice. Two years ago he captured an Iroquois. While the Iroquois was being tortured at a slow fire, he cut off the right hand of the captive at the wrist. This he cured so that even the two nails remain. The other three were torn off at the time of the capture. When this human hand is filled with tobacco it is quite solid. I know because I have touched it. Father Brebeuf told me that if this pagan becomes a Christian he will have him bury this poor captive's hand.

Speaking of hands reminds me of a foolish test of courage the Hurons have. Two young braves, to show their courage, will bind their bare arms lightly together. Then a lighted tinder is put between the arms. The brave who first withdraws his arm or shakes off the fire is considered wanting in courage.

Robert Le Coq, one of the donnés here, whom they call "Sergeant Jonah" because he is always getting into and out of trouble, was challenged to this fine game by a brave. "The Sergeant" let the tinder burn through to the bone. Then the pain was so intense that he had to shake it off. He neglected the wound and would have lost his whole arm, if Christian, the surgeon here, had not attended to it. I am not going to play that game with any Huron boy.

What I will do with any of them is hunt berries. In summer we go after raspberries, mulberries and blueberries. You look to see where the pigeons go and there you will always find plenty of these berries. Very likely a bear is nearby, gorging himself. Near the Residence is a place where strawberries are plentiful. Bigger than any I saw in Quebec.

To the west among the Neutrals a wild apple grows. Last autumn the Hurons brought us many of these. They are delicious. We still have some left in our storeroom.

The Fathers have some prunes and dried raisins that Father Jerome Lalemant sent up last summer. These are a treat for the Huron children who know their Catechism answers.

But I would trade them all for some of the French cakes we ate on Captain Daniel's vessel. Do you remember that day last summer on the "Chasseur"? It was only months ago but it seems years.

I heard a strange rumor from a squaw who was captured by some Hurons who were hunting many leagues to the westward. She does not belong to any tribe near here. I was with Father Brebeuf when he was questioning her. She spoke a little Huron. She told him that she was born leagues and leagues towards the setting sun, where the land is flat like a plain without end. When she was a little girl in her own country—that was before she was captured in a war by some raiding savages—she remembered crossing a very wide river that flows to the southward. Her people call it The Father of All Waters. I forget the Indian word for it, but that is what it means.

Ever since I heard of this mighty river, which must be wider than our St. Lawrence, I have wished when I grow up to go to the west and see it for myself. Would you like to come with me, Louis Joliet?

Father Brebeuf says some day the Blackrobes will go further west into the forests to baptize the savages who live there and if I grow up to be a good boy I will go along. Suppose both of us go to these western lands. What do you say?

But, Louis, that is future dreaming. I just looked out the door. It is snowing heavily and it will be some more days before we will be able to leave the Residence. So I will play some more games of chess with the boys and the soldiers. Father Brebeuf is too good for me.

Anyway, I have written this long promised letter to you. I hope you keep your promise and are writing me just as long a letter, telling me everything that happened in Quebec settlement and at Our Lady of the Angels. Not that I wish to return to school. I never want to go back, but I would like to hear the news.

Now I will finish this letter. It will be put with the Fathers' and when the flotilla starts for the St. Lawrence next June, it will be carried down. I will pray that no Iroquois capture it and that your long letter will be brought to me in the autumn. Better bring it up yourself.

May God and His Blessed Mother bless us both,

Your dear friend,
JACQUES.

From the Residence of St. Mary
in the Huron country.
Finished, Dec. 31, 1648.

Chapter Seventeen

Sergeant Jonah

T HE NEW YEAR, 1649, came in with a break in the bleak weather and the blizzard-bound Residence of St. Mary resumed its winter activities.

Jacques' fellow interpreters, Jean Bonin, Claude St. Leger, Guy La Touche and Nicholas Colivet, were eager to start out on the hunt. Each of the donnés, who hunted for the Residence, was persuaded or nagged into taking a boy with him. Jacques, not less eager, begged Father Ragueneau's permission to go along with Robert Le Coq, for "Sergeant Jonah" had become his latest friend. The other boys were less inclined to hunt with "Sergeant Jonah," for as Claude St. Leger put it, "With the 'Sergeant's' ill luck you stand just as much a chance of being bagged by an Iroquois as bagging a moose. I prefer to take less chances."

But Jacques Bourdon laughed off the warning and with the desired permission granted he and "Sergeant Jonah" started east in the cold of a mid-January dawn. From the ridge they had a panorama of the cold looking waters beyond the shore ice of the bay. Then the trees hid the waters and the two slid along on their snowshoes for a silent hour.

Suddenly Jacques called out, "Look! Look, Sergeant, over there!" The boy pointed to the east where a large moose stood out black against a white background. In a moment the animal broke into flight towards them.

"Sergeant Jonah" stopped and said: "The hunt is on. We will

sight the hunters shortly. Let us watch."

The huge antlered beast plunged and crashed through the brittle underbrush. Then it winded the donné and the boy and abruptly changed the direction of its flight. They could still hear the moose crashing through the pine forest to their left when "the Sergeant" exclaimed:

"As I expected. We have seen the hunted. Here come the hunters."

There, coming out of the fringe of woods where Jacques had first sighted the animal, were three Huron hunters on their snow-shoes. They were travelling faster than the moose, whose bulk made him break through the icy crust whenever the surface was soft and this checked his headlong flight.

"I know one of those braves," said Jacques, "he is Paul, the father of Bernard who was killed on the way up to Huronia."

Without a sign of recognition the Hurons, like wolves on the trail, kept on after the moose. Some new danger must have frightened the animal, for it had changed its direction and came charging directly towards the Huron hunters. When they noted this they dropped behind tree boles and once the animal was within range Paul popped up. Three arrows winged across the snows and the moose plunged forward with a broken foreleg.

From that moment the moose was doomed. He struggled and fell. The crust would bear up his weight and then let him through and he was caught as neatly as a bear in a trap.

The Hurons raced across the white surface. They surveyed the struggling animal for a few seconds, then one of them snapped an arrow into his bow and sent it through the moose's heart.

When Jacques and "the Sergeant" came up the three Hurons were already cutting off the skin. The antlers had been separated and Jacques knew these would hang in one of the cabins and from the prongs provisions would be suspended to keep them out of the way of the numerous mice.

"Sergeant Jonah" asked if they had sighted any other moose tracks and Paul informed him: "Yes, white brave, a league to the east two other moose are roaming. May you get plenty of meat for the Blackrobes."

They thanked the Hurons for the information and set off. Coming over a rise in the trail they heard in the distance the lonesome howling of wolves.

"The Sergeant" listened and estimated. "Maybe three or four wolves. Some other folks are out hunting this morning." He turned to Jacques, "They would like to come on you, my little one. What a tasty breakfast would they have."

"Not while I had an arrow in this quiver," retorted the boy. He added: "And what a good dinner the pack would have on you."

Jacques was feeling gay now that he was actually on a hunt.

"The Sergeant" said nothing for awhile. Then he spoke: "Once you might have made a dinner on me."

"When was that?" asked Jacques, scenting a story.

The going for half a league ahead was smooth and the two slid along easily. The howlings of the hunting pack of wolves had died down and they were a good distance away.

"In a way," began Robert Le Coq, "you might say it was because I wasn't some Frenchmen's dinner five years ago that I am here today, where I am not so sure that I won't end in a wolf's jaws or an Iroquois iron pot.

"It was in '44 that I sailed out of Dieppe in the 'St. Jeanne.' She was a good vessel, bound for the cod fishing on The Banks. But a storm came up when we were a day's sailing from The Grand Banks. The main mast was whipped out of its step as if by an angry giant's hand and before the damage could be repaired it had pierced the 'St. Jeanne's' bottom, as you might put an awl through an egg shell. The water flooded in. All thirty-seven of the crew worked the pumps or carried water in buckets and heaved it over the side, but the 'St. Jeanne' slowly sank, lower and lower. We threw overboard the three cannons we had to protect us from the heretical English pirates, who always cruised the Banks to take a living out of the mouth of honest fishermen. Then the ship's cargo went over the side. The storm had abated somewhat and the blue skies were overhead. But the flood in the hull rose steadily. Finally when the deck was awash, we piled into the three boats we had for the cod fishing and none too soon.

"I saw the last of the 'St. Jeanne' end up and slide down like one of those porpoises, which are forever leap-frogging under the bows of a boat in warm waters. So fast had she sunk that only a little brandy was saved and we thirty-seven in three small boats.

"Then it was, my Jacques, that I learnt what a large place the ocean is. You must see it, day after day and night after night, from a small pitching boat, more than a hundred leagues from any land.

"The third dawn showed us one of the boats had disappeared and I don't know to this day what happened to it. Poor forsaken mortals! May the Good God have mercy on their souls!

"In our two surviving boats were twenty-one souls. No biscuits and no fresh water. We prayed to the most Holy Virgin and good St. Anne during the next thirteen days, eating nothing, drinking nothing, but a sip of that brandy. After the first week we each wetted a stick in the brandy and sucked it twice a day. Five died and we dropped their bodies overboard with scarcely a prayer.

"On the thirteenth day after we saw the last of the 'St. Jeanne,' we talked of drawing lot to see which should serve as food for the others. Some regretted having heaved those bodies overboard.

"I was rather stout, though I had lost considerable weight in that pitching boat, and I offered to the others: 'Do not resort to chance. I see no one in the company better able to afford your nourishment than myself.'

"Just then the ship's boy—he had sharp eyes—saw a sea turtle asleep below the surface and quite near us. It was of monstrous size. With oars we poked it to the surface and some willing hands seized it by tail and flippers. All who could helped drag it on board. We sucked its blood and I for one could feel the strength surging back into me.

"But four more tossing days passed and again the talk came back to the old topic. Another agonizing day and all agreed that it was necessary.

"We drew lots and the lot fell on me, Sergeant Jonah. 'There!' said I, 'didn't I tell you it was God's Will that you should eat me?'

"But we were Frenchmen, not these painted savages, and our abhorrence at eating human flesh and raw too, for, of course, we had no fire on board the boat, made one of the seamen climb to the masthead to take a last look around the horizon. He had no sooner climbed high, when he began to shout, 'A ship to port! A ship to port! I see a ship!'

"I had been making the most fervent Act of Contrition I ever made in my life, but I stopped it in the middle. We in the boat could see nothing yet, but the two boats were turned to port and we rowed with all our remaining strength in the direction the sailor at the masthead directed.

"Then the ship was visible. We all fell on our knees and prayed like a convent of nuns. I was not the least fervent, for even though I had offered myself, the prospect of life was better.

"The vessel proved to be an English one. When they learnt that we were French, they refused to let us come on board, shouting that they had not enough food. They started to pull ahead and then the sails were lowered.

"Later we heard that some English women on board had begged their husbands so hard, even offering to cut their own food supply in half, that the vessel let us come on board. We were so famished that at first they gave each of us only a glass of fresh water and then a little gruel.

"We did not eat much till we were landed on the island of Madeira."

Jacques had listened in silence to the soldier's account. Now he asked:

"Sergeant, when you got safely ashore on this island of Madeira, which I believe is not so far from Europe, why did you ever come back to New France?"

Robert Le Coq was silent for a moment. Then he said: "I did go back to France and in the port of Dieppe I met some good Fathers of the Society of Jesus there. I liked them and I volunteered to go with them to this mission. Soldiering is my trade and when I learnt that soldiers could be used in New France I volunteered to come to the mission as a donné. It was the least I could do after my life had been saved in that almost miraculous manner. But I'm not so sure that I won't be eaten yet. With these Iroquois cannibals lurking in the forests and pouncing on one when least suspected."

The mention of the ever present Iroquois menace made Jacques cast a prudent glance at the nearby bushes, gaunt against the still January whiteness.

Jacques saw no lurking Iroquois, but his sharp eye discerned something moving on the rising ground, a hundred yards away.

"What is that, Sergeant? Look, look over here!"

"Where?"

"There to the east of those four pines."

Robert Le Coq looked. Then he started forward, shouting to Jacques: "There is the moose we have been seeking."

The two detoured into the forest to keep well to windward of the unsuspecting animal. They saw it was a young buck and Jacques knew they were in for a fatiguing chase. Before they got within range of the soldier's arquebus the animal winded the stalkers. It started crashing away.

Two hours they pursued the tracks in the snow. Occasionally they would sight the moose ahead and then lose it for minutes at a time. But gradually they drew nearer as the moose encountered soft snow. At first the hunted beast had flown northward. Then he veered to the eastward, and Jacques, perspiring mightily as he forced his snowshoes over the hard ground was thankful when the tracks told him that the young animal had turned southward. For every step was bringing them now nearer the distant Residence.

It was less than a league from the hillside, where "Sergeant Jonah" and Jacques had first sighted the moose, that the kill was made.

They had been closing in rapidly on the tiring animal when it struck a stretch of thin icy crust on the snow. Its sharp feet went through and it was only able to struggle slowly ahead.

When thirty yards away Robert Le Coq raised his arquebus and it roared.

"It's hit! It's hit!" Jacques shouted and raced ahead of "the Sergeant."

The animal had fallen on its side. Jacques saw above the reddening snows that a right fore shoulder bone had been shattered by the shot. Mercifully he plunged his hunting knife into the beast's heart and its struggles ceased.

The stout soldier had come puffing up. With the chase ended successfully he flung himself on the snow alongside Jacques and rested.

"And now to get this fine fresh meat back to the kitchen of the Residence," exclaimed "Sergeant Jonah."

But the hunter and the boy had hardly started to cut the meat when Jacques, looking up sighted some Hurons coming along the trail towards them.

He pointed them out to the soldier.

"We are in luck!" "Sergeant Jonah" exclaimed, "if what I suspect turns out correct, these Hurons are on their way to St. Mary's for instruction and our problem of transportation is solved."

So it turned out, for the seven Hurons proved to be a party going to the Residence to seek Echon and learn The Prayer. They threw the slain moose on a sled they were dragging and before dark the welcome carcass was in the hands of Little Martin.

Chapter Eighteen

Echon's Orderly

OST OF FEBRUARY, 1649, had been cold, but no blizzard had come and it was possible to carry on the winter's activities at the Residence. The same less rigorous weather had benefitted the Iroquois enemy and there had been large war parties that came from nowhere, swarmed over unprotected palisades—usually when the majority of the Hurons were out on a hunt—and when these same hunters returned it was to find their village a shambles. There would be plenty of grim signs of the enemy, but no sight of him. Jacques Bourdon, like the other boys, had grown accustomed to seeing wounded and destitute refugees come straggling into the safety of Fort St. Mary.

Now on this late February morning Jacques was going with Father John Brebeuf to the Blackrobe's two mission villages of St. Ignatius and St. Louis. These were about three leagues from the Residence on the first snowy ridge to the eastward.

As the gigantic Blackrobe and the boy trudged along on their snowshoes, Echon had been telling Jacques of an experience he had had during the winter of 1640, which he had spent with the Neutrals, a nation away to the westward.

"And for hours," Father Brebeuf was saying, "as Father Chaumonot, my companion, and myself were walking along, we could hear a roar.

"At first I thought it was in my ears, but then I was sure it was not.

"Our Neutral guide said when we questioned him that it was the Great Falls. In mid-afternoon we came to the high edge of a gorge. There below our feet was angry water. More and wilder than any of the white water you and I portaged around coming up to Huronia from Quebec.

"Then the trail went inland again, but always the sound seemed to increase in volume. Finally the guide said, 'Echon, now you soon see.' We came out of the shadows of the forest and stood on a sunswept point. Never this side of Paradise do I hope to look on a more beautiful scene. There was a great horseshoe of falling waters. Millions and millions of snow crystals glinted in the bright light. Mists of spray with several rainbows through them, rose from that white water caldron.

"I gazed and gazed and then, my Jacques, I fell on my knees at this first sight of the Great Falls, that the savages call Niagara. For the thought had come overpoweringly that now for the first time was I beholding a symbol of the power of God. I had never realized the expression 'Almighty God' till that moment and ever since whenever I meditate on the strength of God, I have in my mind a picture of that great falls of Niagara, that sunny winter's day when I first was privileged to behold it."

The two trudged along on their snowshoes in silence for nearly five minutes. Jacques was thinking over the Blackrobe's words and finally he spoke: "It seems to me, Echon, that a sight like that would bring to my mind the smallness of myself in the sight of God."

"It does that, my little one," replied the Blackrobe, "and also His goodness and power. When I saw the Falls of Niagara I felt strengthened for what's ahead."

Jacques looked at the tall priest at his side and noticed that Father John Brebeuf seemed, as he had on former occasions, to have forgotten his presence.

The two walked along, the only sound the sliding of their snowshoes over the hard snow. Then said Father Brebeuf, as though he were thinking out loud: "I always like to recall that vision I had. When I looked and looked, there were my dear companions and instead of their familiar blackrobes, I saw them clothed in red-robes—as it were drenched in bright blood that they had given for Christ's sake.

"I looked down on my own habit and it also was now a ruddy hue. Soon—soon that change of color will come. It cannot come too soon!"

Again the priest lapsed into silence and Jacques felt that he had overheard secret words that betrayed the constant longing of his companion's heart.

There was in Jacques' heart the feeling of the high privilege that was his to be near this beloved Blackrobe and he could have sung for joy. . . .

Now they had come within sight of the new village of St. Ignatius. Ever since the Seneca Iroquois had swooped down and destroyed the old village, Father Brebeuf had been urging the Huron captains to build a stronger village, fortified after the French manner. But it had taken the Seneca disaster to move the captains to action.

Now the palisaded walls of St. Ignatius II were rising. On three sides deep ravines gave a natural protection to the site. These three sides were already palisaded and the ravine cleared. But the strongest wall had within the past week been almost completed on the exposed northern side where the land was level.

It was down the trail to this side, where the gate was now being hung in place by many Hurons, that Echon and his orderly slid.

The Blackrobe stopped and surveyed the scene ahead.

"St. Ignatius village, Jacques, looks strong enough to withstand any Iroquois visitors. But I have one fear."

"What is that, Echon?"

"That our Huron friends will grow careless with their French constructed village. See those bastions at the corners. They are only strong in war if they are occupied by armed men. But some captain may have a dream or listen to a medicine man's foolish prediction that now is a favorable time to hunt the moose. He will tell other captains and practically the whole garrison, captains and braves, will trail the animals and leave this bastioned wall to its own devices.

"That was what the few braves in Teanaostaye did only last July and the wily Mohawks secretly watched through the eyes of their spies the Huron braves depart. Then they swooped down to an easy conquest."

"But a costly one to the Fathers," observed Jacques, "that error gave Father Daniel his martyr's palm."

"Yes; my Jacques, the fourth of last July. Blessed Father Anthony!

"But here comes some one we know."

Jacques also had seen the blackrobed figure of Father Noel Chabanel coming out of the gateway. He waved his hand in recognition.

When the priests had come closer together, Father Brebeuf called: "Father Noel, I bring you an obedience."

"What is that, Father John?"

"Father Superior has directed me to give you this letter."

Jacques watched this younger priest as he read Father Ragueneau's letter. He knew Father Noel was in his late thirties. His medium height made him seem almost dwarfed, standing there alongside the tall Brebeuf. Jacques' admiration for this missioner, who found all things hard, was constant ever since Father Brebeuf had told him of the secret vow of stability. Whenever the boy encountered Father Noel Chabanel he recalled the cruel trick that had been played on him several years ago.

It was common knowledge among the Hurons that Father Noel found their living conditions intolerable. Once, so the tale went, when Father Noel was spending the night in a pagan cabin, he was offered a piece of meat. He concealed his disgust and attempted to eat the nearly raw flesh. Afterwards the malicious host produced the remainder of the meat and showed it grinningly to Father Noel. To his horror, the Blackrobe discovered that he had been eating part of a captive's arm. And, so the tale concluded, "Father Noel was sick for a week after."

This remembrance flashed through Jacques' mind as he watched the Blackrobe quietly reading his Superior's letter.

"Father Superior directs me to return to the Residence. He is sending young Father Gabriel Lalemant to be your companion in these mission villages. God's blessed Will be ever done!"

Father Brebeuf laid his hand on Father Chabanel's shoulder. "Indeed, Father Noel, I'll miss you."

A wistful look glowed in Father Chabanel's eyes.

"And I—I fear I'll miss the palm that awaits you here, Father John. But it's God's Will that I do my little elsewhere."

Simply and obediently, as always, Father Chabanel left some directions for Father Gabriel. Then without entering St. Ignatius village again, he started to walk the league to St. Louis and back to the Residence of St. Mary, where he would learn that his new field was among the Petun nation as companion to Father Charles Garnier.

When the trail side trees hid Father Noel Chabanel from view, Father Brebeuf remarked: "My Jacques, there goes the priest who has found missionary life the hardest and has stuck to it as only a great hero of Christ could. I wish I was as pleasing in the sight of God as is Father Noel Chabanel."

Here Estienne, the Huron war captain, spoke to Echon about some change in the gate that was being constructed and the gigantic Blackrobe strode across to inspect it.

Jacques wandered curiously around between the secondary outer palisades. The latter were easily twelve feet high, rough hewed logs that fitted close together. Between the logs were openings, some of them large enough to speed an arrow through. Beyond Jacques could glimpse the cleared ground before the palisades.

As he came to the corner he noticed how it was built into a square projecting bastion. He climbed the ladder into the inner platform. Loopholes commanded the long sides of the palisades and two Frenchmen or Hurons stationed here with arquebuses could work havoc on any charging Iroquois.

From his elevation Jacques was able to look over the second line of palisades and over the third and lower ones into St. Ignatius village. Indeed, this was a fortified village, thought Jacques admiringly.

Not many Hurons were visible before the long wooden houses. But he could hear voices.

Jacques determined he had made enough solitary inspection and he climbed down. Instead of reversing his steps to the gate, he went along the palisades.

He came to a group of Hurons, braves and squaws, working silently, erecting the last logs. They paid no attention to Echon's orderly. And Jacques, a little further along the palisades' platform, stopped to look down into the deep snowy ravine that fell away below him.

Jacques noted the natural strength of this tongue of land on which the village stood. It was fortified on three sides by deep cut ravines, with almost sheer walls. Any tree that might help a climbing enemy had been cut away.

Tiring of his inspection, Jacques imagined himself an Iroquois and selecting a quiet place, climbed over the inner palisades and dropped into the village. He would have liked to celebrate the fact by a Mohawk war cry, but prudence stilled his lips.

Instead, he walked towards the center of St. Ignatius. The ground had been cleared and the long Huron cabins were erected on three sides of the square. The wooden chapel, cross surmounted, that the donnés had built for the Fathers' use was finished and occupied the remaining side.

Jacques saw the tall figure of his beloved Blackrobe entering the chapel. As usual Echon had to stoop low to escape hitting his head on the doorway. Then the bell that had been brought from the old St. Ignatius village began to ring out. The boy remembered it was the signal for the instruction class for neophytes.

From the cabins the Huron squaws and children came till they crowded the little chapel. The squaws' black hair was tied back neatly with the strips of eel skin, dyed a bright red, that gave them a field-of-poppies effect as they squatted on the earth floor before the wooden altar.

Father John Brebeuf had put on a lace surplice and his biretta and, as Jacques squeezed into the back of the chapel, he caught a part of the Blackrobe's instructions.

Echon had begun to speak about the Blessed Sacrament and his words were—"You, my children, believe without doubt that Jesus Christ is in the Host—that He is near us, within us, when we receive Holy Communion. He has chosen to conceal Himself like an unborn child in its mother's womb. If the mother did not believe that her child had life when it is concealed from her eyes and if she had too much curiosity to see it before its time, never could she see it except dead, and she would cause her own death. Thus whosoever shall refuse to believe, unless he hears Him, that Jesus Christ is in the Host, never will deserve to see Him. Let us wait till He Himself is willing to reveal Himself and then we shall behold Him with as much joy as a mother sees her little new born papoose."

More Echon told this silent Huron congregation and Jacques, as he listened to the Blackrobe's words felt his heart warm to the Hidden Lord in the Host.

Later, as Echon and his orderly toured the cabins, searching out any sick, they came to the last cabin. Among the families having their fire here was a captain. Maurice was his Christian name.

He welcomed Echon warmly and in the course of the conversation, remarked that most of the other families in the cabin were pagans.

Echon said: "Then, Maurice, you must ever be on your guard. There are many invitations to sin here."

"You say true, Echon. But I say to myself and my family, 'My children, the river which goes down from here to the French settlements on the Great River is nothing but rapids. Yet we make few shipwrecks on it, because we are always on our guard and at each turn we fear to lose both our goods and our lives.'

"The more a canoe is laden with precious furs, the more watchful one is to elude the rocks and the whirlpools which are there encountered. Since I have received Saving Waters, all my treasure is in my heart, and my faith is my most precious wealth. I dread sin more than we fear shipwreck. At each step I think that I have much to lose and that I guide a feeble canoe, but one nevertheless laden with the riches which come from Heaven. I foresee the dangers. I pray God to assist me. I distrust myself and trust in His goodness and never shall I believe myself in safety till I have arrived in Heaven. He who should have nothing or little to lose would fail quite easily. I have finished, Echon."

The tall Blackrobe had been listening attentively to Maurice's explanation and from time to time he had nodded approvingly. Now he replied: "My uncle, your heart is right with God. I wish there were many more like you."

As Jacques walked at Father Brebeuf's side, the missionary remarked: "Maurice is one of my consolations. He has faith like a light on a hillside. And many will follow his example. They will need his courage—yea, we will all need it."

Echon stopped in his strides and Jacques, looking up saw that they had come to the center of St. Ignatius II. Three towering pines rose before them.

It seemed to the watching boy as though the Blackrobe was seeing something desirable at the base of the center pine, for he embraced the bole and then kneeling before the tree was lost in prayer.

Jacques stood awkwardly aside, puzzled at Father Brebeuf's actions. Why should the Blackrobe kneel here at the base of the central tree?

The sunshine fell on the grayish hair and beard of Echon and it gave a tinge of glory to his features.

Soon, little Jacques was to remember this scene vividly, when he stood nearby on another memorable morning.

Chapter Nineteen

The Glorious Day

DAWN HAD YET to break—March 16, 1649—and Jacques Bourdon, having served Father Brebeuf's Mass in the little oblong log chapel that stood towards the center of St. Louis village, was kneeling among the devout Hurons, making his Thanksgiving. The afternoon before Father Superior had sent Jacques with a letter to Father Brebeuf at his mission station and when he had delivered it, it was too late to make the return to the Residence so he had slept in a Huron cabin.

Now youthful Father Gabriel Lalemant had commenced his Mass. Jacques would have liked to serve this Mass too, but Thomas, a Huron boy about Jacques' own age, had that coveted privilege. His clear Latin response, "Et cum spiritu tuo" broke the stillness.

Jacques looked up critically to see if his Huron rival was making any mistakes and his eyes fell on the kneeling figure of Father John Brebeuf. The tall Blackrobe had forgotten his surroundings completely. His lips were moving in fervent thanksgiving. Jacques' eyes were held by the priest's countenance. It seemed to reflect light that did not come from the grayish dawn, just breaking in the east. Nor did it come from the two half consumed candles that flickered in the draft, blowing in from cracks near the altar. The boy knew that his favorite Blackrobe was holy and being holy he was near to God. But this morning the boy thought that the veil had dropped from before Father Brebeuf's eyes and he was gazing on and conversing with All Holiness.

There came into Jacques' mind the remembrance of a conversation he had had with Father Brebeuf as they had snowshoed back to the Residence that day two weeks ago, when they had inspected the newly fortified village of St. Ignatius II. The Blackrobe had been telling Jacques of his missionary trip to the Neutral nation, leagues to the south. That had taken place some years before.

Now Father Brebeuf's very words came into Jacques' mind: "I saw a great cross, so it seemed to me. It stretched across the skies till all Huronia lay under its shadow. I looked and looked and I seemed to understand that it meant that by the deaths of some of us, many of these poor Hurons' children would come happily to Paradise."

Just why this scrap of a former conversation came back to Jacques' mind at this present moment he could not tell.

Despite the bitter cold—the boy's skin was fairly hardened to it now, after months in Huronia—it seemed peaceful and calm in this rude log cabin chapel. Jacques felt at utter peace.

Then his mind turned to youthful Father Gabriel Lalemant and something he had remarked yesterday evening as they sat about the fire, the boy remembered.

"My Jacques, whenever you thank the good God for coming into your heart at Communion, stop a few moments and let your mind dwell on the word 'Almighty.' It's a most strengthening word. Good Father Brebeuf, whose companion I am here in these two villages, taught me this. Think on the word 'Almighty' and you will draw strength for whatever is ahead."

Jacques let his thoughts dwell on the all powerful God—He can do all things—He is more powerful than all the Iroquois nations—He would wipe them out in the flash of an eye—Father John knows that—young Father Gabriel too—I shall trust Him too—dear powerful God—all powerful God—I know You will ever protect me—now and at the hour of my death. . . . I wonder when that will be?

Father Gabriel had come to the Consecration in his Mass. The bell was ringing. Jacques looked up reverently at the white Host—"Almighty God, my Lord and my God," he prayed.

Then the boy's prayers were rudely interrupted. There were excited whisperings in the doorway. A Huron burst into the chapel.

"Echon, Echon," he cried, "it is important, Echon."

Father John Brebeuf gave a last look of love at the Host in Father Gabriel's hand. He motioned the captain into silence till the second consecration was over. Then the tall Blackrobe strode out of the chapel.

Curiosity made Jacques dog his heels.

There on the hard snow in the first gray light of dawn lay a Huron brave. A bloody gash showed along his scalp. He had been running and his breast still heaved violently.

Kettle Hound had pushed forward and was sniffing curiously at the brave. The missioner knelt down at the heaving man's side.

"What news, my brother?" he asked gently.

The brave looked up. "Echon," he said, "St. Ignatius village—Echon—our enemies—a large band of Mohawk Iroquois fell on my village before light this morning. There were no Iroquois in the country—then they—they came like the leaves in autumn."

"Where were all the Huron braves?" asked Echon.

"Most of them left yesterday—for a hunt. A runner—had come, saying ten or twelve moose—were sighted three leagues to the—to the northward."

"I am suspicious ever of these runners who come with good hunting news," observed Father Brebeuf, "so were the men of Teanaostaye drawn away before the Iroquois swooped down and took that village."

The wounded Huron was anxious to conclude his news.

"Listen, Echon. We were few. The new defenses were strong. But the Iroquois seemed to know—they avoided these strong palisades and poured into the village through the unfinished wall on the northern side.

"I was awakened by screams of squaws and children in the next cabin. I rushed out. Some captains were making a stand in the northern part of the village. I joined them. But more and more Iroquois came. They were everywhere. I fought beside the few remaining braves. An arrow struck me here and here. Then a tomahawk thrown from the dark felled me. See, I still bleed." The Huron pointed to the cruel scalp wound.

"The fighting had drifted away from where I lay, towards the center of the village. When I became conscious again, I knew the village was taken. I crawled to the ravine side and dropped down. When I was free of the village I took the trail to St. Louis and here I am. You are all dead men——"

"Not yet," cried Estienne, the Huron war captain of the village who had come out of the chapel and stood listening to the wounded runner. "The Iroquois will be here soon and we will be ready for them."

He cried an order and the long conch shell calls began assembling all the villagers to the palisades.

Jacques stayed close to Father Brebeuf and even Kettle Hound seemed to sense dangers and was a nuisance under foot.

In the dawn light the flitting shadows of braves and squaws running softly occupied Jacques' mind till Father Brebeuf called: "Come, my son, we must be ready."

The tall Blackrobe beckoned the boy closer. "Prepare now, little one, and make your Confession while there is yet time."

Swiftly Jacques covered the ten days since his last confession. All the while the Blackrobe was still in fervent prayer. When the boy was ready, he came and stood respectfully beside Father Brebeuf.

The gigantic Blackrobe motioned him to kneel and seating himself on a nearby log heard Jacques' confession. When he had given Absolution he whispered: "Listen well, my very dear little one, we are old friends and one of us stands close to God's eternity at this moment. Let us promise each other, as good friends should, that he who tarries, will invoke the aid of him whom God takes, asking confidently what aid he needs. Will my little one remember that and promise?"

"Yes; my Father," Jacques whispered in an awed tone.

"Always, till eternity?"

"Always, my Father."

"Then you need fear nothing, for valiant years on God's service," Father Brebeuf paused and added, "Father Jacques."

The wail went up as the day was breaking: "The Iroquois—the Iroquois come! We are dead men!"

Quickly Echon rose to his feet. "Stay close to me, Jacques, I'll need my orderly now."

"Echon! Echon!" the cry went up. The Blackrobe strode into the midst of an excited group of squaws.

"Listen, my good aunts. The Iroquois will soon be within the palisades. Flee all of you into the forests and make your way to St. Mary's, where the French soldiers can defend you. Go now, lest it be too late."

"Give us your blessing, Echon, and absolve us." The cry was taken up.

"Kneel down, aunts." All within sound of the Blackrobe's voice obeyed.

"Now, say the Act of Contrition."

In Huron the words, asking God's forgiveness, poured out.

Echon was saying, "Ego vos absolvo. . . ." His right hand rose and made the Sign of the Cross.

"Say after me the prayer that I have often told you to say for our enemies."

Echon began in Huron, "Pardon, O Lord, those who pursue us with undying hatred."

The prayer was repeated like a litany's responses.

"Who murder us without pity. . . ."

"Open their eyes to the truth that they may know You and love You."

". . . know You and love You."

"That they may be friends to Thee and us."

". . . to Thee and us."

"Amen."

"Amen. Amen."

At the conclusion of the prayer, Echon added: "Now go, my aunts, all who can."

A squaw cried out: "Come, come with us, Echon."

"You speak with a foolish tongue, my aunt. You know I can't do that. My place is with the braves.

"Go and hurry before it is too late."

All about were squaws and children, hurrying by, carrying their few valuables.

Another and another runner had come. Both were badly wounded and fell exhausted as they reached the shelter of the palisades. Carried within, from their lips came scant but sufficient details to let Father Brebeuf know that the Iroquois held St. Ignatius and most of its defenders were dead or captives under torture.

Jacques saw Father Brebeuf kneeling at Father Gabriel's feet and he knew the Blackrobes were confessing to each other.

Then the boy's attention was called elsewhere. From the northern woods arose shrill war cries, growing more audible every second. The victorious Iroquois had arrived before St. Louis village.

Echon turned into a nearby cabin. An old squaw—she must have seen a hundred winters—sat peacefully in the doorway.

"Echon," she quavered, "I knew that you would be around. Give me Saving Waters. I wish to go with my children and grandchildren."

The missioner baptized the ancient squaw.

Jacques had run into the chapel and came after Father Brebeuf, carrying a bark dish that contained holy water. He found Echon going from cabin to cabin, baptizing all he found.

Jacques had entered a pagan cabin. He noticed in the comparative darkness two solemn faced papooses. They were strapped to their boards and had been hung to a post—evidently forgotten in the excitement of the coming attack.

The boy dipped his hand into the holy water and hastily baptized each. To the first he gave the name of Isaac Jogues and to the other that of Father Jogues' martyred boy companion, John Lalande. Both freshly baptized papooses began to cry lustily.

Jacques heard his name called and he ran out of the cabin. Above the increasing noises the Blackrobe shouted, to Jacques: "Go, find Father Gabriel and tell him to consume all sacred hosts."

Jacques ran back towards the center of the village. He saw Father Gabriel Lalemant before the door of the chapel. He was trying to speak to the people. Noticing the boy, he called out: "Jacques, my boy, lend me your tongue."

"Surely, my Father."

Jacques flung out his order in fluent Huron: "Squaws, let Echon's boy close to this Blackrobe."

He emphasized his command with vigorous pushes till he stood beside Father Gabriel.

"What are these squaws saying?" asked the Blackrobe. "They speak too fast for my ear."

Jacques turned and listened to the excited talk. Then he translated: "They say Echon is pouring Saving Waters on the heads of all who wish it. We are dead women. We wish Saving Waters. This they say," Jacques concluded and added: "Father John says first for you to consume all hosts."

When Father Gabriel Lalemant understood the request, he said: "Tell them I will be back in a moment."

The youthful missioner dashed into the chapel and before he returned the crowd of squaws and children about Jacques had increased considerably.

"All these say they wish Saving Waters," called out the boy, "they say hasten before they are dead women."

Father Gabriel Lalemant began hastily to pour the water on the heads of the kneeling catechumens and pagans, who held up their papooses.

Jacques always carried vivid memories of that crowded hour of bitter defense. The pitifully small garrison crouching behind the palisades and shooting their arrows at every visible figure of the enemy. The noise of the six arquebuses that St. Louis village possessed. Squaws busy over hastily built fires behind the palisades, heating the kettles of boiling water that would be poured down on the naked bodies of the Iroquois who attempted to scale the wooden walls.

He had left Father Gabriel and was seeking his own Blackrobe. The shouting and cries grew louder as Jacques neared the southern palisades. He recognized the high shrill war cries of the Mohawks. Then he saw Father Brebeuf's figure moving behind the lines of palisades. He ran to catch up with him. Kettle Hound came from nowhere and raced at his heels.

The gigantic Blackrobe had stooped by a dying Huron. There was a ghastly wound in his breast.

Jacques stopped at a distance when he saw that the Blackrobe was hearing the brave's confession. The boy saw the sign of Absolution and he came nearer. The brave stiffened in Father Brebeuf's arms and Jacques knew another Huron had left the fighting.

The boy heard the sound of chopping without the palisade. The enemy were trying to hack an opening. There was a running of feet on the platform above and two kettles of steaming water were emptied on the attackers. Screams of burning agony. . . .

Here the few Huron defenders had three arquebuses. From the woods outside the sounds of at least a dozen reached the boy's ears.

It was clear daylight now and Jacques, peeking through an opening in the palisade suddenly saw several hundred Iroquois charge into the open. A chief with bright red dyed eagle feathers in his hair led them.

"The enemy charge! The enemy charge!" rang the warning up and down the walls. Kettles of scalding water that the squaws had ready were passed up and balanced on the top of the palisade. The arquebuses thundered and the high shrill war cries of Iroquois and Huron mingled into noise indescribable.

Then the waves of Mohawk Iroquois, fresh from their capture of St. Ignatius II, dashed upon the much weaker defenses of St. Louis. Working furiously squaws passed up and braves poured down the scalding water on the foremost enemy, attempting to scramble up the palisades.

A huge Iroquois captain was struck full in the chest by the fiery stream and fell backwards. As he lay writhing on the ground the Huron beside Jacques put three arrows in rapid succession into his breast. They were still quivering when a war club whizzed by the boy's ear and laid the brave low.

Suddenly three posts of the palisades not twenty feet away from where Jacques stood, swayed and crashed inward. Through this small opening burst the first of the Mohawks. A chief's bright red feathers in his hair. Then more, even more Mohawks came through the opening.

Despite the desperate defense of the Hurons who had run to meet this new menace, the increasing swarm of Mohawks within the palisades made them retreat. Hand to hand fighting broke out all along the palisade's platform as other Mohawks scaled the walls.

Jacques had retreated from the palisades and now he heard his name called. He turned and saw Father Brebeuf with a frightened Kettle Hound at his heels.

"The fight is being lost, little one. Let us go towards the chapel."

Once back near the center of the village, all was confusion. Jacques saw youthful Father Gabriel Lalemant. His thick brimmed black felt hat was pushed back on his head and he was wearied from baptizing the papooses that squaws held up.

Jacques looked to the eastward and noticed new danger. Another breach had been made there and Mohawks were already firing the cabins and the wind was carrying sparks towards the center of the village.

A haze of smoke rapidly drifted over the village. In the increasing smoke Father Brebeuf was pouring the waters of Baptism on the remaining Hurons of the group. The smoke began to make Jacques choke and cough.

The next events came so swiftly that Jacques had only confused recollections of them.

War-painted Mohawks appeared to the east and the south of the center. A rim of Hurons, squaws as well as braves, led by the wounded Estienne, were retreating towards the chapel.

An arrow whizzed overhead and Jacques ducked instinctively. Next second another lodged in his thigh. The sharp pain brought him to his knee. He saw the blood spurt and he sat down with sudden weakness.

Then Father Brebeuf was at his side and with deft hands he was bandaging the wound. He was saying: "My little one has shed some of his blood for Christ. Offer it gladly, you fortunate child."

"I did that, my Father," said Jacques simply.

The tall Blackrobe looked on Jacques wishfully, "This wound of yours is not to death, little one."

He stooped low and kissed the boy's forehead, whispering, "Till we meet in Heaven. I shall never forget my Jacques. Remember our promise always."

Then Father John Brebeuf was gone to minister to a squaw whose head was a gaping wound.

Now the pall of smoke from burning cabins was hanging low over all St. Louis village. He knew the fighting was all about him, but the pain of his wound made Jacques close his eyes and the sounds of conflict, cries and groans and prayers came as through a troubled dream.

When Jacques opened his eyes again a band of ten Hurons were fighting five times their number close by the center of the village. Between the fighting warriors and the chapel Jacques saw the blackrobed figures of Fathers Brebeuf and Lalemant. Both were calmly administering to wounded braves.

Every once in a while Kettle Hound who kept at Father Brebeuf's heels, would jump up and receive a reassuring pat on the head from his master.

By looking in the other direction the scene changed. All the Hurons were now on the ground, writhing from wounds or motionless in death.

The two Blackrobes stood unhurt.

Then Jacques heard a voice that he recognized with terror. For there coming through the haze was Hot Ashes, his former captor, and close behind him loomed the form of The Frog.

Hot Ashes was crying, "Here is Echon. We have the white sorcerer alive."

Another voice, evidently one of authority commanded: "Take Echon alive and the other Blackrobe alive."

Jacques looked and saw the bright red feathers of the Mohawk war chief who had been first to come through the palisades.

This order was obeyed, for the approaching Iroquois lowered their arquebuses and bows. In grim silence the Iroquois surrounded the two Blackrobes.

Jacques thought Father Brebeuf never had seemed more majestic than at this moment when he stood silent and erect, looking steadily into the eyes of the advancing enemy. Youthful Father Gabriel Lalemant stood, like a lamb, with downcast eyes. Kettle Hound at Father Brebeuf's knee whined and his master stooped to pet the dog's head reassuringly.

Suddenly Father Brebeuf spoke out: "Yes, my brothers, I am Echon, the white captain of the prayer. You see my companion and I are unarmed. Why do you hesitate?"

Jacques knew that Echon's reputation had spread to the Iroquois Long Houses and he well understood their hesitation.

With a smile and with hands extended Echon advanced towards the Mohawks.

"Do not be afraid, my brothers, we are unarmed." And he held out his hands, palms up.

This last remark seemed to infuriate the warriors for five or six rushed on the missioners to hurl them to the ground. Kettle Hound snarled and then yelped with pain as a warrior kicked him savagely away.

Jacques saw Father Brebeuf dragged close to the Mohawk chief who grabbed his right hand and tore off with his teeth the nail of the missioner's index finger. . . .

Jacques shut his eyes as he seemed to suffer the agonizing pains. He felt a moist tongue licking his ear and there was a whimpering Kettle Hound. Jacques took the trembling dog into his arms and hugged him.

Out of the haze came other Mohawk Iroquois. These drove to the center of the village all the defenders who were yet alive. As each came he was stripped naked, arms bound behind and thrown on the ground. Mohawks leapt on each helpless captive and tore off a nail or two.

A warrior who had come up unnoticed jabbed Jacques with the point of his knife and the boy winced.

"The white prayer puppy is not dead. Get over there."

Jacques rose with pain and hobbled on his wounded leg. Then he heard a disagreeable laugh.

"We meet again, French boy."

Jacques looked up. There was Stripling Tree grinning wickedly down on him.

Said the Iroquois boy, "It is too warm for clothes." And Jacques was violently stripped and pushed roughly to the ground. Stripling Tree grinned and took Jacques' right hand. . . .

It was while Jacques lay there, the maddening pain in his torn finger making him forget his surroundings, that Hot Ashes and The Frog emerged out of the smoky atmosphere. Stripling Tree ran over to them and pointed excitedly to Jacques.

The three Mohawks came over and grinned down on the boy....

"My nephew has how many finger nails left, let me see?" inquired The Frog gently as he took Jacques' throbbing hand. . . . "Too many." . . . "That's better, little nephew."

Later, the order was given to fire the remaining cabins and retreat to St. Ignatius where the main party of Iroquois had stayed to strengthen the fortifications and provide a place of refuge in case of unexpected defeat at Huron hands.

The captives of St. Louis village who were able to walk were herded into a long line, their backs laden with loot from the burning cabins, and they were started on the trail to St. Ignatius.

The two missioners and Jacques were detained till the last.

Jacques wished he had been sent ahead when he saw and heard the unfortunate Hurons, who were unable to walk, being pitched into the flaming chapel.

He turned and saw Father Brebeuf in the act of making the Sign of the Cross and giving Absolution to the burning captives.

Hot Ashes cried out, "Come, Echon's boy, you here before the young Blackrobe. Then Echon last."

So the three took their places in the line and passed out of the ruined gate of smoke-filled St. Louis village. The trail was red marked before them as it lay across the snows. The cries of helpless Hurons, still burning in the village, rang in Jacques' ears. It was with difficulty that he was able to repeat "Jesus, have mercy. Jesus, have mercy," as he was driven along through the morning forests towards the crueler welcome ahead.

Chapter Twenty

Like a Rock

ALL ALONG the league long trail to Saint Ignatius II the line of captives was driven. It had turned into a bitter March morning and now the cold began to penetrate Jacques' bones.

There came into his mind the old familiar prayer that he had said so often since his days at Our Lady of the Angels and he found strength in repeating the words: "Little Master, I thank You for keeping me from morning till now. Keep me the rest of the way. Forget my faults and help me to overcome them. I give You my acts. Give me Your Grace to perform them well."

In the repetition of these words was surprising strength and they made Jacques forget his paining finger tips and whatever pains awaited him in the other village. The sustaining thought had come that like the Blackrobes behind him in the line, he was suffering something for his Faith. For the Iroquois captors had shown their especial hatred of all Followers of the Prayer in the unremitting warfare they waged on them.

At length the captured strong village of Ignatius II was in view. Jacques now saw the main party of Mohawk Iroquois. A large band of them were busy repairing the damages done to the sixteen feet high palisades during the night's assault and already they had made St. Ignatius an Iroquois stronghold into which they might retreat if defeated.

The news of Echon's capture had preceded his approach and

now all work was stopped and the long line of unfortunate Hurons ahead of Jacques and the two Blackrobes began to be driven with cries and cruel blows through the gates of St. Ignatius.

Jacques had been halted a few hundred feet from the village and gladly sank on the snow to rest. He could hear the torture cries of those ahead of him, but the sight of their agony was blotted out by the palisades.

The boy kept repeating a part of his prayer, "Little Master, keep me from morning till now." Then Stripling Tree and The Frog stood over him. The Mohawk boy kicked Jacques up. The Frog gave him a push forward, saying, "Go now, my nephew, our braves wish to caress you." A switch stung his shoulders—and Jacques was running the gauntlet.

He sensed rows of painted faces and tattooed breasts; bodies blackened by pine fires; freshly bleeding scalps dangling from every waist. Grinning demons with cruel fists struck him down; grinning demons kicked him up and forward. The yells of pandemonium about him—above him. He was wrenched to the left and battered to the right. Somehow he stumbled on. Now clubbed and switched, punched and pummelled, always on and on and on. "Jesus, help me. Jesus, help me." The words were knocked out of him. . . .

He was through the gates and seemingly the endless lines of Mohawk tormentors opened a lane ahead of him. Would the gauntlet ever end? Would he live to the end?

Blood was streaming down his face and blinding the way. Rough hands guided him down the lane. At last Jacques seemed to know that he was near the center of the village. He fell forward. He was not kicked up. But some one—Stripling Tree it seemed—was dragging him like a ripped sack across the rough ground.

Ablaze with pains Jacques heard, as though coming through a fog, the voice of Stripling Tree saying, "Lie there, you French dog." He was savagely kicked into a group of groaning Hurons. His torture was over for the time being.

Down the lane of the gauntlet came the high yells and cries of savage hatred, "Echon! Echon! Echon!" Jacques knew that the tall Blackrobe was beginning to run his gauntlet. A mighty roar told the boy that Echon had staggered within the gates. The roar grew nearer—nearer.

With difficulty Jacques turned. There coming towards the center of the village, like a swarm of infuriated bees buzzing around a helpless animal, as Jacques had once seen bees attack an unfortunate bear, was Father John Brebeuf and his tormentors. He was livid and blinded and he staggered drunkenly along. Redrobed indeed!

Jacques forgot his own pains as pity filled his eyes at this sight of his friend and the boy's own too recent running of the gauntlet seemed less painful. The tall Blackrobe was pushed and struck and hurled forward to fall out of breath a few feet away from where Jacques lay.

There was a lull in the tortures and Stripling Tree who seemed to take delight in remaining close to Jacques explained the reason.

"The Great War Captain has ordered fresh stakes to be driven near here for Echon. We caress him now."

Jacques heard him faintly as drowsiness flowed over him from his strenuous efforts in running the gauntlet. He let it carry him on. "Little Master, I suffer for You. . . ."

Jacques was kicked into full wakefulness. Mockingly Stripling Tree and Hot Ashes stood over him. Said the latter: "So our little nephew is sleeping in the day time. It is too cool here. We will put our nephew in a place where it will be warmer for him."

"Much warmer," added the Iroquois boy maliciously.

Hot Ashes was speaking, "The Great War Captain has ordered a chief's place of honor for Echon's boy and the young Blackrobe. Come."

Jacques was jerked to his feet and led across the bodies of the captives. Hot Ashes and Stripling Tree were stepping on them as though they were as many stones under foot.

He saw that they were taking him to the cleared space in the center of St. Ignatius village, beneath the three tall pines. He remembered this spot, but now how changed it was. The cabins that had circled this space were but smoking ruins with half consumed corpses everywhere. A row of stakes, blackened and burnt down to foot high points, told mutely of other horrors enacted here but recently.

Three freshly cut stakes were driven into the ground about fifteen or twenty feet apart. Before the further one the boy saw a bruised bloodied form. The body was swollen and livid and Jacques had difficulty in recognizing Father Gabriel Lalemant.

A tall captain with a red dyed bear skin over his shoulders ordered: "Tie Echon's boy there."

Jacques was dragged to the fresh stake. His arms were wrenched back till he felt his shoulders might be dislocated. Elbows and wrists were tied tightly with deer thong. The position was painfully erect as the rough stake buried itself between the boy's shoulders.

Then Jacques found that he was forgotten.

The hundreds of Iroquois warriors were shouting for Echon. It rose shrilly from all about the square. Father Brebeuf had to be assisted to his stake, though he tried to walk unaided. Like Father Lalemant, the caressing of the gauntlet had almost left his body unrecognizable.

When his arms were pinioned behind, the Blackrobe raised his voice: "My children," Jacques saw that he was ignoring the Iroquois and addressing the Hurons who lay nearby, "my children, let us lift our eyes to heaven and at the height of our sufferings, remember the Good God sees them and that soon they will bring an exceeding reward. Let us die in the Faith and hope for His goodness. I have more pity for you than for myself. Bear with courage the few remaining pains. They will end with our lives, the glory which follows them will never end."

From the heap of bound captives came the voice of the captain Estienne who had been taken at St. Louis.

"Echon," he called, "our spirits shall be in Heaven when our bodies shall be suffering on earth. Pray to God for us that He may show us His mercy."

"We will invoke Him even until death," cried another.

The Iroquois warriors had listened in silence to Echon's words up to this. Now the Great War Captain gave the signal for the torture to begin.

Jacques saw The Frog come up.

"Echon," he called, "do you know me?"

Father Brebeuf turned his head and gazed long at The Frog.

"Were you not in Toanche once?"

"I was born there, Echon."

"And did I not pour Saving Waters on you?"

"You did."

"Why do I see you in Mohawk paint now?"

"Long ago I gave up the lying Prayer. Now, Echon, I am going to do you a kindness. You teach that Saving Waters and suffering in this life lead straight to heaven. I am going to pour Saving Waters on you so that you will go to this heaven sooner."

Mockingly The Frog walked to the fires and taking a kettle of boiling water, he returned. Reaching up on tiptoe he poured the steaming liquid on the head of Echon. Three times he repeated this mockery of Holy Baptism, saying at the end, "Go to heaven, Echon, for you are well prepared with Saving Waters."

Without a murmur the tall Blackrobe endured the pains.

There were a few drops of scalding water in the kettle. As he passed Jacques The Frog grinned and flipped them on the boy's body. He winced with sudden pain. The Great War Captain barked out a command to The Frog to let the white prayer cub alone for the present.

Jacques bit his lips to keep back the desire to yell. When he turned his head to gaze again at Father Brebeuf he saw a circle of tormentors about him. The smoke from the fires floated low and mercifully hid the Blackrobes' agony . . .

When the wind carried the choking smoke in another direction Jacques glimpsed several Mohawk warriors heating hatchets in the fires. One of these warriors was Hot Ashes. Each took out of the flames a red hot hatchet. As each passed close to where Jacques was bound he felt the heat from these glowing irons. These they were applying to the body of the helpless Blackrobe. The boy looked away. . . .

When Hot Ashes passed Jacques again he held at arm's length a long green vine stem. It was looped and the Mohawk brave grasped each end. On the stem hung six glowing hatchets.

Jacques had heard stories of this torture but had never seen it applied before.

Cried out Hot Ashes, smiling mockingly at his silent victim: "Echon, you are a Great Captain. I wish to honor you with this necklace of precious porcelain."

With this Hot Ashes passed the burning hatchet necklace over the head of the Blackrobe and rested it on his shoulders, so that three of the hatchets pressed his breast and the other three his back. . . .

There was silence in the ranks of the watching Iroquois as they waited to hear Echon's cries. But no sound came from his lips. He stood like a rock, rigid against the stake.

Finally the silence infuriated the Iroquois and they redoubled their efforts to draw a cry from him. More hatchets were applied and once through an opening in the circle of tormentors Jacques had a glimpse of the martyr. Great white blisters had formed on the sides of the body. Still the silence of the rock.

Hot Ashes and The Frog brought up a pelt of bark, smeared with pitch and resin. This they tied under the armpits of Echon. It was set on fire. It crackled and burst into flames. . . .

From the midst of the smoke come the hoarse cry, "Jesus, Jesus."

It was the first sound Father Brebeuf had uttered since he had exhorted the Christian Hurons. It seemed to make his tormentors more furious.

The braves around Father Brebeuf completely hid the sight of him. Jacques knew from their polite mockery they were cutting off roasted flesh and asking Echon if he was not hungry.

Jacques had a glimpse of Father Gabriel Lalemant, rigidly bound to his stake. His eyes were blackened and completely closed from his running of the gauntlet and he was mercifully spared the sight of the tortures that awaited him when these demons were done with Echon. Father Gabriel's lips were moving in prayer.

Suddenly Jacques heard the voice of Hot Ashes yelling, "Echon, you will tell no more of your Prayer lies to your Huron friends."

With this he forced open the mouth of Father Brebeuf and he thrust a blazing stick down his throat. So did The Frog and others. . . .

When Jacques was again able to see through the maddening circle about the sufferer, the face was not the face of a man . . . The stake behind the Blackrobe was ablaze. The thongs burnt through and the body of Father Brebeuf fell forward. . . .

Out of the surrounding demons came the Great War Chief. He stopped. His knife circled the scalp and he held the graying lock up. The Mohawks were shouting now louder than ever. "Echon is dead. Echon is dead. Echon is dead."

The Great Captain had raised his arm for silence. He had instant Iroquois obedience. The only sound the prayers of Christian Hurons.

The Great Captain cut open the breast and held high the heart of Brebeuf, crying: "Brothers, I drink the blood of this Great White Sorcerer that we may all get some of his bravery. Drink, brother Mohawks. . . ."

Now fires were prepared all about the center of St Ignatius village and stakes driven and Hurons tied helplessly.

Many of these were made to sing and their mournful notes were often drowned out by the shrieks of a victim tortured beyond human endurance.

Jacques knew that hours had passed since he had been tied to his stake. It was late afternoon and the gray overcast skies held a threat of snow.

The boy sickened with the sight of horrors all about him. Still no further attempt was made to touch him or Father Gabriel Lalemant. They seemed to have been forgotten in the midst of cruelties.

With the coming of night the flames leapt up, giving a more vivid appearance of the infernal regions with helpless prisoners and dancing yelling demons everywhere.

Now Hot Ashes and Stripling Tree stood beside the boy. He thought that his time had come and he said a prayer for strength. But they cut his thongs and he was dragged over burnt corpses to a partially ruined cabin. Here he was thrown heavily to the earth and told to lie still. The air was purer here and Jacques gulped down large draughts of it. He ached in every bone from the hours of rigid erectness against the stake.

From without came increasing cries and Jacques recalled that Stripling Tree had said in departing: "We go to caress Atironta, the other Blackrobe."

Time passed and the boy slept. He awoke to hear the constant yells of Father Gabriel Lalemant's tormentors. Then the realization came like a shock of discovery—Echon was dead. Jacques found himself praying to blessed Father John Brebeuf, "Please give me strength for whatever is to be done to me."

He seemed to feel out of the darkness the strong arms of his Blackrobe about him; the same feeling of protection he remembered from that time in the snows, when he had hit his head and his Blackrobe had built the fire.

Other fires cast their reflections on the side of the cabin. Cries and moans, yells and shrieks of agony, enforced singing marred by pains, all came in one ceaseless confused sound from the center of the village.

Then Jacques heard steps without the cabin. He braced himself for what was to come.

Hot Ashes entered the cabin alone. The Iroquois warrior was dripping from his share in the tortures and he smelt of many pine fires. But he spoke softly: "Listen, little nephew, Echon asked a favor for you when he stood like a Great Captain at the stake. He asked me to spare Echon's boy from the stake. You are my escaped prisoner and I remembered that once you saved my life in the white water. So Hot Ashes grants Echon's favor."

Jacques could hardly believe what words he was hearing. Yet the fierce Iroquois cut his leg thongs. He said: "Stay here till you hear my footsteps no more. Back of this cabin is the ravine and make your way back to the strong village of the Blackrobes. But," he added as an afterthought, "do not let other Mohawks see you. For then I could not help you."

With these final words of warning, Hot Ashes was gone into the night.

Jacques felt stunned by this sudden change in his condition. Blessed Father Brebeuf was indeed helping him. Rapidly, he blessed himself and got to his feet. With difficulty he stood. He rubbed his legs and arms till circulation was restored. The old arrow wound in his thigh began to pain. He found an abandoned elk skin robe in the cabin. Gratefully he draped it over his shoulders. He limped to the opening in the cabin and peered out.

Forty or more feet away were the fires and the Iroquois and their victims. Jacques could see the black shadows as they passed before the leaping flames. Other greater shadows played on the tree tops. A Christian squaw was shrieking under fire torture. . . .

Under the three tall pines, where the largest crowd was, Jacques knew Father Gabriel Lalemant stood. He said a Hail Mary for the Blackrobe's strength and turned away.

He flattened himself against the side of the cabin and worked through the light till he came to the back of the cabin. Here it was a few painful steps to the long black barrier of the palisades.

Jacques felt along in the dark, touching pine upright after pine upright, till he came to two spaced far enough apart for him to squeeze through.

Just then he heard Stripling Tree shouting: "The white cub has escaped. He is not in the cabin." Then The Frog's answering shout: "The white cub has escaped. Then we must tell Hot Ashes and seek him."

Jacques listened for no further conversation. He took a step in the dark away from the palisades. His foot rested on black space and he was falling. His robe caught and almost choked him. He clutched instinctively at a branch which struck his hand. This checked his fall. Then the boy worked his way down the steep ravine side till his feet were wet. He knew that he had come to the stream at the bottom of the ravine.

The anguished cries came faintly down here, as though Jacques was hearing them in a nightmare. The boy knew if he was to make his escape to St. Mary's it would have to be before dawn and that, he felt, would break shortly.

Along the tiny ice banked stream that flowed through the bottom of this ravine Jacques worked his way. The feel of the icy water was soothing to the boy's body. He lay face down and drank and drank. Then he crawled on, low like a bear, to escape the overhanging branches.

The ravine turned to the northward and here Jacques found an overhanging rock. He felt under it and made a glad discovery. The earth fell away to fashion a small cave. Gratefully Jacques crawled into this shelter. Faintly came the sounds from the village almost overhead. Jacques decided that it was too near dawn to attempt to go further and run the risk of recapture.

A bedding of soggy leaves were on the cave's floor. Jacques piled some of these before the entrance and huddled down in the cold. His elk skin robe about him. Cold light was graying the ravine. Jacques put away the disturbing thoughts of possible recapture. Then he remembered his Blackrobe's promise of protection all the days of his life.

Jacques began to think of Father Brebeuf enjoying his first taste of Heaven. Meeting the Good God, the Squaw in Blue . . . Peter of Teanaostaye . . . Father Anthony Daniel . . . the Huron babies . . . many, many others . . . maybe he will forget me in his joy. No; he would never do that . . . he thought of me tied to the stake . . . I'm Echon's boy.

The sleep of exhaustion overcame Jacques, as the morning of March 18, 1649, broke.

Chapter Twenty-One
The Cup of Suffering

JACQUES BOURDON became aware of his surroundings. He saw it was bright daylight and the snowy stillness was oppressive. He felt frozen and had the delusion that if he moved his limbs they might break off.

Then he heard the crackling of a branch. He crouched lower and his heart began to pound. Someone was coming. The paralyzing thought came that The Frog or Stripling Tree had tracked him to this rock cave and his recapture was a matter of moments. He experienced the same trapped feeling he had had that rainy afternoon months before, when he and Louis Joliet were almost discovered at the log in the swamp.

The sound grew louder. Then Jacques heard a whimper and the next second Kettle Hound pushed himself through the leaves and bounded into the boy's arms. At this unexpected reunion, he hugged Kettle Hound and the dog whined with pain. There was a long gash on his right side, evidently a knife wound. He yelped when Jacques touched the clotted blood.

"Kettle Hound, some Mohawk almost had you for his pot that time. I wonder how you escaped and where have you been since yesterday?"

Kettle Hound thumped his tail against the boy's leg and tried to tell of his harrowing adventures. Then Father Brebeuf's dog pushed out of the cave entrance and showed by his actions that he wished Jacques to follow him.

Cautiously Jacques looked out. Nothing but the snow-laden underbrush and the icy banked stream met his gaze. He listened. Not a sound came from the sacked village above.

Jacques felt satisfied that the Iroquois, as usual, had finished their business and departed. So cautiously he crawled out. With difficulty he made his way up the rather steep side of the ravine.

Kettle Hound had found a foothold and scrambled up ahead of him. At the top Jacques stopped. Before he showed himself he lay still a quarter of an hour and then, certain that the village of St. Ignatius was deserted by the enemy, he crept to the base of the palisades. Kettle Hound had disappeared but now he came running within the row of pine stakes. If the dog could find an opening, so could Jacques. Thirty feet away Jacques discovered a stake was down and he was able to squeeze through.

He climbed to the fighting platform and looked over what was left of the Huron village. Little streams of smoke like steam from volcanic ground whirled up in spots where the fire had not completely died down. The fierce heat of the burning had melted all trace of snow within the palisades. Ash blackened figures of Hurons lay where they had died in the ruins of cabins. Down by the gates where Jacques had stood a few days ago, greater heaps of corpses told of the resistance made here before the village's taking, or, what was possibly more correct, the final slaughter of the unwanted captives. Across the cabin ruins Jacques saw the three tall pines still standing towards the center of St. Ignatius. Their boles were blackened by much fire and Jacques' recollections of the sufferings he had witnessed there made him turn away.

As he did so, his foot slipped on a loose board in the platform and he lost his balance. His numbed hands clutched in vain and he was falling. There was a sharp crack as his right foot hit the ground and it bent under him. He cried out.

When he attempted to rise he fell forward with pain. He knew that he had broken a bone. Finally he gave up any attempt to drag himself along. Movement only increased his agony.

The cold numbed his limbs and he began to fear that he might freeze to death. The stillness of death was everywhere. He would never be able to crawl to the Residence now ... it did not matter ...

Half an hour had passed and Jacques felt drowsiness creeping over him. It was all right to lie here. He would close his eyes ...

He opened them suddenly. Certainly it was not imagination. He had heard voices. Their tones carried on the cold air. Some people were coming into the village. Jacques listened attentively. Maybe they would take him for another corpse. Then he heard blessed French words.

There, standing within the palisades by the gate was a group of men. Jacques instantly recognized Little Martin and Christopher Regnaut, the donné. Three Huron warriors were with them.

The boy shouted. He was heard and the men ran behind the gate and disappeared. Jacques called out desperately in French: "Brother Martin! Christopher! I am Jacques. Come, I am hurt. Brother Martin!"

Little Martin came at the head of the party. When he saw Jacques, he cried: "Thank God, you are alive! But what's the matter with this ankle?"

He did not need to ask further for Jacques had collapsed in his arms.

Jacques was barely conscious of pain. He had faint recollection of some one putting splints to the leg. From somewhere a sled appeared. He was lifted gently and wrapped in a blanket and laid on the sled. He did recall Brother Martin saying: "Lie quiet now. A squaw refugee reported that you had been killed in the taking of St. Louis Mission. Then another thought that she saw you among the captives being driven towards St. Ignatius."

"She was right, but why do you come here now?" inquired Jacques.

"Because our scouts, sent from the Residence, reported that the Iroquois war party of over 1200 fled the country as silently as they came. And Father Superior sent us to seek our Fathers and you."

"Can you tell us any details of Father Brebeuf's and Father Gabriel Lalemant's capture?" asked Christopher. "We know from the refugees that they both were taken at St. Louis."

"Both are with God now," said Jacques and briefly he told what he had witnessed.

The small party of searchers listened to this first retelling of the sufferings of the two Blackrobes. He concluded: "And so I saw Father John's martyrdom and I know Father Gabriel died too, sometime early this morning. It took place right over there."

Jacques pointed to the desolate world of ashes that covered what had been the center of the village.

"Let us continue our search," ordered Brother Martin. So the sled on which Jacques lay was dragged through the ruins.

It was gruesomely clear that the departing Mohawks had cast many of the unfortunate captives who had been spared the stake into the burning cabins.

Kettle Hound was nosing ahead of the advancing party. Now he sat back on his haunches and raising his muzzle skyward, began to howl. The weird notes broke that stillness of desolation.

All stopped. They were in the center of the village. The blackened boles of the three tall pines were directly ahead of them.

Christopher Regnaut was the first to speak. "I feel sure that Kettle Hound has ended our search."

He and Brother Martin walked forward through the dust of ashes. Jacques saw Little Martin uncover his head and then kneel down. Christopher came back and silently took a blanket from the foot of the sled. This he laid on the ground and then he and the Brother lifted from the ashes by a half consumed stake a pitiful body and reverently folded the blanket about it.

Kettle Hound was howling his recognition of his master....

"Let us pray to, not for, this blessed martyr of Jesus Christ," said Christopher, his eyes streaming with tears.

"Amen," added Brother Martin. "He rides with the white robed army now."

In the meantime Andrew, one of the Christian Hurons, had been searching elsewhere nearby.

"Atironta, the other Blackrobe, is here," he called.

Brother Martin completed the identification of Father Gabriel Lalemant's corpse and wrapped it in another blanket.

Then the two bodies were put on the sled with Jacques. Kettle Hound whimpered and the boy took the dog in his arms. The party, their search completed, began the return to the Residence of St. Mary.

Over the well trodden trail back to what remained of St. Louis village they journeyed. Ruddy evidence of Iroquois cruelty blocked the way or lay frozen in last agonized contortion on the reddened snows to the right . . . to the left.

Despite the Huron scouts' assurance that the latest war party had left the land, the fear of Iroquois was in the air and the group hastened along, every sense alert.

Andrew had been dispatched ahead to notify the Residence and as the party at length came down from the last snowy ridge and the familiar palisades of St. Mary came into view, Jacques saw that all in the settlement stood awaiting their approach.

There were Hurons, braves and squaws and children, many with wounds but recently dressed. There were the little group of faithful donnés and soldiers and two of the boy interpreters; Jean Bonin and Guy La Touche. Before them stood Fathers Ragueneau and Bressani. Each of the white men held a lighted candle to honor the martyrs' remains.

Father Superior stepped forward and laying his hand affectionately on Jacques' forehead whispered: "Two martyrs of Christ and a little Confessor come home and we rejoice."

Thus under the gate and into the grounds of the Residence, between endless lines of weeping squaws and silent Huron braves, the escort passed to stop before the Fathers' building.

Burly Robert Le Coq brushed forward and Jacques found himself lifted in strong gentle hands and carried within to a cot.

He knew that the blessed bodies had been borne to the chapel and laid before the altar. Soon the strains of the "Te Deum Laudamus"—the song of the Church Triumphant to honor martyrs of Christ filled the house. Jacques joined his voice with the others. "Te martyrum candidatus laudat exercitus."

Jacques recalled Little Martin's comment, "He rides with the White Robed Army now" and his voice choked. Many strong voices were choking with sobs as the "Te Deum" came to its triumphant final praise . . . "In Aeternum."

.   .   .   .   .

Sunday, March 21, 1649, was one of those bitterly cold days with the bluest of blue skies overhead.

Jacques from the confinement of his bed knew that preparations were going on for the burial of the two martyrs. The other boy interpreters had been in with all details and now he learnt that Father Superior was vesting to say Mass. A crowd that overflowed the chapel into the hallway outside his room told him that all the Frenchmen were at this Mass. Jacques would have liked to serve it, but that was not to be, so he contented himself with making a spiritual communion and offering his absence for the repose of Father Brebeuf's soul. But he found himself repeating no prayers for Echon. He was saying happily, "Blessed Father John, help me the rest of the way Home."

He followed the Mass by the genuflections of the congregation and faintly heard the ringing of the bell.

Then the Mass was over. Muffled came the prayers and responses. There was a movement in the hallway and Jacques knew that the procession to the little cemetery had commenced. The smell of lighted candles and incense came to the boy and the regular movement of feet as the chapel cleared.

In spirit Jacques followed that funeral procession out of the Residence, across the settlement towards the snowy northern end of the enclosure. It was silent in the deserted Residence. Jacques felt peace in his heart as he waited for the return of the boys, who had promised to retell all to him. . . .

.   .   .   .   .

It was the same Sunday afternoon and Jacques was retelling for the twentieth time his recollections of the taking of St. Louis and the burnings at St. Ignatius.

All the boys were crowded around his bed, envious of his privilege of having witnessed the martyrdoms.

Christopher Regnaut, the donné, came into the room.

"It is good to see the progress you are making, little one. We searchers thought the other day to find your body in the ruins of St. Ignatius village."

"If you had," put in Guy La Touche, "he would have been a martyr too."

Nicholas Colivet and Claude St. Leger, who had been to Father Garnier's missions for the past week and had returned only yesterday, begged Christopher to tell of his part.

The donné was willing and as though he was rehearsing a piece, he began: "Claude, you and Nicholas only got back for the burials this morning. It was my privilege to help Little Martin prepare the bodies of our blessed martyrs for the chests in which they were buried. Ah, they were pitiful!

"Father Brebeuf had his legs and thighs and arms stripped of flesh to the very bone. I saw and touched a large number of blisters from the boiling water which those barbarians had poured over him in mockery of Holy Baptism. I saw and touched the wounds from the belt of bark, full of pitch and resin, which roasted his whole body. I saw and touched the marks of burns from the collar of hatchets, placed on his shoulders and breast. I saw and touched his two lips which had been cut off, because——"

The boys were weeping openly and Christopher's voice was husky as he went on: "Because he spoke of God while they made him suffer. I saw and touched all the parts of his body which had received more than two hundred cruel blows from clubs. I saw and touched the top of his scalped head and the opening which these savages had made to tear out his heart."

Unseen by Christopher Father Ragueneau had come in to the doorway of the room and was listening with glistening eyes to the donné's account.

"What you say, Christopher, is all true, for I have interviewed the survivors of the two villages who have fled to the Residence, and their stories, and Jacques', bear out each other in every detail. Father John was a blessed martyr, for it was because he taught the Prayer, as even these Iroquois call the Truths of our Holy Faith, that they inflicted their keenest torments on him. He is a great Saint at this moment. May he help us all safely Home."

Father Superior took a sheet of paper from his habit pocket and opened it.

"I believe," he said, "this explains a large part of Father John Brebeuf's heroism. Listen attentively, boys. I found this paper but this morning among his writings.

"'My God and my Savior Jesus,'" he began to read, "'what can I render to You for all the benefits which You have conferred upon me? I will take from Your hand the cup of Your sufferings, and I will invoke Your Name. I now make a vow—in the presence of Your Eternal Father and of the Holy Ghost; in the presence of Your most sacred Mother, and of her most chaste spouse, Saint Joseph; before the Angels, the Apostles and Martyrs, and my blessed Fathers, Saint Ignatius and Saint Francis Xavier—yes, my Savior

Jesus, I make a vow to You never to fail on my side in the grace
of martyrdom, if in Your infinite mercy You offer it some day to
me, Your unworthy servant. I bind myself to it in such a way that
I intend that, during all the rest of my life, it shall no longer be a
lawful thing for me, when remaining at my option, to avoid oppor-
tunities of dying and of shedding my blood for You . . . And when
I shall have received the stroke of death, I bind myself to accept it
from Your hand with all pleasure, and with joy in my heart. Con-
sequently, my beloved Jesus, I offer to You from this day, in the
feeling of joy that I have thereat, my blood, my body, and my life;
so that I die only for You, if You grant me this favor, since You have
indeed condescended to die for me. Enable me to live in such a way
that finally You may grant me this favor, to die so happily. Thus, my
God and my Savior, I will take from Your hand the cup of sufferings and at the end I will invoke Your Name, Jesus, Jesus, Jesus.'"

A hush hung over Jacques' room as Father Superior finished
reading from the sheet in his hand.

"Thus speaks the heart of John Brebeuf and is it any wonder
those savages tore it out and attempted to drink in some of his
courage?"

"No, Father," said all the boys together.

Jacques added: "'Jesus, Jesus, Jesus' were the last words that I
heard Father John ever utter, as he stood like a rock at the stake just
before the Mohawks cut off his lips."

"You were very privileged, my little son, to hear them, for Echon
was verily a Giant of God."

"Amen," said all the boys together.

Chapter Twenty-Two

Huronia Fades

N ALL SOULS' DAY—November 2nd, 1649—the "Chasseur," Captain Charles Daniel in command, was the last ship sailing that year from Quebec settlement. In sight of the whole settlement, waving and shouting bon voyage, she had raised her sails, the guns of Fort St. Louis at Monseigneur's, the Governor's orders, boomed a farewell salute and the "Chasseur" slipped down on the current of the broad-breasted St. Lawrence. Soon Orleans Island, where the surviving refugees from doomed Huronia were to be gathered in a last despairing attempt to save them from Iroquois fury was left behind. Down the ever widening river, into the broader Gulf of St. Lawrence, sailed the "Chasseur." Some days later she crossed the Gulf and leaving behind the green banked forests, was rising and falling on the gray Atlantic wastes. The last landfall of New France had dropped below the stern horizon. Across the weeks of wet leagues lay Old France.

Then it was that Claude Mangre, the stout cook of the "Chasseur" these past three months, sought Captain Daniel's cabin. He rapped timidly.

"Come in," called out the captain.

"Now what, my man?"

"My captain, I have a confession to make," began the cook, nervously rubbing his hands together.

"Why not seek the cabin of our holy passenger, Father Jerome Lalemant. I am not your Father Confessor."

"It is not that kind of a confession, my captain."

"No; then speak up, my man."

"You know the little Jacques, who has grown so tall since he came down from the accursed land of the Hurons?"

"Of course, I do. He and Louis Joliet, his bosom friend, were in this very cabin ten days ago, saying good bye and eating a prodigious quantity of those good cakes you make.

"I saw them go over the side in the last boat ashore."

Captain Daniel looked sharply at the embarrassed cook.

"My captain, you saw the Joliet boy in that last boat. Jacques——"

"What about him, Claude?"

"The little Jacques, who has grown so tall since he came down——"

"You said that once before. What about him? Speak out, cook, and be quick about it."

"The little Jacques was not in that last boat."

Captain Charles Daniel looked long at Claude Mangre, who seemed to lose weight under the inspection.

Then the captain ordered: "Send that stowaway to this cabin at once."

"Yes; my captain. I knew you would understand. I—I hope I acted for the best."

Three minutes later there was an apologetic knock at the cabin door.

Captain Daniel strode across the floor, flung open the door and motioned the boy to enter. The captain closed the door, strode back to his chair, and sat looking at the tall fourteen year old figure, standing at attention before him.

The silence grew embarrassing. Finally Captain Daniel remarked: "Jacques, my lad, some years ago I was given to understand that you ran away from Our Lady of the Angels and fell into and out of Iroquois hands. Then you went up to Huronia and seemed to have escaped martyrdom with the loss of two or three finger nails. Now you board my vessel and out of sight of land I am informed by our cook——"

The master of the "Chasseur" paused. "Perhaps you have a good explanation?"

Jacques Bourdon nodded eagerly.

"Captain Daniel, I have a confession to make."

The captain shook his head. "Your fellow conspirator of the galley used the same expression."

"It's not that kind of a confession."

"He admitted that too."

"Captain, I want to tell you a secret and then you will understand all."

"Sit down there on that chest. Unfortunately I have no cakes handy."

Jacques waved the suggestion aside.

"May I begin at the beginning, please?"

"That is the best place to start, my lad. Take your time. We have weeks at sea before us and the weather is favorable."

"Well, the morning last March my Father Brebeuf was taken by the Iroquois he told me that I was not to die with him. I did not realize what he was saying at the time, but in the months that followed I did. He said whichever of us lived was to invoke the other in all things. You know, Captain, after the martyrdoms I broke my ankle and lay abed mending it all the last days of St. Mary's Residence.

"It was still in splints the day—it was last June 14th—when Father Paul Ragueneau, the Superior, decided to set the torch to the Residence. For days before, under Brother Martin's and the donnés' directions, logs, fifty or sixty feet in length, had been fashioned into four rafts and moored in the River Wye. On these were laden what could be taken.

"There was an island out in Georgian Bay, called St. Joseph's. It had been decided to flee to this island and construct there a new

Residence. Father Bressani had gone ahead and was directing the erection of palisades and buildings.

"Now this morning runners came, announcing a large party of Mohawk Iroquois—'like leaves in autumn,' they reported—were coming to attack St. Mary's. They were on the borders of Huronia already.

"We had expected an attack on the Residence for some time. It was almost the last stronghold left standing in Huronia.

"Father Superior came to my cot. He was carrying a small canvas bag. He said: 'Jacques, I have a task that you will like.'

"'What is it?' I asked.

"'You know we are evacuating St. Mary's within the hour. Little Martin has dug up our most precious possession and here are the relics of Blessed Father Brebeuf. You are to guard them carefully.'

"'That I will,' I promised, taking the small canvas bag reverently in my hands. I was delighted to be assigned this task, for I had been useless in all the work that was going on about me. And now I had the most prized task of all!

"The other boys lifted up my cot, one at each corner, and I was carried out of the Residence. In the yard all was confusion, as lines of donnés and soldiers and Hurons were hurrying to the rafts with bundles of clothing, food and articles that could be used.

"We passed Robert Le Coq, whom they call 'Sergeant Jonah.' He was having a hard time, forcing along three porkers that resisted every foot of the march. The boys had to set down my cot and help Sergeant Jonah capture one pig who suddenly broke away and ran back to the abandoned pens. Sergeant was sweating and not exactly saying his morning prayers when the porker was finally cornered and retied.

"I saw Kettle Hound. He was Father Brebeuf's 'honest hound.' And when I whistled he jumped up on the foot of my cot.

"The cot was carried to the last raft and then the boys went back to the Residence to help. Within an hour all that we could salvage was on board the four rafts.

"Father Superior stopped by my side. 'Jacques,' he said, 'I am asking Blessed Father John to guide us safely across the waters to St. Joseph's Island. Add your prayers to mine, for I have a belief that the prayers of Echon's orderly will be listened to better than mine in that holy quarter.'

"I said the prayer as I lay there. It is easy to pray to a great saint whom you know personally."

Here Captain Daniel put in. "That's a fact I never thought of before. You ask Father John for a safe and quick passage across. Will you, Echon's orderly?"

"Yes, Captain."

"But go on with your explanation."

"Well I looked up and saw tiny clouds of smoke beginning to rise from the Fathers' House.

"'Little Martin is setting it on fire,' shouted Jean Bonin excitedly as he came running up to my cot on the raft. Kettle Hound began to bark too.

"'Yes,' Father Superior told Jean, 'that firing is necessary so that we do not leave Saint Mary's as a fortification for our Iroquois friends to have and to hold.'

"I watched fascinated as the building enveloped in smoke. Soon only the cross over the chapel was visible and I could hear the crackling of the flames. I saw Little Martin and two of the donnés walking through the smoke and they pushed off in the last canoe. When they overtook our raft the heat from the burning palisades was beginning to feel uncomfortable. The heavily laden rafts were being poled down the Wye and maneuvered into the open bay.

"Within the hour St. Mary's was in smoking ruins. That Residence was the only real home I had ever known, thanks to Father John, and it hurt in here to see its end. Then it was I began to feel that my connection with Huronia was gone. But having charge of Blessed Father John's relics I felt sure that all would be safe. And I was right. Sails were set on the rafts and we followed the others and the canoes all that night. Next day we landed at St. Joseph's Island safely.

"We had abandoned St. Mary's none too soon for the Huron scouts brought word that the large Iroquois war party were sighted in the neighborhood the morning after we burned the fortified village down. They had meant to attack St. Mary's that time.

"I do not remember much of the days at the new Residence at St. Joseph's for three days after I arrived I came down with a cold that turned into pneumonia.

"It was a morning in the following August that I awoke from a seemingly refreshing sleep. I was on a strange cot in a strange room of a strange Residence. Outside I could hear the sounds of men working on the palisades and one of our cows mooing. It sounded like Evangeline. Into the room came Father Bressani, saying: 'So the little one is himself again, after all these weeks of raving about "burns, bruises and blood." Thanks be to our prayers to Blessed Father John. You know, Jacques,' he said, 'I am becoming convinced that you have a charmed life, or, rather, the Good God has yet much work for you to do for His greater glory.'

"In the days following as my strength came back I lay for long hours on my cot in the shade outside the new Residence and I learned some of the events that had taken place since my illness. All the villages in Huronia had been captured and the Hurons killed or taken captives. It seemed that when I asked for some brave I had known, I was always told that he was dead or missing or he had fled with the survivors to the protection of friendly nations to the west or east or north. No attempt had yet been made to attack the Island, but it was feared the Mohawks would grow bolder and come at us in canoes, when they learned of the weakness of the island's defences. But what was worse, there was a lack of food to feed the missioners and refugees during the coming winter. For one of the cruel things that the Iroquois did was to destroy all the fields of corn in Huronia to make sure there would be no winter supplies.

"'How many Hurons are on St. Joseph's Island?' I asked Claude St. Leger. He told me, 'There are at present over one hundred cabins and I heard Father Superior saying to Father Bressani only yesterday he estimated there were six thousand Hurons here, mostly old braves, squaws and papooses. There are only a few hundred warriors left.'

"One afternoon Father Bressani stopped beside my cot. 'I bring bad news and good news,' he said.

"'What is the bad first, my Father?' I asked.

"'This morning that "honest hound," Kettle Hound, attempted to snatch meat from a pagan squaw's pot once too often. As I just heard the story, Father Brebeuf's dog was expert at dodging a thrown knife or tomahawk, but this angry squaw picked up a bow and sent an arrow into poor Kettle Hound's ribs. Then the squaw put the dead dog into her pot and so passes Kettle Hound out of this thieving world. Maybe, it is just as well, for there will not be many dogs alive on the island when winter comes.'

"I was sorry to hear this news for Father John loved that dog. He told me once he got Kettle Hound as a puppy, when he was stationed at Teanaostaye. But I often heard Father John warning his 'honest hound' of the fate that finally overtook him.

"'Now for the good news,' Father Bressani went on, 'Father Superior and I were discussing your health this morning and I want you to speak frankly to me. Do you think you are strong enough to make the long canoe trip down to Quebec?'

"'When?' I asked.

"'Very shortly, for unless we have some reinforcements of soldiers and supplies, our Iroquois friends will satisfy their ambition and not have a live Blackrobe or Huron in Huronia by spring. I am to go to Quebec and seek aid. Do you feel well enough to make the voyage now?'

"'I am feeling stronger every day,' I told Father Bressani truthfully.

"'Then I may tell you that you will leave here in my canoe within the week.'

"And four days later I saw the last of St. Joseph's Island from Father Bressani's canoe. The donné, Christian, was also along in the canoe. Besides there were two canoes of Hurons under the command of the captain, Paul. I was sorry to leave the other boy interpreters and the French. But I was happy, for just before the canoe pushed off Father Superior laid in my hands a small bundle.

"'Guard this carefully, favorite little one. I am sending Echon's relics by Echon's orderly to Quebec. Place them in Father Jerome Lalemant's hands. I feel confident that our good Father John will see this canoe party through all the Five Nations of the Iroquois.'

"Father Superior was right for we never sighted an Iroquois all the leagues down to Three Rivers.

"While I lay back in the canoe during those days down from Huronia and guarded Father John's relics I thought and thought and my lifework grew clearer.

"One evening as I lay by the fireside—it was just after we had left the Ottawa River and the wide banks of the St. Lawrence told me that the trip would soon be over—I confided my secret to Father Bressani.

"'Father,' I began, 'may I tell you something secret?'

"'Certainly, my little one, if it is a secret that may be shared.'

"'It is that. Father, I want to go back to school. I will study hard this time.'

"'That's the right ambition, my child. Though once I thought I heard someone say that his school days were over.'

"'Now I have a good reason to study hard and I never had it before.'

"'What is that?' he asked.

"'I know that I am to be a priest and in the future years carry on Father John's work among the savages.'

"'You know this?' Father Joseph Bressani looked at me that searching way he has sometimes.

"'Yes, my Father.'

"'May I inquire how you have this certainty?'

"'Shortly before he died for Christ, Father John Brebeuf as good as told me so. He called me "Father Jacques."'

"'If that martyr of Christ told you so, then, you fortunate child, you need never fear. The Good God will guide you eventually up the altar steps. It is a splendid thing to know one's vocation early. It saves so much waste time.'

"By the time we saw Quebec my health was completely restored, though I was rather hungry looking. Louis Joliet gave me a better welcome than Monseigneur the Governor did. As she had done that time Louis and I came back from Iroquois hands, Louis' mother insisted on taking me into her cabin and fed me and then she fed me some more. Madame Joliet is the best cook in the settlement and it is no wonder Louis is overweight all the time.

"Father Bressani took some soldiers and supplies back to Huronia and I was sent back to Our Lady of the Angels and the Fathers there told Father Jerome Lalemant that I am making great progress in all my studies. Father Superior says he wishes some of the other students there had been captured by the Iroquois and had gone up to Huronia, if my adventures had made this change in me. But Father Jerome knows privately why I study hard. I told him when I put the relics of Father Brebeuf in his hands."

Jacques paused in his narrative and Captain Daniel remarked: "So far so good. You are back safely at Our Lady of the Angels, but I am still waiting for an explanation of your presence on my ship quite some leagues out in the Atlantic. Anything further to confess, Jacques?"

"Yes; Captain, I am coming to that. When I learnt that Father Jerome Lalemant was sailing with you for France, I wanted to go along, but I was afraid to ask his permission. When I came on board with Louis Joliet to say good bye and found Claude Mangre was cook here, the plan came to me. Claude was willing and he promised to hide me in the galley. In fact, he wanted me to stay as he is deadly afraid of Iroquois and he thought I would be safer on your ship than in Quebec settlement. So I confided in Louis Joliet and told him to say where I was after the 'Chasseur' was gone.

"Remember, Captain Daniel, you offered to take me for a voyage once, when Louis and I visited you in company with that other martyr, Father Gabriel Lalemant."

"Bless me, so I did!" remembered Captain Daniel.

"Well then," Jacques grinned triumphantly, "I am not a stow-away but a passenger at your invitation."

Captain Daniel capitulated.

"And welcome, Jacques. The ship's yours. But now let me have an interview with Father Jerome and break this news to him. And you might profitably pass the time in saying a prayer to Blessed Father John Brebeuf that my interview is successful."

While Captain Daniel was gone Jacques stood before the crucifix fish curio that stood under a glass case and prayed fervently.

He was interrupted by the entrance of Captain Daniel and Father Jerome Lalemant. The captain stepped behind the Blackrobe and winked to Jacques that all was well.

Said Father Jerome: "So, Jacques, our good byes the other week were not necessary. Captain tells me that you are a welcome guest on board, so any objections I might have had are cut from under me. But it's God's Will I believe. For I have noticed for some time that our Blessed Father John Brebeuf is showing an active interest in your vocation and I would be the last one in the world to oppose the will of that Giant of God.

"I had planned to send you to school in France next year. Now I will enter you at our college at Rouen when we land."

"Wasn't that where Father John once taught?" asked Jacques.

"Yes; the same college, where the dauntless Echon had so much trouble handling a class of small French boys that superiors had to relieve him of class room duty.

"But," Father Jerome Lalemant turned to Captain Daniel, "I will leave it to you, Captain, to decide what this boy does on the voyage across to earn his passage."

"That is easily decided, Father Jerome," declared the captain.

"Jacques, you are to help the cook. Report to him."

Jacques grinned his approval. "Captain, sir, I have been doing that secretly ever since we left Quebec. Now I will work openly."

Father Jerome motioned Jacques that he might leave the cabin, but Captain Daniel detained the boy a moment.

"Jacques, my lad, when you have finished your priestly studies and desire to return to New France, if this old seaman is still above the waves, please give him the privilege of offering you transportation on his vessel. It will be yours from crow's nest to keel and I'll be the happy navigator that trip, for I will know Echon's boy—pardon, Father Jacques Bourdon—will be my guarantee that that one voyage will be prosperous.

"Now get more of the sea breeze into your lungs. You will need its benefit in Old France."

Jacques thanked his friends and went out on deck. He reported to a relieved Claude Mangre and then sought the bows, where he could peer ahead across the wet leagues.

Evening was coming on fast. The "Chasseur," meeting the waves, seemed to make the half circle of horizon rise and fall.

Jacques was soon lost in happy thoughts. He seemed to see down the years that were yet to unfold. The long road of study in the newness of Old France—priesthood's joys and powers—the voyage back in Captain Daniel's vessel—a Blackrobe in New France—the canoe trips into the distant western wildernesses, possibly with Louis Joliet as companion—of a surety a view of that wondrous Falls of Niagara that my Father John admired.—"Almighty

God"—Why, Almighty God, it was You Who led me, an orphaned boy to my Father John's care.—And Almighty God it is You Who will let me share my Father John's glorious lifework. . . .

The old familiar prayer of youthful days at Our Lady of the Angels came unwittingly to the lips of "Echon's boy" and he found himself repeating in the light of a new and dearer understanding, "Little Master, I thank You for keeping me from morning till now. Keep me the rest of the way. Forget my faults and help me to overcome them. I give You my acts. Give me Your grace to perform them well. Amen."

Future Father Jacques Bourdon, valiant Blackrobe of the Society of Jesus for half a century in the wilderness that one day would be Midwestern America, laughed for sheer joy.

THE END

OTHER TITLES AVAILABLE FROM ST. AIDAN PRESS

View a sample chapter from each title at www.staidanpress.com.

THE QUEEN'S TRAGEDY
by Msgr. Robert Hugh Benson

"Upon the publication of former books of mine several kindly critics remarked that the reign of Mary Tudor told a very different story with regard to the Catholic character. It is that story which I am now attempting to set forth as honestly as I can."

$19.00 — 364 pages. Available at amazon.com.

THE NET
by Agnes Blundell

Roger felt a freezing dew break out upon his forehead. The net was over him it seemed; in vain he told himself that he could establish his identity. His head was worth forty pounds to the vile creatures at the stair foot, and once in their clutches who knew if he could ever communicate with his friends? . . . Gaolers and pursuivants alike fattened on the traffic in human life and divided the spoils. Judges were as careless as callous."

$16.00 — 264 pages. Available at amazon.com.

THE ANCHORHOLD
by Enid Dinnis

Editha de Beauville had all that the world could offer: wealth, wit, and beauty. Yet a chaplain's sermon drove her to give up all this, and enter the religious life. But could a proud, strong-willed noblewoman accept and embrace the poverty and self-abnegation of the religious life, particularly that of full seclusion in an anchorhold? A difficult path lay before Editha. Read on to learn how she fared, and how her life affected those around her, including Sir Aleric, her erstwhile suitor, now a crusader knight; Fr. Nicholas, a young priest who was quite bright, and thought so too; and Fiddlemee, the witty yet wise court jester whose past held a surprising secret.

$14.00 — 194 pages. Available at amazon.com.

THE SHEPHERD OF WEEPINGWOLD
by Enid Dinnis

Sir Robert Luffkyn, rich grandson of a peasant, has purchased the manor of Weepingwold from the noble but impoverished de Lessels, intending to make the renamed Luffkynwold a busy center of his tanning trade. He sends Petronilla, last de Lessels, to Gracerood, intending her for its future Abbess, and plucks little Brother Kit from the cloister to become the new parson of the long-abandoned church. How will Father Kit fare with the parish and his own soul? Will Petronilla find her true vocation? And is there really a witch in the parish?

$14.00 — 202 pages. Available at amazon.com.

SCOUTING FOR SECRET SERVICE
By Fr. Bernard F. J. Dooley

Frank and George are going to spend their summer vacation in the Adirondacks, thanks to Frank's uncle Ed. But once they get there, they realize something fishy is going on. Can they trust Pete, their Indian guide, or is he mixed up in it too? And is Frank's mysterious uncle really behind it all?

$14.00 — 188 pages. Available at amazon.com.

THE MASTERFUL MONK
by Fr. Owen Francis Dudley

Brother Anselm comes back to England to counter the Atheist's efforts to destroy the influence of Catholic morals. Between his lectures he is drawn into a struggle for the soul of Beauty Dethier, who is Catholic but fascinated by the "freedom" of the world and the Atheist. It will take more than argument to save her from disaster.

$18.00 — 342 pages. Available at amazon.com.

WILL MEN BE LIKE GODS? & THE SHADOW ON THE EARTH
by Fr. Owen Francis Dudley

"Men, in their pursuit of happiness, are in danger of staking their all upon the greatest hoax ever foisted on humanity. This book has been written to expose the hoax together with the follies and fallacies of the hoaxers. In place of Utopian dreams the real solution of the problem of human happiness is offered."—*from the cover of Will Men Be Like Gods?, 1949 edition.*

Father Dudley's first two books on human happiness are published together here—his rare collection of essays together with a novel which illustrates the essays and introduces his most famous character, the Masterful Monk.

$15.00 — 216 pages. Available at amazon.com

CANDLELIGHT ATTIC AND ODD JOB'S
by Cecily Hallack

Here are seven true stories in honour of the Seven Joys of Our Blessed Lady, and ten more invented ones about the delightful Barnabas Job, to make a comfortable book for those who are afraid of the dark.

$14.00 — 192 pages. Available at amazon.com.

THE HAPPINESS OF FATHER HAPPÉ
by Cecily Hallack

Shingle Bay did not know what to make of Fr. Savinius Happé. He was a cheerful, rotund Franciscan, a famous author of books on everything from Etruscan civilization to Alpine meadows to beetles, and someone who had never quite mastered the English language. His jovial demeanor concealed a wisdom that alternately bewildered, astonished, but ultimately won over the people of Shingle Bay.

$10.00 — 112 pages. Available at amazon.com.

CON OF MISTY MOUNTAIN
by Mary T. Waggaman

"It had been a long night for Con. Just what had happened to him he was at first too dazed to know. Dennis had flung him into the smoking-room with no very gentle hand, turned the key and left him to himself. And, sinking down dully upon a rug that felt very soft and warm after the hard flight over the mountain, Con was glad to rest his bruised, aching limbs, his dizzy head, without any thought of what was to come upon him next."

$14.00 — 190 pages. Available at amazon.com.

NON-FICTION

THE STORY OF THE WAR IN LA VENDÉE AND THE LITTLE CHOUANNERIE
by George J. Hill, M.A.

The brave French Catholics of the Vendée and neighboring provinces rose up in arms when the revolutionary government replaced their priests with clergy who had renounced the Pope. Though they lacked money, allies, and were divided by disputes, they did not cease to fight until they had secured the open practice of their Faith. Here is the story of their devotion and courage against the advocates of liberty, equality, fraternity, and death.

$18.00 — 342 pages. Available at amazon.com.

CATHOLICISM AND SCOTLAND
by Compton Mackenzie

Much has been written about the desperate fight that English Catholics waged to keep the Faith, but Scotland's Catholic history is little known. Have you ever heard of David Beaton, Cardinal Archbishop of St. Andrews, and his struggles? Or of Fr. Ninian Winzet, who boldly challenged Calvinist champion John Knox to a public debate? Read this book and find out about the Scots who sought to defend their country and their Faith from the onslaught of Protestantism.

$12.00 — 138 pages. Available at amazon.com.

DOMINICAN SAINTS
by the Novices of the Dominican House of Studies

Here are related the astonishing lives of fourteen saints of the Dominican Order, including St. Dominic, St. Catherine of Siena, Pope St. Pius V, St. Rose of Lima, St. Vincent Ferrer, and more. An encyclical on the Dominican Order by Pope Benedict XV and a list of all the Dominican Saints and Blesseds (as of 1921) complete this wonderful introduction to the "Dogs of the Lord."

$19.00 — 392 pages. Available at amazon.com.

www.ingramcontent.com/pod-product-compliance
Lightning Source LLC
Chambersburg PA
CBHW021959260626
47156CB00018B/2364